THE DEVIL'S ELBOW

by

Ed Londergan

Ed Londergan

While The Devil's Elbow is based on historical characters and events, the book is a work of fiction. All characters and dialogue are products of the author's imagination.

Copyright © 2012 by Ed Londergan

Cover photo by author
Cover design by Sproutreach
Author photo by Capture Design and Photography

ISBN 978-0-9893049-0-0

www.edlondergan.com
www.facebook.com/EdLondergan
www.twitter.com/EdLondergan

Published by Indian Rock Publishing

This book is dedicated to
Karen Brown, Kathy Gardner, Vern Lubs,
and Sonny Anderson

July 7, 1695

In the following pages, I will tell you a story. I am older now and some of the things I'll relate happened more than 30 years ago although to me, it seems as if they happened only yesterday.

While I do not consider myself an accomplished teller of stories, I will do what I can with the abilities I have, so that you will know all that happened and why. And while I do not have what many call a formal education, as mine stopped at the time this story begins, my curiosity and attention to detail has always served me well.

Certain memories from this time make me smile, and though it was a difficult existence, there were many simple things and many people that brought me great pleasure. We tend to forget details as the year's progress, and our memories of the good tend to outweigh the bad and I, like all other men, am subject to the same influence.

Chapter 1

The greatest grief that can happen to a boy happened to me when I was 14-years-old. No matter what happened, life was never to be the same again.

My world turned upside down when my mother died while giving birth on the cold and dismal morning of April 7, 1665, leaving me, Jack Parker, an orphan in the coastal town of Ipswich, located 30 miles north of Boston in the Massachusetts Bay Colony.

I've found that there are times in life when you feel all alone, as if no one else cares about your very existence. Although that's rarely the case, it just feels that way. That's how I felt - alone and abandoned, not knowing what to do or even where to start, scared of everything, scared of losing what little I had. It was a terrible time, for my entire world was gone.

My father died the previous fall in a hunting mishap of which I was the cause. I blame myself for my father's death because if I hadn't been so careless, he wouldn't have had to save me and he wouldn't have gotten sick. It is a burden I carried then and carry still.

He and I were hunting one cold, windy, late October

morning several miles from home along the Ipswich River. I went charging down a steep bank, which was slick from two days of rain, to the river to get a fat raccoon he had shot. I slipped and fell, rolling and tumbling, until I landed face down in the cold water. I stood up, took a step, and fell into a deep hole, the water closing over my head. My father jumped in to save me, but as he began to pull me out, he fell and went under, pulling me down with him. By the time he dragged me to shore, we were soaking wet from head to foot, choking on the water we swallowed, water draining from our clothes into our shoes, and shivering in the wind that made it feel much colder. By the time we got home, both of us were shaking with chills; my hands and feet were tingling and my face was numb.

My mother took care of getting us warm and dry, making us sit near the roaring fire in dry clothes, covered in blankets, eating warm vegetable stew and drinking hot cider. I recovered by the next day, but my father developed a cough that came from deep in his chest. For the next two days, he was very sick and unable to get out of bed, burning with a high fever while shaking with constant chills. During the one time he was awake, he called me to his side and told me in a harsh, rasping voice to take good care of my mother, that I had always been a good boy and he knew I would grow to be a good man. The last thing he ever said to me was that no matter what happens to you, there is an inner strength that will never leave you, unless you let someone take it away, and that the measure of a man is determined by how he faces life's difficulties. He passed away that afternoon.

If I didn't have my aunt Charity and uncle Josiah, I don't know what I would have done. My aunt was a wonderful woman - patient, kind, always happy and always smiling. She came from the town of Sandwich on Cape Cod to take care of her ailing sister and met Josiah at the Sabbath meeting soon after she arrived. They began to spend time with each other and when her sister recovered, Charity didn't return home. Josiah was an independent-minded man and had little tolerance for many of the practices of the day. Like my father, he was not a particularly religious man. He didn't like many of the ministers he met, as he believed they thought they were far superior to the rest of us, which they did. Charity, on the other hand, made sure Josiah went to meeting every Sabbath, whether he wanted to or not.

While they had a good but hard life as most of us did, the one thing they did not have was children. After three years of marriage, it was clear that Charity couldn't have children, which was a tremendous disappointment to them both. Because she was barren, there was talk about how God was punishing her and Josiah. No one ever said what they were being punished for, but hints of the various causes, none of them good, surfaced from time to time. Although no one said anything to her, Charity knew the rumors were out there and that she was talked about by other people, mostly women, and it hurt her more than any of them would ever know.

My mother was three months pregnant when my father died. They were excited about it because having another baby was a wonderful thing; especially after losing my little sister three years before to a high fever and whooping cough that lasted almost a month. She was six-years-old when she died.

There were times when my mother didn't feel well for a day or two and as her time came near, she reassured me daily, telling me not to be concerned and that everything would be fine. However, I could see the worry in her eyes when she'd suddenly clutch her belly, grimacing with momentary pain.

My mother went into labor early in the morning shortly after Josiah and Charity arrived. She was very glad to see them. Within a short while, my mother began to have strong pains. Charity sent me to get the midwife and Mrs. Morgan, my mother's best friend, so they could help with the birth. When they arrived, Josiah and I left the house, knowing this was a place for women only. We were outside a few minutes when Charity came to the door.

"Josiah," she said. "Take Jack and go somewhere." With that, she closed the door. He looked down at me knowing there was nothing we could do but leave. He gave a deep sigh as he put his hand on my shoulder.

"Come on Jack. Let's find us something to do." As we walked away, he grumbled for he didn't like being told what to do, not even by his own wife.

We walked around a good part of the town for the first half of the morning. We visited three of his friends' farms but didn't stay long when they asked us to help with some work. Josiah never minded working hard, just not for someone else.

I remember we stopped at the tavern on our way back. It was a low, dark room with a large fireplace that always had a measly little fire burning. There were three or four men drinking rum and lounging about. Walter, the tavern keeper, was a tall, barrel-chested, broad-shouldered man with a black, bushy beard. Walter always doted on children. More than once, he slipped a piece of maple candy into my hand when my father wasn't looking while giving me a wink.

We got back to the house after a couple of hours and were surprised to find that my mother hadn't given birth yet. Josiah went in only to be pushed out by Mrs. Morgan.

A short while later, we heard the baby cry. The midwife came to the door and motioned to Josiah. He went and spoke with her and came back smiling. He told me that I had a baby brother; "a strong and lusty lad" is the exact phrase he used. I saw two of my friends and ran over to tell them.

When I came back, Josiah was talking in low tones to

the midwife, who was trying to explain something to him. He began to step into the house but was stopped by the midwife's assistant. Josiah said something, pushed her out of the way and shut the door behind him.

I wandered in front, waiting for him to come out. When he finally did, he was upset and waved his arm for me to follow him. We went into the back near the barn where he stood facing away from me. He took a deep breath and gave a loud sigh before turning and squatting in front of me.

"Jack, something went wrong after the baby was born. Your mother was hurt very bad inside and something happened. She was bleeding and they couldn't stop it. There was nothing they could do." He took a deep breath and looked at the ground. He raised his head, looked me in the eye, and spoke in almost a whisper. "She died a few minutes ago." I stood there stunned, the rest of the world ceasing to exist for me. I didn't hear or see anything. I began to wander about in a daze, moving as if in a dream. I went to him and looked into his face.

"No, you made a mistake…my mother is not dead…she can't be. I saw her just a little while ago. She can't be dead…she just can't be!" I cried as a shudder ran through me. Part of me was sure they had made a mistake. My mother couldn't be dead. "I saw her just a while ago," I repeated.

Josiah didn't say anything. He just looked at me with sad eyes. I saw a tear come from his left eye and make its way down his cheek. It began to dawn on me that he wasn't lying and that my mother was dead. I ran to the house and hit the door hard, causing it to open and slam against the wall. The women turned and looked at me, all of them crying.

"No!" I yelled and began to cry. They were around the bed so I couldn't see her. "I want to see her. I don't believe you," I said even though I realized that it was the truth.

Charity came and wrapped her arms around me as I began to cry hard for what seemed like a long time. She held me the whole time, patting my back and telling me it would be all right and not to worry. After I stopped crying, she wiped my face with her apron and ran her hand over my hair. She pulled me close to her and started crying, so I joined in. We wept for a minute or two until Josiah put his hand on my shoulder, pulling me away from her. He turned me around and walked me out the door. I remember looking around, seeing Charity in the doorway wiping her eyes with the back of her hand, looking at me in a way that was so sad that I started to blubber again.

Josiah squatted and put his hand on my shoulder. I slapped it away and ran around the corner of the house, not knowing or caring where I was headed. I stayed around the corner for a minute, not knowing what to do, until I heard Charity's voice.

"Josiah…take him away. Go to Minister Trumbull's or to Morgan's or somewhere, but just go. He doesn't need to be here now." At that, I started to run and after a few minutes, found myself by the side of a small stream. I'd come here before many times to sit by myself and watch the birds, skip rocks or just watch the clouds float by. It was my special place, the sound of the gurgling water never failed to soothe me.

I sat down, drew my legs up, and put my head against my knees, wrapping my arms around my legs. I kept hearing my uncle's words, "*Your mother died. There was nothing anyone could do.*" I sat there for at least an hour, wondering what would happen to me now that everything I knew was gone. It was mid-day by the time I got up and started walking, not having any idea where I was going, but I wandered back to the house to see Josiah sitting outside waiting for me. As I got closer, he moved over on the bench, motioning for me to sit down. We sat for a few minutes without talking. After a while, he got off the bench, stood in front of me and squatted so his eyes were at the same level as mine.

"Jack, none of this is your fault. There was nothing you or I or anyone else could have done. She was taken for a reason, although I don't know what it could be." I stood, looked at him and shrugged, listening but not hearing.

We took my mother to the burial ground that afternoon. After I ran away, Charity and the other women put her in the shroud while Josiah got the carpenter, James Gilbert, to build the coffin and James' brother to dig the grave. It only took a few minutes to bury her. I stood at the edge of the grave watching as they lowered her body into the gaping hole. A dozen or so people, friends of my parents or Charity and Josiah's, came to the burial and stood as the dirt was shoveled into the grave. I jumped hard when the first shovelful landed on the coffin, as it hit me that that it was my mother, my own mother, in that box and soon she'd be covered with several feet of dirt. I shivered and gasped at the thought. We stayed for a few minutes, all of us lost in our own particular thoughts. I just couldn't believe she was gone. I was with her just that morning, just a few hours before and now I would never see her again. In all my years, I have never gotten over the suddenness in which life is extinguished. A person is here among the living and then, in a few seconds, they're dead and gone.

I looked up, wiping my eyes with the palm of my hand and saw several of the women crying softly as their husbands put their arms around them to provide some comfort. Charity took a handkerchief from her pocket and wiped her eyes while giving me a weak smile. As we left the burial ground, Josiah walked in front of us, his head hung low. He brought his hand to his face several times to wipe away the tears we knew he was shedding but would never let us see. I walked back to the house with everyone else, lost in a daze of sadness and confusion.

As I went in, I looked around and remembered my

mother sitting at her spinning wheel talking to my father on a cold October night last fall. They smiled and laughed, and it was warm and we were happy. That was the day my mother told me she was having a baby.

Charity went ahead of me and was on the other side of the room when I came in. She turned, looking at me with tear-reddened eyes and put her arm around my shoulders, telling me it would be all right. I missed my mother. I wanted the pain and hurt to go away. She comforted me for a long time before I stopped sniffling, then she gave me a cloth to wipe my face. While Charity reassured me, Josiah went around us and built up the fire, adding three good logs that burned well. We stood in front of the fire, oblivious to everyone else in the room, staring at the flames and wondering what the future would hold.

Later that night, Charity came to sit next to me on the floor in front of the fire. We didn't talk for what seemed like a long time. I was tired and on the verge of falling asleep, my head bobbing up and down. She leaned over and helped me up and walked me to my bed. The last thing I remember is her talking about the baby.

"I talked to Mrs. Fletcher today. The baby is doing well and they'll be taking him. She lost a baby girl a little more than a week ago. The only problem is that they are moving to Groton next Monday. I'm sorry Jack." It made sense but he was my brother and I'd never even seen him. I hoped that maybe, at some point in the future, I would get to see him for at least a little while.

The sadness came upon me in waves, with the pain following. As the days went by, I cried, but only when I was by myself, for I didn't want anyone to see or hear me. I'd go to the barn to stand in a corner, talking to my mother, telling her how much I missed her, and wishing she were here to hold and protect me. I was a sad, lost, and lonely young boy with a broken heart who couldn't understand why his parents were taken away from him. If they died when I was an infant, I would not have missed them, but that was not the case.

A couple of days after my mother died, I was in the barn sniffling away when I heard footsteps behind me. I turned and saw Charity standing in the doorway.

"I was wondering where you went," she said, looking at me. "What are you doing out here?" When I didn't respond, she came over to me and put her arms around me. She held me tight, slowly rocking back and forth.

"Oh, I know how it hurts. We miss her very much too. It will take time, but it will get better, I promise it will. Josiah and I will always be here for you. You never have to worry because we'll always take care of you," she said, wiping my eyes with her apron before giving me another hug. "Come on now," she said, putting her hands on the back of my shoulders and pointing me in the direction of the house, "Dinner's ready." As we sat at the table, I looked across at my aunt and uncle and realized that we were all that was left of our family. The only other family I had left besides my aunt and uncle were several distant relatives I'd never met, and from what I'd heard of them, I didn't want to.

As I lay in bed that night, my mind drifted back to the past. My memories of the time before my father died were good. Our house was not large, but on a cold fall day, it was warm, and the smell of the apple pies and pumpkin muffins my mother made could make me stay indoors all afternoon. I'd sit by the fire making birch brooms or some other thing but that was just an excuse for staying near her. I was cozy, warm, and happy. It always seemed that my father had other ideas for me on those days.

"Come on Jack," he'd say, tousling my hair as he walked by, "Let's go to the woods and shoot some partridge so your mother can make us pie and beans." He'd always say the same thing and then throw me my wool jacket. While I was getting ready, he'd wink at my mother, telling her that he was hungry and that we'd be back soon. This always made her laugh. My mother's beans were wonderful; the smell of molasses and fried salt pork would linger for hours. The thought of it still never fails to make me hungry. My stomach would rumble in anticipation the entire time we were gone. It made walking in the chilly wind on a rainy or snowy day bearable. For my mother's beans and partridge pie, I'd have stood in three feet of ice-cold water all afternoon in a 40 mile-an-hour wind.

One of my greatest joys was my dog Tinker, or Tink for short. He was a black beast of a dog and always seemed to think of himself as still a puppy, even though he must have weighed close to 90 pounds, which I knew well, since he was forever trying to crawl onto my lap. He had warm brown mischievous eyes, a shiny coat, and an unending desire to run and swim. He loved to go hunting with my father and me. He got a great deal of joy out of leaving the house early in the morning in the cool, crisp air. The minute he saw me get my gun, he'd begin to bark and whine because he knew where we were going. He got so excited that his tail would wag hard enough to cause him to move forward when he was sitting. His barking made us leave in a hurry, just to get him to quiet down. The minute he was outside, he would dash off, his nose in the wind, running around just for the sheer pleasure of it. In many ways, he was a big, happy child. No matter how old I get, I smile when I think of him.

We would visit Josiah and Charity often, always bringing good things to eat. Those were pleasant days when we forgot any cares or worries and the food and family made for a wonderful time.

My father and I always had some adventure in the works, whether it was hunting, fishing, or going to visit one of his friends who would take us out into the bay on his small fishing boat. I didn't care what we did because it was great just spending time with my father. Those are some of my most cherished memories. Wherever we went, Tink came along with us whether we wanted him to or not, wagging his tail and giving me that goofy, happy look of his from time to time.

As I recall the events and times of my childhood, more and more memories come to mind. I could go on and on but leave it to say that for the most part, they are happy memories.

Over the next several months, my aunt and uncle discussed what would be best for me; whether to go with them to their farm, or for them to stay here with me, or for us to go to a new settlement in the wilderness out in the western part of the Colony. That excited me to no end with thoughts of adventures, Indians, hunting and all the other things a young boy would love to do. The thought of staying in Ipswich didn't interest me in the least. I wanted to go somewhere - even though I wasn't sure where. They decided to stay at my house and rent their farm. Moving to a new settlement wasn't discussed any further. We stayed in Ipswich and worked my father's farm. This state of things continued for two years until they began discussing my future. I was shocked when I found out their decision.

"Jack, we want to talk to you," Josiah said, motioning for me to sit at the table with them. "We want the best life for you and we hope you know that. Both of us understand how difficult it's been for you over the last two years. We'll always be here for you and do everything we can to help you. We want you to have a better life than we do." They looked at each other and hesitated over what was coming next. My aunt leaned over and put her hand on my arm while giving me a weak smile.

"Your uncle," she said, giving him a quick glance, "talked to Elizur Hapgood about a man he knows in Boston...." she stopped, talking her hand away.

"This man in Boston," Josiah said, picking up where she left off, "is a successful merchant with a coastal trading boat, a warehouse, and a tannery. He employs two coopers and a blacksmith and has a shop where he sells his goods. He's a wealthy man.

"Elizur told me that this man, Goodfield is his name, needs an apprentice, and is looking for the right boy. When Elizur heard of it, he said he thought of you." It took me a minute to understand that they were saying I should become this man's apprentice. The normal term for an apprentice was seven years, although I'd heard of some of four or five years. The thought of all the things and people I'd leave behind went through my mind.

"No!" I exclaimed, "I don't want to, I don't want to be anyone's apprentice." I looked at them bewildered at the possibility of leaving my home. "I want to stay here. Why are you trying to get rid of me?" I asked. "Why is being an apprentice better than farming? If you and my father could do it, then so can I," I said, looking at Josiah.

"We're not trying to get rid of you. Farming is hard work and it takes its toll over the years. We want you to have a better life and more opportunities. This could be a good thing for you."

"I'd be gone at least five years! I'd be 19 when I'm through! No, I won't go," I declared, wondering whether my protests would make them reconsider. They had to know that this was the last thing I wanted and that I'd rather do anything than go away for so long.

"We understand how you feel, but I'm going to Boston tomorrow with Elizur to talk to Mr. Goodfield," he said. "Now go do your chores." I went out to the barn and sat on the floor. Picking a piece of hay out of the pile behind me, I began scratching the dirt with it. It wasn't fair that they wanted me to go away. It was all too much for me to take in at once. My mother and father were gone, my brother was living with the Fletchers who moved to Groton, and now Josiah and Charity wanted me to leave the only home I'd ever known. Gone for five years! Maybe I'd never be able to return I thought, shocked at the way my life could change in just a few days. I began to panic. I wouldn't be able to see my friends and their families as I went around the village or to the Sabbath meeting.

I'd also miss Becky Morgan, the 12-year-old daughter of my mother's best friend, Elizabeth Morgan. I found myself liking her more and more. She and her mother were always very kind to me and even more so since my mother passed away. I realized I'd miss her smile and her laugh, the way she'd make fun of me when I did something she thought to be foolish.

Becky wasn't home when I got there. She was at a neighbor's house, but her mother expected her home in a little while. While I waited, I sat outside on the small rise to the side of their house watching the waves roll across the cove. There was a steady wind blowing off the ocean moving a small coastal trader along at a good clip. I saw her coming down the road and ran to meet her. As I got closer, I saw her smiling at me and realized that I was smiling, too. It was just good to see her. My smile disappeared at the thought that I might not see her for a long time.

"What's wrong?" she asked, grabbing onto her bonnet

as the wind gusted.

"Josiah and Charity want me to become an apprentice," I blurted out.

"What?" she asked with her eyes flying open in surprise. "Where? When? They're just talking about this aren't they?"

"Josiah's going to Boston tomorrow to talk to some wealthy merchant Elizur Hapgood knows."

"I just can't believe they'd do something like that."

"They said they want a good life for me. They want me to learn a trade, something that would give me greater opportunities than staying and working on the farm," I said. "I don't know…this happened all of a sudden…I don't know what to do. I never thought about anything like this."

"What do they mean a good life? You can have a good life without going to Boston or being an apprentice. Have you talked to them? Told them you don't want to go?"

"Yes but it didn't do any good. We only talked about it for a few minutes. I need to change their mind and convince them that I shouldn't go. I just don't know how."

"Oh, you'll figure it out...you always do. Make sure that they know it will be more difficult for them with you gone. They'll have to do more work. It won't be as easy for them as it would be if you stayed."

"But they never had anyone to help out before they

came to live with me so not having me around wouldn't be a big loss for them. I don't want to go," I said, looking at her with her hair blowing in the breeze, "because I'd never see you or anyone else I know for a long, long time. An apprenticeship lasts five or maybe even seven years! I'd be at least 19 when I'm done."

"You wouldn't be able to come home at all?" she asked.

"I don't think so. It would be up to my master. An apprentice has to do what his master tells him, including where he goes, who he sees and when."

Becky squared her shoulders. "I need to talk to Charity about this," she said. "This just isn't right."

Well, she talked to Charity and I pleaded, trying to persuade them to let me stay, all to no end. Josiah met with the merchant and made all the arrangements. I was going to be an apprentice whether I wanted to or not. I was crestfallen when I found out that my hopes for an adventurous life were dashed. Even though I wanted to go somewhere, I did not want to go to Boston. Not that I hadn't been to Boston before; I had several times, but to live there away from my friends and the things that were familiar to me was too much to contemplate. I became resigned to my fate, awaiting the day I would leave with the same enthusiasm as if I was about to be flogged.

Josiah and I left in the early morning, two days after he returned from meeting with Mr. Goodfield. The last people to see me off were Mrs. Morgan and Becky. While the adults talked, I told Becky that I wanted to walk down to the small beach a short distance away. We crossed a small hill and came to a sandy area with dunes and tall beach grass, continuing to the water without saying a word. We walked the small beach and turned when we reached the end, coming back to where we started. After a few minutes of staring at the ocean, I realized I had to get back. When I looked at her, I saw tears in her eyes.

"What are you crying for?" I asked, a little annoyed at her sudden show of emotion.

"Because I'll never see you again, Jack." She was looking at me in a way I had never seen before.

"Don't cry. I have to get back now or Josiah will be mad. He's itching to leave." She reached out and took my right hand in hers and sniffled.

"You have to kiss me," she whispered.

"What? What are you talking about? Why do I have to kiss you? I don't want to kiss anybody, above all you."

"It's the way you say goodbye when you know you'll never see that person again." I had to get back so I decided it would be easier to let her have her way than take time arguing about it.

"Now close your eyes," she said. I did and felt her lips

touch mine. She held the kiss for a moment until I pulled away. It was an odd but pleasant feeling and not as bad as I thought it might be. I realized I enjoyed it.

"Now I have to kiss you back," I said, surprised at myself.

"Why?"

"Because you kissed me and now I want to kiss you." I bent and pressed my lips to hers feeling a strange but thrilling sensation. I held it for a minute before pulling my face away little by little. When she looked at me, I saw how green her eyes were. She had a soft smile. I realized I was smiling too.

"Now we have to get married," she stated.

"What?" I exclaimed, flabbergasted at her pronouncement, backing a few steps away from her. "Why do we have to get married?"

"Because when a boy and girl kiss more than once it means they're going to marry." I didn't know what to say and was relieved when I heard Charity calling us.

"We have to go now Becky," I said. "I'll see you again, maybe sooner than you think." Whether I said that to comfort her or me, I don't know. She gave a slight smile and went up the dune with me. Conflicting emotions ran through me; confusion over what just happened, excitement that I kissed a girl, frustration and anger that I had to go somewhere I didn't want to be.

The Devil's Elbow

Chapter 2

When I got back, Tink was waiting for me with his tail wagging so hard, his whole body moved back and forth. I looked at him and felt a big lump in my throat. How was I going to say goodbye to him? He'd been my best friend since I was six and I might never see him again. I went down on my knee as he came to me. I wrapped my arms around his neck fighting back the tears.

"You're a good boy Tink...always have been. I don't know what I'm going to do without you. It's just not fair! I shouldn't have to leave you, I just shouldn't have to!" He stopped wagging, tilted his head to one side, looking at me with his big brown eyes. It's like he was listening to me. I could tell that he knew, somehow he knew. He put his muzzle into my neck like he did when he was a puppy so I hugged him and scratched his ears. His head went all the way over to one side and his back leg starting moving up and down like he was trying to scratch himself.

"I wish I could bring you with me," I said as a few tears starting to flow. I buried my face in his neck and held him tighter. "You be a good boy for them. I'll come home as soon as I can just to see you," I whispered. He started wagging again as Josiah came out the door. I said my goodbyes to Charity, patted Tink one last time and got into the cart beside Josiah. Charity stood by the door, looking sad as we drove away. Tink sat next to her, looking first at her then at me. I looked back and waved, wanting to shed a tear or two of my own, but I didn't.

It wasn't long before we got to Boston. I've always found that it seems to take longer than you want it to when you're going somewhere you want to go, and a much shorter time to get someplace you'd rather not be. I thought about asking him to turn around and go home but I knew Josiah wouldn't, so I didn't bother.

Mr. Gurdon Goodfield's house was halfway between the wharves and Beacon Hill. It was located on a semi-circular street just up from Bendell's Cove, where the town docks jutted into the cove and ran along the left shore towards Gallop's Point. Mill Pond was to the east just a short distance from the wharves. The house was close enough to the cove so that on all but the coldest days, the smell of fish, seaweed, and muck wafted from the water. As I was to see later, the harbor was a pretty place with several green islands off in the distance. The Common was a short distance away in the direction of Trimountain, or the three hills, Pemberton, Mt. Vernon, and Beacon.

The house was a large, dark brown two-story dwelling

with more windows than I'd ever seen in one house. It was at least four times the size of my house. It was tall, with the second floor jutting out several feet over the first but only on the front side. The door was offset to the right side, making the house look unbalanced.

Goodfield was a short, plump, but not quite fat man with wiry brown hair and hazel eyes. He stood looking me up and down as if trying to decide whether I was worth the time and trouble to take in.

"Well," he said continuing to stare at me as he addressed my uncle, "is he able to work hard? He doesn't eat too much does he? There are others in the family you know. I can't afford to have some boy eating all day long and not working as he should. That won't do. It just won't do. He'll have to work hard, oh yes he will. We'll teach him how to write, read, and cipher. It's God's Providence that you came to me boy."

"I already know how to do all that. My mother taught me to read, write, and cipher," I snapped. Both of them looked at me in surprise; Josiah because of how angry I sounded and Mr. Goodfield because he didn't think a boy like me would know how to read, write and do arithmetic.

"Well, if you already know, I won't have to teach you. You'll have more time to work then," he said with a nasty grin. "And we have plenty of work." At that moment, he reminded me of a fat snake, its flat eyes staring at you just before it strikes. I didn't like the way this was going and I could see Josiah was watching me. Not knowing what else to do, I shook my head back and forth to tell him that I didn't want to stay here.

"Now, Goodman Clarke, come in and sign the papers," Goodfield said motioning to Josiah but ignoring me. I started to follow but Goodfield stopped me. "There's no need of you being here boy. Now wait outside." With that, he closed the door in my face.

I turned and looked around, up and down the street, watching the tradesmen go by. Boys, girls, men, and women were all working at something or other. It was a beehive of activity everywhere I looked. Men were rolling barrels, boys trundling wheelbarrows full of things, girls carrying baskets of cloth and vegetables, and women were tending their gardens on the side of each house. The area near the water wasn't as open as at home with more buildings crowded near each other, making narrow passages for the wind to blow through, bringing all the smells - good and bad - with it. Wood smoke, thick enough to choke you, was everywhere. The sounds of people seemed all around me, calling to each other, some laughing, and serious discussions among deep voiced men as they walked. I noticed that there were not a lot of children playing and yelling as they did back in Ipswich. Boston seemed a stern and serious place, something I never noticed on my few previous trips.

Josiah came back out, saying something to Goodfield that I couldn't hear. "Come on Jack," he called. I went to him and we walked down towards the water. "Mr. Goodfield has decided to make you a cooper. The apprentice who worked for him isn't here anymore so he needs someone to take his place," he said, flashing me a quick smile. "What do you think of that?"

"I don't know," I replied. "I really don't care what he makes me do."

"Now, it's not going to be that bad. He seems like a good man, and he assured me he'll look out for your best welfare. We'll be able to send you letters now and then and we can see you, if you're not busy, when we come into town, which isn't all that often, but it will be good when we do." While it would be nice to see them, the only thing I heard was that I could receive letters.

"Can anyone send me a letter?" I asked.

"Well, I think so but…we only talked about your aunt and me. Why are you asking?"

"Oh, just in case someone else wanted to send me a letter," I said, thinking of Becky.

"And who might that be? How many people send you letters now? Do you expect to start getting a flood of them?"

"No, no I don't. I was just wondering if I could get letters from anyone but you and Charity, that's all."

"I'm sure you'll be able to. I don't see why not. Now let's get your things." He was covering his real feelings by being too chipper about everything. The way he was acting just wasn't normal for him. He was a moderate type; sometimes quiet, sometimes not, but always on an even keel. He was doing a poor job of trying to convince me that all is well. We walked back up the street to the cart. My things consisted of a small bag with all of the clothes I owned, or at least those I wasn't wearing which wasn't many, a blanket and a few personal items. The most prized of them was a small pewter spoon that belonged to my mother. It was the only thing of hers I had taken with me. Just looking at it would bring back the memories of her that made me feel better. Josiah stood by the cart rubbing his neck. He was uncomfortable with saying good-bye.

"Well, you ought to go," I said, trying to make it easier for him. "I have to talk to Mr. Goodfield about the details of my arrangement. I hope this isn't going to be as bad as I think it is." I said that more to myself than to him. I could tell that it stung him the minute I said it. I didn't know what to say so I didn't say anything at all. In a way, I felt that he deserved it since he was getting rid of me by dumping me with this fat old man. Scowling, I could not believe the circumstances in which

I found myself.

"Well," I said.

"Well," he repeated.

"Please ask Charity to send me a letter as soon as she can. I'll write you if Mr. Goodfield lets me. Take care of yourself, Uncle Josiah." With that, I turned and walked into the house, leaving him standing in front of the cart. It was not very nice of me, but at that point, I wasn't feeling nice at all.

Goodfield stood at the other side of the room with his back to me. He turned and looked me up and down, walking around me once. I felt like I was some animal he was thinking of buying. When he finished, he grunted and left the room. A minute later, he came back with a short, plump woman wearing a nut-brown dress with the cleanest, whitest apron I'd ever seen. She was wearing a cap with a widow's peak and had a kind look about her. She looked as pleasant as Goodfield did gruff. He grunted again and turned to her.

"This is Jack," he said to the woman who I assumed was Mrs. Goodfield.

"Hello Jack. I'm glad you came to us. You'll be sleeping in the garret with the other apprentices. There's a good mattress for you that was stuffed with corn and hay just last week. You'll eat your meals in the other room," she said, pointing behind her. "If you have any questions, which I'm sure you will, ask the other apprentices. They've been here for a while and know how things operate. I keep a clean house and don't tolerate any horseplay or rowdiness. I expect you to behave at all times. You do what you're told and you'll get along fine. Gurdon," she said bowing her head to her husband before she turned and walked out the room. Goodfield looked down his nose at me for a minute.

"Well, don't just stand there boy. Put your things in the garret and get back down here. The stairs are over there. Come down right away. The morning's wasted but you can still work for a few hours. Remember this: you have to earn your place in my house. Now go." With that, I went up the stairs to find my place among the apprentices' pallets.

The higher up I went, the hotter it got. Even though it was only June, I was sweating by the time I got to the top of the stairs. The only light came from two small windows on either side of the room. There were four pallets with thin mattresses on each. The three nearest to the stairs each had blankets and clothes hanging on pegs behind them while the fourth was untouched. I put my sack down and sat on the mattress. It smelled of new hay and rustled with old corn leaves. Two small tables stood opposite the pallets. On each was a little candlestick with a fat stub of candle in them. It would be hot in the summer and freezing in the winter, since there wasn't a fireplace. I thought of how on a cold night I would sleep in front of the fire with Tink beside me.

I didn't want to incur Goodfield's wrath so I hurried downstairs, only to find him gone. I went from room to room looking for him. The size of the house amazed me because I didn't realize that one house could be this big and contain so many rooms. Any two of the rooms were the size of our entire house. I found him outside in the back.

"I'm back, sir."

"And it's about time. What took you so long? Now, you're going to become a cooper. You'll be working under Jacob, the best cooper in Boston. He's worked for me for several years," he explained. "He won't tolerate any nonsense. You are here to learn…and make me money. You do everything that Jacob tells you. He's worked with just one apprentice before but the boy got sick and had to leave...I heard he died soon after that. Oh well," he said, dismissing the thought of the poor boy as easy as brushing off a fly. "Jacob is a good man but has a short temper." With that, he began walking towards a building that looked like a warehouse. Before we got to it, he turned to the right, stopping in front of the cooperage. It was a small building, open on two sides to let the light in with stacks of wood all around. Seated at the bench was a thin man with long arms and legs. He wore a gray, sweat-stained hat with a brim so wide that from the way he was sitting, I couldn't see his face. Long, dark hair hung down from under the hat, covering his ears and neck. His hands moved surely and smoothly over a piece of wood. He was making a long barrel stave.

"Jacob," Goodfield said, "this is the new apprentice. Name is Jack. Just got here a while ago. I told you about him the other day. I want him to learn all there is about coopering. Work him hard." Goodfield went back to the house, leaving Jacob and me alone. He continued to work the stave, shaping it until it was just right. I stood watching, since I didn't have much else to do. He didn't speak until he was finished, which was a good five minutes.

"So you want to be a cooper, eh?" he asked, raising his head and peering out from under the brim. I saw only half of his face but it looked long and gaunt. A thin beard covered his pointed chin.

"No, I don't. I want to be a farmer."

"Well, well, Goodfield's given me a boy to teach who doesn't even want to learn. That's not a good way to start, you know. I have better things to do with my time than spend it on someone like you."

"I never said I couldn't be a cooper and a good one at that. I never said I didn't want to learn either. You asked me if I wanted to be a cooper and I said no, which is the truth. But I never said I couldn't be." He leaned the stave against a half-finished barrel. As he sat up, I saw how skinny he was. He looked like he weighed less than I did.

"All right," he said. "That's fair. You answered the question honestly. Now, let's talk a bit so we understand each other. Come over here and sit down," he said, motioning me to a three-legged stool. I moved it so I was facing him.

"Tell me how you came to be here. Did your father send you here?"

"No, he couldn't have…my father is dead. My mother died two years ago giving birth to my brother. I live with my aunt and uncle but they sent me here. They said this would be good for me, that I'd learn more and have a greater opportunity for a better life." He sat there looking at me, considering what I told him.

"What town are you from?"

"Ipswich."

"How old are you?"

"14."

"So you're all alone now?"

"Well no, not really. I have my aunt and uncle. And I have my dog Tink…that's short for Tinker."

"Yes, I'm sure it is," he said, a small smile appearing on his long, drawn face. He got up and began pacing in front of me across the open end. "I want you to know that I'm not like Goodfield. I work for him because I'm a very good cooper and he pays me well. I don't believe in beating people down to get what you want. I'll teach you all that I can but you have to be willing to learn. If you're not, tell me now and I'll speak with Goodfield so he can find something else for you to do." From what little I knew about Jacob, he seemed to be a reasonable man. It occurred to me that I might do worse than to learn from him and that I could work with someone who wasn't as tolerant. I realized that I was stuck here and might as well make the most of it, learning whatever I could. He looked down at me while I gave the matter a little more thought. I stood up and saw that he was a good foot taller than I was and didn't seem as old as I first thought.

"I'll work with you," I told him. "I'll learn all that you can teach me and do the best I can."

"That's good. I'm glad...you seem like a good boy. I will teach you all that I can." He did just that. Over the next two months, I learned much about being a good cooper and became skilled at turning out buckets, barrels, hogsheads, piggins, and firkins. Jacob was pleased with my progress, and never hesitated to tell Goodfield, who seemed like he could care less how I was doing as long as I made him money.

During the next few days, the other apprentices and I came to know each other. We talked of home, friends, things we missed, and hopes for the future as well as the good and bad points of working for Goodfield. John Smith was from

Duxbury, which was south of Boston, Rich Brown came from Roxbury, and Will Preston hailed from the small town of Marlborough, which was 20 miles west of Boston. John, a tall, lanky boy who was training as a blacksmith, didn't want to be here any more than I did. Rich was glad to be working as a tanner, although the stink from the animal hides followed him everywhere, sometimes making conversing with him difficult on a hot day when the wind was blowing from behind him. Will was enjoying himself and learning as much as he could about becoming a good carpenter. He was a short, somewhat chunky boy with a small, fuzzy beard covering his upper lip and chin, who whistled a soft tune most of the time.

There are certain memories that stay with us; ones that bring back the sights, sounds, and smells of a certain time and place. Some of the sharpest from my time at Goodfield's is of heat, sweat, dead fish, and the smell of wood shavings. The warehouse was dark, hot and humid, and the cooperage less so, because of the open sides. It seemed that I was sweating all the time. It ran down my face, neck, back and legs, and my clothes stuck to my body all the time. The only thing that I liked was working with Jacob, because it was outside where the wind blew and the smell of the freshly sawn wood was all around me. It was the one thing that took my mind off the situation in which I found myself.

I was surprised one morning by Elizur Hapgood. I was tidying things up in the cooperage, and when I turned around, there he was. He was a heavyset man with a thick neck and barrel chest. He put his hands on his hips and looked around at all the things I made.

"Jack my boy, how are you? How goes things with Mr. Goodfield? Are you learning anything? Why, of course you are! You're a smart boy…you couldn't help but learn."

"Mr. Hapgood, I didn't expect to see you here. Are you here to see Goodfield?" I asked, suspicious of his reason for visiting. After all, Hapgood was the one who started me on this miserable journey. If he hadn't told Josiah about Goodfield needing an apprentice, I would still be at home.

"I came in on some business and thought while I was here I'd say hello. So, how are things going?"

"They're all right," I answered, shrugging my shoulders. "I'm learning a few things but I would rather be at home."

"I'm sure you would, but it will be good. Just give it a little more time, another year or two. I'm sure you'll come to like it."

"Maybe I will, but more than likely I won't," I snarled. I decided to try to change the subject.

"How are Charity and Josiah?"

"Oh, they're fine. I saw Josiah yesterday and told him

I'd be coming in. He wanted me to say hello and let him know how you're doing. Some people at home have been asking about you," he said with a twinkle in his eye.

"Who?" I demanded. "Who's been asking about me?" I hoped it was Becky but I didn't get my hopes up for fear of being disappointed.

"Oh, quite a few…the Warner boys, Jack Bradbury and his brother Andrew, and one of the Morgans."

"Which Morgan?" I asked, feeling a lump in my throat. I noticed my palms were sweating.

"Just the one I ran into yesterday," he said, keeping me in suspense. "Jack, who would you most like to hear from? Be honest with me now."

"Becky," I responded in a low voice.

"I thought so. I saw her yesterday afternoon. She asked if I'd be going to Boston any time soon and I mentioned that I was today. She asked me to tell you that she hopes to come into town with her father someday soon so she can see you. She also wanted me to tell you that she promises she'll write." I became aware that my heart was pounding and my mouth had gone dry. "Oh, I forgot about this," he said, reaching into his bag and pulling out a letter. "Your aunt asked to give you this." Just at that moment, Goodfield came around the corner. I turned to the side and shoved the letter in my breeches so he wouldn't see it. I was sure that if he did, he'd take it and throw it away.

"Hapgood! Are you taking up my apprentice's time?" he bellowed. Without waiting for an answer, he turned on me. "You! Get back to work! There's no time for idle chatter, not in my business. There's a ship arriving in three days and we need enough barrels to be able to send the cargo out so get cracking. Where's Jacob?"

"He left a few minutes ago, sir. He didn't tell me where he was going." He scowled at me a moment longer and turned on his heels.

"Come on Hapgood, do you want to tend to business or not?"

In the short time I'd been there, it was apparent to me that not many people liked Gurdon Goodfield. He was gruff at his best, even with his family, and mean at worst. He believed that everyone who worked for him was a slave. There were a couple of men like Jacob who were treated better. He continued to work there only because Goodfield paid better than the other merchants did. As I was to learn later, for all of Goodfield's dealings, he wasn't a prosperous merchant.

I wasn't able to read Charity's letter until much later. Just before I went to bed, I sat on the floor of the garret with a stubby candle in one hand and the letter in the other. While it lifted my spirits, it made me long for Ipswich and my home even more.

Jack,

Please know that we miss you. Perhaps I should have been more forceful in my defense of your not going to Boston but Josiah had his mind set. I don't think it would have made any difference. While I think there are more opportunities there than here, it may not be the right thing for you. Tink misses you too. He mopes around all day, waiting for you to come home and play with him.

I visited the Morgans this morning. Becky asked about you. I told her we hadn't heard from you yet. She asked that I give you her good wishes and she hopes your time as an apprentice goes quickly. Perhaps sometime you can write her for I know that she'd like that. I hope you'll be able to come here on some business for Mr. Goodfield. We all want to see you again as soon as we can.

I got a letter from Mrs. Fletcher the other day about your brother. They named him Ethan. She said he looks like your mother but has your father's eyes, is growing like a weed and learning to talk and though most of it is gibberish, he talks a mile a minute. They bought a farm in Chelmsford and moved from Groton a few months ago. If we are ever in that area or if they ever come to Ipswich, we could see him.

Take care of yourself, work hard, and remember that we love you.

Charity

My first thought was of Tink. I could picture him sitting there just inside the door waiting for me. Early in the morning, he would wake me up by pushing me with his big, cold, wet nose. My thoughts turned to Becky. I could feel her lips against mine and see her crying when I left her. I hoped with all my heart that someday I would be able to see my little brother and be with him for more than just a little while. Even though I never even saw him, I missed him. A wave of homesickness swept over me and I wanted nothing more than to sleep. I blew out the candle, found my way to my pallet, and fell onto my mattress.

Before I knew it, it was time to get up. I dragged myself from my bed, made my way downstairs, and grabbed a handful of food before heading out to begin my coopering again.

Jacob was patient and explained things well to me, for I caught on fast. I've always liked to learn new things, and even though I was working for Goodfield, it was interesting and took my mind off all the things and people I missed at home. We made more staves than anything else because Goodfield shipped them to England, where they sold for a good price.

About two weeks after getting Charity's letter and right after I learned how to make several things well, Goodfield came stomping down yelling for me, making me wonder what

I'd done this time.

"Parker," he exclaimed, "you're done with this right now. One of the boys on my coastal trader just finished up. I need someone to replace him and you're it."

"But sir, I don't know anything about boats and I'm learning this well. Jacob said I'm one of the best apprentices he's ever worked with. Ask him for yourself." Since Jacob wasn't there at that moment, as he had gone to collect chestnut wood from the warehouse, my argument fell on deaf ears.

"It doesn't matter one bit. You're on the boat starting today. Mate's name is Quimby. Crotchety old man, but he's been sailing for years and knows the coast waters better than any man in the Colony. Go to the wharf and see him now. I'll let Jacob know. Now move boy, move!" There didn't seem to be any way I could get out of this so I put down my tools, straightened things up as best as I could, and with Goodfield watching me with his hands on his hips and scowling as he always did, I trudged off towards the wharf.

Chapter 3

At the wharf there were several men carrying barrels and boxes of things from the boat to the warehouse. I stood for a minute eyeing the scene while trying to figure out which of them was Quimby. I didn't see anyone who fit Goodfield's description. All of them were young, with the oldest being about 25-years-old. Two young boys were trundling goods off in huge wheelbarrows, almost tipping them over because they were overloaded. My eye fell on one man who was giving directions to the others. I did not know if he was part of the crew, but I approached him.

"Excuse me sir, are you Quimby?" When he turned and looked at me, I saw that he was a tall man with a handsome face, browned from the sun and wind, with light green eyes.

"If there was one person I'd never want to be, it is Quimby. What's your business with him?" The man put his hands on his hips, looking from me to the unloading.

"I'm Jack Parker; Jacob Eliot's apprentice. Mr. Goodfield put me on the boat. He said I needed to see Quimby."

"So, you're the new man. I'm Tom Wiswell, the chief

hand on the boat. Quimby's not here right now but he should be back soon. Have you ever been to sea?"

"No, I haven't. I grew up in Ipswich and have been out a couple of times but just in the bay...nothing more than that."

"Well," he said, with a smile spreading over his face, "this will be a big adventure for you. I want you to meet the other hand. Hezekiah, come here," he said to a tall, gangling youth with blonde hair sticking out in all directions from under his big, brown, floppy hat. He came over and stood next to us. "Jack, this is Hezekiah Usher. He's been on the boat for two years. Hezekiah, this is Jack Parker. He's taking Loell's place." Turning to me he said, "Loell was the apprentice who just finished his term. Goodfield didn't plan it too well and wasn't able to replace him before he left. That's why you're here." While it didn't make me feel any better, at least I understood what was happening.

"How does this work? Where do you go? What do you do?" I asked.

"We travel up and down the coast picking up all sorts of goods that we bring back here," Hezekiah explained. "Goodfield stores everything in the warehouse until a ship is ready to go to England or maybe Spain. Then he sends his goods on someone else's ship."

"What types of goods do you get?"

"Lots of things that can be sold in England...things

they don't have," Tom replied. "The biggest cargo is lumber. They don't have many trees over there and we do, so Goodfield and the other merchants send shiploads of it. One of the other things is barrel staves and hoops like the ones I'm sure Jacob had you make. Thousands and thousands of staves and hoops can be sent on one ship"

"When are we supposed to leave?"

"Next Tuesday," Tom answered.

"You're lucky," Hezekiah said, "I was on board only a few hours before we left."

"Just so you know," Tom added, "its not easy work - especially when the weather is bad. The seas can get rough and you're cold and wet a good part of the time. The ship wasn't built for our comfort, but to hold as much as it can. Goodfield wants a strong return on his investment." Hezekiah chuckled at this.

"Why aren't you working?" snarled someone behind me. I turned and there stood a grizzled, skinny, toothless old man. His face was dark brown, with wrinkles and lines radiating around his mouth and eyes; it looked like old worn leather. He had a scar that ran from under his left eye down to his jaw. His eyes were different colors; the right a startling blue and the left a golden, piercing brown. His clothes were dirty and he gave off a strong odor of sweat and rum. He turned his withering gaze upon me and stepped closer until he was just inches from my face. I was taller than he was, so the top of his head was level with my nose. His breath was horrid; it smelled worse than he did and reminded me of rotten meat. He stepped back and looked me up and down.

"Who are you and why the hell are you bothering my men?" he growled.

"I'm Jack Parker. Goodfield sent me down here. Said I was to take someone's place," I replied, a spark of anger flaring up inside me at the questions from this foul smelling little man. I could see Tom and Hezekiah watching me to see how I handled myself with him. He walked all around me, grunting as he did. As he faced me, he put his hands on my shoulders and pushed me hard. I stumbled backwards a few steps. Without thinking, I regained my balance and pushed him back. He landed on his ass, sitting down hard on the wharf. Looking up at me, he held out his hand. I reached down and pulled him up. While he was so light I almost threw him, I could feel the hard muscle in his arm.

"Quick and strong; big too," he cackled. "I'm Quimby boy. You now work for me. Let him unload the hogsheads," he told Tom, giving me a sly smile as he brushed past me.

The ship was not as big as I thought it should be for one that had a crew of four, counting Quimby. It was a coaster or round ship; 60 feet long and 20 feet across the beam, with two masts and the rudder off the right side. It looked slow and unseaworthy, but it was designed for hugging the coast and carrying great amounts of cargo.

For the rest of the afternoon and all the next day I worked unloading the cargo. I never imagined a ship of this size could hold so much. Huge hogsheads weighing 200 pounds each, barrels filled with who knows what, stacks and stacks of barrel staves and hoops, and lumber of all sizes. Every muscle ached and throbbed; I was sore all over. I ate my evening meal in a fatigued daze after which I stumbled to the garret and dropped onto my pallet already asleep.

Over the next couple of days, I learned the basics about being out on a ship.

I found out on our first trip what a bastard Quimby could be. He put me in the hold to stack all the cargo we got. I got no direction from any of my crewmates even when I asked. They all demurred to Quimby who ignored me, so I did the best job I could. Not knowing how to place cargo, I organized it the way I thought best to get as much on as possible while making it easy to unload. When I had it halfway loaded, I stopped for a few minutes to rest. The sweat was pouring down my face, neck, and back. I was breathing hard and the fetid air made it worse. The cargo area is wide but not high, so being on the tall side, I was always bent over while I lifted and strained. Just as I sat on the top of a barrel, Quimby came down the ladder and stood staring at me, slapping his right hand against his leg.

"Did I tell you that you can rest?" I didn't respond but just looked at him. "Well, did I?" he screamed. "Get moving boy. There's no rest for you on my ship. You'll work as long and as hard as I tell you to." He turned and began inspecting my work. "This is all wrong! Why did you do it this way boy?" he yelled. "Now get over there and begin unloading all this! The staves and hoops go on the top of the hogsheads near the bow. The barrels go along the port side and the lumber along the starboard side." He worked himself into frenzy, screaming and shouting at me about what an idiot I was and how he couldn't believe Goodfield would dump someone as useless and worthless as me on him when there was so much cargo to be picked up and delivered to the warehouse before the next ship left for England. He came at me, continuing his tirade and pulling a leather-covered rod from his belt, hit me hard across my cheek. My head rocked back from the force of the blow and I fell onto my side. I saw flashes of red and white and grabbing the edge of a barrel, pulled myself up. I could feel the deepening sting and tasted blood in my mouth. My face throbbed from ear to jaw. I pulled myself to my full height and looked down at him. Now furious, I flexed my hands and clenched them tight.

"Don't try any tricks or I'll beat you senseless," he said in a flat voice. As much as it bothered me, I decided that the consequences of my punching him until he couldn't stand were worse than just letting it go. I also decided that I would get out of my apprenticeship as soon as I could and I would spend all my time trying to figure out how.

Early the next morning, Quimby put me to work scrubbing the decks. After two hours of scrubbing hard enough that my elbows and shoulders hurt, Quimby came along to see how well I was doing. He stood over me, slapping his hand against his leg but didn't say anything. I knelt there, waiting for him to tell me how I'd done. He looked up and down the deck with a careful eye, searching for anything I might have missed.

"You missed a whole piece down by the bow. Start all over again. I want the entire deck scrubbed and washed again." I sat back on my heels, wiping the sweat from my eyes. "You'll get no rest. Now get going boy." I finished an hour later. Quimby came around again, this time walking up and down the deck, looking from side to side.

"That's better. You did a fair job, but..." He stood facing me as I put the brush in the bucket, glad that I was done with this backbreaking job. Taking a step back, he loosened his breeches and starting pissing all over the area around him. He cackled as he did it, flashing a toothless smile at me. "Guess it wasn't that good a job after all was it? Do it again, boy." With that, he hitched up his breeches and walked away, leaving me to scrub the deck for a third time.

We were in Boston only four days, unloading the cargo and getting the ship ready to sail again. Tom came aboard late in the afternoon and announced that we were heading to a trading post on the Kennebec River to pick up a load of pelts. I found out from Hezekiah that the Indians sold bales of pelts to Goodfield for a few trade goods like kettles, axes, and beads because he was one of the several men in the Colony licensed to trade with them.

We left well before dawn the next morning, heading out on a strong breeze and high tide. The sky was clear and stars were fading as the sky began to lighten. The sun came up, the light sparkling off the water. For a minute, I forgot why I was there and enjoyed the feel of the wind and sun, the motion and sound of the ship sliding through the water. Tom started singing in a beautiful voice, which surprised me. Quimby came on deck and glared at him but didn't say anything, so Tom kept singing. He'd gone through three or four songs we all knew when he broke into one I'd never heard. It was a sorrowful tune about a man who had lost his wealth and the woman he loved. He later told me it was called "The Willow Tree" and that he'd first heard it years ago.

We were busy doing all manner of things as Quimby ordered us about for the next hour or so. Tom stopped his singing as soon as Quimby started yelling at us. With the heavy work done, Quimby retired to the aft deck and Tom began again. The words of this song pulled at my heart and caused an empty feeling inside me. The name of the song, "The Girl I Left Behind Me," made me think of Becky and how I missed her. While I don't remember all the words, there are some verses I'll never forget:

> *"Her golden hair in ringlets fair,*
> *her eyes like diamonds shining*
> *Her slender waist, her heavenly face,*
> *that leaves my heart still pining*
> *Ye gods above oh hear my prayer*
> *to my beauteous fair to find me*
> *And send me safely back again,*
> *to the girl I left behind me*
> *I seek for one as fair and gay,*
> *But find none to remind me*
> *How sweet the hours I passed away,*
> *With the girl I left behind me."*

Wiswell's voice was strong and clear. He told me that he sang whenever he could since it soothed him. I have a strong memory of listening to him as we cut across the slight rolling waves on that sparkling morning. He continued to sing off and on throughout the day, and I can still hear him and feel the spray lift up towards me as I drowsed on that fine summer afternoon.

As we sailed up the coast, I saw the land change from towns with small patches of forest in between beaches and marshes to endless marshes and ponds with spruce trees at their back edge. We passed by Salem, Gloucester, Ipswich and Newburyport. I looked towards the Ipswich River with a heavy heart. It was my home, and I missed everyone and everything there very much. I turned away with a deep sigh.

There were several long stretches of beach, which turned yellow and gold in the daylight. In between there were cliffs of hard, gray rock, some 100 feet high; the waves crashing against them. The coast was dotted with quite a few small bays and tidal rivers that ran back into the dark green pine forest. It was fine looking land. A few small settlements of only three or four houses sat at the water's edge, miles apart from each other. When we reached the Kennebec, what I saw awed me. Small, green islands dotted the blue water like jewels. When we swept around a headland and coasted between two islands, geese and ducks by the thousands rose into the air as we approached. Sailing for an hour through several small bays, we came upon a narrows with rocky points on either side. With a light breeze behind us, we went past a long, narrow island and entered into a large bay. The area was wild and beautiful; the land was rich with trees, marsh, and fields with groups of deer. There was a clean smell and a tang to the air. It was one of the most beautiful places I've ever seen.

The trading post, having been set up by the Plymouth Colony years before to collect beaver pelts, was at Merrymeeting Bay on a point of land where the river split into two sections. Even after so many years, as the annual trapping continued unabated, pelts were still plentiful with the demand for other pelts as high as that for beaver. Deer, bear, wolf, moose, mink, and fox were common, but sable pelts were the most prized of all and sold to the Governor. He would send the best back to England for the King and keep the remainder for himself.

We got there just before twilight, anchoring a hundred yards off the shore. The Indian village that supplied the pelts was just upriver. As we approached the trading post, the trader came out to us in a canoe paddled by two Indians to talk with Quimby about taking on the pelts. He told him that we would begin in the morning since it was getting late. As I watched them return to the trading post, I saw many Indians standing on a headland, silhouetted against the waning light in the western sky, looking in our direction.

The wind was light from the southwest and the sky was clear. As we ate stale bread and salt fish, Quimby began telling us of his adventures. He seemed a different man; laughing and cackling to himself as he remembered certain things and swearing at others. I looked over at Hezekiah who just shook his head. He made the motion of drinking and I understood that Quimby had sucked down more than his share of rum. I learned that Quimby had been sailing since he was a boy over 40 years ago. He told us the same stories of his adventures and voyages to distant ports including England, Spain, and Barbados, going on for at least an hour. We sat there in the darkness listening to him babble. The more he drank the more he repeated himself telling us the stories again and again until we knew them so well we could have repeated them in our sleep. After a while, I turned away from him and lay down on the deck to sleep and looking up into the darkness, I saw bright stars stretching from horizon to horizon. I pulled my blanket up and the last thing I remember is hearing drunken Quimby stagger towards the bow and fall down with a loud thud.

The next morning we found Quimby right where he fell. Tom kicked him a couple of times in an effort to wake him, but it didn't do any good. It seemed like nothing could rouse him, so Tom dropped a bucket on a rope over the side and threw the cold water onto Quimby. He opened his eyes, startled at the sudden dousing. He stood, shaking a bit, and grabbed onto some rope to help pull himself up. He got upright, grimaced at us, and began barking for us to get under way. He looked haggard; his clothes covered with dirt, he was unshaven and smelled of sour sweat and rum. He staggered to the railing and began retching over the side.

An hour later, a canoe came out and took Quimby to shore. He was gone a while, trying to buy the pelts with the axes and copper kettles he'd taken with him. Six canoes came out to us, each full of pelts and Quimby in the bow of the first canoe. The minute he came aboard, he began barking orders at us. He directed most of his nastiness at me, as usual; he was merciless. There have been very few men I truly hated, and Quimby was one of them.

I had just started when Quimby came towards me yelling at the top of his lungs. "Boy! Bring those bales and get them loaded now! Come on, we don't have all day!" I dragged bale after bale into the hold, each weighing almost two hundred pounds. Even though I was used to such work, after the seventh bale I was breathing hard and sweating. Quimby refused to allow Tom or Hezekiah to help me stow the bales into the cargo hold, even though Tom offered twice. I slowed down a bit, trying to load them to balance the weight. I was moving far too slow for Quimby for he tore into me again.

"Boy! What the hell do you think you're doing? Didn't you hear me...we don't have all day to get this done. We need to sail soon on the tide. Move your ass boy!"

"I'm not a boy!" I shot back jumping up on deck as he rushed up to me.

"Oh, yes you are, boy. Don't you talk back to me again you filthy bastard. Didn't you learn your lesson? This time I won't hit you," he said, lowering his voice as he approached me like a cat stalking a mouse. I could see him quivering with rage; tense and ready to strike at the slightest provocation. "No, I won't hit you this time…no, I'll cut off your ear. I won't take your fingers because you need those to work but you can get along fine with just one ear." As if to prove his intentions, he put his hand on the knife he carried in his belt. "You aren't the first and won't be the last to lose an ear to me," he whispered with a wink of his eye. From that point on, I said as little to him as I could since I never doubted that he would do just as he threatened.

We set sail around mid-morning, heading back down the coast with a good breeze behind us. Tom came over to me as I stood in the stern next to Hezekiah, who was manning the tiller.

"Be careful of him Jack," he told me as he nodded in Quimby's direction. "He's taken a real dislike to you. I saw Quimby cut a man's hand off with an axe two years ago when he was drunk. He got into an argument with this farmer at a tavern in the Connecticut Colony. There was an axe next to the fireplace and as they're yelling and shouting at each other, Quimby reaches behind him, grabs the axe, and swings at the farmer's arm. Well, his right hand was on the table and Quimby chopped right through his wrist. I never saw anything like it. Blood everywhere; the farmer was screaming, people are yelling and pushing towards us. The old bastard started swinging the axe at anyone who came near him. I got out the door before anyone else and ran for the ship. We'd only been there a short time and I hadn't talked to anyone so no one knew who I was. I figured there would be a group of angry men chasing us. Quimby ran past me as we got close to the boat. He yelled, waking the others, jumped over the railing and ordered us to get out into the river. As luck would have it, there was a strong wind that night and we were gone in a few minutes…it was a narrow escape. They would have hung us if they caught us." This bit of information frightened me. I vowed to get off this ship as soon as I could, even if it meant I had to run away.

Sometimes we were gone just a day, a very long one to be sure. Other times we were gone for three or four days like the trip we were on. Quimby liked his rum, so he'd spend most of the night, if not all, at any tavern he could find. If he could, he would go to a former shipmate's house for a night of drunken revelry. Whenever he could, Tom stayed with people he knew in the various places we stopped. Hezekiah and I stayed on the ship to guard the cargo.

We'd sleep under the open part of the deck, lying on the hard wood, with a thin blanket over us. We shared the place with a few rats that crawled about at night. In good weather, it was an uncomfortable place to sleep. In bad weather it was horrible, and it was the worst when it rained. We'd only be able to get a few feet in towards the bow under the raised deck. The rain flowed to all sections as the ship went up and down with the waves. We'd be cold and wet and could guarantee that we wouldn't sleep at all that night. If we tried to sleep in the hold, it would be even worse since the stench would almost suffocate us. Plus there were more rats. If that wasn't bad enough, the ship stunk of dead fish and sea mud. It was in my clothes, my skin, and my hair and I couldn't get rid of the overpowering smell. It followed me wherever I went - even back to my mattress at Goodfield's house.

Quimby announced that on our way home, we'd be stopping at the Isles of Shoals, a small group of islands a four-hour sail south from the Kennebec. He wanted to see two of his old friends, Walter Barefoot and Roger Kelly, both of whom had reputations of being coarse, rough men. Rumors were that both had been successful privateers and from what I'd seen of Quimby, they sounded very much like him. Quimby was angry to find that neither one was home. Barefoot was in Boston and Kelly was at sea. He, of course, took it out on me by giving me a tongue-lashing and hitting me a few times with his leather rod. He was relentless and I'll admit that I came close to murdering him that night. I was tempted to drive his head into the deck and throw him overboard. After spending his rage, he announced that we'd stop in Ipswich to pick up a load of salt cod and that we'd spend the night. I thought it was odd since we'd be no more than a two-hour sail from Boston. It didn't matter why we were stopping; just the fact that we were was enough for me. I'd be able to see Charity and Josiah even if it was only for a short while. I thought about trying to see Becky since I hadn't been able to write but didn't know how much time I'd have off the boat. Just the thought of seeing my home made me happy. Quimby proved just what a bastard he was as we tied up at the dock. He ordered me to stay on the ship all night. He knew that I came from town and wanted to go home but he was determined to deny me even that. Quimby, Tom, and Hezekiah all went to the tavern. I asked Hezekiah to go to my house to let Josiah and Charity know that I was here but Quimby heard me.

"You'll get no favors from him boy so stop asking. You're staying on the ship all night so get used to it. I don't care if your family lives just down the road, you'll not be going to see them. And, if I find that you snuck out, I'll whip you to within an inch of your life." With that, he stumbled off the boat and began to make his way to the tavern.

I sat there for a couple of hours, looking up and down the wharves hoping to see someone I knew. Quimby said I couldn't leave the ship, and I had no doubt that he'd come close to killing me if I did, but there was nothing to stop me from having people come to see me. Every time a man came my way, I looked hard to see if I recognized him. I didn't see anyone I knew and began to wonder who all these strangers were and where had they came from. I was sitting there on the rail, the slight breeze chilling me now that the sun had gone down, when I turned and saw Sam Davis, a young boy that lived just down the road from me.

"Sam," I called, "Sam come over here." He came trotting over and stood on the wharf.

"Jack, what are you doing here? I thought you were in Boston?"

"I'm a cooper's apprentice for a wealthy man but he put me on his coaster. I need you to do something for me, Sam. I can't leave the ship. The mate is a mean man. He won't let me leave because he hates me. He knows I want to see my family but won't let me. He told me he'd kill me if I did and I don't doubt him," I said in one long breath. He looked a little puzzled at this rush of words.

"What do you want me to do?"

"Run to my house and tell my aunt and uncle I'm here. Then go to Tom Morgan's house and let Becky know. Talk to her mother if you can. Her father doesn't like me. Please hurry Sam…I don't know how much time I have before one of the crew comes back."

"All right, I'll go your house, but I'm not going to the Morgan's. Mr. Morgan is mean." With that, he took off in the direction of my house. I slumped down onto the deck, excited at the chance of seeing Josiah and Charity but worried that Quimby would come back for some reason. I was taking an awful chance, but I decided it was worth it.

It seemed like Sam was gone forever. I waited and waited thinking that maybe I should just go to my house. Since Quimby wouldn't be back until morning, I thought I should just go, although I worried that if I did, something might happen to the ship and I'd be in deep trouble. Losing an ear would be the least of my worries. I paced back and forth trying to decide whether to go or stay.

"Jack, oh Jack," I heard Charity call me. "Oh Jack, let me see you," she said. "You've lost weight…and you're so dirty. What has happened to you? And why are you here on this boat?"

"Leave him alone," Josiah told her as he came up behind her. "Of course he's dirty, he's been working."

"He's not dirty, he's filthy," Charity shot back at him coming to the railing. "And he smells," she added.

I told them of my coopering and the time on the ship, including how bad Quimby treated and threatened me. I talked for five minutes without stopping to get all the information out as fast as I could. I could see they were trying to take it all in, but the look on Josiah's face showed the doubt he had about sending me to Goodfield.

"I want to see Becky too but Sam wouldn't go get her. I don't know if Quimby will come back. He said he's staying at the tavern but I don't trust anything about him. I don't know how much time I might have."

"You uncle will go and get her," she said to Josiah. He turned and walked away. Charity came onto the deck even though I told her of Quimby's threat. She vowed that she'd make sure Quimby would not hurt me. I'd never seen her in such a defiant mood.

"Is it as bad as you've made it out to be?" she asked, wrinkling her nose in disgust at my smell as she came closer. I wasn't sure how to respond; if I told her the truth, she'd be very upset but there was nothing she could do about it. If I lied to her, I would regret it, knowing that I might be losing an opportunity for her to assist me in getting out of this horrid situation. I decided I would rather have her upset, so I told her every detail of what I had been through. She was shocked by what I related and the way Quimby treated me and singled me out for a punishment that I didn't deserve. What frightened her most was when I told her about Quimby cutting off the farmer's hand.

"He's an evil man. How did you end up with such men? I won't have you working for him or Goodfield," she declared with an unmistakable determination in her voice. "We'll get you out of this Jack, I promise you. I'll do it myself if I have to." she said. We talked for another 15 minutes when out of the shadows came Becky, followed by Josiah. She looked even prettier than I remembered. I stood there gawking at her like an idiot. As she came up to me she noticed my dirty condition, wrinkling her nose at the smell of me.

"Oh you stink! What's happened to you? How did you end up here?" I started to explain, but as I was repeating what I'd already told Josiah and Charity, she interrupted me.

"Why didn't you write me?" she demanded.

"I haven't been able to…I've been working longer and harder than I ever have. Goodfield won't let me have any paper or ink. He said it's too expensive to be wasted on someone as useless as me."

"But I sent you three letters…"

"What letters? I didn't get any letters."

"I sent them to Mr. Goodfield. Elizur Hapgood took them for me. They were addressed to you."

"He never gave them to me." My anger and frustration were growing. I could feel my face get warm and realized I was clenching my teeth. I turned and locked my gaze on Josiah.

"See? Is this what you wanted for me? Is this your idea of what's best for me?" I yelled. "This just shows how they treat me. They work me to death, threaten me with whippings or cutting my ears off…or even branding me," I added, even though the last part wasn't true. I wanted him to know what a terrible thing he did to me. "I don't want to be an apprentice. I want to come home, although I'm sure you'll find some reason to send me off again," I spat at him. He held my burning stare for a few seconds before dropping his eyes to the ground.

"This isn't what I wanted for you," he said. "Please believe that. Goodfield told me how well you'd be taken care of, all the things you'd learn, and how good it would be for someone in your situation." He walked over to Charity's side and stood there looking at me. "You have to believe me, Jack; if I knew it would be anything like this, I never would have agreed to it. I'm not sure what I can do but I'll try. If I can, I'll go talk to Mr. Goodfield this week. Maybe we can get him to release you somehow. I don't know…I just don't know."

Becky just stood there, taking this all in and looking bewildered. She wasn't sure what to do or say. This is not how I wanted our meeting to go. I imagined it as a sweet, smiling, enjoyable time. Instead, it was a mess and I wasn't sure how to make it better.

Chapter 4

One morning, we were docked and unloading the cargo when Goodfield sent his youngest daughter down to the warehouse to get me. When I got to the house, I found him standing in the back near the vegetable garden rubbing his big belly.

"Jack," he called, causing me to stop in my tracks in surprise. He never called me by anything other than "boy" or my last name. "I've made a decision." he continued. "I'm taking you off the ship. Quimby has always said you work hard and can carry twice what the others can." This surprised me even more, since I never expected Quimby to say anything good about me. "But he's also told me from your first day that you were trouble and not worth his time or effort. With the winter coming on, there will be fewer trips to gather cargo…fewer ships go out in the winter so you'll not be needed as much." It was as if in answer to my prayers. I felt like dropping to my knees to give thanks.

"Have you had anything to eat?" he asked.

"Just a stale biscuit earlier this morning," I said.

"All right, go up to the kitchen and get yourself something. Make sure you take your things from the ship up to the garret," he said, walking away. I was puzzled because I couldn't figure out why Quimby would want me off the ship. I did more work than the others. He seemed to enjoy yelling, screaming, and threatening me. The only thing I could think of was that Goodfield needed me somewhere else more than he did with Quimby. However, Goodfield used my name and was in a good mood; two things he had never done before, at least when I was around. I grew suspicious of what his motives might be, for I'd never trusted or liked him.

As I was finishing my meal, he came into the room and sat down with a thump. He looked at me as I ate and, reaching out, ripped off a piece of bread and began chewing.

"I know you said you can read and write but can you do it well? I've had others here who claimed to be able to do both but couldn't. I have a reason for asking you this and want a truthful answer."

"Yes sir, I can read well. My mother taught me when I was young. I'd read the Bible to her every night." He got up, went into the next room, and came back a minute later with a big book in his meaty little hands. It was the well-worn family Bible. Opening it, he placed it in front of me.

"Read this," he said, pointing to a place on the page, "Book of Ezekiel, Chapter five, verses 15, 16, and 17." I looked at him, wondering why he was asking me to read. I pulled the book in front of me and began to read:

"Also, thou son of man, thus saith the Lord God unto the land of Israel; An end, the end is come upon the four corners of the land. Now is the end come upon thee, and I will send mine anger upon thee, and will judge thee according to thy ways, and will recompense upon thee all thine abominations. And mine eye shall not spare thee, neither will I have pity: but I will recompense thy ways upon thee, and thine abominations shall be in the midst of thee: and ye shall know that I am the Lord. Thus saith the Lord God; An evil, an only evil, behold, is come. An end is come, the end is come: it watcheth for thee; behold, it is come. The morning is come unto thee, O thou that dwellest in the land: the time is come, the day of trouble is near, and not the sounding again of the mountains. Now will I shortly pour out my fury upon thee, and accomplish mine anger upon thee: and I will judge thee according to thy ways, and will recompense thee for all thine abominations. And mine eye shall not spare, neither will I have pity: I will recompense thee according to thy ways and thine abominations that are in the midst of thee; and ye shall know that I am the Lord that smiteth."

I laid the book down and sat back in my chair. Goodfield leaned forward, putting his elbows on the table. He had a small piece of paper, quill, and ink next to him. He motioned for me to take them. "Write down what I say. And be exact because paper is expensive." *Don't I know it*, I thought to myself. *After you told me it was too expensive for someone as useless as me.* I wasn't sure if it was as expensive as he said or that he was as cheap as I thought. I put the thought out of my head and concentrated on the task at hand.

"John," he began, "The Argus is due to sail on the 15th of next month. I do not have a full cargo and need additional goods. The bales of pelts you mentioned would add to those I have already bought. I am ready to offer a fair price. I need molasses and will buy one-half of your next cargo from Barbados. I pray to God for your eternal salvation. Your humble servant, Gurdon."

"Let me see how you've done," he said as he took the letter and read it, grunting his approval. "You can do all that I need." He folded the note in half before giving it to me. "Take this to John Pynchon at The Sign of the Dove. It's the tavern at the far end of the Common." I stood holding the paper in my hand, uncertain as to the change in my duties. He saw my hesitation and looked at me. "Well, are you going or are you just going to stand there taking up my time?"

"Sir, why did you ask me to do all this? Do you have a special purpose in mind?"

"Yes, I do. I need an assistant." he said. "And right now you're the only person who can help me. But, don't get any ideas about this being an easy way out of your daily duties. I'll work you as hard as Quimby did," he thundered. I was out the door in a flash.

I've learned through my years of living that things very rarely happen for a single reason. Never did I imagine the effect that simple errand would have on the rest of my life.

I found the tavern without any problem. Mr. Pynchon was there and I was admitted to see him right away. As I entered, there was a well-dressed man of medium build facing away from me in the room on my right. I stood there a moment before he turned. When he did, he looked surprised to find me standing there.

"Mr. Pynchon, sir?" He narrowed his eyes a bit and took a step closer.

"And who might you be?" he asked in a pleasant voice.

"I'm Jack Parker, sir. Mr. Goodfield sent me with a note for you," I told him, holding the paper out to him. He took it but didn't unfold it. His face was of a medium complexion, with a dimple in his chin, a high forehead, and a thin nose pointing down to his bow-shaped mouth. His eyes were light blue and his hair a light shade of brown.

"Well Jack Parker, come in and let's see what Goodfield wants now." He sat behind a great table of dark polished wood and motioned me to a chair at the side. He flipped open the paper, read it, and dropped it on the table.

"Well that doesn't surprise me," he said to himself. He looked up at me with a small smile. "Are you curious why Goodfield sent you here?"

"I already know, sir. You see, I wrote it for him. I mean, what I'm trying to say sir, is that he told me what to write so I wrote it. It was a test to see if I could write."

"I can see that you passed the test. How long have you been with Goodfield?"

"Far too long," I replied, not realizing what I said until it was out of my mouth. "Um, I mean, uh…it's a long story."

"I have a few moments," he said with a chuckle. "Tell me about it. I like a good story. Go ahead," he said, encouraging me to tell him about my life in Ipswich. I related what happened to my parents, how Josiah and Charity took me in, apprenticed me to Goodfield, my working in the cooperage, being sent on the coaster with Quimby, and how I came to be here with him. I realized that I'd been talking for far more than a few minutes, but my story poured out of me. Mr. Pynchon sat looking at me thoughtfully. I began to fidget, not sure if I had told him more than I should have. I wondered how well he knew Goodfield and whether or not what I told him would came back to haunt me.

"That is quite a story for someone as young as you. You seem like quite a boy Jack Parker. Now, as to being his assistant, I'll give you some advice. Do all he tells you to right away and do not make him wait. Try not to anger him. If you ask him for more work, he'll be appreciative. Ask him about the business; he enjoys talking about his success. Take this note back to Mr. Goodfield." He handed me the note after scratching a reply.

"Thank you, sir. It's been very good to meet you, sir."

"It's been good to meet you, too. I've enjoyed our talk. Maybe Mr. Goodfield will have more errands for you and we can talk again."

"I do hope so, sir. I'd like that very much," I said enthusiastically.

This became the most enjoyable duty as his assistant - taking letters and packages to various people in and around Boston, either goods they bought or letters Goodfield had written. I was away from Goodfield, which, in my opinion, was always a good thing, and I got to meet new and interesting people, which helped satisfy my curiosity.

Mr. Pynchon was a pleasant man and treated me well each time I saw him. He always made a few minutes for me so we could sit and chat about anything and everything. He was serious much of the time but had a good smile and laugh. I'm not sure why he took such an interest in me, but he greeted me as a friend every time. Maybe I reminded him of someone or he liked boys who weren't afraid of important men like him. He came from Springfield to meet with the governor and other officials. Most of the time I brought him letters that were left at Goodfield's for him. Over the course of the next year, I saw him each time he came to Boston.

On my second visit with him, he told me to sit and began to ask me detailed questions about Ipswich, my family, my interests, and other things along that line. He looked at me with care and concern as I answered his questions. When he asked what I wanted to do with my life, I thought it was an odd question. No one had ever asked me that before and I'd never given it any thought. After a moment's reflection, I told him that I wanted to be a farmer with a lot of land and have many adventures. He laughed at that and told me that the two, as a rule, did not go together. You could be a farmer or an adventurer, but he'd never known of anyone being both.

"Well sir, if it's quite all right, I have a question for you, if I may?"

"A question for me? Of course, go ahead and ask me your question."

"How did you get to be so important?" I asked with childlike curiosity. At this, he laughed, finding it very funny. After a moment, he recovered himself.

"You'll have to forgive me Jack, but that just struck me. No one has ever asked me that before. Well, it's simply God's will. My father, William, arrived here in 1630 and became the treasurer of the Colony. He was an excellent merchant and started Springfield as a trading post in 1636 with eight families that he took west with him from Dorchester. Since Springfield is on the Connecticut River, it's a favorite stopping point for Indians from all areas up and down the river. Fur trading has been the order of business for many years. About ten years ago, my father wrote a book, *The Meritorious Price of Our Redemption,* a religious treatise that argued points of Puritan teaching. It was condemned by the General Court. He was ordered to retract the statements he'd made and to appear before the Court. He didn't want to, so later that same year, he transferred all his assets in the Colony to me and went back to England. And that is how I started to become so important. So remember, God has a plan for each of us."

"I wonder what mine is."

"I've no doubt you'll find that out when you're supposed to know...all in God's good time."

On what came to be my next-to-last visit to him, at least at that time, I met another man who I'd heard of but never in all my thoughts could imagine I would meet. It was Governor Endecott. He was a stern looking man with dark eyes and stood with a man on either side of him, staring at me for what seemed like a long time, although it wasn't any more than a few seconds. Mr. Pynchon smiled at me, seeing my obvious discomfort.

"Governor, this is Jack Parker from Ipswich. He's apprenticed to Goodfield as a cooper, deck hand, and now assistant. I've met him several times and he's a fine boy," he said, looking at me. I couldn't quite believe that he was telling the governor that I was a fine boy! Governor Endecott continued to look at me, which made me uncomfortable. Again, Mr. Pynchon came to my rescue.

"Come back later at early candlelight if you can. We'll talk then," he told me. The governor and the other two men turned and began talking with Mr. Pynchon. I remember thinking that Josiah and Charity wouldn't believe this when I told them.

I didn't even ask Goodfield if I could go back to Mr. Pynchon's because I knew he'd say that I couldn't. I slipped out of the house and made my way as fast as I could. When I got to the tavern, I was told that Mr. Pynchon was out but would be back soon. I decided to spend a few minutes waiting for him, although the longer I was away, the greater my chances of Goodfield finding me gone and that would cause serious trouble. This was the first time I'd done anything like this and worried more as every minute passed. I was about to leave when Mr. Pynchon came in, hat in hand.

"You were able to come back…that's wonderful," he said, pleased that I was there. I followed as he walked to a table farthest from the door and asked the innkeeper for drinks; rum for him and cider for me.

"So," he asked, putting his hands on the table, "what did Goodfield say when you asked to come see me?"

"Well," I said, "I…uh…never asked if…I…uh… could come because he'd just say no." I wasn't sure how he'd respond to this bit of news. I was pretty sure he'd be angry with me but he surprised me by letting out a chuckle.

"Oh, that's something," he said, shaking his head and grinning. "Goodfield will be very upset with you if he finds you're gone."

"Yes sir, I know that." We talked for almost an hour about various things - he questioned me about home, my parents, my education, my aunt and uncle, friends, and even my dog. There seemed to be no end to the man's curiosity. I enjoyed every minute of our conversations. Mr. Pynchon was someone I could talk to and not be afraid of being punished for speaking my mind. He told me more than once that he enjoyed my honest answers to his questions and as he put it, my "turn of mind."

Looking back, I always enjoyed my visits with him. It was the one interesting thing I had to look forward to because most of what I did was drudgery, for when I wasn't writing letters, I was hauling barrels and boxes and buckets full of anything and everything.

A few weeks after my visit with Mr. Pynchon, a man from Ipswich, a friend of Josiah's, came to Goodfield with the message that Josiah would be here in the morning and wanted to see me. According the terms of my apprenticeship, Mr. Goodfield decided who I could see as well as when and where. He didn't agree to let Josiah see me until after Josiah arrived and then only begrudgingly. He gave us just 10 minutes and we had to stay in front of his shop where he could see us.

After greeting Josiah, he asked how I was and if things were better than when he last saw me on the boat. I told him that things weren't much better and that I was bored. I just let all my frustrations out at once. When I finished, Josiah looked at me, taking in all I said. I also told him in no uncertain terms, that I wanted to go home. He reminded me of the terms of my agreement and that I just couldn't leave because I didn't like how things were. I reminded him that the agreement also required Mr. Goodfield to teach me his business, which he hadn't; and therefore, the terms of the agreement were broken which meant I could leave with Goodfield's approval. Josiah stroked his chin as he always did when thinking hard. After a moment's consideration, he said that he would speak to Mr. Goodfield about the situation and see if he might consider ending my contract early; however, he wouldn't do it until later when his business was finished. I told him that I would like to talk to Goodfield before he did, hoping that maybe he was so unhappy with our arrangement he'd let me go. Josiah doubted that Goodfield would agree, but he told me to try anyway.

I slid off the cart to let him go on his way with the hope that Mr. Goodfield might release me from my apprenticeship. I cautioned myself not to get my hopes up too high for I may be stuck for a few more years. I resolved that if that were to happen, I'd run away. I found Goodfield alone in the shop and waited until he noticed me before approaching him.

"What do you want?" he asked gruffly.

"I'd like to speak with you, sir if I may."

"About what? Unless it's important, I don't want to hear it. I'm busy."

"It's important to me," I replied folding my hands in front of me.

"Yes, well, what is it then? Be quick, I don't have all day." From my time with him, I knew that he really was never that busy, so he most likely did have all day.

"I've worked hard for you during my time here," I told him, standing to my full height and looking him in the eye. "I've done all you asked and more. You've never liked our arrangement. You've never thought I was a good apprentice, which I'm not because I don't want to be here and never have. I came here against my will. I don't want to learn how to be a merchant. I want to be a farmer. You've treated me badly from the day I arrived, giving me new clothes only when the old ones were so worn they were only good for rags. You put me with Quimby, one of the worst men I've ever known. We've never liked each other, that much is apparent. I learned all I could, which wasn't much at all." I expected a thunderous outburst in response but he just stood there, eyes bulging, staring at me, his face turning red.

"I want to be released from our agreement."

"What? What did you say?"

"I said," swallowing hard, "I want you to release me from our agreement." He didn't reply but stood there drilling me with his eyes, his chest heaving as he clenched and unclenched his hands. I waited but he just stood there. "Mr. Goodfield, sir, what purpose do I serve here? Have I been able to decrease your work or increase your business? No, I haven't," I said without waiting for him to reply. "I've just eaten your food and generally got in your way. As I understand it, our contract calls for you to pay me two pounds, ten shillings at the end of my apprenticeship. I will forfeit all rights to that money if you release me now." He turned away from me and walked to the other side of the room. I could tell from the look on his face that he was thinking this over. He stood there, looking at me and rubbing the back of his neck. He paced back and forth several times, appearing to accept then reject the idea. After several minutes' consideration, he approached me.

"I'll consider it only if your uncle agrees to pay me the same amount." Any hope I had left me for I knew that it was less than likely Josiah would be able to pay him much at all, never mind such a large sum. I wasn't sure how best to respond, knowing that my only hope was to buy my way out of the contract. At that moment, Josiah came through the door with a smile for me and a greeting for Goodfield.

"I see you and Jack have been talking," he said as more a question than a statement. He looked at me, trying to get some sign as to Goodfield's reaction to my request.

"Well," Goodfield began, "your nephew has just asked me to release him from his contract. He has agreed to forfeit the two pounds, ten shillings I am to pay him at the end of his apprenticeship." Josiah gave me an approving look, impressed by the fact that I was willing to give up the money for freedom. "I told him," Goodfield resumed, "that I would consider it only if you pay me the same amount. Before you answer, remember that if I agree to his forfeit, I've not gained anything. Now, I should get something for the food and lodging I've provided him, don't you agree? For such a skinny boy, he can eat more than I can," he said rubbing his protruding belly. "I must get recompensed for that at least." Josiah looked from me to Goodfield and back again.

"So, if I pay you now, will you release him this afternoon?" Josiah asked putting the question to him. I think both Goodfield and I were equally shocked by the realization that Josiah was about to do as he asked. Goodfield moved to Josiah's side.

"If you pay me now, our agreement is ended." Josiah reached into his shirt and pulled out a small leather bag. From it, he took the money and laid it coin by coin on the table next to him. After telling us to wait, Goodfield walked into the other room and returned with my contract. He took a quill from the stand, dipped it in ink, and wrote something on the bottom of the page.

"It's done," he told me as he scooped the money off the table and put it in his pocket. "Get your things and be gone with you." With that, he turned and walked out of the shop. I couldn't quite believe it. There are times when you wish for something that seems almost impossible but when it comes true, it's difficult to accept that you got your wish. I could not begin to count the number of nights I lay awake, dreaming and wishing of going home even if it were just to visit, or maybe even for a night. There were a few times when I lay awake all night, tossing and turning, trying to find a way out of being Goodfield's apprentice, feeling doomed to an existence I hated.

I stood there for a few seconds, slightly stunned, not quite believing that I could actually go. Without a word to my uncle, I turned and flew from the shop into the house and up the stairs. Just as I got to the garret, I grabbed my few things and shoved them into a small bag. With that, I took a quick look around and shot down the stairs faster than I came up them and ran out the door. Josiah was waiting for me in the cart so I jumped up and threw my bag into the back while sliding onto the bench next to him.

"Your aunt will be very happy to see you," he said with a big smile and soft laugh. He flipped the reins, the horse began to move, and I realized that I was on my way home.

"Where did you get all that money to pay Goodfield?" I asked, still astounded at my good luck.

"It doesn't matter where I got it. I had it and I'm glad I was able to use it to get you out of something I never should have gotten you into in the first place." I waited for him to say something more but he didn't, at least not then. We rode along in a comfortable silence, as I thought about all that I was going to do now that I had my freedom. I've found that most people don't understand what having freedom really means or how best to use it. I'm sure I wouldn't have known either if I hadn't been thorough the experience. I was going to use it to make the life I wanted; to have my farm and spend my days with my fingers in the dirt, making things grow.

"I'm sorry," Josiah said. "I thought this was going to be a good thing; something to help you. It wasn't and for that I am truly sorry." I accepted his apology, thankful that he recognized the mistake he'd made. We never spoke of it again.

For the rest of the trip, we talked about the various things that happened in Ipswich and Boston. A little ways before we got to Ipswich, the thought occurred to me that Mr. Pynchon might wonder what happened to me. I know Goodfield might not give him a correct version of our discussion and I wished I could somehow get a letter to him, letting him know that I was no longer an apprentice. I also wanted to tell him that I had thought long and hard about his question concerning what I wanted to do with my life and thank him for being considerate to me. I wondered how I could get such a letter to him. Very few people ever went from Ipswich to Springfield; generally, they went to Boston and someone from there took whatever goods you had to Mr. Pynchon's town.

Chapter 5

It was great to be home with all the familiar people and things around me. In some ways, it felt like I'd been gone for years and in other ways, it felt like I never left.

I was greeted by Tink, who came bounding at me full speed, almost knocking me over. I knelt down and rubbed his head and neck and he pushed his muzzle into my shoulder, wriggling all over, happy to have me home. We sat on the floor as I hugged him and he slobbered all over me. We were very glad to see each other and being with him made my heart smile again. After seeing Charity and depositing my things on my mattress, I went out to see my father's horse, Bubs. Seeing me, he stood there, moving his head back and forth. I pulled his head into my shoulder and rubbed his neck just like my father used to.

The first night was wonderful. Charity made fish stew, fresh bread, and a raisin pie, three of my favorites. Everything tasted great. After dinner, I took a walk around, looking at things. Nothing much had changed. The same gray weather-stained clapboard houses, the same dusty dirt roads, the bay and ocean surrounded by the large, flat marshes of tall brown grass.

One house had a new thatched roof, and a family moved into the empty house down past the meetinghouse, but outside of that, it was just as I remembered it. Later, I sat at the table, appreciating what I had in life. When I was tired, I laid on my own mattress and slept better than I had in a long, long time.

One of the first things I did was write a letter to Mr. Pynchon explaining why and how I left Goodfield's. I wanted him to hear it from me; I didn't want him to believe any of the hearsay I was sure was going around about my departure.

> *Mr. Pynchon,*
>
> *I am writing to let you know that Goodfield released me from my contract at my request. I forfeited the two pounds, 10 shillings I was to get at the end of my apprenticeship. My uncle had to pay the same amount to secure my release. I did not want to be an apprentice, I was there against my wishes, and Mr. Goodfield did not want me there. My mother always told me that things work out for the best and now I believe that's true.*
>
> *I appreciate all that you did for me. Our visits meant a lot to me and I enjoyed them very much. I've often pondered your question about what I want to do with my life. I've decided that I want to have both a farm and family, although where, I don't know yet.*
>
> *I hope that we will meet again.*

Your most humble and obedient servant,
Jack Parker

I have often thought that to maintain friendships is one of the more important things in life, for no matter what hardships you go through, friends, good friends, will always make difficulties less so and always be there to offer the help you need. While Mr. Pynchon and I were certainly not close by any means, I felt in him someone who would protect my current interests and expand my future prospects. My father always maintained that to be helped, you must help others for in order to receive, you must give. While I had very little to offer someone like Mr. Pynchon at that time, I believe he looked kindly on me and would receive me warmly should we have the opportunity to meet again. I expected no response to my letter but held out the hope that he might reply.

During the next few weeks, I was able to get dirt under my fingernails again, work in the fields, and feel the soil between my fingers. I inhaled the musty, sweet, rich smell of soil, ready to receive the seeds which would become the plants needed to sustain us. As the season went on, I'd walk the fields of corn, wheat, and rye, holding my hands out to my sides, feeling the tops of the plants as they grew in the warm sun. The soft feel of wheat against my outstretched hands and the rustle of corn leaves brushing against my hips as I walked by gave me such pleasure that it balanced the misery of my time with Goodfield and Quimby. My enjoyment wasn't limited to working in the open air at something I loved, but from all the little activities and events that happen in our daily lives that we take for granted. The smell of fresh baked bread that Charity made twice a week, the laughter and company of friends and family, a beautiful sunrise over the ocean or sunset over the fields, the warmth of a blazing fire on a cold winter's night. These things became more important to me and I cherished each one.

Life returned to the comfortable rhythm I knew before going to Boston. I tried new things that I'd heard about, such as using ground clamshells like the Indians did at the Kennebec. I tried it first in the vegetable garden, and it gave such good results, the plants were full and almost perfect. It was the best harvest we ever had.

Over the next two years, the seasons blended seamlessly, each moving into the next with a grace and simplicity that delighted me. Each season was just what it should be - cold and snowy in the winter, warm and rainy in the spring, soft and warm in the summer, and cool, crisp fall days. Each made you appreciate the last. They came in like an old friend you hadn't seen in a while. The farm grew and we were able to buy another cow, two sheep, and three pigs. That, of course, meant more effort, but it was worth it to see the results of our hard work.

Becky and I continued our romance, realizing how far things progressed between us. I looked forward to seeing her every day. It was the one thing of which I never tired. All in all, life was good.

One soft, early April evening, the sky was clear and the sun had just set, leaving a light blue band of color in the western sky as Josiah, Charity and I sat in front of the fire. We had no work to do, which was unusual since we were always busy from sunrise to sunset.

"This is nice," Charity said with a pleasing sigh, looking at Josiah and me. "When was the last time we just enjoyed an evening?" she asked. "Do either of you remember?" Josiah shrugged his shoulders and I stared into the fire, hypnotized by the dancing flames.

"I have no idea," I told her dreamily. We sat for a while longer until Josiah started fidgeting in his chair.

"Well, I suppose now is as good a time as any," he muttered.

"Now's as good a time for what?" I asked.

"There's something we need to tell you." I got a bad feeling about whatever it was they were going to tell me. The last time they said that was when I found out about going to

Boston.

"Why do I have a feeling I'm not going to like this?" I asked. Charity turned to me.

"Now listen to what it is before you starting judging whether it's a bad thing or not."

"Do you remember when we first came to live with you we talked about a new settlement in the western part of the Colony that some families from here started? Do you remember that?"

"I remember it well. I was excited at the possibility of living on the frontier but we only talked about it once or twice. Since you never mentioned it again, I figured you had changed your mind. That, plus you sent me to Boston."

"We weren't sure of the best thing to do so we didn't do anything," Josiah said, ignoring my remark. "Anyway," he continued, "there are several families there now at the Quaboag Plantation. You know some of them – John Ayres and his family, my old friend John Warner and his, Will Pritchard and his too. Your friend John Pynchon owns most of the land. He purchased eight square miles of land from the Indians; the Quaboag who are part of the Nipmuck tribe." The fact that Mr. Pynchon was involved made me sit up and pay close attention to what he was saying.

"Your aunt and I want to go. It's a chance at a new life for us, something we've dreamed about for years. We'd be able to have a big farm - three, maybe four times bigger than what we, what you, have now," he said. "If we're going to do this, we have to do it now. It's our last chance before we get too old. We want to leave in the next couple of weeks." I sat back, trying to take it all in.

"So you want to leave? I'd stay here to run the farm...that would be all right I guess."

"No, Jack, you don't understand," Charity said softly. "You're going to come with us. The three of us would go there. We couldn't let you stay alone."

"What?" I asked indignantly. "Why not? You want me to go? Leave here for good to go to somewhere where there is nothing? If you remember, I left once before and it didn't turn out so well." At this, they both cringed. "So, I don't want to do it again, especially if it means I'll be gone for good. I would leave everything. I'd have to leave my parents' house, my friends, and Becky! For what? More land? A bigger farm? Even more work than we have now?" I hung my head, resting my elbows on my knees. I stared at the floor, turning it all over in my mind. The full realization of what this meant sparked within me and I didn't like it. I was not going to go away from everything I knew and loved. I wouldn't do it again. I'd have to leave my parents' home and end my connection with them and that was the most painful thing of all.

"I won't go," I told them. "I'm not leaving Ipswich. I'll

stay here. I am old enough to run this place by myself. You go if you want make your new life. It won't include me." With that, I stalked out of the house slamming the door behind me. As I had done in the most difficult moments of my life, I began to walk, not having a destination in mind, but just putting one foot in front of the other. Now and then, I looked up to get my bearings but I never stopped, just kept walking along. There was a bit of a nip in the air and I shivered, realizing it was chilly and I had on only my shirt and breeches. I wrapped my arms around myself and walked faster in hopes of warming up a bit. As I thought about things, the fact that Mr. Pynchon was involved intrigued me. We had a good relationship; I was sure he would treat us well and give us whatever we needed to be prosperous. That, and the fact that I knew several of the families there would make it easier. I stopped in my tracks, realizing that I was actually considering it.

No, I said to myself. *It wouldn't be right, leaving your home and Becky. How can I leave her?* I walked on, thinking as I went. I felt that if I did go I would be somehow betraying the memory of my parents. I realized they would always be in my heart and with me no matter where I went but if I left, I would lose the connections I had with them. There were so many memories I would leave behind that it would break my heart. I shivered again, knowing I would have to go home sometime. I remembered Becky's father talked about going there too with

John Warner and John Ayres, Sr. If there was a chance that Becky would go, then it would be an easier decision, but that wasn't a sure thing by any means. Her father had changed his mind on small and big things at the last minute before so I had to find out what Becky knew. With all these thoughts swirling in my head, I turned back the way I came, understanding I'd have to make a decision soon.

I hadn't been gone long, but when I walked in, Charity was already in bed. Josiah sat by the fire staring off into space. He turned when I closed the door.

"How was your walk?" he asked with a hint of a smile. "Did you figure it all out?"

"No," I replied, "I didn't figure anything out…just came up with more questions. Look, I know you want to do this, but can't you understand that I may not? This is my home, where I was born and lived with my parents. I just don't think I could go. It would be like leaving them. Do you know what I mean?"

"Yes, yes I do. Now listen, this isn't going to happen overnight. These things take time, at least a few weeks or maybe more. Other people from town are there, so it's not like we'd be all by ourselves. They're people we've known for years." He stroked his chin and motioned to the other chair. I sat down and waited for him to begin.

"Jack, this means more to us than anything else we've

ever done. This is our life's dream. I've always wanted a big farm where I could have lots of cows, sheep, and pigs," he said wistfully. "Your aunt and I talked about this right after we got married. If we didn't or couldn't go, it would break her heart. I've never been able to give her much. She's never asked for much either, but I feel bad that I've never had enough money or credit to get her something nice. If I can do this, she'd smile all day every day for the rest of her life. I know you have your own dreams and that's good, that's fine, you should have them. Everyone's entitled to them, but we're not getting younger. Oh, we can get around fine and have no trouble going through the day, but there are aches and pains that were never there before. I need…we need…you to come with us."

"What about my dreams? When do I get to begin making them come true?"

"There are a lot of things you have to do in life that you never planned, including working harder and scrounging more than you ever thought possible. Once you've done that for a few years and if you've been smart, your dreams may start happening, but it's not a given that they will. I know men who've never achieved even one of their life's dreams. They go on with life and keep striving, but inside, day by day, they're breaking a little piece at a time because they haven't been able to accomplish what they hoped for or worked towards. After a few years of that, when you reach a certain age, you start to crumble until one day you just give up all your dreams. You feel defeated and beaten and your hopes fade a bit every day until you almost don't remember what they were. So you go off by yourself and ask what happened…how did I get to this point…what didn't I do…or what could I have done better? Then you start feeling sorry for yourself; thinking about all the problems you had to deal with and the things life threw in your way." He paused and looked at me for a moment before resuming. "I don't want to be like that and I certainly don't want you to end up that way. So, I'll tell you what, you help me achieve this one dream and I'll help you every way I can with all of yours. I know it will be hard work and some will think us crazy, but it's a dream I've always had in me. I'll do as well by you as I know how. Think about it and we'll talk tomorrow. I'm tired," he yawned, "and I'm going to bed. G'night. I'll see you in the morning." He walked by, patting me on the shoulder. I sat there looking into the flames and wondering what my dreams were.

It's odd that sometimes when you can't figure things out, a good night's sleep helps. I woke up feeling better about things and knew I needed to talk to Becky. I also knew that my dream was to have a great farm of many acres with a big family to work it. I didn't care too much about the finer, expensive things like some people do; I just wanted my sons and daughters around, my wife and I working together to make our life better. I wanted to build something I could pass on to my children and grandchildren - something to give them a foothold in the world.

After breakfast and my morning chores, I took off for Becky's house. As I walked, I realized that in thinking about my dreams, the mother of my children was Becky. I never questioned it or thought that it could be someone else. I guess my heart knew it before I did.

Her father, Tom, was a small, skinny man who always had trouble making up his mind about anything big or small. He'd dawdle over whether to buy a pig for so long that by the time he decided, he'd learn that it was sold the week before. He was always complaining about something. It could be that the weather was too hot, too cold, too dry, or too wet. Or that he made a bad deal and got less than someone else did for selling the same amount of the same thing. He liked to blame the world for any misfortunes he encountered. Her mother, on the other hand, was just the opposite. Always smiling and happy and ready to help with anything that you needed, she loved taking care of her family. It was clear that she enjoyed life. You could not have imagined two married people with such different personalities and outlooks on life. I've always heard that opposites attract, and that was definitely the case with Tom and Elizabeth Morgan.

I found Mrs. Morgan in the garden tending the herbs.

She heard me coming and looked up, pushing a lock of hair out of her face with the back of her hand.

"Good morning, Jack. I suppose you're here to see my favorite daughter." This was an old joke between us since Becky was her only daughter.

"Yes, I am. Do you know anyone who might be going to the new settlement out west," I asked. Quaboag Plantation? The place where John Warner, John Ayres and Will Pritchard went." She stood up and came toward me.

"Yes, I know them. Now why are you asking that?"

"Because Josiah and Charity are planning on going. They told me last night. They want me to go with them but I don't want to. I want to stay here."

"Oh, now tell me all about it." There have been times when she acted like a mother of sorts, helping me in times like this. "How did this all come up anyway?"

"Well, Josiah told me that they want to go west and buy land to build the farm of their dreams. He talked about a man's dreams, how this is the only one he has left, and that he's never accomplished any of his others. They want me to go too; they said they need me and can't do it without me."

"Well," she said, rubbing the dirt from her hands, "you have to understand that as you get older your dreams become more important to you. You realize there may not be a lot of time left for you to achieve any of them. And, you have to remember what Josiah and Charity have done for you. Maybe you should think of them instead of yourself."

"And what have they really done for me?" I snapped.

"They took you in when you had no other place to go. They gave you a home, took care of you the best they knew how, and gave you all they could." She continued, stopping me before I could start complaining about them sending me to Goodfield, "Now, is that what's bothering you? The thought of helping them make one of their dreams come true?"

"I can't go. I just can't…"

"Why can't you? I know it would be a big change, but think of the possibilities, the chance to make your own life they way you want it to be."

"I went away once and didn't like it. It didn't work out too well…it was horrible. I don't want to leave all the people I love and places I know. I don't want to go away again…anywhere."

"Jack, what's wrong?" she asked.

"I can't leave," I said, "because I'd be leaving my parents and I can't do that."

"No, you won't leave them. No matter where you go you will never leave them behind. They'll always be with you."

I could feel my eyes getting wet but I held back the tears. As I'd done many times in the past, I thanked her for her advice and went to see Becky. When I found her by the barn, she looked up and smiled at me. I walked towards her, thinking how pretty she looked with the sun shining on her face. She came towards me wiping her hands on her apron.

"I'm a little surprised to see you so early," she said since I didn't usually visit until late in the afternoon.

"I've been surprised all day long," I joked. "We need to talk." We walked towards the field where the cows where grazing.

"Josiah told me they want to go to Quaboag Plantation, where John Warner and John Ayres settled a couple of years ago. It's Josiah's last chance at realizing his life's dream of owning land and building his own farm in a new place."

"Well, that is news," she said. "When are they thinking of going?" I couldn't quite believe that she didn't understand that they weren't going by themselves.

"Becky, they want me to go with them. Josiah said they need me to make this happen, and they can't do it without me. Your mother said I should go and to stop thinking of myself. She said they've done a lot for me so I should give something back to them." She stood there looking at me, different emotions moving across her face.

"I don't know what to say. I mean, this is very sudden. How long would you be gone?"

"I don't know. I think they want me to stay with them…and…never come back."

"When would you go?"

"I don't know when, but soon. Josiah says he can't wait to get away from the fools and idiots," I said, accurately reporting my uncle's thoughts on the character of some of the people who lived in the town.

"Oh Jack, no, I'd miss you so," she in a soft voice. "What if you came back after a year? If you help them get the house and barn built and the crops planted, and then came home to…the town…to me. If only for a year, well that wouldn't be too bad," she said. Before I could answer her, she continued with her thoughts. "But you know," she said, brightening, "My father's talked about going there too a couple of times. So, maybe we'll be moving there too. So it won't be for long…maybe only a few months, that's all," her voice was full of hope but we both knew it may not happen that way at all. Tom Morgan was the most indecisive man I'd ever met. He'd take a month to make a decision another man would make in five minutes, always looking at every angle 40 times before putting the decision off and coming back to it a week or two later to do it all over again and when he finally did make a decision, he'd be proud that he'd been bold enough to do it. Of course, the other side of it was that he almost never changed his mind once he had made a decision, but the chances of him pulling his family out of Ipswich to a frontier settlement were slim to none. Old Tom was not anyone you'd think could go out into the wilderness and survive any length of time. He was a simple man who never gave the impression of having any great sense of adventure.

"Becky, I wouldn't come back. Josiah wants me there permanently. That's what I'm trying to tell you. I don't know what to do. This is like them sending me to Boston all over again." I stood there looking at my feet and shaking my head, feeling lost. When I looked up, she was standing there her hands together with a faraway look on her face. A single tear coursed slowly down her cheek.

"I can't say no to Josiah after all he and Charity have done for me," I said. "I want to help them but don't want to go away." I reached out and took her hand. "I don't know what to do. I do owe them a lot but I don't want to repay them by moving away from town...from you. What if your father decides not to move and stays here? Then what? This just isn't fair." We stood there in silence, staring off into the distance wondering what we could do to satisfy everyone and still be together.

When I got back, there was a letter waiting for me. Charity said a man from Boston on his way to Newburyport delivered it. I was very curious about who would be sending me a letter and why. I broke the seal and opened it, almost falling off my chair with surprise because it was from Mr. Pynchon.

Jack,

It was good to hear from you. I did wonder what happened to you and why you left Goodfield's so quickly. He told me his side of things but that's of no concern for you. I understand your reasons and trust that all will be well with you. I too enjoyed our visits and hope that we will meet again. Perhaps you should consider coming west. It would give you the chance for the adventure you want and the farmland is wonderful. Please remember that there is always a place here for someone like you.

John Pynchon

I read it twice and as I placed it on the table, I realized I'd made my decision to go. I promised myself that I'd come back for Becky in one year so we could be married.

Two weeks later, I was up very early and left the house before the sun rose over the bay. I had only an hour or so before I needed to be back, and before we'd be on our way to Quaboag. Becky and I arranged to meet on the stretch of beach surrounded by tall grass and can't be seen unless you're right next to it. We were happy to see each other but sad that I was going away and we didn't know when we'd be together again. We walked and watched the sun rise over the ocean and into the blue sky over the low band of clouds on the distant horizon. I looked around and seeing no one, I put my arm around her waist and drew her close.

"I'm sorry about this; about leaving you. If it weren't for everything Josiah and Charity have done for me, I wouldn't go. Please know that I don't want to leave you." I just stood there thinking about what it would be like in a new place where I couldn't see her when I wanted. "I'm going to miss you very much," I told her. "I don't know what I'll do not being able to talk to you whenever I need to. I'm going to be very lonely."

"I'm going to miss you too, Jack. Who am I going to tease? Who am I going to horse around with? Who am I going to tell that I love them?" she said with a bit of a smile. Her smile was a thing of true beauty. I remember one fine summer day we were near the edge of the pasture down by the bay and the sun was glinting off the waves like diamonds. I don't remember what I did or said but she looked up at me with a smile lighting her face and it spread to her eyes, which twinkled, full of delight and mischief. She looked at me, wrinkling her nose and then hit me on the arm, laughing as she did. That surprised me and I started to laugh too. We couldn't stop for a couple of minutes, breathless and red with stifling laughter. It was moments like those that I never wanted to forget.

"I think I'll be able to come back now and then," I said. "When I come back I'll bring you a present, but only if you do something for me."

"What?" she asked.

"Write to me as often as you can. It will help me feel less lonely and I can't go too long without thinking of you. I'll send you letters whenever I can and messages with people when I can't."

"I will. I promise. As often as I can get any scrap of paper, I will."

I took her hand in mine and we began walking again. We walked to the end of the beach in silence, turned around slowly, and walked back. I couldn't think of anything to say. Time was moving faster than I wanted it to as I realized that when we reached the other end, I would have to leave. I didn't want our time together to end. I wanted to stay on the beach and I didn't want to leave Ipswich, my home, my friends, and most of all Becky. My heart was heavy and I was very sad. Without saying a word, she pulled me to her and held me close.

"Becky," I said a bit hurriedly, knowing that I'd stayed longer than I should have. "Becky, wait for me. I'll think of you every day and the very first thing I'll do when I get back is see you." I gently held her face in my hands. "I promise that I will come back for you in one year so we can be married." She smiled but it faded fast. "I'll come back for you as soon as I can, to either to stay here or go to Quaboag. I can promise you that much."

"Of course I'll wait for you," she said as if it were

something she'd already decided. I looked around once more and seeing no one, I put my arms around her waist and kissed her very softly at first, then again and again. I knew I couldn't wait any longer.

"I have to go," I said. She dropped her head and nodded. Putting my hand under her chin, I lifted her face up. Silent tears were running down her face. I kissed her one more time and looking into her eyes, I told her I loved her. It was a secret stolen moment. As she began to cry, I held her once more and then left sniffling, feeling the warmth in my eyes as I scrambled up through the grass and up the little rise.

As I left her and began the walk home, I thought about how our childhood friendship had become something much more; something wonderful. I'd never thought about being in love with her; it just seemed so natural. As I walked on, I knew I'd think of her many times every day and miss her very, very much. I began to understand that I'd found the love of my life and that made my heart ache all the more.

Chapter 6

We left less than an hour later. As we were about to go, I told Josiah to wait and jumped off the cart and ran to the burial ground. While I wasn't certain the thought occurred to me that I might never be here again, I wanted to say goodbye to my mother and father. I stood before their graves, thinking of how much I missed them. I began to get a little teary-eyed, since this might be the last time I was this close to them.

"I'll miss both of you very much. Whatever I do and wherever I go, I'll make you proud of me. If I get back here…" I couldn't imagine not coming back. Instead, I whispered, "I miss both of you very much. I love you." With that, I turned and ran back to the cart because I wanted to leave, right then and there.

Josiah sat holding the reins and looked over at me. Charity turned with a questioning look on her face.

"What was that all about?" he asked.

"I had to say goodbye," I told them. He looked at me for a moment, then at Charity. Without a word, he snapped the whip and got moving.

Since the cart was overloaded and the seat was big

enough for only two people, Tinker and I got the chore of herding the animals. He'd keep me company, making sure none of the animals strayed too far. I knew I'd walk a good part of the way because I tied Bubs to the back of the wagon. I didn't want to ride him since, if I had to chase after one of the animals, I'd have to get off him in order to run into the woods.

It was hard to believe that we were finally leaving. As we started out, I vowed I wouldn't look back, but I did anyway. The house was empty and looked forlorn. It was where I'd spent my entire life; some of the memories unfolded as I stood there until Josiah's yell shook me out of my reverie.

"Jack, stop standing there! Get the animals! Those pigs are starting already..." he hollered. I heard him mutter to Charity, "If he can't take care of those animals this could be a long trip." I turned around and began walking away, silently saying goodbye, not knowing when or if I'd see it again.

The trip took five days, and we had established a rhythm for each one: Up at dawn, a quick breakfast, gather the animals, get them moving, an hour-long stop at noon to rest and water them, stopping late afternoon to set up camp, take care of the animals, a fire, a meal and sleep. It was comfortable and somehow reassuring. The only worries I had were losing one or more of the pigs or sheep and meeting Indians. The chance of running into Indians was real and possible. The worst part of the day was trying to fall asleep. I was tired but kept hearing sounds – a crack of a branch here, a rustle in the bushes there, the wind blowing through the trees; all possibly masking the approach of stealthy attackers. My fear was greatest then and to add to it, we'd hear wolves howling every night. On the third day, we spotted two of them loping through a field on a hillside, so Josiah and I slept with our guns by our sides. What really got me was that none of this seemed to bother either Charity or Josiah; they were asleep within a minute of lying down.

The journey could have been made in three days if we pushed the oxen hard, but Josiah wanted to go slower to make sure they were not worn down when we arrived. As we got closer, my anticipation grew. I wondered what it looked like and the type of farms the other settlers had been able to make out of the wilderness. I talked about going to Springfield some day so we could get supplies but also to visit Mr. Pynchon. While I missed Becky very much, especially the further away I got from her, Josiah's excitement began to rub off on me. My dream of having a large farm swelled within me and I realized with a tremendous amount of hard work, I could have that. If I helped Josiah, I would inherit their estate some day, since they had no other close relations. I reminded myself that if Tom Morgan didn't bring his family to Quaboag, I would go back, marry Becky, and bring her to the settlement.

We'd been traveling through a lightly wooded area, the road dappled by the sun coming through the trees as we began to go up a hill that was steeper than it looked at first glance. The road wound to the left, then back to the right before swinging left again. Each time it turned the slope got steeper. After two hundred yards or so, we crested the hill and a wonderful sight was in front of us. Long, wide fields were in front and to the right. Over the edge of the hill, there were higher hills in the distance, lush with corn and grain growing against the bright blue sky.

We continued on the town road and began to go down the other side of the hill. On the left were more hills, somewhat higher than others, rolling off into the distance. As I looked at the scene before me, a large hawk soared above me, climbing higher and higher until it was just a speck in the western sky, floating away on the wind. A loud voice bellowed from behind us.

"Well Josiah, think you can make a good home here?" The three of us turned together, startled at the sudden noise. A short, squat, muscular man stood leaning on the shaft of a scythe, the blade resting on the ground. I could tell there was a smile under his gray, bushy beard.

"John Warner, how are you?" Josiah said, pleased to see an old friend as he climbed off the cart. "I think we can make a wonderful home here." They approached each other smiling and shook hands.

"We finally made it," Josiah said as a big smile spread across his face.

"Well, hold your celebrating until your first crop comes in," he said, turning from Josiah. "Charity, how are you? It's good to see you. Priscilla's been waiting for you. She went in a while ago. She'll be glad to see you. Jack," he said, turning to me, "you've grown quite a bit since I saw you last. How have you been? Have these two been treating you all right?"

"I'm fine sir, thank you. They treat me well...for the most part," I told him with a sly grin. Charity looked at me in surprise before a smile appeared on her face.

"How long did it take you?" he asked Josiah.

"Five days. We took it slow, didn't want to push the oxen too hard. Thankfully the weather was good."

"It's been a fine stretch of weather. Come on now. Priscilla would have my head if she knew I was standing here talking your ear off while she was waiting for you. Since we weren't sure when you'd get here, everyone has been looking for you for the past week. Come on now."

Josiah led the team down the road with Mr. Warner at his side. Within the first few steps, they were talking of Ipswich, Josiah giving him what news he could. We came up to the tavern that was owned by John Ayres, Sr., who was an important man back home before coming here. He and Mr.

Warner were two of the original four grantees of the settlement. Just as we arrived opposite the tavern, a couple of people came out to see who the new arrivals were. Since Ipswich was not a big town and most of the settlers came from there, we knew quite a few of them. Susannah Ayres, Mr. Ayres' wife, and Elizabeth Prichard greeted Charity warmly. A young boy went to tell the other families that we had arrived. I stood off to the side watching everyone come from the houses. I recognized several of them, but didn't want to join the excitement just yet. I was looking everything over and getting a feel for the place when I received a hearty slap on the back. I turned to see Tom and Joe Ayres grinning at me. The brothers were older than me, and Tom was a couple of years older than his brother. I knew them from the Sabbath meetings and was glad to see them. We exchanged greetings while more and more people came to welcome us. Sam Prichard and Mark Warner joined Tom, Joe and me. We made our way over to the rest of the group, which was now 20 or so people. The greetings went on for a few minutes before we all went into the tavern. They asked us for news of Ipswich and of their friends and family. We told them everything we knew, which was much more than we thought it would be. It's amazing the little pieces of information you pick up without realizing it. We in turn, asked them about what was going on in the settlement. They told us about the gristmill that was recently finished and operating, that there was news from

Boston about a new road that would go through the village within the next couple of years, of the crop successes and failures, of the Indians, and of Springfield. I asked them if they ever saw Mr. Pynchon. Most of them stopped talking and looked at me. John Ayres, Sr. leaned on the bar and cocked his head.

"How do you know John Pynchon?" he asked.

"I met him when I was apprenticed in Boston," I told him. "I was there for a little over two years and the man I was apprenticed to, Mr. Goodfield, knows Mr. Pynchon. I met Mr. Pynchon while taking letters for Mr. Goodfield. He and I talked several times; sometimes for over an hour. I got a letter from him just before we left." From the look on their faces, you would have thought I just told them that all the trees were purple because there was complete silence. "He even suggested that I come to Springfield."

"Well, uh, well, that is something isn't it?" Tom Kent asked no one in particular. "I mean, who'd think that Mr. Pynchon would know someone like Jack here." He stopped for a moment and then went on. "That isn't what I meant, Jack. What I was trying to say is that it is a surprise to us that you're on such good terms with him. That's all I meant."

"He's a nice man," I replied as I looked over at Josiah. "As soon as we get the chance I'd like to go to Springfield to see him." Everyone continued to stare at me. Jane Kent broke the silence.

"I'm sure your uncle will take you with him so you can visit Mr. Pynchon."

"Of course, of course," Josiah replied, "but first we have a house to build," he said getting a few chuckles and low laughter.

"Now, you'll stay here while you're building," said Susannah Ayres. She looked at her husband who nodded in agreement. "That's right, we won't take no for an answer. The boys will help you with your things." At that, everyone left, going back to whatever work they were doing when we arrived.

Everyone was very glad we'd come because the original grant in 1660 required 20 families to be living here within five years and there were only 12 before we came. The settlers requested another grant; a regrant, in 1667 that was approved by the General Court.

Several of the leading men of the settlement were important, and in some cases wealthy, when they came to Quaboag. William Prichard was the son of a wealthy Welsh nobleman and came to the Bay Colony to escape some unnamed trouble, either political or personal. He was one of the original settlers. John Ayres, Sr. was a prominent member of Ipswich as well as captain of the militia and a man of substantial means. Richard Coy Sr. owned a successful tavern in Wenham, held several political offices, was a corporal in the militia and an important force in building the meetinghouse there. Daniel Hovey, or "Deacon" as he was called, was perhaps the wealthiest and most influential of all, for he owned land and property in Topsfield, Ipswich, Quaboag, and Hadley. He had a license from Mr. Pynchon to trade with the Indians, something very few people in the entire Colony had. John Warner was a large landowner in Ipswich who was not in good standing with the church, which is maybe why he was the first settler. Knowing his temperament, he probably couldn't wait to leave them behind. The one thing most of the settlers had in common was that they weren't in full agreement with the doctrines of the church and were less than moderate in their religious beliefs and practices. I knew Josiah would fit right in.

After taking care of the animals and bringing some of our belongings into the room we'd have, I went down to the tavern room and as I looked out the front door, I wondered what my new life would be like here. It was a pretty area with rolling hills, open fields, and stately chestnut trees on either side of the town road. I walked up the hill at the back of the house and stood on a great big rock to get a better view. I could see for miles in three directions. I continued up to the top of the hill and going over the crest, I saw a river with wide blue curves snaking between marshes. It looked like a good place to live.

The next day was a busy one. We unloaded the rest of our things, selected the spot for the house and barn, and were visited by some of the people who weren't around to greet our arrival. We also got an extended tour of the village. The highlight for me though, was meeting two of the Quaboag Indians who came to visit Mr. Ayres. We heard stories of the Indians many times of their appearance, way of life, customs, their likes and dislikes. The information was sometimes not flattering or favorable to the Indian or his tribe. Some of them came into Ipswich regularly but these were the more "civilized" ones who had adopted many of our customs, including various forms of dress. To me, these Indians, almost all men, represented those I'd heard so much about. Having no other knowledge, I thought all Indians were like them.

Many of the stories characterized them as "devils" that would not be civilized until they adopted our way of life, including religion. There was a strong belief that God brought us to this land here for that very purpose; that the Indians would become better people by knowing and accepting the word of God. Even though my parents and I went to Sabbath meetings all day Sunday and each Thursday evening, we did not accept all that the ministers said about various subjects including the belief that all Indians were bad. After all, I reasoned there were good and bad people amongst our own townsfolk. I didn't believe that the Indians could be any worse than we were. Both my father and Josiah's passive religious attitudes strongly influenced my own.

It came as something of a surprise when we met our first Indians. Sam Warner told us how the Indians - the Quaboag, Wekapauge, and other local tribes welcomed the earlier families, teaching them ways of planting and other things they'd need to know to survive and prosper. John Warner told us of how several Indians, men and women, came soon after he arrived and showed him how to build a strong, temporary shelter. He explained that communication was difficult at first, with neither knowing the language of the other, but that the Indians learned English quickly but that their language was difficult to learn.

Charity was the first to see them. Three Indians, two men and a boy, were walking towards us coming up the backside of the hill. We stood and watched as they approached.

Their appearance was nothing like we had heard. The men were tall, muscular, and well proportioned, their skin a light bronze and their eyes dark brown. One had long, straight hair, blacker than any I'd ever seen. He had a friendly look on his face and in his eyes. The other had a knot of hair on the left side of his head, a few inches above his ear with a foot-long braid hanging down to his shoulder while the rest of his scalp was bald. He was wearing a long, brown feather tied to the knot, causing it to hang down over his left shoulder. Both men had figures painted on them. The one with the knot of hair had what looked like a turtle painted in yellow on his left cheek and horizontal black lines on his other cheek. The other had a six-inch striped snake in black and red paint on his right breast. The boy was younger than me, although not by much. His glossy black hair was very straight and fell to his shoulders. He had quick, dark eyes and a mischievous smile.

When they got to be about 20 feet away, they stopped and appraised us. The men were on either side of the boy. We each looked at the other for a minute until I made a slight bow not knowing what else to do. They and Charity smiled; Josiah didn't take his eyes off them. All three were dressed alike with only a belt about their waist and a strip of dyed hide placed over the front, between their legs and over the back of the belt. The men wore low moccasins; the boy was barefoot. Their lack of clothing caused us great embarrassment; my aunt dropped her eyes and blushed at their appearance. Mr. Ayres came out of the barn and seeing them with us, walked down to join us.

"Well, I see you met three of my friends," he said, wiping his hands on a piece of cloth. "This," he said, indicating the one with the feather in his hair, "is Conkganasco, leader of the tribe by the two lakes several miles south of here. We met him the first week we were here. We've helped each other haven't we?" he asked. Conkganasco smiled and replied in very good English, better than some of the people from Ipswich.

"Yes John, that is right. It makes no sense not to help one another. We've become good friends." Looking at us intently, he introduced his companions. "This," he said, gesturing to the other man, "is Muttawmp and this is my son Ahanu. What are your names?" Josiah did the introductions.

"I am Josiah Clarke; this is my wife Charity and our nephew Jack Parker." Conkganasco looked at me.

"Why do you not live with your parents?"

"My parents died four years ago, so I went to live with my aunt and uncle." For a moment, he stood there looking at me, his brown eyes fixed on my face.

"Your aunt and uncle seem like good people and I'm sure you've done well by them." He looked at Charity and Josiah then back to me. "There are boys here that you know. Some of them have been to our villages. The one at Wekapauge," he said, pointing west towards the planting field, "is closest. Our village, Quaboag, is at the end of the river between the two ponds. Talk to your friends, Joseph Ayres and Samuel Prichard. Come with them to visit us." He gave me a brief smile and walked away the other two following him. I was excited that I'd been invited to see an actual Indian village and couldn't wait to go but Josiah tempered my enthusiasm by reminding me that we still had a house and barn to build. Any of my social activities, as he called them, would wait until all the work was done. I heaved a big sigh and followed him to the site of our house.

We began building the next morning. Four other men agreed to help us; two of them and I began digging the foundation while Josiah and the other two went to the woodlot and began cutting the trees. The house was to be 24 feet long by 20 feet wide. The foundation had to be six feet deep and lined with fieldstone and the fireplace and chimney took up one entire end. It took three of us five full days to dig it and another two weeks to gather and place the stone. Josiah and I worked non-stop with the others while Charity, with the help of a few other women, provided the food and drink we needed.

Once the foundation was completed, it was time to saw the timber into lumber for the frame. I was stuck with what I consider the worst job when building – working in the sawpit. It was a deep hole; one man would climb down into it while the other stood on the edge. A timber was laid part way across it and they would saw through the wood. We cut lumber of all sizes this way. All the sawdust would fall into the hole and onto the person in the pit. I had sawdust in my hair and on my face, clothes and in my mouth for a week. It seemed that no matter what I did I couldn't get rid of it. The job I wanted was to make the shingles because it was a mindless task; something I could do all day. Once you got the rhythm of it down you could sit there all day pounding out shingles. From start to finish I worked harder and longer than I ever had. My hands were cut, bleeding and swollen, my back ached, and my arms felt like they'd fall off. Of course, everyone else who worked with us was in the same condition.

All in all, it took us not quite six weeks to put up the house and barn. Everyone was glad because anything like a house or barn raising is a reason for a social celebration.

The day was sunny and pleasant with a light breeze and a beautiful blue sky. We began at first light. We laid the timbers along each side and placed the mortise and tenon together. Will and John Ayres Jr. took the augers and began making the holes for the wooden pegs or treenails, which were pronounced "trunnels" for some strange reason.

While we were preparing to raise the house frame, the women were bringing the food, which was set on tables made of planks. Raising a building is hard work, even for a group of men accustomed to such work. This required us to take stop for a few minutes every now and then, to have a small mug of rum or cider and a piece of bread or pie.

By mid-morning, the frame was up and pegged together. The house was finished in another two weeks. As we were moving our things from the tavern to the house, I began thinking of Becky. A wave of loneliness swept over me as I looked around the house and thought of us having our own some day. I was in a bad humor the rest of the day, wishing that

I hadn't left Ipswich and that we were together.

Chapter 7

My mood improved after I received an invitation to join Sam Prichard and Tom Ayres on a visit to the Wekapauge Indian village that was located about three miles west of the village. Both Sam and Tom's fathers traded with the Indians and Sam was bringing two small copper pots to one of the Indian women. They told me that the Wekapauge were part of the Quaboag tribe which itself was part of the much larger Nipmuck tribe.

When we got within sight of the village, I stopped and looked around, taking in all the details. The village stood on a hill that dropped steeply to the shore of a wide lake. On the western side, the village border was a stream coming from the lake that flowed into a broad river a hundred yards to the south. Groups of pine and oak trees were between the wigwams and river while chestnut, elm and maple trees were on the other side of the stream. It was a pleasant spot.

Situated around an open central area were seven wigwams. On one side was a long wigwam twice the size of the others. All the wigwams looked alike; they were semi-circular and about 12 feet high, 20 feet long, and 16 feet wide covered with long, wide pieces of bark. On the outside of each building there were saplings running lengthwise tied together end to end with what looked like vines but what I later found out was woven thin strips of elm roots. These saplings, lashed to other longer, thicker bent saplings, went over the top from side to side. Together the two sets of saplings formed a strong skeleton or support.

A large vegetable garden surrounded the wigwams in a semi-circle from the lake to the river. At first glance, I saw only corn, but then I noticed squash vines intertwined around the stalks and beans growing up the stalks.

"Come on, Jack, let's go see Kanti." I looked at him a bit puzzled. "That's the woman we've come to visit," Tom explained. "Her wigwam is on the other side by the stream." We moved through the village and were greeted warmly by almost everyone. As we got to the wigwam, a tall boy came over to us calling Sam and Tom by name. Like Conkganasco, his English was very good. After greeting them, he turned to me.

"William," Sam said, "this is Jack Parker. He and his family have just come to our village to live. Jack, this is William. We call him that because we can't pronounce his name," he said with a smile.

"Don't listen to them," William said in a friendly tone. "They are too lazy to learn my name. It is Sunukkuhkau."

"It's not that we're lazy," Sam said. "It just takes too long to say." I looked at William and tried to pronounce it correctly. After a few tries, I gave up.

"I hope you don't mind but I'll call you William too. I'm glad to be here," I told him. "I've never been to an Indian village before."

"That's all right. You can call me whatever you want. I know who I am. My mother will be happy you brought her pots. She's been hoping you would come soon." With that, he turned and led us into the wigwam. The inside was bigger than I thought it would be with another sapling framework that supported the bark slabs I'd seen outside. In the middle was a small fire burning in a ring of stones. Running the entire length of the sides and back wall were platforms about three feet wide and three feet high off the ground supported by thick, round pieces of wood covered with thick layers of bear, deer, moose, and wolf skins. Woven reed mats were tied to the sides of the framework from the floor to above the platforms. Woven and leather bags hung from the framework several feet above the platforms.

William introduced me to his mother. She was a very pretty woman, which surprised me because I didn't think Indian women would be that good looking. The only ones I'd seen were old, sad looking women who came into Ipswich with their husbands. William's mother, on the other hand, had a happy look about her. She was of medium height with long black hair that fell to the middle of her back. She wore a dress of deerskin pinned across her right shoulder. Her left shoulder and arms were bare, showing the light bronze hue of her skin. She had short strings of blue and white shells hanging from each ear and wore a pair of deerskin moccasins that came up to her ankles. Although Kanti spoke limited English, she was able to make herself understood to us.

Sitting at the back beyond the fire was a man watching us. I didn't notice him at first because he hadn't moved and blended into the background, his hair and skin the same color as the bark behind him. William introduced me to his father Shattoockquis, sachem of the tribe. He was much older than Kanti, his face showing the lines and wrinkles of age. Still, he appeared a vigorous man. His spoke little English, so William served as our interpreter.

"We have to go," Sam told William. We stayed for only a short time but I could have spent another hour roaming around the small village meeting and talking to the other Indians but we had to get back. Before we left, William told me that I was welcome to visit with them anytime.

Over the next few years, I came to know many of the men and women at Wekapuage and Quaboag. I can say with all honesty, I've never met a kinder, more generous, respectful group of people. They were always friendly and always willing to share whatever they had, which sometimes wasn't much. They were open and honest and wanted to be treated fairly in all of their dealings with us, and for the most part, they were. They laughed often and much. It was common to see the young boys and girls running around, playing some kind of game, smiling and laughing. They enjoyed games and stories of all types. Compared to them, we, the people of the Massachusetts Bay Colony, were a hard-nosed, glum, stern, unhappy group.

I took William up on his invitation to visit and did so whenever I could. During my third visit to the Wekapauge village, I met four of William's cousins - two young men and two young women. The older of the young men was stocky and squat and gave me a hard stare. He looked like he carried a chip on his shoulder and could have a short temper. I learned later that his name was Matchitehew, which means a "man with an evil heart," which I thought appropriate for him. The other young man was slender but had the same intensity about him as his brother did. His name was Wematin or "brother." The two young women looked like there were several years between them. The older one, who looked to be the oldest of the four, was rather plain and uninterested in meeting me. The younger one, though, was very different from the others. She was of moderate height with skin the color of golden copper. She had a very pretty face with black eyes that shone, long, black hair down to the middle of her back and a beautiful smile that never left her face. Compared to the other three, she was a shining jewel. Her name was Oota-dabun, which means "day star." Her smile was infectious. After a minute I realized I was smiling too because I couldn't help it. She had a special quality about her that the other Indians I'd met didn't.

Over the next few months, I would come to visit William as often as I could, although I was less interested in seeing him than I was in seeing Oota-dabun. I used these visits as an excuse to be with her. Had I told my neighbors in the village that I was going to see her, it would have be frowned upon and might result in a mild censure during Sabbath meeting.

She seemed glad to see me each time. We began to spend more time together, sometimes walking down by the lake, and other times on the other side of the stream. The land on that side sloped up gradually to a level area with big fields on all sides of the path. I'd help her pick berries or plants to be used for medicine. She wanted to learn English, so I taught her more each time I went. She was a quick learner and within a short time was able to carry on a conversation in English. She made a few mistakes, but did well. After she learned English, she began to teach me her language. It was difficult and I had trouble because it was a bit guttural.

It got to the point where I was spending so much time with her that I began neglecting my work at home. I never told

Josiah or Charity who I was visiting, although I think they knew. As far as I know, most, if not all of the other people my age who knew the reason for my visits never mentioned it to their parents or other relations. It was our unspoken although open secret.

Josiah took me aside one day and told me that while it was good I made friends with the Wekapauge I was spending far too much time there and we couldn't afford it; I had to carry my share of the work. He also mentioned that others were beginning to talk about why I spent so much time away. I realized I had to curtail my visits but told Oota that I'd meet her at the edge of the Great Field when I could, which I did.

One evening after a visit to the Indian village, I related my latest adventure to Josiah and Charity during supper. I told them about the way the Indians farmed, smoked their fish, and made a food from fat, ground corn, and berries. I went on and on, not realizing how long I'd been talking until I saw they were through eating. They looked at each other, grinning.

"You have not stopped talking since you got out of bed," Charity told me. "You haven't done this in quite a while. Sometimes I don't know what gets into you," she said shaking her head as she got up from the table.

Josiah surprised me by announcing that we were going to Springfield in three weeks. "Now, that's if everything that needs to be done here is done. You and I will go to see your friend Mr. Pynchon to settle for the land and buy some supplies."

The next week I went to see William and Kanti to ask about some herbs they used to stop itching. Josiah and several others got a bad rash that itched terribly over their arms and neck. None of the normal herbs we had did much good. As I got close to the village, I noticed that there were very few people around. It was a quiet, misty, cool, slightly foggy day, a good day to stay in the wigwam.

Kanti was glad to see me as always. In some ways, she reminded me of my mother. She was kind, even tempered, and smiled quite a bit. She told me that William was off fishing down the river with a couple other men from the village.

After I left Kanti, I walked towards Oota's wigwam unsure whether I should visit her. As I got closer, I was surprised when she stepped out of the wigwam.

"Oota, I was just coming to see you."

"I'm glad," she said, a smile lighting up her face. She had the most beautiful smile I'd ever seen. I'd come to realize over the last few weeks just how much I liked being in her company. A few of my friends reminded me that, while everyone had a good opinion of me and thought Oota was a wonderful young woman, anything more than friendship with her would be going too far. That thought was quietly whispering to me, telling me that we couldn't be more than friends. I realized that I wanted more than that and I thought she did too, although I couldn't be sure.

Without saying anything, we turned and began to walk towards the Great Field, away from the wigwams. On a couple of our other walks, we'd gone to a place down by the river; a small, secluded spot. That was where we headed to be away from any others. There was a very large pine tree with a wide trunk and around the base was a thick carpet of soft, dry needles that smelled good. We sat down next to each other, our backs against the trunk.

"I can't stay too long. I need to get these herbs back to Charity so she can make something to help the rash some of us got." I said, "But I'll stay as long as I can." She turned toward me, her dark eyes warm and inviting. I noticed how her lips were soft and pink and how pretty she was. Without thinking, I put my arm around her waist and gently pulled her to me. I leaned over, my lips coming towards hers. She moved toward me until we were almost touching. There was a moment of uncertainty, an unspoken question if this was wrong. I touched my lips to hers, kissing her softly, hesitantly.

Our lips touched for a brief moment before she pulled away from me. I leaned in and kissed her again and she surprised me by kissing me back. When I tried to kiss her again she moved her head back and sat up. I could see the emotions through her face; she was frightened because she'd done something she shouldn't have, excited at her first kiss, and scared about the consequences. I watched her face, thinking about how pretty she was with her black hair and long eyelashes against her soft bronze skin, and her warm brown eyes were intelligent, questioning, wanting.

"Jack," she said, "we shouldn't have done that." I looked away from her, the thoughts rushing through my mind, slowly realizing that a relationship between us would cause trouble for both her and me. I pushed the thoughts aside, not wanting to get involved thinking about what's right or what's best for her, preferring to feel only that I wanted to stay with her, be with her.

"Jack," she said raising her voice a bit, "I have to go. I can't stay here with you any longer. We'll do something we shouldn't." With that, she got up hurriedly and started towards her wigwam. I got up and brushed the pine needles from my clothes.

"Oota, don't go…don't be mad at me. I didn't mean anything by it. I just wanted to be with you." She turned and put her hands on her hips.

"I know that, Jack…I want to be with you too but we can't have it this way…we can't." She turned and started walking again. I stood there watching her go, not sure what I did to upset her.

As I began for home, slowly plodding along, I thought

about what happened and realized that I may have ruined a young friendship. I didn't understand how I could have done something like that. None of my neighbors could find out because that would be an awkward situation at best and very bad at worst. I realized that men who had improper relations with an unmarried girl or married woman received 15 lashes plus a fine. I also realized that Mr. Pynchon as the magistrate would be the one to determine my punishment. I'd be ashamed for him to hear of this and knew that he'd never speak to me again.

I thought of Becky and my heart ached. I felt like I'd let her down, that I'd done something wrong, and should have known better but it didn't feel wrong at the time; it actually felt very nice. I wondered about what might happen with Oota now, if she would speak with me when I went to visit William or Kanti or if she was as confused as I was.

Realizing that it would take me time to figure this all out, my thoughts turned to our upcoming trip to Springfield. The next two weeks did not move fast enough to suit me. I worked at anything and everything to be certain that no job was left undone that would delay our going to Springfield.

Chapter 8

At last, we were on our way. We left just after sunrise while the heavy dew was on the grass. I got a bit of a jolt when the thought occurred to me that Mr. Pynchon might not be there; he could be in Boston. I might not get back to Springfield for months or maybe longer so if he wasn't there, I'd have no chance of seeing him before then. I decided that if he wasn't there, I'd leave him a message.

It was not quite midday when we came down the long hill overlooking the town and river. Beyond the broad river, wider than any I'd ever seen, was farmland that looked rich and fertile stretching up and down the valley for miles. It looked like anything you planted would grow well. To the west of the farmland, rounded hills rose in the distance, rolling one behind the other like waves in the ocean.

Springfield was a good-sized town set back a couple of hundred yards from the eastern side of the river. The town, fortified with a tall palisade running around it, was several acres square. Houses lined both sides of the palisade with the meetinghouse in the middle at one end. At the opposite end was a tall brick house with a barn on the left side and the tavern on the right. A wide, open area was in the center. The brick house had to be Mr. Pynchon's home, for it was the largest and nicest. People were moving about the town as we entered, going from place to place with a sense of purpose. A man was walking away from us, herding several sheep as he went. I watched him because something about him seemed familiar. He was on the short side, skinny with small shoulders. He was a slovenly sort; his clothes seeming not to fit well and almost falling off him. His hat was dirty and crushed and he had a hunched way of walking.

"Doesn't something about that man seem familiar to you?" I asked Josiah pointing at him.

Josiah stopped the cart. "He does remind me of someone…I'm just not sure who," he said as he got the horse moving again. "Let's get our business with Mr. Pynchon done before we start getting curious about anyone." I jumped out as we pulled up in front of the barn and stood looking at the house for minute.

It was the largest home either of us had ever seen - even larger than Goodfield's - a two-story brick building with a large porch in front with a room over it, a steep pitched roof, chimneys at either end indicating fireplaces in every room, and more windows than in any house I'd seen in Boston. It was the type of house in which you would expect a wealthy man to live.

Josiah went up to the door and knocked. A young

woman with soft brown eyes and long black hair opened the door. After listening to our explanation as to why we were there, she led us into a long hallway and told us to wait. There was a mirror on the yellow painted wall just past a wide staircase. The floor was a dark wood with a beautiful carpet running most of the length of the hall. The door to the room across from where we stood was closed. Down the hall on the same side was another doorway. I could see another door at the back of the house with three panes of glass letting in the bright sunlight. We heard men's voices in the room with the closed door getting louder as they moved toward the hallway. A tall, fair-haired man emerged from the room followed by Mr. Pynchon. As they walked out the front door shaking hands, the young woman reappeared.

"Father," she said, "this is Josiah Clarke. He's here to see you about the land at Quaboag." Before Mr. Pynchon came out of the room, Josiah stepped in front of me so Mr. Pynchon couldn't see me. As they were shaking hands, I moved out from behind Josiah. Mr. Pynchon's head snapped up, his eyes wide in surprise.

"Jack!" he said with a wide smile coming to his face, "What are you doing here? You're the last person I expected to see," he said, shaking my hand warmly.

"It's very good to see you again sir," I told him happily. "I've been looking forward to this for some time." He looked me up and down.

"You've grown a bit, filled out some. You look good. It is good to see you my boy! You did get my letter didn't you? As I told you, there's always a place here for someone like yourself."

"Mr. Pynchon sir, Josiah is my uncle."

"Ah, your uncle, of course! Josiah Clarke, that's why I never connected the two of you. Of course, of course. Josiah, your nephew is a fine boy, no, a man now. I'm impressed by his curiosity, straightforwardness, honesty, and the fact that, unlike many his age, has dreams of a better life for himself." Josiah was a little taken back at such an important man having such a high opinion of me.

"My wife and I always thought the same," he said flashing a smile at me.

"Well, come in," Mr. Pynchon said, ushering us into the room. A wide fireplace was on the left side opposite a heavy looking table with ornately carved legs. On the wall behind it were two windows flanked by floor-to-ceiling bookshelves filled with a mixture of what looked like ledgers and journals. Another table stood against the far wall with two candleholders on it.

"Please, take a seat." Josiah seemed ill at ease, not sure what he should do while in the company of one of the richest men in the entire Colony. He fidgeted in his chair for a minute then seemed to relax a bit. Mr. Pynchon put him at ease by asking me a question.

"So Jack, you've come to Quaboag with your aunt and uncle. I'm interested to know what you think."

"Yes sir, I have. It looks like a good place for a farm," I said, "And...I met some Indians. I'd never seen any real Indians before. I made friends with several of the Wekapauge, a couple of boys my age and a pretty girl." I felt my face flush a bit at the thought of Oota-dabun. "But," I added, my enthusiasm dropping a bit, "I left some good friends in Ipswich who I'll miss very much. They may be coming here, though." Mr. Pynchon shot Josiah an amused glance, a hint of a smile on his face.

"Well Josiah, now, about the land...20 acres in the western town plot. That's one pound, five shillings, hard money." Josiah took out his little leather bag and counted out the money onto the table. Mr. Pynchon took one of the ledgers from the edge of the desk, opened it, and began to write, talking as he did so.

"Josiah Clarke, 20 acres of land at Quaboag, one pound, five shillings, paid in hard money." Putting the quill back in its stand, he looked up at me. "One day I hope to be able to write this same thing for you Jack, whether it's at Quaboag, Northampton, Westfield, Hatfield, Hadley, Deerfield or somewhere else."

"Thank you, sir. I'd like that too. But where are those places?"

"Hadley, Hatfield, Northampton, and Deerfield are north of here, up the river. Westfield is a few miles west of here." Leaning across the table towards me, he asked, "How's that girl of yours? Her name is Becky right?"

"Yes, sir, it is. She's doing well, at least the last time I saw her just before we left, but that was over three months ago. Her father, Tom Morgan, said they may join us at Quaboag but I don't know if it will ever happen. He's not a man to make big decisions quickly. It usually takes him quite a while, sometimes a very long while," I told him, my thoughts turning toward Becky.

"Well, then," he said with a smile, "you'll be very surprised and pleased I'm sure, to know that he has made the decision. I received a letter from him just yesterday. He asked to buy 20 acres of land at Quaboag…said he hoped to be here by September or early October." I was stunned. Never did I think that he would actually move his family to Quaboag. I couldn't quite believe such wonderful news. Becky would be coming to the village! It was almost too good to be true. I'd be able to see her every day, to look at her face, into her eyes. I was speechless for a moment.

"That's just like Tom Morgan," Josiah said, leaning forward in his chair, putting his elbows on his knees, "He plans on coming to a new place a month or so before the cold weather begins. Sometimes he acts as if he has only half a brain. Coming here just before the snow starts…doesn't surprise me though. But that fact that they're coming here, well I'd say that's good news, eh, Jack?" he said, giving me a big wink.

"I'm going to write him today," said Mr. Pynchon, "and suggest that he wait until next spring since, as you said, it makes no sense to come so late in the year."

"Morgan, Tom Morgan," I muttered to myself. "That's who the man reminded me of, the one we saw coming in," I told Josiah, "the dirty one with the sheep." At this, Mr. Pynchon chuckled.

"Yes, he is a bit slovenly. His name is Morgan too. The talk is that he came from the Ipswich area but has been in Connecticut for a few years, at least that's what he told me."

"You know," Josiah said, bringing his right hand to his chin, "Tom had a brother that went off years ago…just left one day. No one ever knew where he went. There were reports of him going to New Haven, but I also heard that he went to England. I wonder if that's him." At that point, I didn't care if the dirty little person was the governor's sister. All I could think of was that it would be less than a year before Becky would be living in our village. I shook Mr. Pynchon's hand three times all the while telling him how good it was to see him again and hoping that I could come visit him as we did in

Boston, thanking him again for the good news. Josiah finally got me out the door.

"You were chattering like a chipmunk! I've never seen you so worked up. You were so excited I wouldn't be surprised if you pissed your breeches," he laughed, getting in to the cart.

Chapter 9

The Morgans coming to join us was big news back in the village. Adding another family was very welcome indeed. Everyone agreed that the more families and the more people, the better. Charity was pleased, both for me and because she and Elizabeth were good friends. I knew the move was more difficult for Charity than Josiah thought it was. She'd been quiet and keeping to herself lately. When we told her what we learned, she brightened. It's not that she didn't know the women already in the village, but just not as well as she knew Elizabeth. She needed someone to confide in, someone she was comfortable with; a good friend.

I was back in Springfield less than two weeks after Josiah and I went. In my excitement, I'd forgotten to get two sacks of dried peas so I went with Judah Trumble very early one morning. Now, I know that I didn't need to go, that Judah could have brought them back, but I wanted to see Mr. Pynchon again and spend some time by the big river. Rivers have always fascinated me. As I watch the water sliding by, I wonder where it comes from. Was it from rain 100 miles away or was it from an underground spring that no one knew about? That, and I liked the peaceful feeling I got sitting by a river or stream listening to the splashes and gurgles.

When I got there, I saw the scruffy man who was possibly Tom Morgan's long lost brother. As I came up to him, he was tying sacks together that were in the back of a wagon. He grumbled something about the knots being all wrong and began re-tying them. I stood watching until he turned around giving me a baleful look, his eyes boring into me.

"What do you want?" he spat at me.

"Mr. Pynchon says he thinks you're from Ipswich. Are you?"

"What business is it of yours where I'm from? Or for that matter where I'm going to? Just who the hell do you think you are anyway?"

"I'm from Ipswich too. We just moved to the Quaboag settlement. Most of the other settlers are from Ipswich too…you might know some of them."

"That may be. But what makes you think I'd care even if I was from Ipswich?"

"Well, you remind me of a man I knew. You look a lot like him. I just wondered, that's all."

"Yeah, well, do your wondering someplace else. I have things to do, now leave me be."

"Do you know my uncle Josiah Clarke and his wife Charity? Or Mr. Ayres, Coy, Prichard, Warner, Wilson and…"

That was all I got out before he cut me off.

"I know most of them. Never had much use for any of them...including your aunt and uncle." He was a mean, grumpy, nasty man who wanted nothing more than to be left alone. Before I left, I had one other thing to ask him.

"Are you Tom Morgan's brother?" At that, he stopped working and stood up, wiping the dust from his hands. He climbed down off the wagon and came toward me, stopping when he was two feet away.

"Whether I am or not is no one's business but my own." While he looked angry, I could see curiosity in his eyes.

"I know him and his family well," I said, putting my hands on my hips.

"Good for you."

"Since you haven't seen him for so long, you couldn't know that they're coming to Quaboag in the spring." I said. He looked at me with a stern gaze.

"Did you say they're coming here?"

"Well, not here but to Quaboag, to farm like the rest of us." He didn't say anything but looked thoughtful before turning and walking away.

"Don't mind him," a man behind me said. Turning, I recognized him as the tall, fair-haired man at Mr. Pynchon's house. "He's a strange man. He doesn't seem too happy knowing his brother is moving here soon."

He wore no hat, but a tan shirt with a wide collar, brown breeches with light yellow socks and good leather shoes with silver buckles. He carried a hickory walking staff in his hands. He was a good-looking man with a firm jaw and sharp blue eyes.

"I was walking by when I heard you ask about a brother of his. I always assumed he didn't have any family. He is a loner who doesn't like anyone. I'm Thomas Cooper. Didn't I see you at John Pynchon's a while ago?"

"Yes, you did. I'm Jack Parker," I said extending my hand. "I'm on my way to see him now." He looked at me for a moment, obviously thinking about something and measuring me at the same time.

"John mentioned you yesterday in a conversation about the trouble we've had getting good messengers. Do you ride well?"

"Yes I do. I have my own horse. It belonged to my father. His name is Bubs."

At that, he chuckled. "Bubs...that's a wonderful name for a horse. Go see Mr. Pynchon. He'll want to talk to you. It was good meeting you Jack."

"It was good meeting you too, sir."

As I walked along, I thought of Mr. Pynchon's interest in me. I was no one special; I met him by chance. He was one of the most powerful and wealthiest men in the Colony. In addition to Quaboag, he owned five other plantations of varying size, several ships in the coastal trade, a huge number of sheep and cattle, and a sugar plantation in Barbados. He owned more land any other man in the Colony. He was a successful merchant, magistrate, and Assistant to the General Court who met with the governor at least four times a year. I marveled at the fact that he was bothering with someone like me.

His daughter answered the door and showed me into his office without waiting. He was sitting at the desk with his back turned towards the window, letting the light spill over his shoulder onto a letter. He finished and looked up.

"Jack, how are you?" he asked getting out of his chair to shake my hand.

"I'm fine, sir. How are you?"

"I'm busy as always. There is more to do than there are hours in the day. I am going to Boston the end of next week and there is much to do before I go. I want to ask you something. It's all right if you say no, although I hope you don't. It's an opportunity for you, something I can do for you." I was intrigued and wondered what it could be. "I need men to serve me as messengers. Your neighbor Richard Coy, the father, not the son, does it now and then as well as others from Northampton, Hatfield, and Westfield but they are not always available when I need them for one reason or another. We've known each other for a while and you're a good man, honest and responsible. I want you to be a messenger for me. Now, I know your uncle will object because he needs you at the farm but I need you too, Jack. I'll need you for two days every other week. I'll pay you four shillings each time you ride." He looked at me waiting for an answer but I just stood there. Finally, I realized he was waiting for me and I blurted out "Yes, sir. I'll be a messenger for you."

"Fine," he said, "I want you to take a letter to Lancaster. You must wait for the answer and return it to me immediately. I want you to leave this afternoon and be back here no later than noon on Friday. I'll have the letter ready in a little while."

"I came with Judah. He's around here somewhere. I'll find him and let him know we'll have to go right after you give me the letter."

"My guess is that you'll find Judah at the tavern," he said without looking up from his desk. "Come back in half an hour."

As I walked towards the tavern, I was pleased that one of the richest men around wanted me, a farm boy, to be a messenger, to work for him. I knew Josiah might be upset because I'd be gone for two days but for four shillings, he'd think it was worth it.

Judah waited at the cart while I went to Mr. Pynchon's

for the letter. I was ushered into his office by his daughter. He didn't look up from his writing. After a few moments of me standing there listening to his pen scratching the surface of the paper, he folded it and poured blue wax from a little dipper on the edge where the folds met and pressed a stamp into the wax to seal the letter.

"Here's the letter," he said. "Deliver it to William Hutchinson in Lancaster. His house is opposite the tavern. Wait for his response. I want you back here by Friday afternoon. Do you understand?"

"Yes sir, I do. I'll be back by Friday afternoon," I said with a little more confidence than I felt.

"If you can be here by mid-morning, so much the better. Now be off. I'll give you your four shillings when you return."

"Yes sir. Thank you, sir." With that, I ran and jumped into the cart surprising Judah. I told him to go as fast as he could because I needed to get back quickly.

When I got back, Josiah and Charity were just sitting down to dinner. They didn't expect me so soon, at least not until mid-afternoon, and were surprised at my getting back so early. Charity saw me through the open door and came out.

"Jack, is everything all right? Why are you back so soon?"

"Everything's fine," I said jumping off the cart and walked towards her. "Nothing is wrong. I got the peas and spoke to Mr. Pynchon."

"Why were you talking to him? Or rather, why was he talking to you?" Josiah asked coming out of the house chewing on a piece of bread. "All you had to do is get the peas."

"I wanted to say hello to him. He asked me to be a messenger for him," I said proudly.

"He did what?" Charity asked. She was as surprised as I'd been.

"He asked me to be a messenger for him when he needs me. Others like Mr. Coy aren't always available. He's going to pay me four shillings and not in trade either...hard money."

"Four shillings? For taking letters back and forth? Did he say when he wants you?" Josiah asked.

"Yes. This afternoon."

"What? You can't go this afternoon...we have work to do repairing the fence."

"He wants me to go to Lancaster to deliver this letter to William Hutchinson," I said, taking the letter out of my shirt to show them. I'm to wait for his answer and be back by Friday morning."

"Friday morning? You'll be gone two whole days? Now, I don't know if that's worth four shillings hard money or not."

"Josiah, I think he ought to go," Charity said. "Mr. Pynchon thinks highly enough of Jack to ask him to do this. He's old enough and can take care of himself. He's a good rider and can be there and back in little time. Besides, it's four shillings. From what I've heard, Mr. Pynchon doesn't always do that you know." Josiah shoulders slumped and he let out a long sigh.

"I know, but it won't happen every time," he said. "If Jack does it again, Pynchon will give us credit. I know he will."

"I know that but four shillings is four shillings. It would help us. How could Jack say no to him?"

"Well, it's done and I know you'll do your best for him," he said, turning to me. "I'll need to figure out how to get everything done while you're gone."

After I ate, I went out to get Bubs and found him down by the woods. I saddled him after getting a leather jug of beer, my hat, my pouch filled with Indian meal to eat on the way, and my gun, powder, and shot. Then I made sure I had the letter in my other pouch. Josiah and Charity were waiting outside for me to leave. I got on Bubs and rode over to them. They looked worried about my never having gone on a trip of this distance by myself. I tried to reassure them.

"I'll be back early tomorrow night. Then I can go to Mr. Pynchon's early Friday and collect my four shillings," I said, trying to be cheerful. My effort failed since their expressions didn't change. Josiah put his arm around Charity's waist and raising his other arm, pointed his index finger at me.

"Be careful."

I'd taken three shillings, all the money I had, to pay for food and stabling Bubs. With that in my pouch, I rode down the Town Road.

The first several miles were easy and pleasant. It was a sunny day, warm but with a touch of coolness in the air. White, fluffy clouds moved slowly from west to east. Bubs was running easily but covering distance. I was excited about this job since it paid so well and allowed me to get away from the endless chores. It was different and I was enjoying it.

I reached a place where the path narrowed, barely wide enough for me and Bubs to get through it. Tall pine trees grew close to the path on both sides, which made it dark and foreboding. It was much like a smaller area a few miles back since both had a swamp and a brook on the left and a hill on the right. This area was much narrower and longer than the other had been. There were several bends to the path so it wasn't possible for me to see too far ahead. This dark, close, menacing area continued for a distance, longer than I thought it did. I had my gun resting across my legs, and for no particular reason, I slowed and checked the priming. I realized that I didn't like this part of the path; it gave me a chill and the sooner I was out of it the better. It was all in shadow, getting darker and deeper as I went along until it was almost pitch black. It was much cooler, almost cold in fact, than any part of the path so far.

After a mile or more, I came out on the top of a hill that sloped down and away from me. I could see other hills far in the distance. I rode on, feeling much better being in the open. I went down this hill and up another larger one. Open fields stretched out on both sides. As I came up the top, I saw a river below me at the back of a wide, flat area that went along the river for a mile or more. At the far end to my left, I saw a small group of wigwams, smoke curling out of them. For a moment, I thought of riding down there, but the sun was moving to the west and I didn't have time to visit so I pressed on.

As I rode on, lulled by the rhythmic rocking motion Bubs made as he walked, my thoughts drifted to Becky.

I saw her standing next to our table the day my mother died. She was helping her mother put out food for the people who came to visit us after the burial. She was wearing a brown dress, white apron and a short, white cap. She was quiet and helpful that day, but she wasn't always like that.

Once, when we were down by the river, she pushed me into tidal mud that stunk of decay, and laughed and clapped when I pulled myself out covered in brown, slimy muck.

Another time, I was taking three sheep my father sold to a man on the other side of town. Becky came out of nowhere, running at the sheep, yelling, and waving her arms. They scattered to the four winds so it took me over an hour to herd them back. She thought it was funny as hell.

I almost clobbered her one Thursday when they came over for a simple supper before we went to the Sabbath lecture. She would not stop bothering me but did it only when we were out of sight of the adults. The first thing she did was pinch me so hard it hurt, then she "accidentally" hit me with a huge wooden cooking spoon, and then, when we were on our way to the lecture, jumped with both feet onto the instep of my right foot; it hurt like hell for a few days. I chased her but she was too quick, even for me. I told her she was lucky I didn't catch her because I would have smacked her. She stuck her nose in the air and told me that I would have done no such thing because she was a girl and boys were not supposed to hit girls. She shot me a sidelong glance full of the knowledge that she had me beat and there was nothing I could do about it.

Sighing, I shook off the memories and picked up the pace.

I arrived in Lancaster after dark and rode down the road looking for Mr. Hutchinson's house. It was a dark night; it had gotten cloudy, so there was no moonlight. After a short time, I found the house, went up the stairs, and knocked on the door. While I waited, I looked up and saw it was a house several times larger than ours with four gables and a shingled roof.

While it was very nice and from all appearances, the home of a well-to-do man, it was not as imposing as Mr. Pynchon's.

No one came to the door so I knocked again, a little louder this time. After a moment, the door opened. A young woman dressed in a spotless skirt, apron, and headscarf and carrying a basket came into the hall from a room behind the stairway.

"Good evening," I said as politely as I could. "I have a letter for Mr. William Hutchinson from Mr. John Pynchon of Springfield."

"He's not here. He won't be back until tomorrow. Leave the letter and I'll see that he gets it as soon as he arrives," she said, holding out her hand.

"I can't leave the letter. Mr. Pynchon instructed me to wait for an answer. When tomorrow is he expected?"

"He should be here before midday." With that, she closed the door, leaving me standing there. Not knowing what else to do, I took Bubs and walked across the road to the tavern. It was larger than Ayres tavern with several tables against a long wall and three or four around the hearth. There were six or eight men drinking and talking amongst themselves. A tall man with a gray beard wearing an apron across his big, round belly was the tavern keeper. He looked up from wiping the table.

"What I can I do for you, young man?" Considering how little money I had and how I didn't want to spend any more of it than I had to, I pondered his question for a minute. I had a little bit of my Indian meal left so I didn't need any food, although the roast chickens two men were eating made me realize just how hungry I was. I would need a place to sleep and to stable my horse. I decided to start with a drink.

"I'll have a pint of beer please." He poured the drink into a wooden mug and put it in front of me.

"That's the best beer you'll get for quite a distance. Of course, the fact that there's nothing for miles around helps," he said with a belly laugh.

I looked around at the mostly empty room and moved towards one of the tables by the windows. On the wall to my right was a sign of the five Alls. There were five human figures, each having a motto under him. The first is a king in his regalia with the motto: I govern all; the second, a bishop with the motto: I pray for all; the third, a lawyer in his gown with his motto: I plead for all; the fourth, a soldier in his regimentals, his motto being: I fight for all; and lastly, a poor countryman with his scythe and rake and the motto: I pay for all. I chuckled at the jest and took in the room. A red-haired man, older than I, sat two tables beyond. He looked up as I sat down and nodding to me, raised his mug. I nodded back to him to be polite. He got up and came to my table.

"Just passing through on your way to Boston, I suppose?" he asked as he pulled a chair out and sat down. Not knowing anyone and seeing I'd be here waiting until morning, I was glad for his company, even if I hadn't asked for it.

"No, I'm not going to Boston. I'm here to deliver a letter to Mr. Hutchinson but he's not here so I have to wait until morning."

"Well, Williams here," he said indicating the tavern keeper, "serves good food and drink but his lodgings are the worst you'll find between here and Boston. I'm Robert Wilson," he said extending his hand.

"I'm Jack Parker," I said, shaking his hand.

"How about another mug?"

"Thank you but I can't spend any more. I need it for a bed and stabling my horse."

He offered and I accepted, for me to sleep in his barn, and after finishing our drinks, we left for his house. It wasn't far since nothing is in a settlement of that size. His house was at the west end of the village, smaller than most with the barn being almost the same size as the house. While it was not the first time I'd slept in a barn and probably won't be the last, I slept well.

The next morning after he'd given me a small loaf of coarse bread, I thanked him for his hospitality and rode the short distance to the village and since I didn't expect Mr. Hutchinson to be home for a while, I tied Bubs at the tavern and walked through the village. It was three times the size of Quaboag with a big meetinghouse at one end of the road with large two-story houses on both sides of it. Pigs, cows, and sheep roamed about as at home but in greater numbers. Two women were grinding corn while a bedraggled looking man was in the stocks with a big red "D" hanging from his neck, the sign that he'd been very drunk on more than one occasion. At the side of each house was a garden with a fence around it to keep the animals out. Several young women were working there, weeding and hoeing. There were several men about with a group at the meetinghouse and another smaller group outside the tavern.

I decided to see if Mr. Hutchinson had returned yet since I wanted to get back as soon as I could, the trip already taking a day longer than I thought it would. When I got to his house there were three horses tied up in front, raising my hopes that he was there. I knocked on the door and it was answered by the same woman as last night. She acted as if she'd never seen me before.

"I'm here to deliver a letter to Mr. Hutchinson from Mr. Pynchon of Springfield. Is he here?"

"Yes he is. He arrived a short time ago. I'll tell him you're here." Giving me a sour smile, she closed the door, leaving me standing there for several minutes. I began to wonder why it was taking so long and started getting anxious and impatient to be on my way homeshe finally opened the door, motioning for me to come inside. She led me into a small, dark room that contained a table, two chairs, and a shelf against the far wall with books and journals on it. I turned to look around and was surprised by a small, shriveled looking man standing beside me; he'd been behind the door.

"Good day, sir. I've come with a letter from Mr. John Pynchon." He held out his hand, moving his fingers impatiently. As he took the letter and walked by me, I noticed how small he was; his long pinched face held a short, gray beard. He held a stick in one hand that he used as a cane. He crossed the room with a shuffling walk before sitting with a groan, opening the letter, and grimacing as he did.

"If you think you're going to get anything from me young man, you're wrong! You will not! Nothing!" he shouted, even though I was not more than 10 feet away. This outburst surprised me, not only because it was unexpected, but it was said with such vehemence in a dry, grating, cranky voice.

"I didn't expect anything, sir," I said, somewhat meekly hoping to avoid another outburst. He harrumphed and began to read, mumbling as he did so. His long, bony fingers looked like claws. Every moment or two, he'd stop reading and gaze at me with a sharp, hawk-like look.

"So," he said with a slit of a smile, "John Pynchon wants an answer now does he? I've a mind to send you off without one. Who does he think he is?"

"I don't know, sir. But…"

"Don't talk, young man! I don't want any back talk from you, do you understand?" I stood there wondering what business Mr. Pynchon might have with such a strange old man. He stood up, tossing the letter onto the table and scrabbled around the chair with his back to me. He walked to the window and looked out at the street, slightly hunched and crablike, his hands behind his back. He turned quickly, surprising me.

"God will punish John Pynchon! Yes, he will. So successful he thinks he can order me to give him my cattle on his terms. It won't happen, no, it won't," he trailed off, looking at the floor. "Did you know," he said, turning an inquisitive eye at me, "his father was a heathen and blasphemer? He wrote a book that was heresy and stood before the General Court he did. His book was burned in Boston. He went back to England before giving an answer for his heresy. He was a coward as well as an old fool."

"No sir, I didn't know any of that," even though Mr. Pynchon told me all this the second time we met, I didn't want to get into a discussion with him.

"Mmmm…yes…well…my granddaughter said you came last night. What did you do while waiting for me?"

"I went to the tavern, met Robert Wilson, went home with him, and slept in his barn.

"Where do you live?" he asked.

"At Quaboag. We have a farm of 20 acres. My uncle and I work it. We have 10 acres planted and 10 for pasture and the biggest garden at the plantation. It's a fine piece of property."

"And how did you get this land?"

"Why, we bought it from Mr. Pynchon like everyone else."

"Does that man own everything in the western colony?" he asked more to himself than to me.

"Yes, sir he does," I replied. He sat at the table and drummed his fingers as he read the letter again. He gave me a sly look as he picked up his quill with his right hand and scratched his chin with his bony left hand. He wrote only a few words, blew on the ink to dry it, folded it three times, poured wax on it, and put his seal on it. He stood and handed me the letter.

"What's your name?"

"Jack Parker, sir."

"You seem like a good lad," he said, appraising me once again. "How long did it take you to get here?"

"I left Quaboag at noon and got here quite a while after dark."

"Take my answer to John Pynchon. You seem a much better messenger than I usually see."

"Thank you very much, sir." With that, I left. I put the letter in my pouch, untied Bubs and climbing on, took a last glance at the village of Lancaster before riding off. Bubs was rested, fed, and watered and he too, wanted to get home. It being a little past midday, I thought that with a bit of hard riding I could be at Quaboag not too long after dark. It was a warm, partly sunny day and as I rode, the wind blew in my face. It felt good to be on my way home at last. I rode easily, and Bubs enjoyed it as much as I did.

As we moved along, I began to think about my first trip as a messenger, not sure whether if it was worth all the trouble. It had been a long trip, longer than I thought it would be, and four shillings didn't seem like much in the way of compensation.

After a few hours, I approached four rolling hills that I knew were about eight miles from home. The sun wasn't far from setting so I spurred Bubs on, hoping I might be home earlier than I planned. I wanted to cover as much distance as possible while there was still enough light. A chilly breeze sprang up, feeling even cooler when I was in the shadows.

As Bubs and I came over the second hill, the area below us was mostly in shadow. At the edge of the path where the sunlight and shadow met, two wolves were eating the remains of a small deer. I raised my musket but they were too far away for a killing shot. Getting the bounty of four shillings for a wolf would make the hardships of the trip more bearable. The bigger wolf stopped eating, lifting his head as he did, and glared at me with eyes that glowed green in the dying light. He growled at his companion, a smaller, younger looking animal, who, with a bloody piece of meat in its mouth, took a few steps in my direction. My hope was that it would come close enough for a shot, although judging from their response to me I doubted it. Wolves were quite common and it wasn't unusual to see at least one every third or fourth time I went hunting. Jim Travis from our village shot 14 in three years time. They weren't fearful of us to any degree and didn't always run at our appearance, although they are always wary.

I rode down the hill going directly for them. The larger one backed up several yards while continuing to glare at me. The other started to move around to my right, loping up the hill near the trees. Because it was in full shadow, it was difficult to see it. My concern grew that they would try to get behind us and try to stalk Bubs. I'd heard of it happening a couple of times from people in Springfield but it always to the west of there. My concern grew when I saw a third wolf, much bigger than the first, at the far end of the field. It was at the very edge of light and shadow, and the light was fading fast as the sun went over the hill. It began to move at an easy pace down the hill directly towards me. Bubs began moving back and forth, side to side, neighing constantly, showing his fear of the wolves, having picked up the scent. The smaller one kept getting closer although moving slower and more cautiously than it did before.

It moved behind me to my right so I turned Bubs to face it, keeping the other two in sight. I believed that if I galloped away, they'd chase me. I wasn't having a good feeling about this since they seemed more menacing with each moment and began to stalk us. I waited, as each got closer, not daring to move forward up the path. Seeing the smaller one moving, head down low, covering ground quickly, I turned in the saddle and shot. I was surprised when it fell to the ground with a howling, wailing noise. I shot so fast that I didn't think I'd hit it, only hoping to scare it away. I began to load my gun, not knowing what would happen but believing that I'd need it again soon. The wolf didn't stay down but got up with difficulty and dragged itself towards the woods. I looked and saw the first wolf moving up the slope, running at an angle, never taking its eyes from me. It headed in the direction of the third wolf that was now gone; I lost sight of it while shooting at the small one. I marked the spot where the injured one entered the woods and planned on coming out when I got back from Springfield to look for the dead animal to get the bounty.

The colors were fading as it got darker, with everything turning a light gray. I was concerned that there would be more wolves ahead since we'd be in the long, dark stretch with the thick, heavy pines trees on each side. I kicked Bubs' sides now wanting to be home as soon as I could because I was tired and sick of riding for so long. Once we went through the scary place, I could gallop all the way, since it was open ground and the path was easy to follow, even at night.

I was filled with foreboding as we approached the dark place not only because of my experience on the way to Lancaster but I also remembered various Quaboag and Wekapuage men talking about how this area is frequented by evil spirits that were responsible for evil deeds and mischief. Quaboag Sachem Conkganasco told several of us one night about a group of Indians coming back from a successful hunt that went into a place like this and disappeared without any trace. I'm glad I didn't remember this on my way out or I'd have found a different route. Now it was too dark and too late to try to find another way. I'd just have to ride through, trusting to God.

I kept a sharp watch for the wolves. We started up the slope on the other side of the hill; the dark section looming ahead of us. I rode into the first part of it, the huge pines closing in on both sides, making it as dark as could be. It was like having my eyes shut. I let Bubs find the way since I couldn't see the path at all. Going back was not an option, since I didn't know another way, and if I tried to find one, it could take me miles out of my way and many hours, which I didn't have.

I stopped when I heard a noise off to the right about 50 feet or so into the woods. It stopped when we did. Bubs got jittery again, making me fear the wolves were near and that he could hear and smell things I couldn't. I thought that if it was the wolves, they'd wait until there was a good place to attack. I gently kicked him on, going slow , listening for any sound. We traveled a short distance when I heard a shuffling noise behind me. I thought, as unlikely as it might be, the injured wolf was behind us limping along. I didn't want to think that it might be something else more sinister and threatening than a wolf.

I decided to push through as fast as I could and be out of this place as soon as possible. I gripped my gun with my right hand and held the reins tightly in my left, leaned forward and kicked Bubs in the flanks. There being almost no light, he couldn't see to go any faster than a slow walk. I knew from my earlier trip that the path rose to an area that had sharp, hard thin pieces of rock like knife blades sticking up a few inches out of the ground. As we got to where I thought it was, I reined in to prevent him from stepping on it and being hurt. The last thing I needed at this point was for Bubs to get hurt, leaving me to walk the remaining eight miles. If that happened, I'd have to lead him the rest of the way, which would slow me down, and I had get home, eat, sleep, and be in Springfield all by mid-morning, which was in 12 hours.

We moved along slowly, feeling our way in the dark. I knew the path curved to the left as it went up a small rise. The sun having set quite a while ago, the thick pine trees caused the road ahead to look even darker than before. I was on edge listening for any sound. I felt the hair on my arms stand on end as a wolf howled close by, joined by two more. It was an eerie, wailing sound that brought out fear in the strongest, bravest man. Suddenly, I felt something press against my side and brush my face. I let out a scream that was swallowed up by the trees.

I put my hand out, dropping the reins and felt the soft brush of pine needles. I let out a loud sigh when I realized I'd gone too close to one side and brushed against a branch. A wolf howled again louder and closer and another followed a second later off to my other side. I heard a scraping, shuffling sound behind me like someone was dragging a heavy sack. I leaned forward to grab the reins but couldn't reach them. They'd dropped to the ground when I put my hand out so I had to get down to find them. The darkness was overwhelming and I got a strong feeling that something or someone was watching me. I slid off the saddle little by little, holding my gun tightly. I put my hand on Bubs' withers and felt my way to his head, reaching down, feeling his muzzle. I found the reins, gathered them in my hand and moved back, feeling for the stirrups, grabbed the top of the saddle, put my foot in the stirrup, and swung myself up. Something was running through the trees parallel to the path. When it got past us, it suddenly stopped and I thought I heard ragged breathing. A strong gust of wind came through the trees, blocking all sound. It stopped as quickly as it began. When I heard the noise in the trees, I brought my gun up and fired in that direction. The noise was deafening in that enclosed path; the shot seemed to echo again and again. When it stopped, everything was still and silent. I tapped Bubs with my heels and he moved on at a slow walk. I could sense his fear, his breath coming in and out in quick bursts and feel his quivering muscles in my legs as he slowly danced from side to side. I felt a wave of fear and anxiety run through me. It seemed like we'd never be out of this place, as if we entered it hours ago although it was only a few minutes.

I got Bubs calmed once again. I rode down the middle of the path and saw a lighter area up ahead, went down a slight hill and found myself out in the open. I could feel a light wind and saw the stars in the sky. After I went a short distance, I stopped and turned Bubs around, so I could look at the stand of trees and the edge of the path going into darkness. My shoulders were tight and my legs hurt; I was glad to be out of there. Just as I was about to turn to leave, I saw two eyes glowing green, staring out of the woods at me. The hair on my body stood on end and fear washed over me in waves for the eyes were too high to be those of a wolf. They had to be something the size of a man. I turned and rode as fast as I could, leaning over Bubs neck, crouching as low as I could get, urging him on with kicks to the flanks. As we pulled away, I heard a wild, lonely, mournful, haunting sound that seemed to turn to wild laughter.

Several days after it happened, I told William and Kanti about it. They exchanged a meaningful glance before William left the wigwam. "He went to get the shaman. You must tell him what you told us. It's very important that he know about this," Kanti told me in a serious tone. The shaman, an old man with long, gray hair and wrinkled skin came in wearing a fox pelt on his head. His eyelids were painted yellow and there was a black streak running diagonally across his face, from the right cheekbone to under his nose, down across his mouth and to his left jawbone. William said he'd only told the shaman that he had to hear my story but told him nothing of it. The shaman sat in front of me, waiting for me to begin. I explained to him, through William's translation, what I'd seen and heard that night, beginning with spotting the wolves. The shaman looked at me with a mixture of curiosity and respect. He began speaking, gesturing wildly, making signs of animals with his hands, then standing and stamping around like some hoofed beast. He stopped, put his head up, and howled like a wolf, only it turned into the same heart-stopping sound I'd heard that night. I fell back in surprise, not expecting to hear that again. He stopped howling and sat next to me. He began questioning me about that night.

"He wants to know if that was that the sound you heard," William asked.

"Yes, it was," I told him. "It was almost the exact sound."

"And the eyes, they were green? Too high for an animal?"

"Yes, they were a glowing green, like a dog's in the firelight only blazing. They were at the same height as my eyes." The shaman began speaking again, only this time directly to me trying to explain something. William told me what he was saying.

"He says you are very lucky that you escaped alive. It was Abamacho, coming to steal you away. You must never go that way again at night, for if you do, he will get you, and you will never see anyone again."

"But, if I got through there once, I could do it again. Not that I would want to, but I could." William told the old man what I'd said. He looked at me shaking his head back and forth and went speaking on for a while.

"If you were to go there again," William explained, "he says you would not get very far before you were taken. You are marked; Abamacho knows you now. You cannot hide from him. He was the third wolf coming to see you and claim you for himself. It is not safe for you to go there ever again. You must find a way around that place. If you ever want to see your family or friends again, you must go another way. If you hear his wicked howl again, you are doomed." The shaman stood and touched the first two fingers of his right hand to his chest before raising his hand and opening his palm, their sign of good luck, and left us. I didn't know what to think but Kanti explained that this was not to be taken lightly, that it was a very serious thing, and that they did not want one of their good friends taken by the most evil of creatures known to them.

However, I didn't learn any of this until later. I never went through that area again, having found a way around it by going through some fields, open woods and a small swamp. The new route, longer but much safer, joined the old road three miles past the dwelling of the devil.

As I rode on towards home that frightening night, I realized how tired I was. The whole experience drained me; the tension and anxiety washed over me and I felt exhausted. My eyes adjusted to the night after leaving the haunted forest. I guided Bubs over and around the few obstacles along the way – two small brooks and a swamp. Once I reached the millpond, I began riding at a fast trot to cover more ground.

The clopping sound of Bubs' hooves seemed very loud against the silence of the village. When I reached home, I was physically and emotionally exhausted. I slid off and led Bubs to the barn; he needed as much rest as I did. I rubbed him down and gave him a big pile of hay and a bucket of water. I tried to enter the house as quietly as possible, but the door squeaked when I opened it. I hadn't taken more than three steps when Charity greeted me. She was sitting by the small fire in the hearth. Josiah was sleeping soundly, snoring away.

"Jack, you're home! We were worried about you; we thought you'd be back yesterday. What happened?" she asked. Josiah grunted and woke up but didn't get out of bed. He threw his legs over the side and sat up.

"We thought the devil's own demons got you. I told your aunt that even though you'd be a day late you'd be fine, but I'll admit I was getting a bit concerned when you weren't here by dinner. Charity, he needs something to eat. You're hungry…," he said, more as a statement than a question. She lit a small candle that guttered at first, the light flickering against the wall, took a trencher, and filled it with corn mush from a pot on the hearth; I was hungry and ate it fast, shoveling it down like I hadn't eaten in a couple of days. She spooned out more as I got a mug of cider from the barrel. I sat there with the fire burning, my stomach on the way to being full and took a long drink of the cider. It was good to be home.

Since it was just several hours before dawn, I related the various parts of the trip and after answering their questions and promising to tell them everything tomorrow, I went up the narrow stairs to the loft and lay down on my mattress. I must have fallen asleep as soon as my head hit the pillow because the next thing I knew Josiah was calling me to get up. It was one of those nights when you're so exhausted, you sleep well but it feels like you didn't.

Half awake, I dragged myself out of bed and down the stairs and sat at the table while getting dressed. I put on a clean shirt and breeches since the clothes I'd worn for the last three days were dirty and I wanted to be presentable for Mr. Pynchon. I was anxious to get to Springfield and collect my four shillings.

I rode easily at first, not wanting to tire Bubs so early in the trip since neither of us was fully rested. I wanted him to warm up slowly because I planned to gallop most of the way. I went through the Indian village of Wekapauge and saw Oota hoeing the corn, Kanti making a basket, and William just coming out of the wigwam, waving to them as I went by. A couple of hundred yards past their village, I saw Matchitehew just off the side of the path. As I got closer, he stepped in my way and began yelling and waving his arms to frighten Bubs. I crouched low and kicked Bubs hard, riding right at him. It was as if Bubs didn't like him either and picked up speed, bearing down hard on him. Matchitehew stood his ground daring me to hit him and I was happy to oblige. A second before we got to him, he took a step to the right before reaching out and trying to pull me out of the saddle. I pulled my foot out of the stirrup and kicked at him, catching him in the jaw. The impact sent him sprawling. I looked back and saw him picking himself up and dust himself off, all the while glaring at me. While it gave me a moment of satisfaction, I knew he'd make me pay for that in some way, for he was lazy, mean, brutish, nasty, and seemed to enjoy being that way. I shook off thoughts of any retaliation and put my attention on getting to Springfield as fast as I could.

The rest of the way was very familiar and we got there quickly, even though Bubs was tiring as we neared Springfield. I promised him that he could walk all the way home.

When I got to Springfield, I went to Mr. Pynchon's house but he wasn't available, so I sat outside and waited. It was windy with a patchy blue sky and dark clouds off to the west. I thought that with the luck I'd had it would start raining halfway home. After a while, he opened the door.

"Jack," he said in a firm voice, "I hoped you be back by yesterday. Where's the letter? You did see Hutchinson didn't you?"

"The letter's here, sir," I said, taking it out of the pouch and handing it to him. "I didn't get back sooner because Mr. Hutchinson was gone and didn't get back until noon yesterday. I saw him as soon as I could and left there early yesterday afternoon. I didn't get home until late last night and came as soon as I could." He read the letter as I explained this to him and as I finished, he dropped the hand holding the letter and raised his head.

"Hutchinson's a shrewd man and drives a hard bargain. But, he has what I want and since no one else does, I have to pay his price. He turned and made his way into the house.

I followed him in. I was tired and wanted to collect my money and go home.

"You did a good job even though you ran into a few difficulties. I'll need you again next week. I'll have letters and a package that has to go to Marlboro."

"Thank you sir, but I'll have to talk to my uncle first. He needs me at the farm. I don't know if I can do it." He looked at me for a moment before going to a chest against the far wall and with his back to me, opened it and began to count coins. Counting them again as he came back to me, he stopped before giving them to me.

"Instead of hard money I can give you credit for four shillings. Your uncle can use it for any goods you need. It might help him be more agreeable to you working for me now and then." I thought about this for a minute and realized it may help satisfy Josiah, especially if I had to go to Marlboro next week, for I didn't intend to say no to Mr. Pynchon.

"How much will I earn next week?" I asked, glancing up at him.

"I'll pay you five shillings but you'll pay for feed and stabling of your horse yourself."

"Can I take half of my earnings in coin and half in credit?"

"You can have all of it in credit," he said, apparently not wanting to part with any money if he didn't have to.

"Mr. Pynchon sir, I'll take half in credit and half in coin." He chuckled as he counted out the two shillings.

"You're a good businessman," he said as he dropped the coins into my hand. He went to his desk, picked up his quill, and dipped it in ink.

"I'm putting in the credit for two shillings under your name with a note that it can be used by your uncle for any reason."

"Thank you, sir. When will you need me next week?"

"I thought you said you wanted to talk to Josiah?"

"I think my earnings from this trip and next week's will prevent him from having any objections," I said with a smile.

"You'll be gone for two days. Be here early Wednesday morning." With that, I left, but before turning for home, I rode down to the river and stopped in a field between two pastures. For some reason, the sight of that big river always pleased me. I walked to the water, knelt, and dipped my hand into it, moving it back and forth. It was cool and soft and felt good. I stayed for a few more minutes, reclining with my knees up and my arms behind me my elbows resting on the grass. I saw the dark clouds getting closer and realized I should start back so I wouldn't be caught in the rain. It would be a long, uncomfortable ride if I were soaking wet.

The dark clouds followed me, seeming to move at the same speed I did. When I got about halfway home, it started to rain lightly for a few minutes, then stopped. After a mile or so, it started again a little bit heavier. That lasted a few minutes and lightened to a drizzle. I rode on through these sporadic showers when about a third of the way from home, it began to rain hard. My clothes were completely soaked in a short time as the rain poured off my hat and down my back. I pushed Bubs hard, knowing how tired he was but that he would be able to rest for the next few days. I thought about stopping to see William and Kanti and maybe Oota, but decided not to since it was close enough to home that it wouldn't make much difference in how wet I got.

As soon as I got home, I unsaddled Bubs and put him in the barn with some forkfuls of hay. As I went in, I realized how hungry I was, and even though wet to my skin, couldn't help but smile at the smell of the bread Charity baked and the sight of a stew bubbling on the hearth. I went to the basket of bread, tore off a great big piece, and stuffed it in my mouth. I grabbed a mug and filled it with cider from the barrel. Charity came in with her arms full of wood; her dress was wet and water was running off her hat.

"Jack, are you eating my fresh bread? It came out of the oven just a while ago," she asked, looking over the pieces of wood.

"Yes, I am...I'm hungry. I haven't eaten since this morning," I mumbled around a mouthful of bread.

"Listen to you. The way you eat people would think I never feed you. Dinner will be ready soon."

"Mr. Pynchon wants me to ride for him again next week. He'll pay me five shillings to go to Marlboro," I said between bites.

She looked at me in surprise. "Five shillings? That's nine shillings in one week. That's a lot of money."

"I'm taking only half in coin. I'm leaving the rest as a credit for us to use when we need it."

"Your uncle will be pleased with that," she said as she stirred the stew. The smell made my mouth water. "He's had to work even harder than he does when you're not here."

"I know. I'll work hard tonight and tomorrow until the Sabbath. Mr. Pynchon wants me in Springfield early next Wednesday morning."

"Josiah's down at the Field. Go help him now for a bit. I'm sure he'd like to hear about the credit. I know we could use it." I put on my hat and walked out the door and back into the rain, although it had slowed to a light drizzle.

Chapter 10

"It's about time you got here instead of riding all over the country," he said with a touch of anger in his voice. "When did you get back? Have you been sitting at the house waiting for me to finish your work?"

"No, I haven't. I came right down here," I said a little defensively.

"Well, get busy," he said holding the hoe out to me. I began to hoe, knowing enough not to say anything that might provoke him. We worked in silence for a while. I was angry at being treated as if I wasn't doing anything and just wasting my time when I was earning money for us. I could tell Josiah was upset by the way he moved, grabbing at the weeds and ripping them out with a grunt. We continued on this way until I stopped hoeing and looked at him.

"Josiah." He didn't respond.

"Josiah."

"What?"

"I wasn't trying to get out of work. I was just trying to help us by earning some money."

"Damn it Jack, I know that. It's just if he wants you to

do this more and more I don't know what I'll do. I can't do all this work by myself and I can't ask others to help when they have work of their own. I could hire one of the Ayres' boys or Coy or Hovey or Wilson but it would just be more work to get enough to pay them. You know that we've never had a lot of money and your aunt and I appreciate what you're doing…we really do. I don't want you saying no to Mr. Pynchon too often. If you do, he might find someone else. When does he want you again?"

"Next Wednesday. He wants me to go to Marlboro. I have to be at his house early in the morning. He'll pay me five shillings for that trip." He looked up in surprise.

"Now that's a good deal of money for riding to Marlboro and back. Of course, Rich Coy gets a pound to go to Boston."

"I told him that I'll take half in coin and half in credit. We can use it for anything we need. If I ride two or three times a month, it will be good money. I'll try not go too often so I can still do my work."

"We'll talk about that at dinner. Grab your hoe and start working. We have to finish this half of the garden this afternoon."

With that, I started hoeing between and around the rows and lost myself in the repetitive motion of moving the hoe back and forth over and over again. The sun came out, casting warm rays as the sound of the birds lulled me into a drowsy state where I let all my worries and cares drop.

At dinner, the three of us agreed that it made sense for me to continue to ride for Mr. Pynchon as long as Josiah could manage all the chores. If it got to the point where he couldn't, I'd stop.

During the next three months, I rode five times; going to Marlboro and Lancaster twice and Boston once. For my efforts, I was paid 28 shillings. Josiah was pleased at this since I wasn't away for more than two days at a time, except Boston, which was three days, plus I worked on the farm as I always did.

The conversation turned to the Morgan's arrival sometime in the next couple of weeks and after they got here, how I was going to approach Tom Morgan, something I would rather not do but knew I would have to at some point.

"You're going to have to face him sometime you know. What are you going to do?" Josiah asked, standing with his hands on the back of his chair. Charity turned in her chair and looked up at him.

"If Jack is going to try to convince Tom to let him court Becky, if might be best if he doesn't see Jack much, at least at first."

"Maybe, but what are you going to do to get Tom to

even talk to you," Josiah asked, taking his hat off and scratching his head. 'You have to do something. Things aren't just going to turn out fine if you do nothing."

"He's right you know," Charity told me. "What can you do to get him to at least listen to you?"

"I don't know. What do you think would help?" Charity stopped as she began to take the trenchers away. Her eyes got wide and a smile crossed her face.

"Why don't you help them build their house?"

"What?" Josiah asked. "Why would he want to do that? If Tom couldn't stand being around him much, why would he want Jack's help? I don't understand what you're saying."

"It's simple…they have to build their house. Now, since you're so handy you could help them with a lot of things." I was surprised at her suggestion, probably even more than Josiah was, but the more I thought about it, the more sense it made. Although I'd have to figure out how to do my regular chores and help them at the same time. No matter how I did it, it wouldn't be easy.

"Even if he needs my help, why would he agree to it? Other men will help. We know that," I asked, wondering why Tom would even entertain the idea of my helping them. I was handy and could work with wood doing everything from hewing timbers for the frame to building the fireplace and chimney.

"Because you'll be able to spend more time than anyone else. I'll do most of the work so you can help them. It'll only be for a couple of weeks," Josiah said as he adjusted his belt and put his jacket on. "I'll talk to Tom about it. Mention it to Nate, too. Let him help convince his father. I might talk to some of the others and bring up that maybe they shouldn't offer to help too much. That'll make your offer more attractive to him. If he lets you, and you work hard, he might look a little kinder on you when you ask permission for Becky. Although he may not. He's a hard man." With that, he walked out the door. Charity came over and put her hand on my arm.

"He's right, you know. Tom Morgan is lazy at times, especially when there's work to be done. I think he'd like any help he can get, even if it comes from you." She took both of my hands in hers. "You'll be able to court Becky and get married. Elizabeth and I already know this. Tom and Josiah don't; at least not yet. Just have patience. Now go do your work. He's waiting for you." I started for the door and hesitated before turning back and giving her a kiss on the cheek.

"Thank you," I said. Surprised at my show of affection, she smiled when I pulled away.

"You're welcome," she said.

The next three weeks went by very slowly. When you wait for something important in your life, it always seems to take more time than it actually does. Time flies by with wings made of lead. During this time, I kept busy helping not only Josiah and Charity, but also anyone else who needed help. I went to Springfield twice with Judah and went hunting two or three times a week. I worked liked I was in a fever, doing all that I could to make the day of her arrival come as soon as possible. I, like all other men, cannot make time move any faster than it does, so I was frustrated that it seemed to be moving slower than I thought it should. With each day, my anticipation grew. Charity reminded me to have patience with Becky's father and that everything would turn out well.

One thing that made these weeks more bearable was that the days were very pleasant. Each day there was a clear blue sky, a comfortable temperature, and a light breeze. It rained only twice during this time. Such perfect weather heightened my feelings, as it seemed like the beautiful weather would continue until they got here. During these days, I thought of the life we would build together; we would have our own farm and a good number of children. We would live a good life, and I would grow old with the woman I loved.

While we didn't know what day they'd be there, we had a good idea because Charity got a letter from Elizabeth a month before they planned to leave Ipswich. After all the waiting, the week in which they would arrive finally came. My hopes rose with each passing day. On the fourth day, there were a few puffy white clouds in the sky, but otherwise it was another perfect day. The good weather seemed like an omen to me. I was up much earlier than usual, not being able to sleep because of my excitement. I was full of nervous energy. I had many of my chores done in half the time it usually took. Charity couldn't help notice my anxiety and impatience.

"Jack, sit down and eat your breakfast. Fidgeting and pacing back and forth won't get them here any sooner." I sat and tried to eat but I wasn't very hungry. Josiah came in from the barn; I saw him and Charity exchange looks.

Josiah stood just inside the door. "What are you going to do if they don't get here until late? Are you going to sit around all day waiting? What if something happened and they don't get here for a few more days?" The thought that they might not be here when I expected never occurred to me since I was so caught up in their arriving hopefully today. I knew Josiah was right and that I couldn't sit all day moping around, but I didn't want to miss Becky.

"I don't know. I guess I need to get to work," I said, slumping my shoulders. "I never thought they might not be here today."

I made my way down to the lower field and began cutting the hay with the well-worn scythe. Having something to work on took my mind off Becky's arrival, at least to a degree. The rhythm of the blade slicing through the grass and the swishing sound it made calmed me. I concentrated on the sound and motion of each cut.

I began to think of my life since my mother died. As I get older, the faster time seems to move. Though it was hard to believe, it had been 12 years since she passed away. I still felt loneliness in my heart for both my parents. I smiled at the memories and wondered what it would have been like if they both lived.

I remembered the first time I saw Becky when she and her mother came to visit us. She was a small, freckle-faced girl dressed just like her mother in a brown dress with a matching doublet, white apron and a cloak with a hood. I thought about our first kiss in the dunes so many times, it was as if it happened thousands of times instead of just twice. That moment stayed with me, seeming as though it was happening again and again. Now, I know I have a good imagination and may have made it something bigger than it was, but I don't think so. I never tired of feeling her lips against mine and seeing the freckles on her face or her green eyes looking deeply into mine. Every time I thought of her telling me that we had to get married because we kissed twice made me realize how true it was. I wondered where life would take me from here. I knew that from this point on, I'd been able to determine what I did, when, and how. After we married, we'd build a house on the land I'd buy from Mr. Pynchon and begin our life together. I was so lost in the reverie that I didn't hear Josiah until he was right behind me.

"Jack!"

"Ahh! What? You scared me," I said, startled out of my reverie.

"They're here. Elizabeth and Becky came over a little while ago. Tom, Nate, and young Tom are at the tavern." I looked at the sun and saw that it was almost directly overhead. I didn't realize I'd been out there so long.

"Come on, now. Go see Becky," he said with a grin. "I'm sure Nate wants to see you too. You can finish this up later. It's time for dinner anyway." I ran up the hill as fast as I could. As I came over the top, I saw several women standing outside our house, talking excitedly. I looked for Becky but didn't see her. As I got closer, I saw Charity standing with Elizabeth Morgan, Susannah Ayres, Jane Kent, Martha Coy, Mercy Travis, and Abigail Hovey.

As I got closer, I still didn't see Becky and wondered where she might be. Charity saw me and nodded towards the house. Nothing else needed to be said. When I was at the back of the garden fence, Becky stepped out the door, looking around. Charity caught her attention and pointed in my direction. Becky turned and saw me standing there with a big smile and then she began to cry. I walked toward her, wanting to take her in my arms and hold her but didn't dare. As we got closer to each other, I noticed that everyone had stopped talking and were looking at us.

"Hello Jack," she said softly, crying and smiling at the same time. She reached for my hand but stopped. I moved as close to her as I dared, looking into her eyes, taking in her face, and seeing the beautiful golden dusting of freckles across her nose. I wanted to kiss her so very much.

"Hello, Becky," I said with a huge smile. "You don't know how good it is to have you here. I can't believe it…I just can't…finally…after all this time." I couldn't stop looking at her. "My, you are beautiful! I missed you so much every day," I said a little above a whisper. My love for her came rushing up from the place where I kept it all these years; I desired her so much I was tempted to hold her and kiss her then and there regardless of the consequences. I could tell she knew what I was thinking.

"Jack, not now…it would only cause trouble," she whispered, leaning towards me. "We'll be alone later…I promise." Several of the women smiled at us, while others wore a stern look of disapproval at our public display of affection. I looked at the group and saw Becky's mother with a hint of a smile on her lips and in her eyes.

"Hello Mrs. Morgan. How was your trip? I see that you got here in one piece."

"Thank you, Jack. It is good to see you. Charity told me you've been doing well…I'm glad to hear it."

"I have been doing well, but I'm doing much better now. Boy, am I glad you're here."

"I can see that. Nate will be glad to see you too. He's been looking forward to this almost as much as his younger sister," she said with a wide smile. Some of the other women twittered and giggled, a nice departure from their normally stern behavior. They looked like they were enjoying themselves, something that didn't happen very often.

I looked at Becky again and couldn't stop smiling. Her eyes sparkled at me, her hair hung to her shoulders, soft and moving ever so slightly in the light breeze, surrounding her face and making her look even more beautiful than the last time I saw her. I still couldn't believe she was here. My enthusiasm was short lived, for Josiah came up the hill and stood there looking around at us.

"Jack, the men are at the tavern," he said. I took the hint, looking at Becky once more as if I'd never see her again. Charity came to my side and in a soft tone so she wouldn't be heard by anyone except us, said, "It's all right. You'll be able to see each other later. Now go." Without a word, I turned and walked with Josiah. I could sense that he wanted to say something and waited for it to come.

"I need to know something. Are you willing to do whatever you have to in order to marry Becky?" he asked.

"Of course I am. You know that."

"Does that include groveling in front of Tom? Even if you helped with their house, he's going to act as if you never did anything. He'll probably ignore you and make it plain to everyone that he has no interest in speaking with you. You have to be prepared for that; he may not let you see Becky." I stopped, surprised at what he said. I waited for Becky so long, the thought never occurred to me that he might still say no. Josiah put his hand on my shoulder.

"Do what he asks. Don't say anything that he might make him mad at you. Try not to set him off because he's looking for any excuse to embarrass the hell out of you in front of everyone. It's the way he is." As we started towards the tavern, I realized that in a matter of 150 feet, I went from the woman I loved who made me feel so happy to her father, the man who didn't like me and controlled our future. He could refuse me permission to court Becky. As we got to the tavern yard, I turned and looked Josiah in the eye.

"I will do whatever it takes, regardless of how hard it is or how long it takes, to make Becky my wife." I opened the door and stepped into the room. It took a minute to adjust to the darkness after being out in bright sunlight. Most of the men had a mug in their hand, standing around Tom, Nate, and young Tom, who were sitting at a table.

John Ayres, Sr. motioned to us. "Jack, Josiah, come join us. I'll pour a mug for each of you to help us welcome our new family." I liked him, for he was a good, hard-working man who held several important offices in the village and always had time for me, no matter what he was doing. I always enjoyed his company and advice.

Nate got up and came over to me, holding out his hand while giving me a big grin. I returned it and shook his hand, realizing how much I missed his friendship. He had been away, apprenticed to a sea captain out of Portsmouth.

"How have you been?" he asked with a mischievous look in his eye, knowing full well that I just saw his sister. "Let's go outside, we've got a lot to catch up on," he said, starting for the door. I got my mug from Mr. Ayres and followed him outside, taking a big swig before sitting on the ground. He sat down and began picking up some grass and twisting it in his fingers. I smiled for it was an old habit of his, one he had since we were children.

"To answer your question, I've been well...working harder than I'd like to but that isn't going to change anytime soon. So, how have you been and where have you been? It's been what, four years since we've been together? It is good to see you."

"Has it really been that long? I sailed all over – to England, France, Spain, Honduras, Jamaica, Barbados...you name it, I've been there. While some of it was exciting, I realized I'd rather be with my family and friends than sailing all over the world. I'll tell you all about it once we get settled. It's good to see you too."

"How was the trip? I asked. "Did you have any problems?"

"No, only one of the cows wandered away and it took me over three hours to find her. She just walked away into the woods. My father was not happy about that, I can tell you. A couple of things like that but nothing to cause us any trouble. The day after the big cow got lost in the woods the other one walked into a small pond and couldn't get out. She was stuck in the mud so I had to go in and drag her out. I got soaking wet and covered with mud. That and the pigs were just plain mean. If it were up to me, I would have sold them.

"It did take us seven long days, though. I didn't think we'd get here today when we started out this morning, but we made better time than we thought we would. It took so long it seemed like we would never get here."

"I am having a hard time believing that Becky and you are here. Does your father still not want to see me? I have to talk to him soon."

"Give it a couple of days. Let him get settled and see everyone. Maybe a week or so…that would be good. I need to say hello to Charity…come on," he said, rising to his feet and brushing his pants off.

"I'll be there in a minute. I want another mug," I said,

heading back inside the tavern. Josiah stood next to Tom and all talk stopped when I came in the door. All the men were watching me to see what I'd do since I had to go right by Tom to get to the bar. I walked straight to it, glancing at them as I went and ignoring Tom.

"John, I'd like another mug if you please," I asked.

"Of course, of course," he said, filling my mug and putting it on the counter.

"Thank you." I turned, took two steps, and stopped in front of Tom who was talking to Tom Wilson and Jim Travis. He turned around when they looked at me. I decided that I was not going to let him fire the first volley as it were. I squared my shoulders and being several inches taller than him, looked down at him, right in the eye.

"Hello Tom." He looked at me for a moment, as if he couldn't decide whether to say anything or just ignore me.

"Jack," he said, no more of a greeting than that. I continued to look at him, not giving off anything other than confidence. I made sure that even though it was unspoken, any troubles we had or any hard feelings he had for me were not going to bother me. We stood there looking at each other for a moment; quiet filled the air. Judah finally broke the silence.

"Tom, tell us, did you have any trouble with the animals? How was the swine? They always give me trouble. Miserable beasts, though they taste good." At this, everyone went back to talking, some sitting at two tables while Tom, Josiah, Tom Wilson and Jim stood near the bar. Josiah shot me a disapproving look that let me know that he didn't like my confronting Tom. Nate was just coming up the road as I came out the door.

"They're all talking about women things. I'll say hello later." We walked down the road a bit, enjoying the pleasant day.

"You know, it's good to finally be here. I thought we'd never leave Ipswich...it was one thing after another. Then we were on our way. My father was mad the whole trip, although that's nothing new. I think he thinks that it was the wrong decision...that he is having second thoughts about moving. Of course, Becky couldn't wait to get here...to see you."

"I'll tell you, the last few weeks have dragged because I wanted you to get here as soon as you could. Your sister means the world to me."

"I know she does...we all know. Your only problem is my father and he is a stubborn man. You are going to have to wait on his decision and you know he doesn't make them quickly. It took him a long time to decide for us to come here and that was only because Charity kept telling my mother how wonderful it would be here. Now I know what she meant," he said, looking around. "If it were up to me, we would have been here three years ago," he said with a laugh. I was about to tell him how I planned on dealing with Tom when I remembered who I met in Springfield.

"Your uncle lives in Springfield. At least I think he's your uncle…he looks like your father and is from Ipswich."

"What? My uncle is in Springfield? How do you know that?"

"I met him. He works for Mr. Pynchon tending his livestock and helping at the warehouse and on the river. He didn't seem too happy when I found out who he was and told him you were coming."

"Well, that's a surprise. He and my father haven't seen each other in, oh, at least five years, maybe longer. They had a big falling out; each of them is as stubborn as the other one. My uncle left town a week or two after the argument. We didn't know where he went, at least until now. His name is Wait by the way. He was married, but that was years ago when I was young, no more than three or four. Her name was Judea. I have no idea what happened to her and never asked. It was one of things that you wanted to find out about but you knew that you shouldn't ever ask about it."

"Josiah and I were out there maybe a couple of months after we got here," I told him. "When we saw him, it was from the back and he reminded us of someone but we couldn't figure out who. I went back with Judah a couple of weeks later and saw him again. When I asked him if he was your father's brother he said that it was none of my business. When I told him you were coming here, he was surprised and looked a bit curious. From what I found out, the selectmen were only going to let him stay for two months and were about to make him leave when Mr. Pynchon hired him and posted a bond. Your uncle seems grumpy and mean."

"That sure sounds like him. I'm not sure how my father will take the news of his brother being so close. We'll have to see him when we go there. Let's not tell him now. Let's wait."

"Do you think that's a good idea? If he's not in a good mood now how more upset can he get? Besides, he won't make a scene in front of his new neighbors, will he?" I asked. Nate squatted down picking at the grass. He thought this over for a minute playing with the grass in his fingers.

"You're right. He might get upset but there is nothing he can do about it. His brother's in Springfield and it's better he knows now so he can decide what to do."

When we got back to the tavern all but a couple of the men had left so it was Tom, John Ayres, Sr., Judah Trumble and Jim Travis seated around a table near the fireplace. Tom had several drinks under his belt and it was plain that he was celebrating his family's arrival in the best way he knew how. He looked pleased with himself and smiled as we came in the door. It left his face as soon as he saw me.

"Well, look who's back," Jim said, leaning back in his

chair. "John, I think they need another drink."

"No, we're fine," Nate said as we pulled up chairs from a nearby table.

"Jack just told me some news that you might want to hear. It's about uncle Wait." At the mention of his brother's name, he bristled reminding me of a porcupine spreading its quills.

"What about him?" he said giving me a malevolent stare.

"I thought you should know that he's living in Springfield. I met him two months ago. He works for Mr. Pynchon."

"What's his name?" Judah asked Tom who was staring at the floor.

"Wait," replied Nate.

"I know him! He's the dirty little man with a bad temper. Gets mad at the slightest thing. Grumpy old fart. Mr. Pynchon thinks highly of him…he doesn't hire just anybody and I should know," he cackled.

"What does he do there?" Tom asked.

"He tends Mr. Pynchon livestock, helps at the warehouse and unloading the boats. He does odd jobs too."

"I think I know who you mean," Jim said turning to Judah. "He always wears the same clothes day in and day out."

"Jim, in case you haven't noticed, most of us do the

same thing. Maybe he doesn't have anything else. Tom, it sounds like you need to take a ride to see him," he volunteered, not knowing of the trouble between them.

"I may see him when we go there. Then again, maybe I won't." With that, he got up and staggered towards the door. "I'll see how the rest of them are making out getting us unloaded." A couple of the village boys were helping unload their wagon, taking things upstairs to a room and the rest to Ayres barn. The room was quiet for a minute as each of the men were thinking about Tom's crusty ways.

"Sure doesn't seem too interested in knowing his brother is here," Judah said, shaking his head.

"Well, I know why he's not happy about it," Nate said as he moved his chair a little closer to the table and the three of them leaned in a bit to hear what he had to say. "My father and his brother are pretty much alike - stubborn and hard-headed. They had a big fight six, maybe seven years ago and haven't spoken since. My uncle left town a couple of weeks later and no one knew where he was…until now. I guess my uncle wouldn't be too happy to see my father."

"No wonder he's not too excited at the idea," John said, pushing the chair back and standing up. "If I were in his shoes, I wouldn't be too happy either." At that point, I left and headed home.

When I got there, all the women had gone, leaving only

Josiah and Charity. She was knitting me a new pair of socks and he was making a broom out of a birch sapling. It was late candlelight and there almost no light in the sky. I hadn't been there two minutes and had just taken a bite out of a piece of bread when Charity looked up from her knitting.

"Jack, Nate said he wants you to meet him by the barn."

"I just saw him a few minutes ago and…"

"He told me that he needs to see you," she said extending her hand towards the door.

"But," I said a bit confused. She looked at Josiah, who hadn't taken his eyes off the broom and seemed like he wasn't paying any attention to what we were saying.

"Becky," she mouthed silently. Now I understood and was out the door as fast as I could. I ran to the barn and looked around inside but didn't see her so I went outside and around to the back. She was not there either, so I turned back thinking that maybe I didn't hear Charity right. I got no more than a few feet when I heard a soft whistle. I turned around and went the few paces back.

"Who's there?" I whispered. There was no answer.

"Becky, are you there?" No one answered. I crept around the side of the barn, gave the same soft whistle, and heard it answered from around the corner. It was full dark now, and while my eyes had adjusted to the darkness, it was still difficult to see things at more than 10 feet away. As I got to the corner, I heard a noise behind me and as I spun around, I heard the soft whistle again, followed by a low laugh that I knew was Becky's. She came out of the darkness and slid into my arms. I wrapped them around her and held her tight, thanking God that we were together.

"I told you we'd be together later, didn't I?" she said with a giggle. We held each other for several minutes and the smell of her hair and curves of her body was something I waited to feel for a long time.

"Oh, Jack," she murmured in my ear, "I've wanted to hold you for so long…oh, hold me closer, don't ever stop." I held her for what seemed like a long time, kissing her cheek and neck and then her lips. She responded with a soft moan and held me tighter. I felt her trembling with excitement. She kissed me, full of passion and built up longing. At that moment, we heard someone walking nearby so we stepped apart, listening intently. All we needed was to be caught like this by someone other than Charity, Elizabeth, or Nate. After a minute, we heard Nate softly calling our names.

"Jack? Becky? Where are you?" Without responding, we walked around the side of the barn and almost ran into him.

"There you are!" he said in a low voice. "Becky, you have to get back now. Father wanted to know why you've been gone so long. I came out to find you so you wouldn't get in trouble."

"All right, I'll be along in a minute." He turned and walked towards the tavern, leaving us alone again. I took her hands in mine and kissed her on the tip of her nose.

"Oh Becky! I love you so much. I've thought about you, dreamt about you, and wished you were here so I could hold you and kiss you. And now I can…," I said with a big smile, happier than I had ever been. I was also frustrated because I didn't want to stop but knew I had to. I knew she felt the same way.

"Maybe I could stay a few more minutes…I don't want to go."

"No, you have to go. I don't want you to get in trouble and have your father suspect something. That's all we need…as though I don't have enough trouble with him already. I'll see you tomorrow," I said, pulling her against me and kissing her softly on the lips. She gave another soft moan and broke away but still held my hand.

"After all this time waiting, I want to be with you…always and forever," she said.

"We will be…soon. I want us to get married before the end of the year."

"Oh, yes! I want that more than anything in the world," she said excitedly.

"I'm going to talk to your father in the next few days.

I'm not going to wait any longer...I've waited too long already." She stood on her toes and kissed me.

"I love you."

"I love you, too." With that, she walked off into the darkness.

Chapter 11

Nate came over the next morning to talk about building their house. We had beer and bread while I explained our idea about my helping them. He laughed, thinking it was a fine idea but was certain his father would say no to my offer. He agreed to do all that he could to get his father to agree, not only because he knew they needed the help, but also as a way to help Becky and me.

Over the next couple of days, Josiah talked to Tom several times about how handy I was, what a great job I did on our house and that I had helped several others build their barns. He also reminded him that it was a lot of work and they needed to get it built as soon as they could. Nate told him the same things; making a strong case for me working with them. At last, after hearing the same thing from Elizabeth and Becky, to everyone's surprise, Tom agreed to the idea.

At first, he worked me very hard, doing the things that no one wanted to do like digging and hauling cartloads of rocks for the foundation and chimney while he and Nate dug the cellar hole. As Tom worked on the fireplace and chimney with some of the other men from the plantation, Nate and I chopped chestnut and oak trees and squared them for the sill, posts and beams. A one-room house needed four timbers for the sill and eight for both the posts and beams; 20 in all. We used their oxen to drag the trees to the area where we squared them. The whole process took us five full days.

Nate and I cut more trees and dragged them to the sawpit, sawing them into boards for the floor and walls. Each board was long and wide and we loaded them into their cart to bring to the house. Tom came down two or three times a day to make sure we were cutting the boards the way he wanted. He also wanted to be sure that I was down in the pit doing the hardest job, getting pounds of sawdust in my hair, ears, eyes, on and under my clothes and even down my throat. He seemed to take pleasure in my discomfort. I just worked all that much harder, hoping to impress him.

There were a few times when I almost told him that I was done, that he would get no more help from me. I held my tongue, remembering why I was doing all this work; it was all for Becky. I vowed that no matter what job he gave me or how bad he treated me, I wouldn't quit. I needed to get him to view me as someone who was worthy of courting his daughter. There were times when I thought my labors would mean nothing to him. I would help build their house and he'd say no anyway. I knew he could be like that but I thought of what Charity told me about having patience. Even though others from the village helped as they could, I made sure I worked harder and longer than anyone else did. Now and then, Tom would stop what he was doing to look at me for a minute. We didn't talk much because he didn't say a lot to begin with but his hard feelings toward me were still there, although perhaps not as strong as they had been. The only time he talked to me was when he wanted me to do something. So it was a surprise when he walked over to me when we took a rest one afternoon from pounding pegs through the floorboards into the joists.

"Josiah was right," he said stone-faced. "You are pretty handy and aren't afraid to work hard." With that, he grunted and walked away. Nate came over smiling and looked at me.

"I think he's not as upset with you as he was. I don't think he likes you, but you are making an impression on him. You keep it up and someday he might talk to you twice in the same day," he chuckled, handing me my mallet.

Early the next morning, Charity was pleased to see Oota and Kanti walking up the town road. Most of the time they came to give us certain types of food or implements or trade for small goods, while other times they came just to visit. Charity liked Kanti the first time she met her and I know the feeling was mutual. Most of the people in the village liked Kanti. She was open, honest, friendly, and always looking to teach us new and better ways of doing things as we taught her some of our ways. It was a practical and beneficial relationship that grew into a village friendship. Oota and I had become good friends after our bumbling romantic start. She had grown into a fine young woman and was as admired as Kanti. I took a special interest in her and helped in any way I could and protected her when necessary. I became something of a big brother to her; this pleased both of us. We saw each other often, enjoyed each other's company, and now understood what was best for our relationship. A romantic relationship between an English man and a young Indian woman would never be tolerated.

This was Elizabeth and Becky's first introduction to the two Indian women. They'd come over to help Charity spin and weave. Becky took an instant liking to both of them and them to her. I was on my way over to Morgan's to help finish the last of the work on the house when I came up to them as Charity was making introductions and explaining to Becky and Elizabeth how we knew Kanti and Oota.

"Jack has known Kanti since right after we got here. He's become a good friend of her son William. I'm sorry Kanti, but I can never pronounce his name correctly." Kanti smiled at her and in good English said, "It is Sunukkuhkau. It means He Crushes. I chose his name because as an infant, he was always crushing his food. His father wanted his name to be Huritt; that means he's handsome. I didn't see how an infant could be handsome so I told him we would not name him that." They pondered this for a moment before I explained the difference between English and Indian names.

"Many of us are named after one of our direct relatives – our father, mother, grandparent, aunt, or uncle. The Indians name their children on a quality or characteristic of the child. They can also change their name to whatever they choose at any point in their life. I've only known three of them that have done that. We give them English names because they are easier for us to pronounce. They don't care what we call them, as long as we treat them openly and honestly. The greatest wrong anyone, even another Indian, can commit besides murder, is to lie or cheat one of them. They will no longer have anything to do with you and will never forgive you."

"What does your name mean, Kanti?" Becky asked.

"It means She Who Sings," Kanti replied with a smile. Charity, Elizabeth and Becky all smiled at such a pretty name.

"Oota, why don't you tell them what your name means?" I asked. She stood there smiling her happy smile, pretty as she could be.

"My name is Oota-dabun. It means Day Star."

"What a beautiful name," Becky told her. "I wish we named our children like that." Her father stood there looking like he had just bitten into a sour apple and shook his head.

"No you don't," he said. "You could have been named something you wouldn't like. You weren't a happy child," he grumbled.

"That is not true," Elizabeth cried. "She was a wonderful baby. Why don't you get back to work instead of standing here?"

"All of you should get to work too," he said in an unpleasant tone. He walked away. I left them and followed Tom to his almost finished house. Becky told me later how much she enjoyed meeting Oota and Kanti and that they visited for over an hour. She and Oota became good friends, which I was glad to see. Over the next couple of years, the three of us developed a special relationship. Oota was like a close cousin; a member of the family.

Looking back, these are pleasant memories that never fail to make me smile. That year we had a bountiful harvest as the weather was good and crops grew well. I spent much time with Becky, and Oota joined us quite a bit. I made money riding for Mr. Pynchon, game was plentiful, and I always got some kind of animal when I went hunting - either a raccoon, deer, turkey, and once a bear. I found that since Becky arrived, Sabbath services were not as boring and tedious as they had been. Overall, it was a plentiful, prosperous, happy time but as I am sure you know, the good times never last as long as you want.

Chapter 12

John Ayres, Sr., as First Sergeant, commanded our militia, assisted by Second Sergeant William Prichard and Corporal Richard Coy. When the village was first settled, the militia drilled every other week on Friday mornings. As time went by and the Indians seemed much less of a potential threat than they might have been, they drilled once a month. When we arrived, muster was every six weeks or so and didn't follow a set schedule. I, like all the others, looked forward to it since it was a welcome rest from our daily labors. Boys under 16, and some of the girls, helped with the farm work on muster day. Ed Ayres called us to muster by drumming, as he did on the Sabbath, which could be heard for quite a distance on a quiet morning. Josiah Kent was the flag bearer, carrying the colors of the Massachusetts Bay Colony. In other settlements, the minister, clad in a black robe, began the training session with a prayer. When Rev. Younglove was living there, he presided. After he left, we dispensed with the opening prayer. We were required to bring our musket, a pound of powder, and at least 20 balls of shot. Each of us wore a bandoleer over our shoulder and had a short sword or long knife in our belt. Some of the men had pistols.

We trained on a large, flat area behind the meetinghouse. Orders were given for us to move into various formations as well as how to hold, aim, and fire our muskets. All of this was very military looking, but I wondered how useful it would be if we found ourselves in a fight. I kept these questions to myself as our military leaders took these preparations seriously.

Every now and then, Sergeant Prichard would organize us into groups of six for a shooting drill that in all ways was a contest to see who the best marksman from each group was. Jim Travis was the best shot of all of us and always won. This shooting drill was down behind the hill in an open area next to the biggest meadow. We did not do this often, as it was a waste of powder and shot. Each of us was required by the General Court to have at least one pound of powder and two pounds of lead at home to defend ourselves in an engagement. On this particular day, Sergeant Prichard ordered us to the shooting area, told us we would each take two shots at trees standing in the middle of the field. We marched for a short while, covering about a mile.

Sgt. Ayres moved to the front and addressed Corporal Coy.

"Corporal, form these men into groups of six," and turning to us, said, "The groups will shoot in order starting with the group on the right. Each man will take two shots."

I was in the third group with Will and Nate, so we all sat down on the side of the hill overlooking the flat area. While there was some joking and talk, most of us took our shooting seriously, for it was a sign of our skill with a musket. Should we ever find ourselves in a fight with the Indians, we wanted to be as ready as we could.

The shooting went quickly with a few remarks to those who missed the tree with either one or both of their shots. We got into formation again and marched around to the right and up the hill. We were quiet and I was thinking about how, while we made light of the muster days, it was something we may need to do at some point. There were incidents north of Springfield and west of Northampton with the Pocumtucks or an occasional foray by small groups of Mohawks. While these were isolated incidents involving drunken Indians, it kept the possibility of an attack before us.

We reached the village and headed to the tavern. Sgt. Ayres always had good rum on hand, and on muster days, gave us a little more in our mug than we paid for. As we settled ourselves into chairs and on benches around the room, Sam Warner asked Sgt. Prichard about the recent Indian problems.

"Will, do you think these drunken Pocumtucks and Mohawks will lead to more trouble?"

"Well," he replied, "I don't think they will. It seems, at

least from what I know, these Indians were sold rum, and we know how drunk they get even on a small amount. John, have you heard anything else?"

"No, I haven't. Mr. Pynchon told me that they were young men determined to cause trouble. No real harm was done, a few sections of fence were broken and a pig killed and such, but nothing else."

Will, one of the quieter people in the village, shifted on the bench and asked no one in particular, "Would our Indians ever attack us?" We had talked about this before and it seemed very unlikely, given our good relations with the Quaboags in particular and the Nipmucks in general. It would take a series of strong, violent acts on our part to drive them to such an action. There was no reason in the world why we would ever do anything to harm them, not after they had been so good to us.

"I can't see where or why they would," Jim Travis offered. "We know them very well and help each other whenever it's asked or needed. John, you visit with Conkganasco often. Has he ever been anything other than friendly and helpful?"

"No, he hasn't. I respect and admire him, especially since he saw the way, accepted religion, and became a Christian. We never had any trouble and I can't see why we would."

From the table next to the fireplace, Judah related his

last trip to Springfield. "When I was in Springfield last week some of the men at the warehouse were talking about the tribes and if they'd ever attack. Most believe it is as you said John, that there are a few young Indians who are causing some trouble. There were one or two men who held that the Mohawk might attack before the year is out, but I can't see that happening," he continued, "at least not by any large group. I don't think they'd come this way when they know we could get the militia after them."

"Jack, you're friends with William and Kanti. Have they ever said anything about this?" Deacon Hovey asked.

"Kanti mentioned how the Pocumtuck cause trouble now and then with the Quaboag, Washacum and some of the other smaller, weaker tribes but it's nothing unusual to them. This has happened for longer than any of them can remember. William has never said anything about them at all. From my dealings with them, I can't ever see anything happening like this with the Quaboag.

"Of course, the one who causes the most trouble is Matchitehew. He's always angry with us about everything we have and do. Every time I visit the Wekapauge, he finds ways to taunt me…he and his brother. All of you know the damage he's caused either at the Great Field or the mill. If anyone were to be their leader, it would be him. I think he'd enjoying attacking us."

Hovey had been sitting too long and stood to stretch. "I know the Quaboags would never harm us in any way. I just can't see it ever happening." Judah stood and began walking to the bar, but stopped halfway.

"We all know how good they've been to us. Without them, it would be more difficult than it is. I've plowed the fields for half of the Wekapuage women. I got two nice beaver pelts for it last time. If they trade like that, I'll help them whenever they want." We all laughed at this since each of us had done something for them and been paid with nice pelts or small belts of blue wampum. Josiah was quiet during the conversation, which wasn't like him. Others noticed it, too.

"Josiah," Tom Parsons said turning to face him, "you've been quiet today. What do you think of the possibility of us ever being attacked?" He didn't answer for a moment, but sat looking at the floor.

"I don't think we'll be attacked by the Quaboag or any other tribe, but I may be wrong. Everyone said they're confident in their friendship and respect for us. Other tribes are more willing and capable to attack settlements. From what I've heard, the Mohawk will attack anyone they can to avenge a slight or wrong. The Pocumtuck might also, but they wouldn't do it on their own. They would have to join with another tribe. Even though the chance of attack might be low, we have to be serious about our training. Most of us enjoy it because it's a day away from our work but we can't be foolish because if we are ever attacked, it will be swift and brutal." This caused us all to consider that it might be possible and to take muster seriously. From what we heard of past attacks, the Mohawk struck without warning in the early morning before dawn, and were interested more in taking captives than in killing, although they didn't hesitate to put a tomahawk in someone's head.

As we sat there drinking our rum, we talked about how lucky we were to live near the Quaboag; a peaceful and friendly tribe. We had heard stories of how the great sachem Massasoit came to live with the Quaboag many years ago after a war with the Pequot. He helped the Plymouth settlers survive and took a great part in the first feast of thanksgiving. He died a very old man four years before John Warner settled at Quaboag. Conkganasco told stories he heard as a child from his grandfathers of how strong the Quaboag were years ago before the great sickness killed most of them. They took part in an attack against the much-feared Mohawk. When the Mohawk retaliated, the Quaboag didn't ask the other area tribes in the area for assistance, but sent a messenger to Massasoit asking for his help even though the Wampanoag lived two days journey away at the ocean. The two tribes had a special relation for Massasoit's wife was a Quaboag.

Chapter 13

The next two weeks went by quickly with work of all sorts as we prepared for winter. We cut wood to add to the many piles in each yard since it took many trees to keep us warm during the long winter. The women canned and dried pumpkins, squash, herbs, and apples. They made cider, dug potatoes, gathered beechnuts, chestnuts, acorns, and berries. We smoked meat and fish to store in the loft. Many of our neighbors thought we, or more specifically, I, was odd for smoking it as the Indians did. Several of them even agreed the meat was good, but refused to try smoking it themselves. Most of our neighbors salted food to be stored. Charity and some of the other women made Indian meal so that it could be used in porridge or gruel. It was always good on a cold morning, steaming on the trencher with the crushed nuts giving it a wonderful taste.

During this time, Becky and I continued to see each other as often as possible. Many times, I would leave some chore half finished or not put something away in the barn. Then I would remember to do it after dinner, usually as it was getting dark. At times, we didn't care if we were caught; in some ways it would have been easier. Other times, though, we took every precaution to make sure no one except Nate, Charity and Elizabeth knew. It was near the end of October that I decided to ask Tom for the third time if I could court Becky. The first time didn't go well with him telling me to leave and not ask again for he'd continue to say no. The second time he at least seemed to listen, although whether he did or not I don't know. The next day he came up to me and said he decided not to let me court Becky. When I asked why he just walked away.

It was a chilly night with a bit of a nip in the wind. We met behind the barn as we usually did since no one could see us.

I had been waiting for her a few minutes, thinking of what I would say to Tom next time. I was getting angry because he was being so bullheaded and stubborn, even though he knew she wanted to marry me. In spite of all the reasons he heard from his wife, Charity, Nate, and Becky, as well as a few others from the village, he continued to deny me. Just as I was rehearsing for the 50th time what I'd say when I saw him next, Becky came around the side and walked into my arms.

"Oh God, have I missed you. You know, whenever I see you during the day, no matter what you're doing, I want to go and hold you. Sometimes I just stare at you, realizing how very much I love you and miss you because we're not together."

"You're so funny! When I see you," she murmured snuggling against my shoulder and wrapping her arms around me, "I think of what it will be like when I can take care of you, cook for you, hold you in our bed…even more than that," she said with a giggle.

"Listen to you! I've haven't even thrashed your father yet and you have us married and playing games in bed! You improper woman you…" I kissed her mouth softly, pulling her close to me. "I can't wait either."

"Mother and I have been talking to him and I think he may really listen this time. I'm not sure why but I get the feeling he might. Charity isn't very subtle or easy on him. Yesterday she told him he had better make a decision faster than he normally did because if it took him his usual amount of time, some of us might be dead by the time he said yes. Can you believe her?"

"Yes, I can. What did he say?"

"He just grumbled and asked her if there wasn't something she needed to be doing at home. She told him to stop being so selfish and to realize that his children were growing up and had lives of their own to lead and the sooner the better. Then she walked out slamming the door. He didn't quite know what to say." I didn't say anything but took her face in my hands, kissed her nose, and put my arms around her. She shivered with the cold and pressed herself closely against me.

We stayed that way for a couple of minutes, just holding each other. It was almost time for us to go. We didn't want to stay out too long and arouse suspicion. Neither of us ever wanted to leave and my heart ached that she couldn't stay with me.

"I've decided I'm going to ask your father again tomorrow," I blurted out. "I'm going to handle it a bit differently this time. I have always asked him if I can see you. Now, I am going to tell him how much you want to be with me and that he shouldn't deny his own daughter. If he pushes me, I'll have it out with him. I am tired of waiting and of his foolish games. I am not going to take it anymore, Becky. We have a right to be together. If he says no, will you marry me anyway? We can go to Springfield. I am sure Mr. Pynchon will do it…he likes me well enough. He knows how your father can be. He is not that different from your uncle so he knows."

"Oh, Jack, I don't know…I don't want the two of you to fight! That wouldn't help anything. Just talk to him tomorrow…please? For me?"

"I don't know. I'm getting sick and tired of the runaround. I want him to make a decision…I want him to say yes and I can't figure out how to get him to do that. What do I have to say? What kind of argument should I make? What will it take? Why can't it be easier than this? I just want to be with you." We held each other again, feeling the warmth against the chilly night air. She pulled away and touched her forehead to mine.

"I love you."

"I love you too." With that, she started to walk away, but I reached out and slapped her on the behind. She gave a little squeal, slapping at my hand as she did, and laughing as she walked away.

The next morning during breakfast, I told Josiah and Charity that I was going to speak to Tom again that night. Charity asked me to think about what I wanted to say to him and be prepared because I had to make a strong argument. I had to give him good reasons that would benefit him in order for him to agree. She gave me something to think about when she asked what I'd learned from my first two unsuccessful meetings with him and what I'd do differently this time.

All that day as I worked, I watched the red, yellow, and orange leaves slowly fall from the trees like tears. I thought how appropriate that was since it was a sign that they didn't want the season to end and were sad that winter was coming.

When we came in for supper a little after dark, Charity told me that she and Elizabeth would make sure Tom was home alone. The two of them and Becky were going to Prichard's while Nate was taking his little brother to see Rich Coy's new pigs so Tom and I would have an hour. After all the aggravation I'd been through with that man, I'd be damned if I'd sit talking to him about this for a whole hour. I had wasted more than enough time talking to him.

Charity told Josiah that she, Elizabeth and Becky were going to Prichard's, and that he'd have the house to himself for an hour or two.

"Why? Where are you going?" he asked, pointing his fork at me.

"Take a guess…I'm going to the Morgan's."

"But Becky will be at…oh, that's right you're going to talk to him again. Don't you ever get tired of it? I know why you're putting up with it. I'll give you all the help I can but you have to remember that he's a miserable bastard to begin with."

"Josiah Clarke! I can't believe you said that. Now, Tom may be a curmudgeon but he goes to meeting every week and Thursday lecture now and that is a lot more than someone else I know," she told him, giving him a stern look.

"Oh, just because he goes to meeting doesn't change the fact that he's a cranky old man. He's been an old fart since I first met him 25 years ago. Besides, when I don't go there's a good reason, at least most of the time."

"The reason is usually that you'd rather pay the fine with money we don't have and be thought a lazy, godless man than come with me. At least Jack goes. What do you have to say to that?"

"Charity, my love, my darling, I have nothing to say to it. Now, when will my hour of peace and quiet be starting?" he said with a grin.

"Oh, you…," she said not able to stay angry with him.

"Now," he said turning to me, "what kind of an argument are you going to make tonight? Anything he hasn't already heard? Or do you figure to just tell him the same thing over and over until he gets tired and says yes?" All of this was said with a smile.

"No, I'm not going to talk about how much we should be together, or any of that. I'm going to ask him why he wants to hurt his daughter so much…why he doesn't want her to be happy." Charity and Josiah looked at each other and nodded agreeing that this may work better than before.

"I can't wait to hear his answer to that," Josiah said, getting his pipe out. Charity put her cloak on and picked up her basket of knitting. She came over to me and put her hand on my shoulder.

"He's going to say yes tonight…I just know it. It will all go well." I looked up at her and she gave me a wink as she headed for the door.

"I may as well get the argument started," I said, getting out of my chair and reaching for my jerkin.

"You never know…he might surprise you," Josiah said, settling into his chair by the fire.

"I doubt it," I muttered going out the door.

It was a clear, cold night and the stars covered the sky.

The moon wasn't up yet and a frost was forming on the ground. It was a good night to sit by a warm fire after spending time outside. I made my way to the Morgan's house, trying to figure out the best way to begin. I made sure he knew that I was coming, having told Nate in the afternoon. He promised to make sure his father knew. I knocked on the door and waited, half expecting no answer. To my surprise, Tom opened the door and asked me in. That definitely threw me off balance.

"Elizabeth and Nate said you'd be coming over. I figured as much when I heard about her and Becky joining your aunt at Prichard's. That and Nate taking young Tom to see Rich's pigs...like they couldn't do that any other time. No mind, sit down and let's talk," he said, taking a mug off the table and filling it with cider before handing it to me. All of this was making me suspicious because he had never treated me this well. I couldn't figure out why he was doing it.

"Surprised that I haven't laid into you yet?" he said, as if reading my mind.

"Yes, I am. Why not?"

"Well, I thought we might as well be comfortable. Even though I'm not going to say yes."

"There you go again," I said, putting the mug down hard, "not even willing to listen to what I have to say. Will you at least have the decency to let me talk?"

"I'll listen but you're not going to change my mind."

"All right, let's get down to brass tacks," I said, putting my elbows on the table and leaning in towards him. "Will you agree to let me court Becky?"

"No."

"Why?"

"Because you're not the man I want for her."

"Who is? Does he actually exist? Or is just someone other than me?" Tom just gave me a hard look and said nothing. "What the hell do you want from me?" I asked calmly.

"I don't want anything from you."

"Then why all of this? Yes, everything you've told me is not true and you know it."

"Don't get smart with me son or I'll toss your ass out the door."

"I don't think so. You couldn't if you wanted to," I said, knowing that I was taller and heavier than him. I stood there staring at him sitting at the table for a minute.

"You know," I said, sitting down and folding my hands with my elbows on the table, "I've done everything I can to help you. I did a good bit of the work on this house. Hell, I practically built your barn by myself."

"That was your decision to help. I wasn't going to say no when I needed all the help I could get."

"You never had any intention of agreeing to me courting Becky, did you? You just wanted to work me like a slave."

"Maybe I didn't. What of it?"

"You're a miserable, selfish man. Always taking and never giving. Always thinking of yourself. I don't know why I'm so surprised. It takes you years to make decision," I said with a sarcastic laugh. "By the time you make one here, I'll be an old man myself. Becky and I don't want to wait that long."

"Oh, you don't, do you? You'll wait as long as I want you to."

"No, we won't. We've talked it over and we won't wait. She's 18 years old! Don't you think she should have a say in who she wants to marry? I love your daughter and she loves me. I want her to be my wife and she wants me to be her husband. We'll go to Springfield and have Mr. Pynchon marry us."

"The hell you will!" he said angrily, springing out of his chair and approaching me.

"Watch me," I replied, standing so I could look down on him.

"Pynchon wouldn't do that, not if he knew I didn't give you permission."

"He might employ your brother but that doesn't mean he'll bow to your wishes. He has known me a lot longer than he's known you. What business have you had with him? You bought some peas and corn? So what? I met him in Boston when I was an apprentice; I ride for him and have been for a while. I helped build the mill and work for him there too. I've taken care of his livestock. I have more influence with him than you do. He'll listen to me long before he would you. And your brother probably hasn't put in too many good words for you either."

"I wouldn't bet on that. You think you know exactly how this will work out, eh? I don't think you do."

"Should I keep talking or will the answer always be no?"

"What have I been telling you all this time? Haven't you listened? You're not the man I want for my daughter," he said scornfully.

"Why? Why not?" I couldn't hold my temper any longer. "How dare you...after all this time, the letters, the hopes and dreams, the hard work and sacrifices we're willing to make to be with each other. You don't want us to be happy because you've never been," I said pointing my finger at him.

"What do you know about me? Huh? What do you know about me at all?"

"I know you've always had a chip on your shoulder. Even when I was little you were a cranky bastard. Everyone said so and you know it. Because you've never been happy you'll deny us the dreams we've had for so long? If that is true then your daughter will hate you for this, your wife will never forget it and be ashamed, the men won't respect you, and the women will snub you. You'll be spoken of at meeting and more than once. Do you want to sit there listening to that? Becky and I have a special relationship unlike any other two people in this village or in Springfield for that matter and everyone knows it." I took a deep breath realizing that I was standing in front of him, clenching my fists, getting angrier by the moment. "Do you dislike your only daughter so much that you'd rather see her go through life unhappy and heartbroken? What do you have against me that would make you act this way?"

"I have very little against you."

"Then why?" I cried. He sat down, took a deep breath, and stared at the table. He looked up and started to say something but stopped, waving his hand at me. Finally, after a minute or two he turned in his chair and looked at me.

"It's none of your business," he said flatly. "It happened a long time ago before you were even born, before you were even thought of, that's for sure."

"Then if it happened so long ago, why is it bothering you? Why is it interfering with my life?" He sat there silently staring into the fire, lost in the memories of something from long ago. I waited for him to say something. After a good long time, he began, not changing his expression or lifting his gaze from the fire.

"Your father…," he started, but stopped. "It was years

and years ago when we were children, old enough though to be mean and hurtful. We were very poor, sometimes not having much, if anything, to eat. Our land was poor, rocky, and hard. My father wasn't a good farmer but, then again, I'm not much better. Oh, I know it, I always have." He shifted in his chair seeing events from his childhood pass before his eyes. "The number of nights I went to sleep hungry and woke up even hungrier. I did the meanest jobs just to earn a few pence a week! My father drank himself into a stupor spending what little money we had. My mother was a sickly woman barely able to take care of herself, nevermind us. My brother stole to keep us fed, even though it meant a whipping or worse. We didn't have a choice. Your father's family," he continued, putting a shaking hand to his mouth, "had more than we did…not much, but enough." I saw the sorrow in his eyes and waited patiently for him to continue. "Your father," he said sitting back in his chair, the spell broken, "treated my family like dirt. He always made fun of my brother and me because we were so poor. Always looking down at us, telling everyone how we were like brute animals because we had nothing. Nothing! He made fun of us. He never let up...ever. His talk made our life a hell because everyone listened to him. Hardly anyone would help us. He never got in trouble for saying those vicious things. I swore I would never forgive him. I haven't and I won't! Since he's dead and gone, you get to carry his burden."

"This is what it's all about?" I exclaimed, hardly believing what I was hearing. "You're punishing me, punishing your daughter, because of something my father did years ago? Because he's gone, you're unloading all of your pent up anger and hatred on me now? I can't believe this!" I sat down across from him. "Tom, Becky and I want to get married. We want your permission and blessing. I know nothing of my father's past except what I've heard from others. I ask you, no, I beg of you, not to let whatever my father did years ago, however wrong it was, however much it hurt you or your family, to stand in the way of our beginning a life together. I am not responsible for how he treated your family. Don't hold me accountable for something I didn't know about until a few minutes ago. I will do all in my power to make your daughter happy and to give her a good life, a good family…to give you and Elizabeth grandchildren. Please think about this and let me know tomorrow." I left quickly before the rest of the family returned, which is just as well because I really was not in the mood to talk to anyone, even Becky.

That night, I hardly slept at all. I was awake in the small hours of the morning alone with my doubts and my fears. I was hopeful Tom would give us his permission, but I wasn't completely sure. I didn't know what I'd do if he said no. I laid awake thinking of all he said, about my father being so mean to them, not believing my father had done those things because he was always a good and decent man. I just couldn't imagine him being mean to anyone; even Tom and his family. Another thing was Tom's family being so poor they had to steal which was about as bad as you could get. While things are a little less severe than they were in those days, there were several ways of dealing with a thief from having his nose split, to being nailed by the ears to the stocks, to wearing a big red "T" around your neck for a year. If a child did the stealing, most likely the parent would be punished too with both of them getting a sound whipping of 15 lashes with a cat o' nine tails.

Becky came over very early, just as I was getting a good fire burning. She wanted to know how my talk with her father went since Tom hadn't said anything to her yet. She saw the look on my face.

"What happened, Jack?" she asked.

"Well, we talked for quite a while about some things we never talked about before...," I didn't know how to bring up the topic of my father's behavior to her family.

"Well, did he say yes?" her voice filled with hope but half expecting to hear no.

"No, he didn't," I replied, moving close to her, "I asked him to give me his answer today. I don't know if he will, but I hope so. I think he will anyway."

"What is it, Jack? There's something you're not telling me."

"Well," I said clearing my throat, "uh, he, uh, told me things about my father...things I really can't believe but I could tell he wasn't lying. Your father has been holding a grudge against my father for over 30 years. It seems that when they were young, my father made fun of how poor your father's family was. It really hurt him because he's carried it with him all these years. He said he has very little against me. Not giving me permission was his way of getting back at my father. I still can't believe my father would have done that." She stood quietly looking at me. She took two steps, put her arms around me, and laid her head on my shoulder. She stepped back a bit, and looked into my eyes.

"Jack, I love you, and that's all that matters. Not what your father did to mine or what mine did to yours or anyone else's for that matter. As long as he says yes, I don't care about anything else." I gave her a kiss on the forehead. As I started away, she grabbed my hand and squeezed it three times. I looked at her, unsure as to why she did it. She did it again only this time telling me "I love you" – one word for each squeeze. From then on, it was our secret way of telling each other; something no one else could see.

I spent most of the day helping Charity boil soap - a nasty, smelly, sweaty job if ever there was one. God, it was awful.

Josiah and I carried the big cauldron outside and hung

it on the log that rested in the Y-shaped center of two posts with a chain over the log and through the handle of the pot. I then got load after load of wood and started a big, hot fire under the kettle. While I was doing that, Charity took all the ashes we saved and put them in a barrel, building layers of ash and straw. She poured a little water in, leaching the lye from the ashes. This was collected in a big bucket under the barrel. Every now and then, she would pour the lye into the kettle. Once she had enough, I dumped the grease from all our cooking in and started stirring.

Now, soap making is an imperfect art and it didn't always come out right. Sometimes it was too watery and other times it had so much lye, it burned your skin. The result each time might be different even though you did the same thing as the times when it came out fine. Anyone who passed by during the process always wished you luck because that's what it seemed you'd need to get a good batch. The way in which it was stirred made a difference too. You could stir in only one direction and it couldn't be too fast or too slow. All the while, the smell of rancid grease and burning lye got into your eyes and nose. The women usually made soap on cooler days because on a hot day it was even worse, if that was possible, and you could easily be overcome by the smell. The whole thing took us all morning and by the time it was over, we were tired, sore, and sweaty. Before she scraped the soft soap out of the kettle, Charity threw in a small handful of salt which helped harden it. After a few minutes, she put it into a barrel that I moved to just inside the door.

Just as I came back outside, I saw Josiah talking to Tom. It looked like a serious discussion until Josiah tilted his head back and gave a good laugh. I knew something was going on because Tom was smiling too which didn't happen often. Josiah saw me and motioned for me to come over. As I got closer, they turned serious again, although there was a hint of a smile on their faces. They were like little children who tried to stop laughing but couldn't. Finally, Josiah settled down and looked at Tom and then me.

"Jack, Tom has something to say to you." With that, he took a step back. Tom turned to face me and when he looked up, I saw his wrinkled, lined face for what it was: that of a tired, beaten, stooped old man.

"Jack, I've thought long and hard about all that we talked about over the last few months, especially last night. I have to say, I'm impressed by the fact that you never backed down. You never let it drop as some men would have even after I said no to you so many times. That told me you were serious about Becky. Now, I know you might think I'm a mean old man, but I'm not. You made me realize that my feelings, the hurt I still feel from long ago, shouldn't get in the way of you and Becky starting a life together." He stopped and looked down at the ground for a moment. "I was wrong," he said, looking back at me. "I'll admit it. I was stubborn mainly because I didn't want to see my daughter go, even if it was to a good man like you." He took my hand in his and shook it firmly. "Jack, you have my permission to court Becky." I was stunned. Even though I wished for this to happen for so long, after all this time of asking and pleading and pretty much begging, I was close to losing hope. I came back to reality and looked at both of them.

"Does Becky know?"

"Not yet," Tom said with a grin, "I thought you'd like to tell her yourself. She's at the house polishing the pewter. Go see her." I headed off to the water bucket to wash the grease and lye smell from my face, hair, and hands before going to see my future wife.

It's amazing how you remember the smallest details of some of the biggest moments in your life. This was certainly one of mine. I remember how crisp and sweet the air was on that fine mid-October day, and how the light had a sharp, clear quality to it, making everything look good. I remember hearing Susanna Ayres telling her youngest, Ed, to stop playing with the dog and to take some wood inside and that it was going to be a cold night. I remember seeing Sam Prichard chopping wood, the smell of wood smoke, how clear and blue the sky was and the crunching of the faded red, yellow and gold leaves under my feet. I remember that Becky's mother had just baked bread and I can still smell it, even now. I also remember how Becky was standing when I opened the door without knocking, trying to be quiet and surprise her, but not being too successful because of my excitement. I think it also had to do with the fact that I smelled so bad.

She was standing next to the chest with a pewter dish in her left hand and a cloth in her right slowly polishing it. She didn't hear me at first but turned when her mother stood up quickly from the hearth. I can see her now, her face framed by her cap, how it lit up when she saw me and right away understood the news I brought. Her face gleamed, her eyes sparkled, and for a minute, there was no one else in the world but the two of us. The spell was broken as she rushed toward me. I caught her in my arms and twirled her around, both of us laughing.

"He said yes!" I told her as I held her. She had the happiest smile I'd ever seen and she was more beautiful at that moment than at any other time since we first met.

"I knew he'd agree." Mrs. Morgan beamed, almost as happy as we were. Nate came over, shook my hand, and kissed his sister.

"It'll be good to have you as a member of the family…finally," he said, grasping my hand firmly.

"Thank you."

Up to now, Becky hadn't said a thing. She looked at me and her eyes got wide. "This means we can get married," she said as if realizing it for the first time.

"Yes, it does and we will be...by the end of the year."

The next few weeks went quickly and happily. While it was cold during the end of October and into the first two weeks of November, it got very cold towards the beginning of the third week. Fires were kept blazing all day and through a good part of the night. It was so cold that if cider and beer were not kept on the hearth, it would freeze. The wind whistled and whined all the time, slicing through you whenever you went outside. The worst thing I remember about that time was going for wood, which was seven or eight times a day because we used so much. More than once, I could hear the wolves howling close by, though the sound would fade and come back because of the wind. It sounded like they were just over the hill a hundred yards away. It was almost too cold for it to snow but the little that did fall turned into sharpened flakes that stung your face and hands. Only someone who has stood in air so cold it hurts when you breathe, where your face and ears begin to freeze within a minute of leaving the house, and the wind blows so hard and so sharp that it has a deathly edge to it knows how dangerous and frightening such weather can be. For eight days, the weather stayed the same.

On the eighth night, Josiah, Charity and I sat close to

the fire, bundled in our warmest clothes, as we had for the past week. Each of us were staring into the fire watching the flames dance up and down, licking their way around the logs. Josiah looked at us and cocked his head.

"Listen." We sat and tried to hear above the roaring and crackling of the fire. "The wind stopped." I jumped up and went to the door, listening before I opened it to make sure a gust would not come sweeping in. I heard nothing and went outside, followed by Josiah and Charity. The wind had stopped completely; there wasn't so much as a whisper of a breeze. All was deathly still, like we were the only people in the world. I stepped out to look at the sky, the snow crunching loudly under my feet. To the west, the night sky was clear and the stars shone like brilliant gems. The quarter moon was above the western horizon casting a soft glow on the snow. None of us said anything but just stood and looked at the scene.

"Too damn cold to stay out here," Charity said with a shiver as she quickly went in. Josiah and I looked at each other in surprise because she swore only about once every two years.

"How do you like that?" he asked, shaking his head as we walked to the door.

In late November, Becky and I decided to get married as soon as we could. Our intentions were read at the next three Sabbath meetings. Even though Mr. Ayres, the leading member of the village, offered to marry us, we decided to go to Springfield to have Mr. Pynchon do it. I told Mr. Pynchon when I was there a few weeks prior that Becky and I wanted him to marry us. He thought it a wonderful idea and said he would be happy to do that for us. While we were there, I could talk to him about the land I selected for our farm. I had enough in credit with him to buy the land and a cart full of supplies, including some tools that I would need.

We planned to go the last Wednesday of December so we could be back before Sabbath started Saturday afternoon. Becky was excited because she had only been to Springfield once just after they came to the village. The weather had been good; cold but sunny with light winds from the west. There were a few inches of snow on the ground but not enough to keep us from going.

On that Wednesday, our wedding day, December 21, 1674, we left early enough in the morning to get there before dark. The day started cloudy but turned out to be beautiful with clear blue skies and bright sunshine - a perfect winter day. This matched our mood for we were very happy. Even though we didn't say it, we both knew that this was our dream that started so improbably years ago in a sand dune in Ipswich. It all seemed like such a long time ago although I can still see every moment and every detail clearly.

We smiled and laughed much of the way and were able

to truly be ourselves without any of the stern older folks glancing at us all the time making sure we didn't do anything they'd find offensive, which was just about everything. In between the laughter, there were moments of silent pleasure. Becky sat close beside me with her left arm through my right as I held the reins. We didn't say much, but enjoyed each other's company as we never had before. I realized that in a few short hours the woman beside me would be my wife. It gave me a thrill to realize that I would have a wife. Even though Josiah and Charity had given me a wonderful home and loved me, it was time for me to start my own family.

It had gotten much colder since we left the village and as we topped the long hill above Springfield, it began to snow. It was a very soft, almost magical snow through which we could still make out the river and the fields just beyond it. The storm was approaching. The low, dark clouds hung ponderously over the fields and the hills to the west, so we went into town quickly. We found Mr. Pynchon at his house near the fort. We received a warm welcome from him and his family. Even though they had seen me many times, this was their first time meeting Becky. The happiness in their voices was unmistakable at our marriage. Marriages were a low-key affair in those days, nothing more than a quick civil service. It wasn't unusual for the husband and wife to go back to work after the ceremony. Their friends and relatives usually had a gathering at the tavern or one of their houses the same day of the wedding or within the next couple of days.

Mr. Pynchon and his wife Amy, a petite woman with a pleasant face, greeted us warmly. Even though Mr. Pynchon was the most powerful landowner in the Colony, you would never know it from his look and manner. He appeared to be a successful trader and merchant but nothing more. However, for all his appearances, he has bought huge tracts of land and along with several other investors, started six new settlements, including Quaboag.

The man was amazing in his civil service, military commitments, business interests, and as promoter of the western Bay Colony. He was or had been a selectman, treasurer, magistrate, town recorder, town moderator, town clerk and served on many town committees. He was also an assistant to the Massachusetts General Court and advisor to the governor. He was the principal military officer and at the time of our wedding, a colonel of the 1st Hampshire Regiment. His business interests were many; he, along with his brother-in-law, Samuel Wyllys and Richard Lord of Connecticut owned a sugar plantation in Barbados. He owned five vessels in the coastal trade as well as several sawmills, grist mills, and an iron works, and kept up a very busy and lucrative trade with all the Indian tribes from the north, south and west of Springfield. He raised hundreds of sheep and cattle every year for the Boston market and financed many local tradesmen who could provide goods or services to the Indians. Overall, he was a remarkable man and I was very pleased that he took such interest in me.

"Jack, it's good to see you again," he beamed at me. "And this must be Becky," he said taking her hand. "I'd like you to meet my wife Amy."

"It's good to finally meet you sir," Becky said making a slight bow.

"Welcome to our home, both of you," said Amy.

"Thank you," I replied, "As always, it's good to be here...especially today," which drew a laugh from them. I was more nervous than I thought I would be and hoped it didn't show. Becky looked nervous too and slightly uncomfortable at being in the company of such a wealthy and important man.

"It looks like you got here just in time," Mr. Pynchon said, looking out the window at the snow that was falling heavier and faster than just a few minutes before. "I hope you're prepared to spend an extra day," he continued. "This looks like it's not going to stop anytime soon." I looked at Becky who smiled coyly, her green eyes twinkling at the thought of being together for an extra night.

"Yes, we are," she said softly, looking at me. Just then, I caught a glance between John and Amy followed by a smile. I felt the warmth creep into my face, embarrassed that they knew what Becky and I were thinking and hoping. A second night away from the prying eyes of the village would be wonderful.

"Well, shall we get started?" he asked, looking at us. "After the ceremony we'd like you to be our guests at the tavern for dinner. A little celebration feast."

"Thank you very much, sir. We're grateful to you." Mrs. Pynchon began moving into the next room.

"We'll have the ceremony in here," she said. As we were going in, there was a spirited knock upon the front door and in stepped Tom Cooper.

"Good evening, John, evening everyone," he said jovially, taking his coat off. He put out his hand as he approached us. "Jack, congratulations!" he said as he grasped my hand firmly in both of his. "It's good to see you again," he said with a smile. I always enjoyed Tom, for he had a favorable view of the world and was always cheerful and optimistic. When you saw him smiling, which was most of the time, you couldn't help but smile back. He was the type of person who could light up a room as he did now; his good spirit was contagious.

"This must be Becky," he said, standing in front of her. "It's very nice to meet you. Jack has told me many good things about you. You're a very special person to make him feel the way he does. You two are very lucky. Jack is one of the best men around. There are very few like him, you know."

"Tom," Mr. Pynchon said, placing a hand on the

shoulder of his good friend and business partner. "You're just in time...you can be a witness." I stood next to Becky on one side of the fireplace where a nice fire was burning and crackling and the warmth felt good. I took Becky's hand in mine and squeezed it three times. She leaned against me and I put my arm around her.

"I can't believe we're actually about to be married," she said softly, looking up at me. Her face was radiant, a wonder that filled my heart with overwhelming emotion at how much I loved this woman. "We've been waiting for this for so long," she said, looking at the three of them. "We've wanted to get married for years and now we will," she told them earnestly, "and now we will," she repeated in a whisper. Mr. Pynchon cleared his throat and began the short ceremony.

"Rebecca Morgan," he said formally, "In the sight of our most gracious God, this man, John Parker, asks that you be his wife, from this day forward, until the Lord removes you from one another by death. How do you answer him?"

She turned and looked into my eyes. I could feel her love for me and it felt so good, so strong, and so wonderful.

"In the sight of God, I will be his wife," she said never taking her eyes from me.

"John Parker, the Lord has given you this woman, Rebecca Morgan, to be your wife until death parts you. In the sight of God, do you accept her as your wife?" I looked at this woman, this girl that I loved for so long and was filled with a joy and happiness I had never known before.

"Yes, in the sight of God, I take her as my wife."

"May the Lord in all ways be good to you. You have our heartiest wishes and prayers. You are now husband and wife."

"Thank you," I replied. I turned to face my wife and took her hands in mine. "I will love you forever. You are everything to me Becky and I could never live without you." She began to cry softly and I noticed Mrs. Pynchon wiping away a tear. I was so lost in my thoughts about my wife that I had almost forgotten about Mr. Pynchon and Tom. I turned to them. "Thank you sir," I said to Mr. Pynchon.

He took my hand and shook it firmly. "You are perfectly welcome. We are very happy for both of you. I don't always get to do what I want these days with the demands of the business and my government duties but this is one thing I've certainly enjoyed and I'm happy to share in your day. I want both of you to remember that, as God shall enable me, I shall be ready to do my utmost for you."

Tom offered his hand and showing his infectious smile, said, "May God bless you both. Mr. and Mrs. Parker," he said happily. "May we escort you to the tavern for a small celebration?" Becky and I smiled at hearing that and the realization that we were two separate people but a married couple.

"Yes, you may," my beautiful bride replied.

Bundled up in our heavy wool garments, we made our way to the tavern through the blowing wind and the snow, which was coming down sideways. When we entered the tavern, a large, well-built structure that was located in the southwest corner of the fort, the warmth immediately chased away the cold. There were six or eight men in the room sitting next to the big fireplace at one end, a small bar and several tables scattered about with a mixture of chairs and benches. The light from the fire danced on the walls and ceilings. There were candles on some of the tables that burned giving off a strong odor of tallow.

Mr. and Mrs. Pynchon, Lt. Cooper, please come in," said Jeremiah Butler, the tavern keeper. He was a barrel-chested man with a full head of gray hair and a bushy beard of the same color.

"Good evening, Jeremiah," replied Mr. Pynchon. "We're here for a celebration."

"Jack," Jeremiah replied, recognizing me, "what are you here for on this cold winter's day? How are you?"

"We just got married and will need a room," I told him. "It's too late and snowing too hard to go home tonight."

"I have a nice room I'll get ready for you."

"He's fine today," Tom joined in. "Especially being

married to Becky."

"Good evening, Mr. Butler," Becky said.

"Please, no formality. My name is Jeremiah. Good evening to you too," he said with mock formality. "Congratulations and may the Lord bless your marriage."

"Mary!" he yelled loudly towards the back of the room. "Mary! Come out here." His wife was a good-sized, rather frumpy woman who made everyone feel at home. She came out of the back room wearing a dingy gray dress and worn brown boots. Unlike most women, she didn't wear any head covering and her hair was black with streaks of white here and there, which she always wore pinned up on the top of her head.

"What?" she yelled back. "What do you want now?" she gave her husband a hard look.

"Stop yelling woman! They'll hear you at the other end of the village."

"So?" she said in a lower tone, slinging a linen cloth over her left shoulder.

"Mr. and Mrs. Pynchon and Tom Cooper are here with guests; Jack Parker, and his new wife Becky. Mr. Pynchon is having a dinner for them."

"Oh," she said turning towards us, looking as if seeing us for the first time, "Mr. Pynchon sir. Good evening Mrs. Pynchon, Lt. Cooper."

"Good evening Mary," Tom replied, "We're here to

celebrate. The ceremony was short but good," he said, casting a warm smile and happy look at Becky and me.

"I'm sure it was. Jeremiah and I were married 26 years ago," she said to Becky and me. "It doesn't seem that long ago but it was and I wouldn't trade any of it," she said wistfully, flashing a smile at her husband that revealed several missing teeth. "I'm sure yours will be as happy as ours has been."

"Thank you," Becky replied, taking my hand and giving it three squeezes. "I'm sure it will be."

"Jeremiah," his wife directed, "build up the fire while I arrange the table." He complied and soon had a blazing fire that warmed the room. She arranged chairs around one of the longest tables and brought out wooden bowls and trenchers, spoons, knives and napkins.

We had a fine meal of carrot, potato and venison stew, roasted goose, apple and pumpkin bread, cider, beer and flip. It was a great celebration; far more than we ever imagined. We were planning on a quiet simple dinner, which was all we could afford. The food was so wonderful I can still taste it, and the company pleasant. We talked about many things, with Tom giving us accounts of his adventures amongst the Indians to establish trade. Mrs. Pynchon talked about her trip to Boston in September and some of the new fashions and amusements she had seen. Her husband told us about a new settlement he was planning to establish in southern Connecticut. Becky and I talked of life at Quaboag and about how hard but rewarding it was to make a life for yourself and your family with your own two hands in the wilderness. We also spoke of our hopes and plans for the future - a good farm, a big happy family and growing old together. Towards the end of the meal, Mr. Pynchon asked about our relations with the Quaboag tribe.

"Have there been any problems lately? Judah told me that several of the young men got drunk again and were fighting. From what he said, it sounded like a couple got hurt."

"There have been a couple of problems," I replied, trying to make sure he understood that these were minor problems and that Judah had a tendency to exaggerate a bit. "But they're small and don't happen too often. There are two or three of them that always seem to be causing some trouble, but you find that no matter where you go. I think I've had probably more interaction with them than anyone else except Mr. Ayres, and almost all of them are good people, always willing to help, of a strong nature, and a loving family people."

"That's fine to hear," he responded, obviously relieved that the situation wasn't as bad as he thought. "Isn't it Tom?"

"Yes it is. The last thing any of us need is any sort of major trouble with them since everything is going so well, particularly at Brookfield. There have been a few other incidents," he said to me by way of explanation, "with the Pocumtucks that have been a bit more serious than a few drunkards. One of them was killed by his brother-in-law because he'd taken something of his." Tom stood and patted his stomach.

"That was a wonderful meal and couldn't have been for a better reason. Congratulations again to both of you. You make a fine couple, you know. Unfortunately, I have to go," he said as he put on his heavy wool coat. "Jack, I'll see you next time you're in. Becky, it was a true pleasure meeting you," he said with his usual smile. "I hope to see you again. Tell him to bring you with him next time," he said with a wink. I stood and shook his hand.

"Thank you for joining us. It meant a great deal to both of us to have you with us on such a nasty night. I'll definitely bring my darling wife next time."

"Fine. Goodnight, Amy. John, I'll see you in the morning. I want to talk about that land up in Hatfield."

"Goodnight Tom," said Amy.

"All right," replied Mr. Pynchon. "I'll see you in the morning. Don't come around too early. I have some correspondence to catch up on." He opened the door and a big blast of cold air came in with a trail of snowflakes that landed on the floor before slowly melting . Mrs. Pynchon put a hand on her husband's arm.

"John, we should be going too." He stood and took her hand.

"Yes we probably should. I want both of you to know," he said, leaning forward towards us, "that I will certainly help you in any way I can. You're a good man Jack and you have a beautiful wife. I may need you to do a few things for me in the next couple of months. We'll talk next time you're in. Congratulations again." With that, they were out the door and into the storm. Another blast of wind and snow came in causing us to shiver, even though we were wearing heavy wool clothes. We sat and looked at each other for a moment before I stood and took her hand.

"Mrs. Parker, may I escort you to our room?" I said with a flourish.

"Of course you may, Mr. Parker," she replied with a nervous laugh. As we walked to the stairs, Jeremiah and Mary were by the bar, he arranging bottles and she wiping mugs with a big, brown linen cloth.

"It's the room on the right overlooking the river." Jeremiah told us. "I got a nice fire going a little while ago so it should be warm."

We wished them a good night, slightly embarrassed because they knew what happens on the marriage night. Putting her cloth down on a nearby table, Mary smiled and ran a hand over her hair.

"Now you have a good night and I'll have a big, fine breakfast for you in the morning."

Our room wasn't large but comfortable. I watched the show of the fire dance around the room. After I closed the door, I took Becky in my arms.

"I want you to know that I love you more than life itself and that without you I'd be nothing. You are my world. I can't tell you how much you mean to me." She held me tight with her head on my shoulder. I felt her begin to cry softly. I stepped back and lifted her chin.

"What's wrong?"

"Nothing, nothing's wrong," she said, small tears coming down her face. "It's just that we've been waiting so long for this," she said in a tone slightly above a whisper, "and now it's come true. I'm finally your wife. I love you and want to spend the rest of my life with you. I want to be by your side and grow old with you. I want to build a good life; a happy life with children and a farm…but," she began crying again, "I thought of our first kiss on the dunes and how I waited for you, how much I missed you when you left, how my heart ached for you every day and how I'd lie awake at night thinking and dreaming about being your wife. And now I am," she said with a smile through the tears. That night was the most wonderful of our lives. It was a soft surrender and a happiness we'd never known. It was a great way to begin our new life.

The Devil's Elbow

Chapter 14

The snow had stopped by morning, but the blustery wind continued. In some places, the ground was bare and in others, there were tall windblown drifts. A man with a team of horses and a sled made of rough heavy boards went down the middle of the road trying to flatten the snow as best as he could or failing that, to at least push it to the sides.

Mary was as good as her word and served a big breakfast of roasted pork, apple and nut bread, fish balls fried in lard, and Indian meal – ground corn, dried berries and nuts mixed with lard – one of my favorites. We filled ourselves to the point of bursting.

We didn't know what to do with ourselves for unlike at home, we had nothing to get up early for and no work to do. Between that and our slow meal, the morning was half gone by the time we finished breakfast.

The sky cleared shortly after and it turned out to be a beautiful, bright, sunny day. While it was still cold, the wind had stopped and within an hour or so, some of the snow began to melt. We put on our coats and took a walk. The snowdrifts didn't allow us to go to every part of town so we made our way down to the river along a cart path to the wharves. The river was a big, blue ribbon cutting through the pure white snow that covered the large, flat lands on the other side of the river. The sky made the river look even bluer than it was; the bright sunshine made the snow seem even whiter to the point where it hurt your eyes. Becky had never seen a river this big or this wide.

"This is much bigger than the river back home," she said, grabbing my arm to keep herself from falling on an icy patch.

"Yes it is," I replied, putting her right arm through my left. We admired the view for a few moments.

"Whenever I come to Springfield, I always come down to the river," I said, lost in the memory of those times. "It's peaceful and restful." I held her arm as I looked up and down the river. "The morning my mother died, I ran off behind the house and through the field on the other side. I went over the hill behind Adams' farm and down the path to the stream. I sat there for a long time; I don't know how long but it must have been two or three hours. I cried and cursed God and everyone and everything. The murmur of the stream made me quiet. It soothed me. I fell asleep for a while but finally got up and went home. Josiah and Charity were worried sick."

She turned and faced me. "You never told me that."

"I never told anyone until now."

We stood there quietly for a few minutes, enjoying being together, the winter air, the bright sunshine, and the beautiful view.

"I'd like to have our farm on this river someday," I said, dreaming of the future. "Nice, deep, rich soil where I could grow just about anything without breaking my back every day fighting rocks. Our sons would help."

"And daughters," she added.

"And daughters," I agreed. "I'd like to have something to pass down, something that will stay in the family so that two hundred years from now our family, our great, great grandchildren, will be working that land."

"That would be nice, wouldn't it?" she asked.

"Yes, yes it would." With that, we turned and walked back to town, enjoying our first day of marriage and the hopes and dreams of our future.

As we wandered around the village, I introduced her to all the people I knew that we ran into. By the middle of the afternoon, I had shown her everything there was to see, so we went back to the tavern. Surprisingly, we were the only ones there. Jeremiah got us mugs of his new beer and we had a couple each. We went up to our room for a rest and as we started up the stairs, I saw Jeremiah out of the corner of my eye, shaking his head and smiling at us. I caught his eye and he just nodded and smiled even more.

The next morning was clear and warm. After another one of Mary's delicious breakfasts, we went to the barn and hitched Bubs to the cart. After paying Jeremiah and saying goodbye to Mary, we headed to the warehouse to pick up our supplies and we were on our way home by mid-morning. For a good part of the way out of town, the road was clear but once we topped the long hill, things got a little more difficult. The were quite a few snow drifts over the next few miles, but not so high that Bubs couldn't get us through without any extra effort. In between the drifts, which were every 100 feet or so, the ground was almost bare with the wind having scoured it clean of snow and blown it into the drifts. As we went on, the drifts got higher but we still had no trouble going through them. I was pleased and surprised we were making such good time. That came to an abrupt end about halfway home. We came around a bend and up a small hill into an area with tall oak and pine trees on either side for a few hundred feet. The hill went up to the left. Snow had drifted up against that side to a height of six feet and spread across most of the road. The drift went back at least 10 feet and I knew there'd be no way Bubs would be able to get through it. We got out and considered the situation.

"We'll have to dig it out," I said with a sigh, frustrated at not being able to continue our easy travels.

"You don't think we could get through? Becky asked hopefully.

"No, we'd just get stuck and then we'd be in worse trouble. We'll just have to clear it. I guess we're the first ones to travel this road."

Luckily, we'd brought a wooden shovel I made to have it tipped with iron. We had also gotten a new hayfork. The good thing about the drift was that because it was in the shade from the trees it hadn't melted and was still soft, fluffy, and easy to move. I backed Bubs and the cart down the road and after getting the tools, tied the reins to a small tree.

I took the shovel and Becky the hayfork and we started at it. It was light enough so we could push it to the side without much effort and after another while, it was clear enough for us to get through.

"The rest of this part looks all right. I hope it will be like this all the way home," I told her.

We were fortunate that it was easy going for the next several miles. We had to stop twice more to clear the road, but the drifts weren't anywhere near as bad as the first. It was a pleasant trip even with the unexpected snowdrifts.

Becky was as pretty as she could be. She took her hood and cap off when we stopped, her hair framing her face and blowing softly behind her showing her neck. Her green eyes were bright and happy. She was excited all the way back. She was talking but I really wasn't listening because I was looking at her smiling and happy. She finally stopped talking and looked at me.

"What?" she said.

"Nothing…"

"Why are you looking at me like that? What are you smiling at?" she said with a playful laugh. I reined Bubs to a stop and put the reins around my boot. I leaned over and kissed her softly. When I pulled away, she still had her eyes closed. I leaned in and kissed her again. She pulled away and leaning in, put her cheek against mine.

"Oh Jack," she whispered, "I love you." I kissed her again in reply. She started laughing, looking at me with love in her eyes. "What am I going to do with you?" she asked with another wonderful laugh.

"Love me forever."

"That's easy," she said with another silly laugh. She kissed me on the cheek and looked at me. "All right my husband, let's get ourselves home. It will be dark soon and time for bed," she said playfully with an inviting, slightly mischievous look. It was full dark when we got home. The sky was clear and the light from the half moon reflected off the fresh snow, showing us the way.

Chapter 15

The winter wore on with a couple of blizzards in between bouts of milder, sunny weather. Spring returned slowly; the feeling of faint warmth in the softer breezes with the smell of moisture in the air. Everyone was outside much more with the increasing warmth and light, working in the gardens or around the barn doing things that we had waited all winter to do.

Our life changed one fine late April day. Becky and I were leaning against the barn watching the last light leave the sky as the evening star came out. The sunset had been beautiful with streaks of orange, red and purple reflected off the clouds. I put my right arm around her waist. She gave a smile that reached her eyes and leaned against me, pulling my arms around her. We stood like that until it got dark and then walked to the house. As soon as we entered, she turned to me.

"Jack," she said softly, "I'm going to have a baby." I stood there stunned, not quite understanding what she said. My dazed expression caused her to laugh and take my hand in hers. "You're going to be a father, hopefully to the first of many." I recovered from the news.

"I have to get our house built. We can't live with Josiah and Charity forever. And…there's a lot of stuff that has to be done!" I exclaimed, realizing the implications of having children. I was going to be a father; we were going to be parents, with a little boy or girl or maybe both. I looked at her; she was smiling and crying at the same time.

"Oh, come here, mother of my child," I said, opening my arms. She scooted over to me. I wrapped my arms around her and held her for what seemed like a long time. We stayed there not saying a word, her head on my shoulder as a thrill shot through me at the thought of having children.

"This is wonderful," I whispered.

"This is one of our dreams, to have a family. I've never been so happy. To be married to you, the best man on earth, and to be having your baby.

"When should we tell Charity and Josiah and all the others?"

"Charity already knows. So does my mother. She asked me if I was pregnant when I was over there last week. It was right after I found out. I'm due in November." I put my hand on her belly and kissed her softly. She radiated happiness and joy.

Everyone in the village congratulated us over the next few days. Becky had plenty of company as Mary Trumble, Jane Kent, and her daughter Sarah Coy were all pregnant. Mary was due in late July and Jane and Sarah were due around the middle of September. They formed a little club of sorts – the expectant mothers of Brookfield. We had never had this many women pregnant at the same time before. Jane had seven children, six of which were twins, including Sarah. Jane was ten years older than Becky was, while Mary was about the same age and Sarah was young, only 14-years-old. She and Richard Coy, Jr. were married three weeks before Becky and me. Charity and Elizabeth, as well as several other women, believed Sarah was pregnant and they had to get married, which certainly was not unheard of during our time there.

As the months went by, Becky got bigger. She complained that her back and feet hurt all the time and she wasn't able to do all that she had before. I did what I could to comfort her but no matter what I did for her it did not seem to make much of a difference.

I had gotten permission from the selectmen to cut the trees I needed to build our home. Josiah, Nate, young Tom, Sam Prichard, Jack Ayres Jr., and Rich Coy Jr. helped when they could with a few hours here and there. While it was a tremendous amount of work, it was very satisfying knowing that I was building a home for my wife and child. I felt the need to hurry, to get it done as soon as I could, because I wanted a place of our own.

I finished the foundation, chimney, and fireplace in the next two weeks and began squaring the timbers. With Josiah's help, it took another week to get all the timbers ready and peg the three for each end together. The house was 18 feet wide and 24 feet long with a cellar and loft. It gave us plenty of room for the three of us and any other children we might have.

We held the house raising in early June on a clear, warm day. Everyone in the village came to help so it was a real social occasion. Becky, Charity, and Elizabeth put together a good assortment of food and drink. Each of the women from the village brought something, usually the thing for which they were known. Susannah Ayres made delicious apple pies, Elizabeth Prichard had pork and vegetable stew, Jane Kent made a thick, sweet raisin pie, and Mary Trumble had an Indian pudding made from corn and molasses, the tastiest corn pudding I ever ate. The men drank rum a good part of the day - before, during and after working on the house.

We were halfway through, just having raised the last of the timbers, when Matchitehew and Wematin came strolling up the road looking everything over as if trying to determine the value of each item, whether it was a wheelbarrow, pitchfork or bucket. We stopped working and stood there waiting for them. They saw us and continued sauntering in our direction.

I was annoyed at having our day interrupted by these two troublemakers. The women moved back a step even though there wasn't any reason to do it. They seemed to sense trouble. The men gathered and advanced to meet them. Matchitehew came to within two feet of me and stood looking around at the framing while Wematin stood next to him, looking doltish as usual.

"Good, good," Matchitehew said in an approving tone. "You do good work...maybe you build a house for me," he said with a big laugh.

"What do you want?" I asked briskly.

"We came to see our friends, all our friends," he opening his arms towards us.

"You can leave now," I told him. His body stiffened as he lowered his head a bit, looking me in the eye. It was a hard stare; I could feel the hatred simmering in his eyes.

"I'll go when I want to go, not when you tell me," he spat at me. "Besides, maybe we'll stay for some food." he chuckled.

"No, you won't. Now leave. We don't want you or your brother here."

"We don't want you here either English," he snarled, looking at each and every one of us. "I will make sure you leave some day," he growled before turning and walking back the way he'd come.

We had begun early in the morning when I assigned each man his place and we finished around mid-afternoon and began the celebration. For the rest of the afternoon we ate, drank, and visited. Becky and I stood admiring our house. I still had a lot of work to do, but it wouldn't take more than another three weeks. I intended to make it a strong house that would give us shelter for years to come. Little did I know that it wouldn't stand more than two months before disaster struck.

Chapter 16

Nate and I went to Springfield the third week of June, soon after the house was finished to pick up supplies and bring two ox calves to Mr. Pynchon. Nate and Rich Coy, Jr. raised them since October and Mr. Pynchon agreed to buy them. As we usually did during our trips there, we stopped at the tavern after finishing our business. Several men were there, including my friend Tom Cooper. Over a mug of beer, we fell into a discussion of the Indian troubles; particularly about Metacom, called King Philip by the English, the sachem of the Wampanoag tribe that lived south of the Plymouth colony. Philip's father was Massasoit who helped the Plymouth colony get through their first winter and was friends with them until he died a little more than ten years before the troubles started.

"I heard that the Wampanoags are gathering near Swansea and Plymouth. A rider came in yesterday and said that Governor Leverett was warned by Benjamin Church that they might start a war," Tom said in a worried tone. He was normally a calm, steady man but you could tell from his tone that he was concerned about the situation spreading to the western part of the colony. Jeremiah leaned his beefy arms on the bar and gave me a hard stare.

"Have your friends the Quaboags or any of the other Nipmucks been giving you any sign that they might join Philip?" he asked with an edge in his voice.

"No, they planted their fields...everything is fine," I told him. "Conkganasco, the Quaboag sachem, and his son Ahanu were at the village yesterday. We talked about our hopes for a good growing season. He brought a big basket filled with smoked fish and a bucket of blueberries as a gift to Josiah and Judah for plowing their fields. I just can't see them joining with any band of Indians to cause trouble. We have been on good terms since we came here. There is nothing wrong. Whatever is happening down in Plymouth doesn't affect us."

"Have you seen any Indians you don't recognize?" Rob Digby asked. He worked for Mr. Pynchon now and then and lived ten miles south of the Springfield. "Philip might be sending them to meet with the tribes. There was a couple here the other day that none of our Indians recognized. Joe Quannoponit said they looked like Wampanoags but he wasn't sure. He didn't like the look of them."

"No, I haven't seen any that looked like they didn't belong but I haven't been to Wekapauge in almost a week and to Quaboag for a couple of weeks. I've been too busy. Any number from other tribes could have been there and I wouldn't know about it. I just can't see it," I said.

"What I don't understand," Nate said, shifting in his seat, "is why the Nipmucks would be angry or upset about something that's happening in another part of the colony. We treat them right, always welcoming them when they come to visit, give them food, and even buy food from them.

"I think Jack's right." Tom said, running his right hand over his face. "I don't think we have anything to be worried about. Besides the occasional drunken Indian, we've never had real trouble with any of them."

Jeremiah came around the bar, settling his bulk into a chair. "I think it's more complicated than that," he said, folding his hands over his big belly. "From what I hear, all the tribes, around Boston anyway, feel that their land has been taken from them and they've been cheated out of it. That, plus all the drunkenness from the rum they buy is not helping. Some of them will trade their clothes, all their pelts, and anything else for a pint of rum. Most of the tribes think we're doing it on purpose so we can take advantage of them. We all know that isn't true, at least not out here because Mr. Pynchon and the selectmen wouldn't allow it. I know some of the traders around Nashaway haven't dealt with them fairly and that upsets them, as it should. No one likes to be taken advantage of or treated poorly. The other thing to keep in mind is that the men from all the tribes travel all over the place so they know what's happening in just about every part of the colony." He crossed his feet and slumping down in the chair. "And I know for a fact that people like John Eliot and those other missionaries have been pushing them to give up their heathen ways and a lot of them have become Christians, but I don't think many of them like it."

"That's probably true," Tom replied, "but Eliot and those others haven't gone any farther than Quaboag and even then didn't spend much time. They were more concerned about the tribes around Boston."

"There have been a few Pocumtucks around here lately but no others, at least that I've seen," Rob mentioned, trying to downplay any suggestion that we could have trouble here. "They seem fine…not angry or anything." Nate looked at me and nodded his head in the direction of the door.

"Should we get going?"

"Yeah, might as well. Let's go see Mr. Pynchon."

"He may ask you to go to Boston, Jack," Tom said as he stood up and stretched. "He's writing another letter to the governor asking for someone to come out and meet with tribes to make sure they don't join Philip. Since Massasoit was sachem of the Wampanoag before he came to live with the Quaboags, was their grand sachem for a time and the fact that his wife was a Quaboag means that they might join Philip the first chance they get. The Quaboag are Philip's cousins. We have to make sure none of the other tribes cause trouble. We're concerned that they might get the Nipmucks riled up. That's what we have to make sure doesn't happen. Anyway, he may want you to go."

"All right, I'll ask him when I see him," I said, not looking forward to a trip to Boston, not with Becky pregnant and the house just finished. I really wanted to be home, but I couldn't refuse him.

"Well, he's over at the meetinghouse, at least he was when I saw him last which was a little while before you got here."

"Might as well get going," I said with a sigh while Nate paid for our drinks. As we walked through the door, I wondered where all this trouble would take us.

Mr. Pynchon told us he was going to write letters to Governor Leverett as well as to the Connecticut Colony governor to express his concern about the possibility of an Indian uprising. He was also sending a letter to the militia commander at Marlboro to get his feelings. Like us, Mr. Pynchon didn't think it could or would happen, but he wanted to let the people in Boston know his thoughts. He said he was concerned, as we all were, although he had a greater reason than we did. He traded with most of the Indians throughout the western Bay Colony, Connecticut Colony, and part of New

York and had a significant financial stake in keeping the relations good.

He said that he planned on Elizur Holyoke's son John to go to Marlboro but he fell and broke his leg so he couldn't ride and that he wanted me to take the letters to the militia commander. I wasn't very happy and for a minute thought about telling him I couldn't but realized, as I was about to open my mouth, that I owed him a great deal and couldn't refuse when my doing this might help to avert or minimize any attacks. Since he needed me, I told him I'd go, even though all I really wanted was to go home to Becky. After he gave me the letters, Nate and I headed back to Quaboag. Becky was not happy when I told her.

"Why you?" she demanded. "Why couldn't he use one of the other men, someone from Springfield? Why does he have to use you all the time?" He really didn't use me that much anymore but I didn't dare say that because the last thing I wanted was for her to get upset.

"He trusts me," I said taking a step closer to her. "I've ridden for him for a few years and he knows I'm reliable, I do what he asks, I do it well and always on time. I'm probably the best rider he has...plus, he likes me," I said a little defensively. "And, he's helped me, helped us, so I couldn't say no if my riding might help prevent an attack somewhere." She just looked at me, torn between wanting me here and knowing how important this might be.

"I'm afraid," she said quietly.

"Afraid? Afraid of what?" I asked, getting next to her and putting my arm around her waist.

"That something bad will happen when you're gone. I don't like you to be away…now that I'm pregnant," she said, looking at me with her soft green eyes.

"There's no need to worry or be afraid," I told her as I took her hands in mine. "Even if I'm gone it won't be for long…I'll be back tomorrow night. Even if something did happen Josiah and Charity are here, and your mother and father, why, everyone is here for you, you know that."

"I know," she said pulling me close to her. "But it's different. I know they'd all help me but I don't want them to…I want you to be here. I know I'm probably acting like the crazy, pregnant wife, but…," she trailed off. I kissed her softly on the forehead.

"You'll never have to worry my love, I promise." She gave me a weak smile as I went out the door to the barn.

I left early the next morning, riding hard and fast. The sky was clear and a soft wind came from the west. It promised to be a beautiful day. I watched the fields and trees, listening for any strange sounds and was on edge the first few miles expecting unknown Indians to come screaming out of the trees or jump out from behind some bushes. I settled down and realized how foolish I was, that while some of the Indians made me uneasy, most were good friends and wouldn't harm us. It didn't take much time to get to Marlborough. When I arrived, it was still almost two hours to noon.

I made my way to the small garrison, asking the first man I saw where I could find the commander. He directed me to a small room on the left just inside the fort. There were two men in the room, a fat man behind a desk, and a brown-haired man of medium height and a wiry build. They stopped talking as I entered.

"Excuse me, I didn't mean to interrupt but I'm looking for the commander."

"And who are you?" harrumphed the fat man behind the desk.

"I'm Jack Parker with letters from Mr. John Pynchon of Springfield."

"I'm the major in charge," he harrumphed again.

"Then these are for you," I said, taking the letters out of my pouch. "Uh, you are William Crandall aren't you?" I asked as I held them out to him.

"Yes, yes, that's me. Hand over the letters then." I gave him the letters, turning to look at the brown-haired man and saw him smiling at me. He had a friendly face and didn't look to be more than 20-years-old.

"I'm Ephraim Curtis," he said, getting out of the chair and extending his hand. "I live at Quinsigamond." He was not a tall man but wasn't short either. He had a slim build with an intelligent face and watchful eyes. I got the impression he was constantly observing everything and didn't miss a thing.

"I'm Jack Parker, but you already knew that. I'm from Brookfield."

"Brookfield? Then you know the Quaboags?"

"I know many of them well. I also know the Wekapauge. I live near them."

"That's where I'm going. Governor Leverett ordered me to visit the Nipmuck villages and see if they're preparing for war. Can you go with me? I know several of the sagamores but not as many regular Nipmucks as you must."

"Well now," I said caught totally by surprise. "I really have to get back to Brookfield. I was in Springfield two days ago and now I'm here and my wife is pregnant and I don't know...where exactly are you going?"

"When I leave here I'm going to Hassanamesit, Packachoag, Chaubunagungamaug, and Quaboag. The governor wants me to talk to them to find out their intentions. I have to report to him as soon as I can. I could use someone like you."

"Crandall," he said abruptly, causing the fat man to look up at him with his tired, hound dog eyes, "those letters that have to go to Pynchon, who will be taking them?"

"Um, the, uh, the rider, um, from Roxbury…I don't remember his name."

"I have letters for Pynchon that are to be taken to him at Springfield," he said by way of explanation. "We can have the rider stop in Brookfield and tell your wife that you'll be with me."

"I don't know…she's expecting me to get back. I told her I would be back today. She didn't want me to come here, nevermind taking time to go visiting Indians. I don't know…this is very sudden."

"You didn't ask me but I'll give you my opinion anyway," wheezed Crandall. "You should go with him. There's too much at stake here. If you know some of these Indians and can help him," he said motioning towards Ephraim, "then you must help. People's lives may be in danger." He sat back in his chair and folded his chubby little hands across his big, round belly.

"How long did you think it will take to visit all of them? Three days? Four?"

"Depending on what we find it might take only two. I don't plan to spend a lot of time at each one. I want to see what they're up to and get on to the next. The governor wants me back in four days at the most."

"In that case I'll go with you. But I have to write a letter to Becky…she's my wife," I said. "When's the rider leaving?" I asked Crandall.

"He can leave whenever I want him to," he said sharply.

"Good. How about now?"

"We have to get going Crandall," Ephraim told the major. "Those letters have to get to Pynchon and his letter has to get to his wife. How about we get this boy moving?"

"He's at the tavern across the road…," he said shifting his bulk around in the chair.

"Do you expect me to go get him?" Ephraim asked sharply; his voice rising. "He's your rider. You go get him." The fat man heaved himself out of his chair after a moment's effort and lurched forward as if having trouble balancing his weight. He regained his step and waddled off to the tavern.

"Now, let's talk while he's gone," Ephraim said sitting on the edge of the desk. "What do you know about the Indians?" He slid off the desk and sat in the chair. "They are going to attack. I am positive about it. Everything I have seen and heard leads me to believe it. What I am really doing is trying to find out where and when they might attack. The Governor wants to be as prepared as possible."

"I know the Quaboags better than any other tribe," I told him. "I can't say anything about the other Nipmuck but it might be possible that the Quaboags won't attack. While I feel something may not be quite right, I can't put my finger on it. I thought about it on my way here; there were little glances I got from some of the men while a few of the women seemed a bit reserved, which is out of the ordinary for them. Still, I just can't see them attacking, at least not at Brookfield. We've become friends with many of them and always had good relations with them. We've always treated them with respect and honesty. I had better write my letter."

"I'll go see that everything is ready. I want to leave in fifteen minutes or so. We've some ground to cover."

I went around and sat at the desk. I took a sheet of paper and began to think about how best to tell her that I would be with Ephraim. I didn't have much time so I just started.

July 12th

Becky,

I won't be home today. Right after I got here, I met Ephraim Curtis who the governor sent to meet with the Nipmuck tribes. He's to find out their intentions. Because I know many of the Quaboags, he asked that I go with him. If this weren't so important, I'd be on my way home to you now. We're going to Hassanemesit, Packachoag,

Chaubunagungamaug, and Quaboag. We're leaving in a few minutes. I'll be home in two days. Ephraim has to get back to Boston as soon as he can to report to the governor.

Jack

Ephraim and I set out shortly after the rider left for Brookfield and Springfield. Even though Ephraim spoke the Nipmuck language fairly well, he brought a guide who also acted as an interpreter, a tall, lanky Wabaquassett Indian named Black Tom. The name fit him for he wore a tattered black coat and an old floppy, stained hat over his braided hair with a feather hanging down on the left side. Tom wouldn't go further than Marlboro without at least five of us so two other Indians came with us. Three other Indians also joined us; Uncas, the sachem of the Mohegan tribe, and two of his men on their way back to the Connecticut Colony. Uncas had been in Boston meeting with the governor discussing the possibility of attacks. He pledged to not participate in any uprising and told the governor he would do all he could to prevent it from happening. As he told me, if war did start, he would side with the English for we had been very good to him and his people.

"What do you know about all this?" I asked Ephraim. "You've talked to the governor and some of the others in Boston."

"They're very concerned that this will break out into a full-fledged war. So far, it's been only the Wampanoag attacking Swansea, Taunton, Middleborough, and Dartmouth. Those attacks indicate it could be moving this way." As we rode on over the hills and fields, he told me about his buying land from the Nipmucks at Quinsigamond and building his house. He was originally from Sudbury, but decided to try his hand on the frontier. As far as I knew, he was the only person living between Brookfield and Marlborough. He was 33 and had been on his own for 13 years.

I told him about my life; my mother and father passing away when I was young, being taken in by Josiah and Charity, my apprenticeship in Boston, how I developed a friendship with Mr. Pynchon, coming here to Quaboag, building the farm and about Becky and me getting married last December. How wonderful life had been until a few weeks ago when we started hearing about these attacks. I also told him about Becky and the three other women being pregnant and how concerned I was that if something did happen, if the Indians attacked us, they could be hurt. After that, we rode quietly, thinking about our upcoming visits with the Nipmucks. Uncas and his two companions lagged behind us plodding along, looking as if they were asleep.

We went to Hassanamesit and were startled to find no one there, not even any of the women or children. Everything but the frames of the wigwams was gone. We found the same thing at Packachoag.

"I don't understand this," I said, bewildered at this sudden abandonment of a place where Christian Indians lived for years and years.

"They've gone somewhere else. It's not a good sign, Jack. Something's happening and I'm not sure exactly what although I can guess."

"You're not sure? How do you think I feel? If these Indians left, I wonder if my Indians went somewhere too."

"Your Indians? Since when did they get to be your Indians?"

"I mean the Quaboag. I can't believe they'd get involved in something like this."

"One thing that really bothers me is that the Quaboags are cousins of Philip. Did you know that? They'd join up with him pretty quick if you ask me."

"I know…his mother was a Quaboag. Massasoit lived both at the village on the lake and at Asquoach, or Quaboag Old Fort, until he died 10, maybe 12 years ago."

"Is Philip's mother with the Quaboag now?"

"I don't know. I'd have to ask one of the Indians…if we can find them." With that, we fell into a glum silence as we rode on searching for the Nipmuck tribes. For my part, I wondered what kind of trouble the next couple of weeks would bring.

I told him about my recent visits to Wekapauge and Quaboag. When I visited both places, everything seemed normal for the most part. Men were lounging around as usual when they weren't hunting. Women were working in the fields while a few others were doing various chores near their wigwams. Some of the children were fishing while others were playing as they always did. I told him that I was received well and everyone seemed glad to see me. Yet, my senses picked up something, like a very slight breeze of disquiet or anxiety floating through the air. Two of the men shot sharp glances at me, and one of the older women, who'd always been friendly and open with me, was quiet and reserved. I got the sense they didn't want me there, something I'd never felt during any of my many previous visits.

"So what do you think is happening?" he asked.

"I'm not sure," I told him. "Something's changed but I don't know exactly what. Even though everything seemed fine, I get the feeling that my friends aren't telling me everything, even though they'd like to and feel bad about it. It is as if they'd be disloyal to the tribe and their family if they did. Have you ever seen anything like this?"

"No, I haven't but that doesn't mean anything. I think there's plenty to worry about though," he said. "So how well do you know Muttawmp or Conkganasco? Or any of the other Quaboag sachems?"

"Well, on our first day at Quaboag I met Conkganasco, his son Ahanu, and Muttawmp. I have a few very good friends at Wekapauge. I became one of their favorites I guess. Many of them and those from Conkganasco's village on the lake come to visit us often. I helped one of the women when her husband was very sick by killing two raccoons for her. She was very happy and always feeds me whenever I go to visit and sometimes she'll bring us things. She has become familiar with the women in the village.

"My friend William has two cousins, Matchitehew and Wematin, who are brothers. If any trouble started with the Quaboag, it would be Matchitehew who would lead them. He is a mean, angry man always looking for a fight. Some of the younger men and boys look up to him so they'd follow him."

We rode on in silence for a while, each of us carefully considering the consequences of trouble from the Indians. I couldn't think of anything good that might come of it and, judging from the look on Ephraim's face, neither could he.

Chapter 17

Chaubunagungamaug was as empty as all the other villages. It was here that Uncas and his men said goodbye to us and went on their way. They had been very quiet during the trip, talking low amongst themselves every now and then. Uncas broke his silence now, looking at Ephraim and me.

"They are gone to meet somewhere," he said. "They must talk about what is happening and how they'll respond to it. It is not an easy thing to decide because there are many things for them to consider. I've chosen to stay out of the war when it happens but I can't speak for anyone but my people." The matter-of-fact way he said this startled me. He was not questioning whether there would be a war but only when it would begin.

While we looked around the village, Black Tom went west to look for any sign as to where they might have gone. He was back in a short time.

"There's a wide trail, one that many people made, heading west," he said pointing towards a large field.

"All right, let's follow it and see where it goes," Ephraim said, clearly concerned about three whole villages moving so suddenly. We went west for a few miles and came upon an even wider trail. It looked like hundreds of people went this way, dragging their belongings behind them. There was a big swath of flattened grass in a meadow with trampled bushes along the edge. They were heading northwest.

"The only place they could be going is toward Quinebaug," I said.

"There is no other place," Black Tom said, riding along side us.

"Why would they leave like this?" I asked.

"It's simple really. They went to join other Indians. My guess is they are forming a war party. Some have probably gone west to talk to the Pocumtucks and Squakeags, maybe even the Mohawk, trying to get them to fight. This is trouble…no doubt about that. If everything was fine they wouldn't have left their village." We were a mile or more from Quinebaug when Black Tom saw two Indians a hundred yards ahead of us on the road.

"Look!" he shouted. We spurred our horses making for them as fast as we could, Black Tom riding in front with Ephraim and me behind him and the two Marlboro Indians twenty yards behind us. One of the Indians ran into the woods that was choked with heavy brush and disappeared; the other one tripped and fell. Black Tom was on him like a flash. He dragged him up, grabbed him by the arm, and held him. The

Indian struggled for a minute then stood still. Ephraim and I got off our horses and approached him.

"Ask him why he was running away," Ephraim said to Black Tom, who in turn, posed the question to the Indian. The Indian was scared and couldn't talk for a minute. Tom asked the question again, this time shaking him a bit. The Indian stammered again, which was making Tom angry.

"Tell me!" he shouted. The Indian finally found his voice and answered Tom's question.

"He says that they are afraid you've come to harm them. He ran to warn the others."

"Where are they?" Ephraim asked in the Indian's own language, surprising the little man.

"Just ahead, on the island near the swamp," he replied.

"Take him with us," Ephraim told Black Tom. When we had gone a hundred yards, I saw several Indians, all with guns, by the side of the path.

"Tom," Ephraim said, "take him and go meet with them. Find the sachems and tell them I come with a message from the governor and have no intention of harming them in any way."

I slid off Bubs and rubbed my neck, which was sore and stiff. The Marlboro Indians sat glumly on their horses looking like they wanted to be anywhere but here. We stood there for 20 minutes waiting for Black Tom to return. He came back walking fast. As he got close, Ephraim stepped forward.

"So, what did they say?"

"They don't believe it. They think you've come to tell them bad things, to hurt them in some way."

"Let's just go down there," I said with a mix of frustration and anger. I was tired of all this and wanted to find out what happened.

As we went down the path, several Indians stood blocking it, each of them holding a new gun. When we were about 50 feet away from them, they cocked the guns, aiming them at us. I realized that there was no breeze and it was very quiet; the sound of the guns cocking was loud. The five of us stopped, the reins in our hands, looking at the Indians. I had never stared down a gun barrel or had one pointed at me before; it was a particularly unsettling experience. You could see the anger in their faces and in how they stood, leaning forward as if to hit us. Black Tom stepped slowly back towards us while keeping his eyes on the group. From behind them came a shout from another Indian, older than the rest, running towards us. He yelled at them and they lowered their guns. He stood next to them and said something in a low voice that we couldn't hear. They turned and followed him down towards the river. Ephraim and I looked at each other, shrugged our shoulders, and followed them. Black Tom wasn't comfortable with the situation.

"This is too dangerous...they'll kill us. We should go back. Nothing good can come of this."

"I'm not sure we should go down there," I volunteered, not wanting to be captured by a band of angry, murderous Indians. "Maybe we should go back and try again in a day or two." Ephraim shot a hard look, first at Black Tom, and then at me.

"No, we're not going back," he said with determination. "We're here and I mean to meet with them just like the governor ordered me to. You can stay here if you want but I wouldn't recommend it. If we separate, we'll be easier to capture. If we turn and run, they'll probably kill us." With that, he started walking to the river. Not knowing what else to do and not wanting to stay there by myself, I followed him. Black Tom was a little hesitant but he fell in behind me. It did not get any better when we reached the river.

There was an island about four acres total in size, longer than it was wide, on the far side of the river. The river narrowed as it bent around the island and there were a swampy, marshy area in front and to both sides of the island. Most of the island was open with scattered blueberry bushes, a few scraggly pine trees that enclosed a small hill with grasses and cattails on either side of the path leading to the water. We stopped a hundred feet from the edge of the river. The Indians began to hoot and yell at us; several could speak English, calling for us to come over.

When we halted at the edge of the swamp, a huge cloud of small, black flies descended on us, biting our hands and faces, getting into our eyes and mouths, flying up our noses, and covering the horses' necks and heads. The humidity, which had been bad for the last couple of days, had gotten even worse in the last few hours. Between the sweat running down my head, arms, back and legs and being covered with biting bugs, it was agonizing.

Ephraim looked at the group of 50 warriors assembled on the island. They began screaming and yelling again, even louder than before. Ephraim tried shouting them down but couldn't. After a few minutes, they quieted down. Two of the sachems, Muttawmp and Sagamore John, came to the water's edge. Ephraim recognized several other Indians and called out to them but none acknowledged him or returned his greeting. Several of them raised their guns at us and, if Muttawmp hadn't stopped them, would have fired. After a short, heated discussion he had with several of the warriors, they lowered their guns.

"English, come and see us! Come to the island so we can meet," a tall Indian standing near the water yelled. This caused laughter and general howling.

"What do you want? Why did you come here?" asked Sagamore John.

Ephraim looked at them for a long minute. "I come from the Governor with a message for all Nipmucks." He got no response to this; they just stood there giving us a hard stare. "Sachems! I want to talk to you…to meet. Our governor has sent me all the way from Boston to speak with you. Cross the river so we can talk," Ephraim yelled in order to make himself heard as they began making noise again. One of the Indians translated this for the others. Many of them stopped yelling and stepped forward as if to rush us. I looked behind and saw that Black Tom didn't follow us. "Sachems, come to this side so we can talk. I will give you the message then," Ephraim yelled.

"Put down your guns and cross the river!" Muttawmp yelled. "If you want to meet with us, you must come here! Put down your guns and cross!" He stepped forward, gesturing with his right hand in a slashing motion, "No, we will not come over there. Cross the river and we will talk here."

"There's no way we're crossing this river," Ephraim said to me in a low voice. "It's the only thing that's keeping us safe." He turned and yelled back at them. "No, we won't come across or put down our guns. If the sachems come over here we will put our guns down." There was some discussion about this although several shook their heads and walked away, talking loudly at those who were considering it.

We sat there for a few minutes, us looking at them and them looking at us.

"What do we do now?" I asked.

"Let's try it one more time. If they refuse I'll see if they'll send most of their men here while I go over to talk to them," he said, looking straight ahead.

"Wait a minute! You'll ask them to come over here so you can go there? That will leave me with a hundred mad Indians who are just waiting to take our scalps. I am not staying here. You go, I go."

"Everything will be fine. I know it will."

"I hope to hell you're right. I want to see my child born," I told him. "I don't know why I agreed to come here with you," I muttered to myself.

"If we come over there will you send your men over here?" Ephraim hollered at Sagamore John.

"No, everyone stays here. You must come here. Put down your guns."

He turned to look at me; I could see the worry in his eyes. He turned around to face Black Tom who was still behind us. "We have to go over," he said as he began walking his horse towards the river before climbing on. I didn't reply but kicked Bubs gently on the flank and followed Ephraim. I looked behind and saw Black Tom sitting on his horse watching us. When we got to the edge of the river, Ephraim stopped and, looking across at the island, told them what would happen if we were hurt in any way.

"The governor knows we are here. If we do not go back today he will send many soldiers and you will not be safe. Do not harm us, or you and your people will be harmed. Guarantee that we will be safe and we will cross." Muttawmp looked at some of the others and they talked for a moment.

"You will be safe," he said, turning and walking towards the small hill.

"I don't want to do this but we have to," Ephraim said, turning to us. "Come on." I stayed there for a minute, not sure that I wanted to be on an island with all those warriors threatening me and us being outnumbered many times over. I looked back at Black Tom.

"I don't like this," he said a wary look in his eye. "I don't like this at all."

"I don't either," I replied, hoping Ephraim would change his mind.

"Our only chance is to go to them and deliver our message. Let's go," he said as he entered the swamp. I took a deep breath, let it out, and followed him into the muddy water. The river wasn't deep. Once we got through the marshy area, the bottom was rock and gravel so our horses made it easily. The water came up a little more than halfway up their legs. I rode into a pocket that was several feet deeper but Bubs swam easily and made it to the gravel without any problem. As we made it to the island, half the Indians rushed to the water and grabbed our horses who jerked up in fright.

"Let go of my horse! Let go! Let go!" I yelled as loudly as I could, kicking their hands away with my boots. Sagamore John yelled something and to my surprise, they stepped back and stood staring at me with fiery anger in their eyes. One still stood close to me on the left; I could see the muscles in his jaw working as his hateful look bored into me. He said something under his breath that, even though I didn't understand it, I knew was a threat. He made a grab for the halter and without thinking, I lifted my leg, planting my boot on his shoulder and pushed. It caught him by surprise; he fell hard, landing on his rear. Some of the Indians laughed at this while others advanced on me. Sagamore John yelled once more and they fell back again. Ephraim looked at me and moved his head from side to side.

"Jack, don't do anything like that again or they'll come for us," he said sharply.

"I didn't mean to…I didn't think. I just did it." He didn't respond but got off his horse and stood in front of the sachem.

"Jack Parker," Muttawmp said looking hard at me. "You visited us many times as a friend. What do you have to do with this? Why are you here with him?" he asked, motioning with his head at Ephraim.

"We met in Marlboro and he asked that I go with him because I know some of you."

"Your knowing us will not help you today or any other day. You are not our friend anymore," he said, dismissing my years of friendship with a wave of his hand. Even though I did not know Muttawmp well, his statement felt like a slap in the face. I was too stunned to respond.

"Why he's with me doesn't matter. Let us talk," Ephraim said. Muttawmp stared at me for a minute then indicated with a wave of his hand that we should sit on the rocks at the base of the hill.

"What does your governor want with us?" Muttawmp spat out.

"He wants you to remain neutral in any fighting that may happen. He wants you not to fight. Your tribe pledged not to go against the English laws when you asked for protection years ago."

I turned to look back across the river. Black Tom was still on the opposite shore looking like he was about to turn and gallop away. After a long minute during which Ephraim, all the warriors and me stood looking at him, he finally began to cross. As he entered the water, all the Indians let out another horrendous scream that was deafening. When they quieted,

Black Tom was next to me. Muttawmp came toward us, stopping in front of Ephraim's horse.

"Get off your horses…now," he said in a commanding tone. "Put down your guns."

I got off Bubs slowly, followed by Ephraim and Black Tom. I held the reins in my left hand, my gun in my right. We held our guns tightly, not wanting to give them up, not that it mattered much at that point; we put them on the ground. The three of us stood facing the warriors, all of whom were wearing loincloths with various decorations of colored porcupine quills or beaded deerskin headbands or other like things on their body. All at once, they began shouting.

"I come with a message from the Governor," Ephraim said loudly so everyone could hear him. "I come from the Governor," he repeated. At this, they quieted and began to listen. "The governor sent me to you with a message. He wants your promise that you will not fight against us. We mean you no harm and are concerned about the attacks in Swansea. We will not harm you or make trouble with you. We have always been friendly with you and want to keep that friendship. We want your assurance that you will be loyal to us and not join Philip's warriors." At this, there were various mutterings, a few beginning to object but were silenced by Sagamore John.

"Enough! We will hear what he has to say. Let him speak."

"Will you give us your word that you will not attack us or harm us in any way?" Ephraim asked, looking directly at Muttawmp and Sagamore John. They didn't respond but looked at each other briefly, then around at the warriors assembled beside them.

"We do not believe you," Muttawmp said, giving Ephraim a hard look. "One of our men was killed by the English two days ago at the Merrimac. He did nothing against them so we do not find your words truthful. Your governor may want us to be peaceful and not harm you but that is not how we've been treated." Sagamore John sat forward, placing his elbows on his knees.

"I do not believe you either. Your governor must send us a gift to prove his words."

"What type of gift do you want?" Ephraim asked cautiously. The two sachems looked at each other and Muttawmp spoke.

"Three bushels of gun powder. If he sends that to us, we will believe him." Ephraim pondered this tracing his finger in the dirt at his feet.

"Why gun powder? Why not something else?" I asked, looking at Muttawmp then Sagamore John.

"Because that is what we need!" Muttawmp answered shortly. "The English, you and the others, want to destroy us, the Nipmucks, and all the other tribes. We cannot fight you without gun powder!" Ephraim straightened up, looking around at all the warriors.

"We have no intention to harm you or any of the other tribes. We do not seek war with you. There are some bad English just as there are bad Nipmucks. We cannot be held accountable for the actions of those few, anymore than we can hold you for what some of your men do. We want your promise that you will not fight any English and will not attack any of our villages. I give you the word of the governor and the great council that we will not harm you. Will you give us your promise?" At this, they grew quiet, many of them sitting on the ground forming a circle around us. The others stood at the back of the group intently watching us.

"There are others," Muttawmp began, "that want to fight the English," he said, obviously referring to King Philip's attacks on Swansea, Taunton, and Rehoboth. "We do not plan to fight but are afraid that the English will want to fight us. We've done nothing wrong. We've allowed you to use our land, to buy much of it from us, we learned your language, and some of us live in Christian praying towns. We've done all that the English have asked of us."

"Yes, you have," Ephraim replied softly. "We can ask no more of you. I will tell the governor of your promise."

"That's good," Sagamore John replied. "Stay and have food with us. We killed several deer this morning and the fishing has been good."

"Stay with us for tonight…we'll talk more about this in the morning," Muttawmp offered. The change in tone and demeanor was surprising at least to me, although Ephraim and Black Tom seemed to take it in stride.

"Thank you for your offer but we must go," Ephraim replied. "I need to get back to Boston to tell the governor of our talk. And he," he said, pointing his thumb at me, "was just married and his wife is pregnant so he must get home. She told him he must come home tonight." Those that understood English laughed at this, explaining it to those who didn't which brought more laughter. I felt the blush run up my face and shot Ephraim a look. He was smiling too while I found myself chuckling. At that, we rose and thanking them again, picked up our guns, mounted our horses, crossed the river and headed home.

It was mid-afternoon when we parted ways. Ephraim, Black Tom, and the two other Indians left for Boston through Marlboro. I headed home to Brookfield riding through the fields and open woods. The last couple of days were hot and very humid, causing you to sweat even when you weren't moving. As Bubs walked on, the breeze felt good. After a couple of miles, I came up a large hill and looking far to the west, I saw white clouds towering into the sky. There were others nearer; dark, heavy, threatening clouds. I sat looking at them for a minute; a big thunderstorm was building. I was tired and wanted to get home. I dug my heels into Bubs' flanks and galloped hard all the way home. As I rode on, I hoped this thunderstorm was the only storm coming our way, but deep inside I knew differently.

Chapter 18

I was surprised when, four days after I left him at Quinebaug, Ephraim rode into the village. It was early afternoon when he stopped at the tavern. Ed Ayres came to our house to tell us he had arrived and wanted to see me. I couldn't imagine why he was here so soon after going to Boston.

A different Indian was with Ephraim who was well proportioned, clean, and had a pleasant face. His clothes weren't ragged and fit well. He was the opposite of Black Tom. When Becky and I walked in, Ephraim was standing at the bar with a mug of cider in his hand. I noticed at once that he looked tired.

"What are you doing here? I thought you went to Boston just two days ago?" I asked.

"I did. When the governor heard my report, he told me to get back out here to give the Nipmucks a letter from him and to ask some of the sachems to go to Boston to meet with him. I left within two hours of my getting there. One of my tasks was to give letters from Major Pynchon to Constable Ayres, which I just did. Now I need to go to the Indians. Do you know if they are still at Quinebaug? William here," he said indicating his guide, "heard that they moved to Menameset."

"I hadn't heard anything about them moving. As far as I know they're still at Quinebaug."

"All right then; that's where we'll go. That one who told you," he said to William, "might have been trying to fool you." He looked from me to Becky. "Is this your lovely wife you spoke about so much?"

"Oh, I'm sorry. Yes, this is Becky. Becky, this is Ephraim Curtis."

"It's very nice to meet you Becky. Your husband is a good man."

"Yes," she said, smiling at me, "yes he is. He's told me about you. You seem to know all the Indians around here."

"I do know many of them, but not all. Jack, I need you to go with me and we need to leave now. Can you be ready in a few minutes?" Becky and I looked at each other. I was behind in my work because I spent two days with him and hadn't made much of a dent in it.

"Uh…I don't know. I have a lot to do; I'm behind from our last visit." Becky put her hand on my arm.

"The governor and Council need to know what's going on. Go with Ephraim. It's not as if you're going to be gone for a day or two. It's just this afternoon. The work can wait until tomorrow," she said.

"Then I guess I can leave now," I told Ephraim. "Let

me get Bubs saddled."

"I'll be waiting out front for you." With that, Becky and I made for home. She saddled Bubs while I grabbed my gun and powder.

"We should be back after dark," I told her as I went out the door. I kissed her goodbye and rode to the tavern.

When I got there, Ephraim and William were sitting on their horses waiting for me. Several of the men and a few of the women were standing near the tavern door.

Ephraim spun his horse around so he was facing the group. "I am here," Ephraim began, looking around, "because the Governor wants the Nipmucks' pledge to be neutral. With all the Wampanoag trouble down in Swansea, Taunton, and Rehoboth, he wants to be certain there is no threat here. I'm going to Quinebaug to talk to them. I've asked Jack to go with me as he did a few days ago. The governor wants me to get back to Boston as soon as I can to let him know the Indians' response."

"We should go," William said in perfect English, looking at the angle of the sun. He must have been raised at Natick, the largest of the Indian praying towns, to be able to speak so well. Ephraim nodded.

"Some Nipmucks attacked Mendon just two days ago," he continued, his horse moving back and forth as if itching to be on the way. "We think it was Matoonas and Sagamore John from Packachoag. They killed several settlers and their animals and burned the houses. The governor knows of the connection between the Quaboags and Wampanoags. The Quaboags look to the Wampanoags for protection, even though they submitted themselves to our government years ago. The governor's concern is that they will join together and bring these attacks here."

"Now, look, we know these Indians real well," John Ayres, Sr. said, "and they wouldn't hurt us. We have respect for each other and in some cases," he looked at me, "have become good friends with them. Conkganasco, the sachem at Quaboag, is known to us. He and some of his family visit us every week or so and we visit him. Sometimes he'll bring his wife, sons, and daughters too. We've known him and the others for ten years. They'd never hurt us. I consider him a thoughtful, even-minded man who wouldn't take part in anything like what you're suggesting."

"John's right," Will declared. "I can't see any of these men fighting against us. With the ten good years we've had here, I just can't see it. Why would they?" he asked.

"Because all of the tribes are getting angry and are attacking different places," Ephraim replied quickly with a tone of anger in his voice. "Just because you've had good relations with them doesn't mean you're safe from harm," he said looking directly at John and Will. "The trouble started at

Swansea, then Mendon and now it seems to be moving in this direction. Think about it; if the Nipmucks ever went to war, Brookfield would be their first target."

"I just don't see it," John replied sharply, shaking his head.

"We can't stay any longer," William told us. "We must go." The three of us turned our horses and started down the road. We'd gone a mile or so when I slowed Bubs down to a walk and turned to Ephraim.

"So what does everyone in Boston think about what's happening? I take it they're worried since Mendon was attacked."

"They're getting more worried by the day. The governor and Council are convinced they'll attack somewhere else. At first it seemed that all the attacks were down in the Plymouth Colony but since they destroyed Mendon, they could attack anywhere next. No one here seems to take the threat you people face seriously. There are a lot of angry Indians ten miles from here and if they are going to attack anyplace, it would be here. Brookfield is the closest settlement. You know that. They wouldn't attack Springfield…it's too big and well defended. Maybe Northampton, though I doubt it. I just can't understand why no one here thinks the Nipmucks might attack."

"You have to understand," I told them, "we've been here ten years without any trouble at all. The people here can't imagine the Indians attacking us anymore than we'd attack them. I know a few men, myself included, who see things differently. But I'm still not convinced that Conkganasco or the others would bring war against us." William, riding on the other side of Ephraim, turned and looked at us.

"They will attack here sometime, maybe not now, but in the fall or next spring. There will be a war." We stopped talking, kicked our horses, and broke into a gallop.

Chapter 19

It took us almost two hours to get to the Indian camp. Ephraim sent William ahead to tell them we were coming. He came back a short time later saying that they yelled and made noise when they heard what he had to say. It made me think of the greeting we got on our earlier visit a few days ago. When we got to the river, we called for the sachems to come over to us. As they did before, they said that if we had business with them we must come across to them. After asking them again and getting the same response, we crossed the river. Ephraim asked to see Muttawmp as he spoke to the other sachems on our first visit. They told us that he wasn't there but might be back tomorrow. If we had to talk to him then we should come back then.

We told them we must speak to all the sachems that were there. Ephraim pointed out those he knew - Keehood of the Wabaquasett; Willymachen, also known as Black James, of the Chabanakongkomun; John Apeckgonas of the Packachoag as well as Samuel, sachem of the Washakim tribe. They came down to meet with us. They treated us well and unlike the first meeting, without any anger. Ephraim read the governor's letter and they accepted all that it said very well. They promised that Keehood and at least one or more other sachems would go to Boston in four or five days to speak with the governor. They asked many questions which we answered as best we could. We told them that if any of them were not satisfied with our answers then they should go to meet with the governor who would treat them kindly, feed them well, and tell them all that they wanted to know.

We asked them why they were so abusive to us last time. Keehood and John Apeckgonas told us that Black James, who was sitting right there with us, told them that the English would kill all of them because they were not Praying Indians. Ephraim asked Black James if this was true. Knowing that he could not lie, he said that it was. In his own defense, he said that he heard this several times from other Indians. I scolded him because he was the constable of the Praying Town at Chabanakongkomun and should know better than to say such things in times like these. He looked at me, agreed that he was wrong in saying it, and added that he would consider things more carefully in the future. We explained to the entire group that this was definitely not true and that none of us would harm any of them that were not Praying Indians. At that point, we left them and headed back to Brookfield.

We'd been riding for a few minutes when William said that one of the Indians told him as we were about to leave that another Indian there had been with Philip and came to them three days ago. He came with English goods, which all of them knew he'd gotten from robbing some settlers. We asked him why he didn't tell us this sooner. He was concerned, he told us, that if he'd let us know, there would be a fight that we would lose because we were outnumbered. We understood and Ephraim said he would include it in his report to the governor and Council.

It was about an hour before sunset when we got back. I invited both of them to stay with us for the night. Ephraim was hesitant because he wanted to start back to Boston after they had gotten something to eat. I told them that even though there was a last quarter moon, they really wouldn't make such good time at night and were better off staying with us, having a good meal and a few hours sleep. They both looked tired and hungry and without too much more persuasion on my part, decided to stay. Ephraim and William left very early the next morning, their stomachs full of Becky's corn porridge and nut bread. Before they left, I told Ephraim that I hoped we would see each other again, although given the troubles that were going on it didn't seem likely. Ephraim said hoped to see the governor by mid-afternoon before writing his report.

Life went on as usual for the next week, giving me a chance to catch up on all that I hadn't done, although the weather didn't cooperate; it was humid and rainy.

On Sunday, August 1st, everyone was in the meetinghouse for the Sabbath meeting. The morning service had just ended and many of us were about to go home for dinner when we heard the loud sound of hooves pounding towards the village. We ran outside to see how many men there would be to make such a noise. As we stood there, people didn't speak but waited expectantly, realizing that it must be a large number of horses because after a minute, they still hadn't arrived and the noise got louder as they got closer. As we looked down the road toward Prichard's, a line of men on horses came around the corner and stopped in front of the tavern, dust rising around them. There were 20 of them, each looking tired and worn. After they dismounted, Ephraim and two militia commanders walked toward us. One was tall and slim, his face brown and creased from wrinkles. The other man was shorter and barrel-chested with a firm look and a handsome chiseled face. The fact that Ephraim was back so soon was not a good sign.

"Who are the selectmen?" the older one asked. John Ayres, Sr., Will Prichard, and Rich Coy, Sr. walked over and stood in front of them.

"We're the selectmen," John said. "Who are you?" he asked rather brusquely, obviously not pleased with the arrival of so many militia.

"I'm Captain Edward Hutchinson, and this," the older man said, motioning to the other, "is Captain Thomas Wheeler. The governor ordered us here to meet with the Indians because there have been reports of 100 Narragansett moving into the Nipmuck territory. We came to ask them why they have come here and their intentions. We are also here to demand from the Nipmucks an explanation as to why they haven't sent their sachems to Boston as they promised last week. There have also been reports that some of the Indians who attacked and killed settlers with Philip are the Narragansett, including Matoonas, who planned and executed the attack on Mendon." No one spoke for a minute. All of us stood looking at them trying to understand that some of Philip's men could be consorting with the Nipmucks and the Quaboag in particular. To everyone but Ephraim, me and maybe a few others, it didn't seem possible. I could tell from the look on their faces. After what I'd seen at Quinebaug, I didn't doubt what Hutchinson was saying.

"I can't believe it," Rich said, advancing towards the militiamen. "I said it many times and will say it again that we've known these Indians for ten years and never had a problem with them. Now you're telling us that in just the past few days they've aligned themselves with Philip and a group of Narragansett? I just don't believe it."

"It's not a group, but over 100 Narragansett who've come to do us harm," Captain Wheeler explained. "This is serious and should not be taken lightly regardless of your past experience with them. The governor and Great Council would not have sent us unless they believed there was a significant threat to you." Ephraim and I looked at each other knowing that the threat was real.

"Why don't we go to the tavern where we can discuss this better?" Will suggested as he started moving people in that direction.

"Yes, yes, that's all well and good but we can't wait," Hutchinson replied. "We must send men to the Indian encampment with the message that we have not come to harm them but to make a treaty of peace and that we want to meet with them tomorrow. We've directed Ephraim, since he's been involved with them already, as well as two of our guides to go to them. We think it would be a good idea for one or two of you who they know to go with them as a sign of our peaceful intentions."

"Jack, will you go with me again?" Ephraim asked. "I think it would be good since we've been to them the last two times."

"I'll go but they are not at Quinebaug," I told him. "I learned yesterday from my Wekapauge friend Oota that most of them have moved to the villages at Menamesset. I'm not sure how many."

"Ephraim, you need to go," Captain Hutchinson commanded. "Give them the message and come back as soon as you can. Remember, we need to meet with them tomorrow."

"I understand," Ephraim responded. He turned to me. "You ready to go?"

Before I could respond, Becky put her hand on my arm. "Jack, please...don't go. For me...please."

"It will be all right. There's nothing to be worried about," I said with a false confidence, knowing that there might be plenty of worry ahead. "We'll be back around dark."

Two of the guides were Sampson Petuhanit and his brother Joseph, both Indians from Hassanamesit. Their father, Robin, was a faithful Christian Indian who was the ruler at Hassanamesit. The brothers were both teachers, Sampson at Wabaquesett and Joseph at Chaubunagungamaug. They were well educated by John Eliot, a missionary who had established Praying Indian towns throughout the Colony. They mounted their horses. "We know where the village is," Sampson told the captains. "Joseph has been there before." The third guide who stayed with the soldiers, George Memecho, a Christian Indian from Natick, indicated that he'd been there too. Josiah and I ran to the house; he got Bubs saddled while I grabbed my gun, ball and powder. Leaving like this was becoming too familiar for me. By the time I got back into the yard, he had Bubs ready and waiting for me. Just as I was about to mount, I saw Becky coming towards me tears in eyes.

"Please don't go. I'm afraid for you…something might happen. I don't want you to get hurt…or worse. Please stay here with me."

"It will be all right," I told her, wiping the tears off her face with my hand. "We're just going to talk to them. It's no different than before."

"Yes it is!" she said angrily. "The soldiers show that this is dangerous Jack. They wouldn't be here if it wasn't. Other villages were attacked and some of those Indians are here now. The governor would not have sent the soldiers out if he didn't have a good reason. You don't have to go."

"You're my wife and I love you," I told her. "I waited for you all those years and miss you every time I'm away from you. Do you really think I'd put myself in danger? I have a very strong urge to survive and come back to you. Now, I have to go." I gave her a quick hug; she gave me only a half hug, her body tense. I kissed her on the forehead and climbed on Bubs, putting my gun across my lap and rode to the tavern. Ephraim, Sampson, and Joseph were waiting for me. We turned our horses and rode down the road on our way to the Indian village.

When we came to Menamesset, we encountered about 150 Indians, yelling and hollering at the top of their voices while waving their guns and war clubs. As 20 of them came rushing at us we stood our ground, moving our horses together so we were side by side. The Indians came to a sudden stop 10 yards away. The tension was building as they continued to yell, making a tremendous noise for several minutes. The five of us sat searching their faces to see if we knew any of them. While I recognized quite a few from the Quaboag, some Wabaquasett and Packachoag, but there were many we didn't know.

"Most of them are Narragansett. I think the ones on the far right are Wampanoags," Sampson said, glancing at Ephraim and me.

"I think you're right," Ephraim replied, never taking his eyes off them. "We'd better be careful. It looks like Hutchinson's report was right. Joseph, go tell them that we mean no harm, we come in peace, and want to meet with their sachems." Joseph rode towards the group blocking our path and they moved apart slowly, menacing him with angry taunts and hateful stares as he came to them. He rode through taking his time, searching for any danger or ambush. You could feel the tension, as he got closer to the main group, stopping in front of them. Several of the Indians began shaking their heads in disagreement as he began to speak while others were gesturing to a group behind them. Joseph said something to the three closest to him. They turned and walked away, motioning for him to stay where he was. They went to the back of the group and started talking to several Indians - two of whom I recognized.

"There's Muttawmp on the left," I said.

"And the tall one behind him is Keehood," added Sampson.

One of the Indians standing with the sachems walked to Joseph and they spoke for a minute going back and forth. Joseph turned and rode toward us as the Indian walked back to his group.

"They'll send someone to talk to us but we have to wait so they can decide who it will be," Joseph said as he came up to us.

"This could take a while," Sampson said with an air of frustration. "They could argue amongst themselves for an hour."

"We'll give them a few minutes and see what happens," Ephraim said. We didn't have to wait long which surprised us. The Indian who met with Joseph came to us and announced that Keehood and Muttawmp would meet with us now. We got off our horses and led them to where a small group had gathered. As we got closer, both sachems and a few others left the group to meet us halfway.

"We have come," Ephraim began, "with a message from our Great Sachem the Governor. He sends us in peace and means you no harm. He has sent other men who are now at Brookfield who want to meet with you. They want to talk about a treaty of peace between your people and us. We ask you to meet them tomorrow. The two men, Captain Hutchinson and Captain Wheeler, asked us to wait for your answer. Will you meet with them tomorrow?" They walked a few paces away, turning from us so we couldn't hear what they were saying. Both men gestured in our direction several times, as they began arguing over how to answer Ephraim's question. Finally, Keehood came to us and told us that they would give us an answer today but that he and Muttawmp couldn't answer for all the sachems so they needed to talk amongst themselves. We were forced to wait.

After more than an hour Keehood returned and told us that they agreed to send some of the sachems to meet with us early the next morning at a wide, flat area half a mile from the grist mill. He turned and walked away, not giving us the chance to ask why he and some of the others had not gone to Boston as they said they would. We rode home quickly, anxious to get their answer to the captains.

We walked into the tavern and found many people waiting for us including Hutchinson and Wheeler, the three selectmen, most of the soldiers, Josiah and Charity, Tom and Elizabeth Morgan, Richard Coy, Jr. and his wife Sarah, her parents Tom and Jane Kent, Susannah Ayres and all of her children and quite a few of the other villagers. All in all, there were probably 50 people crowded into the room. They all turned as we entered and I remember standing there looking at everyone, feeling tired and drained, wishing we had good news, but knowing it was not going to be what they wanted to hear.

"What did they say?" Hutchinson asked eagerly.

"They said some of the sachems would meet with us tomorrow but didn't say which ones," Ephraim answered. "We've agreed to meet at a place past the mill early in the morning."

"How did you find them? Were they agreeable?" Wheeler asked. Ephraim looked at me as I began to answer.

"They didn't receive us well," I began. "There are about 150 men, all armed and defiant. They screamed and yelled, taunting us when we got there; they threatened us with their guns and clubs, pointing and waving at us." I could feel the tension rising, everyone giving me his or her full attention.

"We spoke with Keehood and Muttawmp," Ephraim chimed in. "What other sachems were there?" he asked Joseph and Sampson.

"Samuel from the Wabaquasset and Quacunquasit from Packachoag," responded Sampson.

"Your reports were accurate Captain, many of them are Narragansett. Sampson thinks a few are Wampanoags. We couldn't identify quite a few of the others. My concern is that the Quaboags listened to Philip's messengers." No one spoke for a moment, everyone digesting the news we had given them.

"So what happens now?" Jane Kent asked, breaking the silence.

"We meet with them tomorrow and deliver the message the governor charged us with delivering," Hutchinson said in a tone showing that he didn't want to be questioned by a woman. Jane wasn't easily intimidated and went back at him.

"So you tell them what you're supposed to tell them. What then?"

"I'm sure they'll pledge their fidelity and allegiance to us. We'll then return to Boston to report to the governor," Wheeler cut in, obviously trying to prevent Hutchinson from causing any hard feelings with Jane or the rest of us. I saw many of the others in the room looking at Ephraim and me for confirmation of Wheeler's belief. I caught Josiah giving me a questioning look knowing that things would not be that simple.

"It may be a little more involved than that," Ephraim told Wheeler. "They may make demands of us for gifts of powder or guns. At least that's my guess anyway." John Ayres, Sr. made his way to the front of the crowd. "I suggest that everyone go home now. Those of us that will be going, meet here early tomorrow morning." With that, the meeting broke up, people filing out talking in small groups when they got outside. As I walked home, I couldn't shake the feeling that there was going to be trouble tomorrow. Little did we know that it would be the last night some of us would sleep in our beds, with our families, in our homes.

Chapter 20

It took us an hour to get to the meeting place. We expected the Indians to be there but they weren't. A couple of times, when we met with them before, they sent a messenger ahead but not this time. There was no sign of Muttawmp, Keehood, or any others. After waiting 20 minutes or so, some of the soldiers started getting uneasy since Sergeant Ayres and Corporal Coy assured us that the Indians would be waiting for us, as they were as anxious to meet with us as we were to meet with them. Several of Captain Wheeler's men were looking at each other and shaking their heads. I could not hear what they were saying but it was clear that they wanted to go back to the village. John, the long-legged soldier from Concord, looked worried.

"I say we go back. It just doesn't feel right. Why take chances with strange Indians coming to join them and the troubles in Mendon and Medfield. I don't see any reason to stay here." I caught Hutchinson and Wheeler glancing at each other as if to ask the other whether they should turn back.

Captain Wheeler adjusted his musket lying across his legs and looked at Hutchinson, Ephraim and me. "What if this is a ruse? What if they never planned on meeting us?" Sergeant Ayres walked over to join the conversation followed by Coy and Prichard.

Richard Coy seemed annoyed at the implication. "Now why would they do that? What purpose would it serve? I can't see them doing such a thing. It just doesn't make sense." Several of the closest soldiers drifted over. One of them, Zechariah Philips from Boston, sat back in his saddle.

"What if they are attacking the village and the meeting was a trick?" he asked. "Could they have deceived us to do something somewhere else?" None of us had ever thought of that and it caused us to consider the Indians might have a malicious motive for this meeting. At this, we all looked around wondering if he was right. Sergeant Ayres and Corporal Coy were shaking their heads once more. By now, all the other soldiers gathered around us listening to what was going on.

Corporal Coy had gotten off his horse by this time, and was moving his right foot back and forth in the grass before looking up at Wheeler. Sergeant Ayres stared ahead and motioned with his arm in the direction of the Indian villages.

"Ephraim, Jack… do you think we should we go back and try to set up another meeting for tomorrow or go ahead to see if we find them?" Captain Hutchinson asked. Ephraim and I looked at each other knowing the Narragansett we saw yesterday had to be aligned with Philip's warriors and could only be here to cause trouble. Ephraim looked again at me and sighed.

"I think we should send a couple of men ahead to see if they are coming," he said. "If they don't see them in a mile or so then we should turn back."

"I agree," I told him. "Sitting here waiting is not good. It doesn't accomplish anything. If we're here to meet with the Indians then let's meet with them," I said as my frustration with the lack of decision beginning to show. "Hell, I'll go try to find them. Who else will go with me?" I asked looking around at the soldiers. "I don't think there will be problems but if there is, why risk more men than we have to?"

"That's not your place to decide," Wheeler said in a firm voice. "Captain Hutchinson and I will determine who goes if we decide to even send someone." Sampson and Joseph had been hanging at the back of the group now came forward.

"I agree with Jack," Sampson said. "Joseph and I will go since they know us. We'll ride up a mile or so to where the road crosses the brook. If we don't see them by then, we'll come back. It won't take us long." Without waiting for a response, they rode off. The rest of us sat and waited, some grumbling about just sitting around. Others were worried about the possibility that the Indians might be doing something behind our backs. For a couple of the men, it was their first trip into the wilderness and the emptiness unnerved them. The fact that there were no other settlements for 25 miles in any direction frightened them. Sampson and Joseph came back with the news that none of the sachems or any of their men was to be found.

The short, fat soldier who blustered last night about how he would deal with all the raids wiped his brow with his hat. "I say that if they want a fight we should find out where they are and attack them. Philip may have hundreds of Indians coming here from all over. We need to attack before they all get here." The heat was affecting him and he sweated heavily, fidgeting as he spoke. Josiah leaned over towards Ephraim and me, rolling his eyes. "There are some people a lot dumber than others and he isn't one of the smart ones."

One of the soldiers, Sydrach Hapgood from Chelmsford, a powerfully built man with a square jaw and chin, shifted in his saddle and shook his head. "As far as we know, they haven't done anything yet. Just because they didn't meet us doesn't mean they're up to no good. That's not to say that they aren't; they might be. It's up to you captains to decide what you think is best for us to do."

Sam Smedly, a soldier from the town of Concord, spoke up. "I think we should wait here for a while longer. If they don't show up, we go back and set up another meeting with them." Last night I spoke to Sam a bit and found him, as I did most of the men, to be friendly and fair-minded. They considered his suggestion for a moment until Sergeant Ayres began to address the captains but spoke to all of us.

"There is no need for us to wait here or go back. Sergeant Prichard, Corporal Coy, and I have told you several times that the Indians, especially those under Conkganasco, wouldn't harm us or you, for that matter, even if some of Philip's men came to them. We don't have to be afraid of them and should go to their village because I'm sure they're on their way and we'll find them. Then we can meet with them and get these issues resolved once and for all."

"John's right," Corporal Coy added. "I'm getting tired of telling you this over and over but we've known these people for years and never had a problem with them. You don't seem to understand that. Conkganasco and his people have become our good friends. We have nothing to fear from them, nothing at all. Sergeant Prichard, don't you agree?"

"I certainly do. Captain Hutchinson, Captain Wheeler, let us move on. We'll never meet with them if we just sit here." Captain Hutchinson looked around at the soldiers who said they wanted to go back.

"Well, what do you men have to say about going forward?" No one answered and most just looked at the ground. Captain Wheeler sat up straight as he turned his horse to face Ephraim, George, and me.

"Well, what do the three of you think we should do?"

We looked at each other for a second as if trying to discover what each of the others was thinking. For myself, I was thinking of the surly, aggressive greeting we got yesterday from the sachems and their men. I was leaning towards going back but realized that we couldn't go on like this for much longer. We had to have a resolution to these issues - not only for the political concerns, but for our everyday safety, security, and peace of mind. I could tell that Sampson and Joseph were for going ahead. After a long moment of consideration, Ephraim spoke up.

"I think we should go find them and meet with them." I looked at Hutchinson and Wheeler.

"I think we should find them too. We can't keep on like this. We have to have a resolution to this." Captain Hutchinson nodded.

"All right, get on your horses. Ephraim, Jack, and George, get out in front." We rode on for several miles, sometimes in little groups or side by side, depending on the width of the road. We crossed a muddy stream that ran between two swampy areas and saw several sets of fresh moccasin prints in soft mud. It showed that a couple of people had come that far, turned around and went back the way they came. Sampson and Joseph waited there while we came up to them. George stayed with them while Ephraim and I rode back to Hutchinson and Wheeler.

"We found some footprints ahead. Looks like a small group came this far and then turned around," Ephraim reported. Both men looked thoughtful for a moment before Captain Hutchinson ordered Ephraim to go back and send Joseph ahead to see if he could find them in the next mile or so. The rest of us made our way to the stream. Joseph rode ahead and we waited for him.

When Joseph came back he told us he'd seen more tracks a few hundred yards ahead and met three Indians that were a half mile up the path. He asked them where the rest of the Indians were and they told him they were up in the area near the big swamp. He asked if they had any idea why the sachems didn't meet us and they said they didn't know. Joseph said he didn't believe them because they looked like they were hiding something and were wary of him.

Ephraim went to Hutchinson and Wheeler to relay Joseph's information. Hutchinson ordered us to proceed to find the Indians and determine why they did not meet us earlier in the day. As we approached the open area near the swamp, we didn't see any Indians. Thinking they might be in the fields beyond the swamp, we continued onward. After two hundred yards, the path narrowed to no more than a few feet wide. On the right side was a steep, rocky hill covered with bushes of various sizes, and on the left was the swamp. Just to the left of the path was an area that was between the solid ground and the swamp. It was a bog and while it wasn't solid ground it wasn't swamp either and would not support the weight of a horse and rider. It was another hot, humid day and the closer we got to the swamp, the worse the mosquitoes got, so each of us was swatting and slapping. We rode on perhaps another 50 yards when all hell broke loose.

I heard several screams and saw 15 or 20 Indians rise out of the swamp and shoot at us. Sergeant Ayres was hit in the chest and fell to the ground moaning. Corporal Coy went up to help him, was shot in the face, and fell over on top of John. The attack had come so suddenly it took us a minute to react. I couldn't believe what was happening.

Captain Wheeler yelled for us to fire and we did as best as we could. Bubs was startled by all the noise and commotion and backed up into Ephraim's horse. I took a bead on the closest Indian, who I didn't recognize, and fired, hitting him in the left arm. For the next few minutes everything seemed to happen slowly with each action and movement burned into my memory; I remember it all as much as I would like to forget it.

Ephraim's horse continued to back up towards the hill and trying to control it, he yelled,

"Look out! There's more coming out of the swamp!" Another group, twice as many as the first, came out from behind fallen trees and bushes. Two of the soldiers fired and missed. I was trying to reload and couldn't get powder in the pan as the yelling and screaming went on all around me.

"Jack! Don't let him get near your horse!" Will Prichard yelled to me. I looked up and saw a tall Indian running at me with his war club raised above his head. As he swung, I shifted in the saddle, lifted my left foot, and kicked him in the side of the face. Dazed, he hesitated a minute before starting to fall and seeing a chance to grab his club, I reached down, almost falling out of the saddle, and pulled it from his hands. He fell backwards with his arms outstretched and hit the ground facedown with a thump. I jumped down and standing over him, hit him in the back of the head as hard as I could; he made no noise as he went limp. Our guide George was pulled off his horse by two Indians and put up a tremendous fight, knocking one down but not able to get away from the other. They hit him in the back with a club and began to drag him away.

Of the soldiers, Zechariah Philips, was killed falling off his horse that reared up when shot by an arrow through the left flank. I don't know how Tim Farlow was killed but Sam Smedly was shot in the throat and tumbled off his horse. Ed Coleborn was dragged off his horse and clubbed by three Indians. Sydrach Hapgood's horse reared and he fell off somehow, landing on his feet ready to defend himself. He killed two Indians before he was shot in the leg and fell onto his back. Another Indian came up and leveling his gun at Sydrach's chest, shot him and then turned toward me.

My gun was empty so I turned it around, grabbing it by the barrel to use as a club. Just as I was bringing it back, I felt a sharp sting in my left side. Looking down I saw my shirt ripped just above my rib cage, a small stream of blood darkening my side. I couldn't worry about it now as the Indian came charging at me. He dropped his gun and grabbed his war club from his belt. He swung viciously, giving a loud grunt as the club whistled through the air missing me by no more than an inch. As he was drawing back for the next blow, I flipped my gun, letting go with my left hand and turning it with my right so the butt of the stock faced him. I grabbed the grip with my left hand and pulling it back as far as I could, slammed it with all my might into his throat. His eyes opened wide in surprise as the club fell from his hands. He fell to his knees gasping for air, his hands clutching his throat.

I felt the sting in my side again and looking down, saw more blood. While the wound was only a few inches long, it felt like it was two feet long. I realized it was not much of a wound, knowing it would be the least of my worries if we didn't get out of here alive. I'd reloaded by now and was looking for the best shot when Captain Hutchinson ordered us to retreat. As we turned our horses around, there were a dozen more Indians standing in our path. They had let us pass on the way in and were now preventing us from going back the way we came. It looked like they had us trapped with no way out.

Captain Wheeler ordered us up the hill and as he was moving to the right, his horse was shot out from under him. The horse fell, landing on top of him, on his right side. He screamed in pain but not from the fall. He'd been shot in the left arm just above the elbow, blood pouring out of the wound. As I moved towards him, I saw Ephraim kicking at an Indian with a black hand painted on his face, the sign of a fearless warrior. I brought my gun up and fired at his head; the Indian went backward in the air and landed with a splash, a bullet hole in his forehead. Wheeler's son was yelling for help, trying to get his father out from under the horse. Several of the enemy saw a chance to kill both of them. Tom, Jr. slipped and fell onto his side as he tried to get his father from under the horse. He rolled onto his other side and fired at an Indian hitting him in the chest. The wounded horse was grunting and whinnying loudly, all the while trying to stand. He raised up just enough for Wheeler to scramble out from under him as we charged up the hill.

"Where's Will?" one of the soldiers yelled as he searched amongst us trying to find him. A couple of Indians let out a yell and we heard a scream and looking down the hill, saw Will in the middle of the brook, being beaten with war clubs. None of our guns was loaded, and as we tried to pour powder and ball down the barrel, an Indian brought his arm up and with terrific force, hit him in the back of the head. We knew he was dead.

Even more Indians were pouring out of the other side of the swamp coming towards us yelling and howling, some stopping to aim their rifles while others swung their war clubs. I know others had bows and arrows because an arrow flew by just inches from my head, sticking into a tree just behind me.

We moved up the hill and quickly took stock of our situation. Richard, John and Will were dead as were several soldiers - Zechariah Philips of Concord, Tim Farlow of Billerica, Ed Coleborn of Chelmsford, Sam Smedly of Concord, Sydrach Hapgood of Sudbury. Others were hurt, some badly, including Captain Hutchinson, Captain Wheeler, his son Tom, Corporal French of Billerica, and John Waldoe of Chelmsford. Although most of the horses were uninjured, three were in great pain, whinnying and grunting, their breath coming hard, their eyes wild with fear, as they tried to make it up the hill. Those of us lucky enough to be on our horses lifted those without onto the back of our saddles and set off at a frenzied gallop.

Sampson was leading us, his brother not far behind him.

"Keep to the fields! Keep to the fields!" Wheeler yelled. "The devils will be hiding in the woods. Stay in the open!" I slammed my heels into Bubs flanks furiously urging him to move as fast as he could; he responded by galloping faster than he ever did, the ground underneath us flying by. My side burned with every breath I took, the searing pain getting worse. I starting feeling woozy and could feel myself lolling in the saddle, my head dropping onto my chest. My sight was going black and I felt like I was going to fall off. I grabbed the reins hard, shaking my head three or four times trying to clear it while breathing hard now, the pain constant. I saw most of the others ahead of me, realizing I was falling behind. I kicked Bubs and started galloping again in agony with each stride he took. After a while, the pain helped clear my head. My thoughts turned toward Brookfield, my wife and baby, and home.

I had a bad feeling that while our battle was going on, other Indians had attacked the village. The thought of them being savagely attacked, and possibly killed, was more than I could bear. A lump rose in my throat as I felt my gorge rise thinking about what might have happened. We could be too late to help; it could all be over by the time we got there. I would make sure that the others and I got back to the village as soon as we could. If the Indians did attack then we could help defend the village if we could get through. I wanted to get back to make sure Becky was all right. The thought of her, my beautiful pregnant wife, and the others being attacked like we'd been made me angry and afraid at the same time. Several of the soldiers began yelling to each other.

"We were pulled away so they could attack the

village," Tom Wheeler Jr. yelled. "That's why they lured us so far away!"

"We don't know that," Captain Hutchinson hollered back at him.

We had been riding for several minutes when we saw a group of the enemy on the top of a nearby hill. They were looking at us, several pointing in the direction of the village. It took only seconds to realize they were trying to cut us off before we could get back to Brookfield. Captain Wheeler ordered everyone to ride away from the Indians, to keep as much distance between us as we could, to give us a greater chance to get back without another fight.

Corporal French was riding in front of me and I saw him leaning over his horse's neck. His right thumb had been shot off and he was also hit in the left shoulder. He was sliding out of the saddle and was about to fall off so I drew Bubs up and jumped down, the pain in my side shooting up my back and neck, doubling me over for a moment, and ran over to grab him as best I could.

"What the hell do you think you're doing?" Wheeler yelled, seeing me stop. He looked pale, his wounded arm dribbling blood onto the horse's side.

"I have to bind his shoulder. He's losing too much blood. If I don't help him he'll die before we get to the village," I yelled back at him. I wrapped French's shoulder with a piece of cloth I ripped from the hem of my shirt and tied it as best I could. I put his hands on the saddle horn and told him to sit up. With a grunting effort, I jumped on Bubs and took the reins of his horse. After a hundred yards or so, he revived and I tossed him the reins. We were the last two in the line and falling farther behind. After another mile, I saw Sampson riding towards me.

"I'll take him," he hollered. "Go ahead…catch up with the others." I didn't wait but dashed forward, pushing Bubs as hard as I dared. Bubs was already blowing hard and I was afraid that if I pushed too much, he'd drop dead and leave me on foot. I caught up with the others farther on, looking for Josiah but didn't see him. I rode up next to a tall, lanky soldier and yelled, asking if he saw the old man with the floppy hat.

"He's up there," he hollered back, pointing to the right front of the line. I saw his back and the hat bouncing up and down. I dug my heels into Bubs' flanks and rode by several soldiers whose horses were fighting for breath and got up near the head of the line and next to him.

"Hey! Josiah!" He didn't hear me so I yelled again. "Josiah!" I hollered as loud as I could. At this, he turned and slowed a bit. We were getting close to the town road and were no more than couple of minutes from the village. "Get Charity and Becky and bring food to the tavern," he bellowed at me.

With that, I rode past him just as the field was

narrowing, the road swallowed up by big trees on either side forming a dark, almost black tunnel. The thought occurred to me that I had no idea what I would find on the other end.

While this was just one ambush, it was part of the beginning of a war. Of that, there was no doubt or argument. War is not glorious or honorable. It is bloody, gritty, painful, and horrible. Anyone who tells you different is either a fool, a liar, or both.

Chapter 21

The Hovey, Trumble, and Travis families lived on the lower part of the road. As we flew past, we yelled that we were ambushed, the Indians were coming, and to grab their children, food, guns, powder, ball, and get to the tavern as fast as possible. Josiah yelled for us to go ahead, that he'd make sure they got there safely.

We came pounding up the hill, turning onto the town road, the horses were strained and breathing so hard they were spraying foam from their mouths, blowing like they were about to drop. The road was only wide enough for two of us to ride together so we were strung out 10 riders long. We came to the place known as the Devil's Elbow, a short section of the road that went up a hill, and turned sharply to the right before dropping down over 30 feet in a 40-foot length. As we were turning the sharp corner, two horses went down hard, sliding into each other before hitting ridges of rock, sticking out of the ground like sharp knives on the downhill side. Both let out loud, piercing, high-pitched screams of pain; we did not have time to stop to shoot them so we rode around them in our desperate dash to the village. Our horses were so winded, we didn't dare stop to pick up the two soldiers who lost their horses for fear ours would drop too; they wouldn't have been able to carry another rider anyway. I thought I heard screams coming from ahead but couldn't be sure because of the noise the horses were making. The soldiers were unhurt and grabbing their guns, ran swiftly behind us. At that moment, with the horrendous noise behind and the possibility of finding the village destroyed, I thought that this is what it must be like riding into hell.

"I'll go to the meetinghouse," Ephraim hollered at me as we came up near Prichard's house. "We'll go to the tavern," shouted Captain Wheeler at the rest of the soldiers. Captain Hutchinson slowed his horse as he came into the open road between Prichard's house and Ayres tavern.

I saw Susannah standing outside the tavern door looking for John, her hand to her face covering her mouth, not wanting to hear what I think she already knew. Elizabeth Prichard came running to her.

"Jack! Where are John and Will? Where are they?" Susannah asked. I didn't have time to get into all the details.

"The Indians ambushed us way out…ten miles from here. They didn't meet us…we thought they attacked here."

"Where are they?" Elizabeth screamed.

"They were killed," I told them. "Richard too…," They clung to each other as they began to cry. John Jr. came out of the tavern and saw his mother crying.

"John, you're father's been killed. The Indians are coming. They're behind us. Get everyone you can into the tavern. Get guns, powder, and shot. Water too," I shouted.

Sampson rode up with Corporal French beside him; Joseph came up behind them. When they stopped, French fell off his horse and landed in a heap. Hutchinson told them to ride around the hill to see if anyone was out in the fields. If they found anyone, they were to bring them in. Without a word, they took off, Joseph going west and Sampson heading north. I rode away to find my wife and aunt.

There was no one outside as I rode up to my house. I jumped off Bubs before he stopped moving and hit the ground running. Kicking open the door, I saw the empty room and began looking for Becky. She didn't answer my calls so I ran outside looking for her, calling her name as I ran to the barn. The barn was as empty as the house. I rushed around to the back of the house but she was not there either. I ran back to poor Bubs, standing there, sweating, foam at his mouth, sides heaving in and out as the air whistled through his dilated nostrils. I scrambled into the saddle, the burning sting of my wound making me grimace in pain, and dashed the short distance to Charity and Josiah's house. My prayer that I would find both of them there was answered as they came hurrying out the door as I charged into the yard.

"We were ambushed! John, Will, and Richard were killed. The Indians are coming. Grab food, water buckets, the rest of the powder and shot, and get to the tavern! Becky, I'll get things from our house. Go with Charity! Hurry! Now! I don't know how much time we have." Charity came running towards me.

"Where's Josiah? Did he...get hurt?" she asked.

"He's getting the Hoveys, Trumbles, and Travises to the tavern."

I barreled back to our house and sliding off Bubs, ran in to get what I could. I stuffed the powder, shot and three loaves of bread down my shirt. A bag of ground corn and another of dried apples sat on the table; I threw it into the bucket I grabbed and bolted out the door. As I got to the tavern, Becky and Charity were just getting there. People were streaming into the tavern in small groups, all moving fast with a shocked look on their faces. Some girls and women were crying; others moved in a stunned silence. We knew we had no time to waste.

We got the wounded men off their horses and into the tavern. Captain Hutchinson was seriously hurt and unable to stand. He insisted that we put him where he could see all that was going on, intending to continue to command us. I saw Captain Wheeler out of the corner of my eye; he moved his head from side to side indicating that Hutchinson was in no shape to command. Wheeler was badly hurt too, his arm bleeding much less but it caused more pain, and it was starting to stiffen up on him. Someone, I'm not sure who, put all the horses in the small stockyard at the right front of the tavern. Three of them were gravely wounded while the rest were so winded they were near collapse.

Unless I moved quickly, my side didn't hurt but now it began to throb while a burning feeling went the length of the angry red slash. I saw Becky and motioned for her to come over to me. She saw me holding my side and the blood on my clothes. Without saying a word, lifted my shirt and looked at it. She left and came back a minute later with a wet cloth and placed it on the wound. I clenched my teeth as the pain shot up my side into my neck. After a minute it subsided. She gave me a worried look and held the cloth out to me.

"Hold this against it...I'll be right back," she told me. I stayed there feeling a bit dizzy but it passed as fast as it came. When she came back, she had something on her fingers and, lifted my shirt up before slathering the smelly, greasy concoction on me.

"There, that should make it feel better," she said. "Are you all right Jack? Do you want to sit down, maybe on the stairs?"

"No, I'll be fine. It hurts but not that bad. Not as bad as the wounds some of the others got." I looked at her and put my right arm around her waist. "Thank you for taking care of me."

There was a moment when all we could think to do was done, all the preparations made. Most everyone brought what they thought would be useful. However, in the confusion, several people brought blankets, even though it was a hot August day. I had a cold, empty feeling, listening for the sounds I knew would come, and we, like prey, were what the hunters were seeking. That thought caused me to break into a cold sweat, and the thought that we could all be dead, that my life, Becky's life and that of our unborn child, could be over before the sun set in a few hours, hit me like a strong slap in the face, shaking me to my very core. Was it possible that I would die here and never again know the sights, sounds, and smells of those things I loved?

We waited five minutes but nothing happened; the Indians didn't appear. With each passing minute the tensions got stronger and the air thrummed with growing anxiety. After 15, 20, and 25 minutes they still didn't appear. Several people began shouting out suggestions as to other things to get - supplies, more food, more buckets of water. Each suggestion melted into the quiet that overcame us as we saw three Indians appear on the road behind the meetinghouse. The number grew steadily, coming like waves onto a beach, 20 more, then another 30, until after a half hour, 150 stood facing the tavern silently watching us. Our fear increased as the number of them grew still greater. We recognized some of them. As I looked out at them, the grass was deep and green, blowing around the attackers in the gentle breeze. The quiet was unnerving and from the big chestnut tree across the road, a bird sang its cheerful spring-like song, so out of place on a hot August day.

The bird's song reminded me of a day in Ipswich when I was 8-years-old. I was walking through the woods one summer afternoon when I came out of the trees into an opening, a circular area maybe 100 feet across. In the middle was a dead apple tree, its branching sticking out in all directions. Sitting at the end of one branch was a songbird preening itself. All of a sudden, out of the woods flew a big hawk and in the space of three wing beats had the bird in its talons. The hawk dropped to the ground, spreading its wings to protect its kill. The songbird flapped its wings feebly two or three times before dying. The hawk turned its piercing look in my direction, grabbed the bird tightly in its claws, and flew off. Looking out at the Indians gathering around us, intent on our destruction, I wondered if I would be that songbird and the enemy the hawk.

We expected them to attack, but they didn't. Men and boys were yelling back and forth trying to get ready for whatever was to come. Women were going from room to room counting all the children.

"Where's little Priscilla?" Mercy Warner asked, looking for Priscilla Hovey. She was a cute but simple-minded little girl who always got extra consideration and attention paid to her. Everyone went out of their way to help her and would always stop what they were doing when she came wanting to chat. Several women began looking in the rooms trying to find her. Sue Ayres came running into the room.

"Oh my God, she's up by the rock!" she yelled, fear filling her voice. There was a large round rock at the top of the hill behind Ayres' barn where the children would go to play. Priscilla was no different, often taking the wooden doll her father made with her. She was a cute little girl, straw colored hair, and round blue eyes with an impish smile.

Sam Prichard burst out the back door and made a mad dash up the hill. He grabbed her around the waist, scooped her up, and ran back with the girl bouncing on his hip. The women took her from him as he made his way back into the house. Everyone congratulated him on saving little Priscilla, a favorite of all of ours.

"Get Simon Davis, Jim Richardson, and John Fiske," Captain Wheeler told Ed Ayres. "I need to talk to them," he told Ephraim and me. When the men came Wheeler explained that neither he nor Captain Hutchinson were well enough to be in command. He appointed them as the top militiamen while he and Hutchinson were disabled. Hutchinson was taken into the back room and laid on the floor, still bleeding from his wound. Wheeler looked like he was about to faint so some of the women came over and began tending to him. Simon, Jim, and John looked at each other, none of them sure as to what to do first.

"This is a hell of a situation," Richardson said. "There are only a dozen of us soldiers good enough to fight. We need to see how much powder and ball each man has with him." Josiah was standing nearby rubbing his hand over his chin.

"That's been done. There's plenty of ball…each of us has 50 or so. There are two five-pound blocks of lead so we can make more. We don't have a lot of powder, though. Ed Ayres thinks they have a keg or two, and went to look but I haven't seen him. If they have it great, if they don't, well…," he said leaving the thought unspoken.

"No need to say anything to anyone yet," Ephraim said in a low voice. "Find Ed to see if he located those kegs," he told Josiah.

"I'll be right back," Josiah said as he headed towards the stairs.

I went to talk to Charity and a few others. Everyone wanted to know about the ambush, what happened to John, Rich, and Will. Most were in disbelief that our friends, the Quaboags and other Nipmucks, who had been so good to us for so long, could turn on us so quickly and brutally.

As the siege started and I saw the Indians running towards us screaming and yelling, intending to kill us, I thought of that muster day when we all agreed we had nothing to fear from the Quaboag or any other tribe. We were wrong and the other militiamen were thinking the same thing, for I could see it in their eyes.

"Oh my God," yelled Priscilla Warner. "Look!" she said, pointing out the window. We all crowded to the windows to see what frightened her. There were too many people to be able to see out so I grabbed my gun and ran up the stairs to the second floor followed closely by several others. There were perhaps 10 to 12 people in the room facing west. I went in, scurrying to the window to get a good view of what was happening. Several asked what was going on but I was too intent on what was taking place to answer. I heard them ask again and someone at the top of the stairs told them what they had seen. They crowded into the room hoping to get a glimpse of the action. Ephraim pushed them back as I opened the window and brought my gun up.

Looking out, I saw a man and boy running hard. They were in front of Kent's house, 150 yards away, when the boy fell. The man looked back, grabbing the boy by the arm, dragging him to his feet. You could tell they were winded but they began to run again, both of them looking back as they did. A few seconds later our guide Joseph rode over the crest of the hill behind them. He stopped and turning back in the saddle, yelled something that we couldn't make out. He sat there on his horse as the man and boy came running down the road. I recognized them as Tom Wilson and his son Billy. Joseph rode a few yards ahead and stopped, measuring the progress they made. Eight Indians came over the crest of the hill running at full speed, guns and war clubs in their hands. Two stopped and fired but both shots missed.

"Two of you get to the attic above here," I yelled. "Wait until I shoot then aim at their heads. We'll slow them down so the other three can get here." Two of the men scrambled up the stairs to the other room. As I brought my gun up I heard the attic window bang open. Tom and Billy were now about 100 yards away. Joseph saw that they were getting nearer the tavern and rode hard after them, putting distance between himself and the Indians. Billy began to run slower as they got closer. Tom grabbed him by the arm, flinging him ahead. The Indians were now 70 yards away. I took a good aim at the lead Indian and fired. The shot seemed very loud and I could tell from the noise downstairs that it startled everyone. The Indian fell hard, sliding a few yards before stopping. I heard the guns erupt in the attic and the Indian on the far left spun around grasping his right arm but didn't fall. The rest came rushing on, not breaking stride.

Ephraim came up to the window and putting his gun up, took quick aim and fired. I could see the dirt fly as his shot hit the ground just in front of the Indians. They slowed a bit but did not stop. I pushed him out of the way and took a bead on the one in the middle now not more than 50 yards away. As I did, they stopped suddenly, looking at the tavern as if trying to figure out what to do next. I recognized two of them as Oota-dabun's cousins, Matchitehew and Wematin. I aimed at Matchitehew, took a breath, held it, and squeezed the trigger as I let it out. Just as I pulled the trigger, one of the others stepped in front of Matchitehew. The shot hit the Indian in the upper back, and he fell forward, landing in a heap. Four of the remaining five turned and ran back towards Kent's then veered off towards the burial ground. Matchitehew stood looking at us, showing no fear or concern. He began to walk towards us then stopped. I stood up and leaned out the window so he could see that it was me who killed two of his companions. We stood like that for what seemed like a long time, although it was not more than a minute before he slowly turned and walked away; I watched him until he went over the crest of the hill.

We could hear the hubbub as Tom and Billy came stumbling into the house. I realized that the attack had begun and that I had fired the first shot in our fight for survival.

I went down the stairs and Becky came over looking rumpled and afraid, her dress dirty and hair falling out of her cap on one side.

"Poor Susannah!" she said. "I can't believe what's she gone through today...not only did she lose her husband just hours ago but now everything she has in the world is on the verge of being destroyed." She touched my arm and drew me into a corner. "We don't have enough food for everyone even for a day. There's a small barrel of pork, a couple of small hams, a barrel of dried apples, and a couple small bags of dried corn and peas but it's not enough. Even with what everyone brought, I know it's not enough. Susannah said they're low because we expected the harvest to start soon. John was supposed to go to Springfield this week too for other supplies."

"We'll make it last somehow...I don't know how but we will. How many barrels of cider do we have?"

"There's only two...," she said. "Jack, I'm scared. The others are too. What's going to happen? How long will they attack? Will we get out of this?"

"Yes, I think we'll be all right. We have plenty of powder and ball. John had two small kegs his son Ed found. The thing that worries me most is the water. If they fire the house, we'll run out of water soon. It's not the bullets that worry me but the house burning with all of us in it." As I said this, I realized I shouldn't have because it would make her more frightened than she already was. I sighed and, when I gave her a small hug, she started to cry but then caught herself. Sniffling back the tears, she wiped her eyes with her sleeve and lifted her head.

I looked at her and thought of how she was a small,

annoying girl back in Ipswich who stole my heart and didn't even know it. I remember well the heartbreak of leaving her and not knowing when I'd see her again. I saw her when she came to Brookfield and now she stood before me, my wife, and soon the mother of my child.

"I'm afraid for the baby…," she said looking into my face and starting to cry again. I couldn't lie to her and tell her everything would be all right because it might not. I didn't want to tell her all the facts because that would upset her even more. The only thing I could do is hold her and tell her I loved her. Raising my head, I saw Charity a few feet away looking at us, her hand on Josiah's arm, a sad smile on her face.

As I held Becky, I began to think of my Indian friends William, Kanti, and Oota. I had not heard from William in two weeks and wondered where his sympathies lie. Did he join with the Wampanoag and Narragansett against us? How could he have avoided not joining the war party? The pressure from the other men to become a warrior against us would be intense. As Becky moved back from me, she looked at my face.

"What's wrong?" she asked.

"I was thinking of William and Kanti and Oota. I hope they're all right. I think William would be forced to join against us. I hope I don't see him. I can't tell the other men, the soldiers, not to shoot at him because he's my friend. I just hope that he's safe from harm."

"Where do you think Kanti, Oota, and the other women are?"

"I don't know," I replied. "I'm pretty sure they've moved to somewhere away from the fight. I'm not sure where that would be," I said with a sigh. "I just pray that they're safe. They've been good friends over the years and I don't want anything to happen to them." We stood there, lost in thought for a moment until Ephraim came over to me, a look of concern on his face.

"Wheeler just ordered Henry Young and me to try to get to Boston to let the governor know what happened. We're leaving in a few minutes." I didn't know what to say. I saw the need to get word to the governor but we could use both these men when the attack came. He put his hand on my shoulder.

"If we have to go, and we do, then now is the time…before more of them get here. We should be able to get around them." He got his gun and spoke to Wheeler and Simon Davis again before walking out the door. I grabbed my gun and followed, keeping an eye on the fields, houses and barns as I went around back to where he and Henry were saddling their horses. Henry didn't say much, at least in the short time I knew him, and now wasn't an exception. He moved a few yards away and waited for Ephraim.

"Listen, my friend," I told him, "be careful. Some of them know you but that doesn't mean they won't shoot you as soon as anyone else."

"I like being alive," he said with a smile, "and I intend to keep doing just that. Don't worry…you'll see me again." With that, he wheeled his horse and set off with Henry down the road. It wasn't long before we did see him again. I was upstairs keeping a lookout with several others when Eleazer Warner flew up the stairs.

"They're back! More Indians are coming! Your friend and the other man are back…," I went down the stairs to find out what happened. Henry was talking for a change, giving his account of their short mission.

"We got to the other end of town and saw some Indians going through one of the houses, pulling stuff out and throwing it everywhere. It was the second house past the Elbow." I heard a small noise and looked behind me. It was Mary Trumble looking sad and angry at the same time.

"Those bastards!" she said, turning away. I saw the look of shock and fear on her face as she held her day old infant son close to her breast.

"Mary, it will be all right. We'll make sure everyone stays safe," I told her, trying my best to give her a measure of encouragement though Henry wondered if they'd all survive.

"Judah's on his way back from Springfield," she said. "What if they catch him?" she mumbled as she turned away.

"Anyway," resumed Henry, annoyed at the

interruption, "one of them turned and saw us and started hollering at the others so we fired on them. Ephraim hit one in the leg and I think I got one in the chest or shoulder…I couldn't tell which. After that we came back here as fast as we could."

"They're right behind us," Ephraim said. "We better get ready." No sooner did he say that than a deafening roar of screams and howls erupted outside. I ran back upstairs and looking out the windows in the front of the house, saw several groups advancing on us. My guess is that there were at least 250 of them. They came to within 75 yards, stopping by the edge of the meetinghouse. Others ran across the road and up the hill to get behind Ayres' barn. Within a minute all of them, as if on command, shot at the house. Bullets thudded into the walls, sending splinters flying into the rooms, and one small window in the front room was shattered. This caused everyone - men, women, and children to drop to the floor, yelling and screaming. When the Indians heard us yell, they screamed even louder, cheering what they believed to be a successful assault. When all those bullets came at us at one time, some piercing the outside walls, we were like little animals scurrying to their holes, afraid of everything, the women and children shaking with fright, and the rest of us not knowing how to feel. That moment was as if hell itself erupted outside the door, and the devil himself was at our very elbow.

All of the men gathered on the first floor. Those of us

on the second floor had to stand on the stairs because there was no room for us. Captain Wheeler was sitting in a chair slumped to one side his injured arm hanging down.

"Men should be in every room," he said, grimacing in pain. "They'll come at us from every direction. Have plenty of shot and powder ready. The boys are making more bullets from the lead blocks so don't spare any. Take careful aim but don't hesitate to shoot. Now decide who should be in what rooms." I went back to the room on the second floor. Ephraim and several others were on the opposite side. Becky's brother Nate, Henry Young, and Sam, Joe and Mark Ayres were with me, which worked out well because three could shoot while the other three reloaded. By doing this, we were able to keep up a rapid fire that not only killed a good number of the enemy but also prevented them from getting too close to the house. There were four windows in the room – one on each of the front and back walls and two on the wall facing west, which worked to our advantage.

"Henry, Nate, and I will shoot first. Sam, Mark and Joe you'll fire while we reload," I told them. Two of the younger boys brought in buckets of water for us to use if they should try to burn the house. I took the front window, Nate one of the west windows and Henry the rear one.

"Any of them out in back?" I asked Henry.

"No more than 10 or so. They're just standing there

looking at us."

"Nate, what's on your side?"

"There's a few...up past Younglove's house. Some just came out...wait...there's more. There's at least a dozen now," he paused a moment before continuing. "There are at least 50 right around the meetinghouse." All the while, the Indians continued yelling and screaming, making the most awful sounds you could imagine. Several shots were fired from the men on the first floor and I saw two of the Indians in front of the meetinghouse fall. One crawled back towards the building; the other one didn't move – he was dead. I decided not to wait any longer.

"Sam, get ready. I'm going to shoot and you take my place after I do. Nate you're after him. Joe you go next. Don't stay in the window for too long or every one of them will shoot at you. Make each shot count. We're shooting down on them so aim a little high. Now get ready." I peered around the open window and saw a short, chunky Indian standing at the front of a group to the right of the meetinghouse. I stepped up, took aim, and fired, hitting him in the left leg. He fell, yelling in pain, which caused many of them to shoot at us; bullets slapped against the house outside our window like hail as I turned to Sam.

"Shoot now while they're reloading. They'll shoot at us again after you do. Nate, that's when you'll go." Sam stepped near the window and took a good look.

"The one with the braid on the side of his head…," he said more to himself than to us as he brought his gun up. With his target picked out, he fired, but missed. Meanwhile, Henry wanted a better look at what was happening on his side so he leaned out the window. He pulled his head back and turned to us.

"There are three Indians trying to sneak up on the back side, right at the corner where they think no one can see them."

"Let me take a look," I said, anxious to see what they were trying to do. I went over and peeked over the edge of the window. I saw only two of them and one was trying to light a small pile of hay they placed against the corner of the house.

"They're trying to burn the house. Mark, go tell Captain Wheeler. Let him know that they should be ready to put it out as soon as we get the Indians away. Now go." With that, he flew down the stairs. Henry brought his gun up and stood on his toes so he could see them since they were almost right under us. As the flames began to grow, the Indians moved away. As they did, Henry fired, hitting one in the right leg. The Indian howled in pain. His accomplice turned and looked up at us and grabbed his friend before running up the hill as fast as they could. Henry leaned out again and hollered after them.

"Got you, you savage bastard! Come close again and I'll…," his words were cut off when he fell back into the room with a thump, shot in the left shoulder. There was some blood but not as much as I expected to see. He tried to sit up but fell back to the floor grimacing in pain.

"Sit still. Don't move or it'll hurt more." I told him. "Sam and Joe, get him downstairs. Ask Mrs. Coy and Mrs. Prichard to take care of him…it will take their minds off what happened today. Tell your brother Tom to come up to take Henry's place." They lifted him as best they could and carried him down the stairs. Ephraim came into the room.

"What happened?" he asked.

"Henry shot an Indian in the leg and was leaning out yelling after him. He was shot in the left shoulder. I think he'll be all right. The ball went right through," I told him, pointing to the ball stuck in the wall behind him. He pulled his knife out of the sheath, dug it out, and stood looking thoughtfully at it, hefting it in his hand.

"I heard you shooting. Are they doing anything on your side?" I asked.

"There's a few up on the hill and down the road past Prichard's taking pot shots. Most of them are at the meetinghouse."

"They're starting to burn the houses and barns. We saw them go over the hill then smoke came up. Must be from Parsons or Warner's."

"Wheeler's already asked me to go again. Wants me to

leave tonight after its dark and before the moon comes up." I was about to respond when we heard the front door slam and men yelling. We both went to the front window.

"It's Sam Prichard," yelled one of the men in the other room. "What the hell is he doing?" We stood and watched with guns at the ready as Sam ran across the road to his father's house and disappeared inside. I heard people pounding up the steps; Joe came in followed by Tom Parsons and Tom Wilson.

"He went to get supplies," Joe told us.

"He's a fool," Tom Wilson declared.

"He's going to get himself killed," Tom Parsons spat out. Ephraim ran back into the other room and told his men to be ready when Sam came out.

"Everyone's gun ready?" I asked. "When he comes out we'll shoot one after another if we have to...let's hope we don't." It was a few minutes before Sam reappeared, his arms full with buckets and sacks stuffed with various things. As he got to the edge of the road, whoops and screams came from the Indians as they charged out from behind the meetinghouse. There were 20 or 30 of them shooting at the house as they came. The minute they saw Sam, a group split off and ran for him. He dropped everything and started to run but wasn't fast enough.

Between all of us on both floors, we got off a dozen shots before they caught Sam at the edge of the road just opposite the tavern. As we reloaded, we watched them surround him. For a second, he stood in the middle of all of them looking at us. Matchitehew, standing behind him, brought his war club up and slammed it into his head. We heard the loud thud and saw him fall. They whooped and screamed. Guns went out every window and fired, hitting several of them as they stood there. Ephraim shot the savage who had hold of Sam's shirt.

They grabbed Sam and rushed back towards his house, leaving their dead and wounded where they fell. I recognized one of the wounded as a husky, mean-spirited man from Packachoag I'd seen at Wekapauge a few times. He was shot in the left leg and tried to stand while holding the back of his leg. I whistled loudly and as he turned at the noise, I shot him in the chest. He hit the ground with a thump.

We could hear the women downstairs crying at Sam's horrible plight and uttering curses at the savages. It was about to get much worse. They took him to the far corner of his father's house and held him by the arms. His body was limp. His feet were just touching the ground and his head hung down. Matchitehew yelled at them to hold him steady. He then pulled out his tomahawk and with one swift motion, cut Sam's head off. Elizabeth screamed and fainted. The poor woman lost both her husband and third son that day.

Matchitehew picked up Sam's head, blood dripping from the severed neck, and held it up to us.

"We see you! We see you English!" he yelled at us. "I see you John Warner! I see you Jack Parker! I see you Sam Kent! We will kill you, all of you, like your friend Sam," he said, holding Sam's head higher, "and drive you back to the water, back where you came from!" He let out a scream as his hatred boiling over. He took Sam's head and tossed into the road where it rolled several feet before stopping on its left side, the vacant eyes rolling up in the sockets, staring at us as if pleading for help that we couldn't give.

The Indians laughed, kicking Sam's head around like a ball, as if they were playing a game. It was horrific to watch but I couldn't take my eyes away from the grisly scene. Everyone in the house began to yell and shout curses at the enemy. Sam's body lay across the road no more than 150 feet from the front door of the tavern. Laughing, they kicked his head down the road behind his family's house. As soon as we were reloaded, we began shooting again at those that were anywhere within range of our guns. Several ran from the back of Prichard's with Sam's head on a pole they'd found in the barn. They stuck it right in front of the house facing towards us. There was nothing we could do about it; every time we looked out we saw his lifeless body lying there and his head, eyes open, staring at us, on that damn pole. Each morning it was the first thing we saw, the sunrise illuminating it in a horrible, ghastly way.

The Indians retreated in the direction of the burial

ground, leaving us to rest for a bit, which we sorely needed. Suddenly, I felt very tired. Lt. Davis came up and told us that he wanted to talk to us so we all went downstairs. It was very uncomfortable, hot, and muggy with the pungent smell of sweat and gunpowder hanging in the air. The heavy perspiration smarted in our eyes and turned to a salty film over our bodies. Ninety-nine people were crowded into that house on a hot and very humid day. Unlike the last time, I didn't stand on the stairs but made my way down to the big front room and found Becky. When I asked about Henry she told me he wasn't doing well.

"His breathing is harsh and ragged and he's lost quite a bit of blood. Ephraim is with him now."

Simon told us that we would need to be ready for the next attack, which he thought, like the rest of us, would come soon. We talked for a while about what we should do to be better prepared, and decided the women and children should stay in the middle of the rooms and the men would be by the walls and windows. Buckets were checked to make sure they were full of water and placed where we could get to them quickly. Some of the women passed around mugs of cider that tasted good, which made me realize just how thirsty I was. Time passed slowly; everyone was on edge expecting another attack. There was talk of trying to get Sam's body and take his head down so we didn't have to look at it every time we stared out the front windows. After some heated discussion, the decision was made to leave it, for while it would have been for the better, the chance of one or more of us being killed was too great.

The sun was almost set. Some of the houses were still burning, having been torched by the savages. I'd gone back to the second floor and with some of the other men, sat for a while watching the fires burn. The Indians were at Wilson's barn, whooping and yelling as they jumped up and down, throwing burning sticks in through the doors. The fire caught quickly and the flames rose. Soon flames were shooting through the upper portion of the front wall as the thatch roof caught quickly, showering burning embers onto the ground and igniting the dry hay near the side. As the barn became engulfed, the Indians turned their attention to the house. A small group ran across the road towards Younglove's with burning sticks in their hands. Seeing the destruction of the houses and barns that we all worked so hard to build and maintain was difficult for all of us.

The sunset was one of the most spectacular I'd seen in years, the clouds pink and red with stripes of orange sweeping across the western sky. The burned buildings were a ghastly profile against the beautiful sunset. Shortly after dark, we heard Indians talking from all around the house. Our eyes were accustomed to the darkness and we saw small groups of them 150 feet away. They were close enough that we could hear them, but far enough away not to be able to make out what they were saying. Mark came in from the other room, telling us to look out the back. On the hill behind us, fires were burning in a line along the entire crest of the hill. I saw the figures of men silhouetted against the dancing yellow and orange flames.

"Take a look out front," I told him. "See if there are fires out there too." He came back in a minute.

"There's at least a dozen all along the back of the meadow...looks like they're on this side of the road."

"All right, go to Lieutenant Davis and tell him what you saw. Ask him if we should do anything or just wait." I was sure I knew the answer but I'd let him make the decision. Others had seen the fires too, so more and more people came to the second floor to get a glimpse of them. The fact that we could see that we were surrounded by the enemy only added to our sense of helplessness. Mark came bounding back into the room.

"Lt. Davis says to wait...not to do anything now. Save our ball and powder until we can see what we're shooting at to make it count." There was yelling on the first floor so I ran halfway down the stairs.

"What happened?" I asked.

"They're trying to burn the house!" someone yelled as Simon came into view. He was an active man with plenty of character and spirit who certainly didn't lack courage. He wouldn't hesitate to face the enemy in the open or ask one of us to do something he wouldn't do.

"We have to get outside! Grab buckets, form a line. It's around at the back corner!" he yelled. There was a scurry of men out the back door. Others took aim at the Indians through the windows to protect those outside. The fire was growing larger by the minute, the flames shooting up the side of the house and the light allowed the Indians to see our men. They lost no time in shooting several volleys at us. Simon went to the door and looking out, shook his fist at the savages gathered around their fires on the hill.

"God is with us and fights with us! He will deliver us from your heathen hands! He will not let you triumph!" he yelled with all his might. "Do you hear me? God is with us!" Several of them came down from the hill and shouted back at him.

"Now see how your God delivers you!"

A minute later, shots poured in upon us from all parts of the hill, from behind the rock and barn. These were followed by derisive yells and taunts of all sorts. Miraculously, only two men were slightly wounded. All of us at the windows on both floors shot at the savages, killing several and wounding many more, their cries of pain filling the night. They retreated up the hill to their campfires, taking their dead and wounded with them. The fire to the house was put out with little damage done.

Captain Wheeler told Ephraim to leave before the

moon rose, which was around 3 a.m. He was to go on foot since that would give him the best chance of getting past the various enemies gathered along the road, in the fields and woods. I worried for him because the number of Indians seemed to be increasing with every hour. The plan was for him to try to make his way to Marlborough as quickly as he could. He figured that if he made good time, running most of the way, he would be there by the middle of the next afternoon. I wished him well and saw him slip away into the darkness. He was back in a short while.

"There are too many of them for me to get through without being caught or just shot outright. I can try again in a little while," he told us. He sat on the floor and leaned against a wall with a big sigh. I could see the weariness on his face. He turned and saw me looking at him.

"Yes, I'm tired," he said, the sleepy tone of his voice matching the look on his face. "But I bet I look better than you do," he added in a small, weak attempt at humor. "You look like you haven't slept in a week. "

"I feel like I haven't slept in a month," I responded as I felt the waves of exhaustion go through me. "Why don't you get what sleep you can?" I said. "You won't leave again for at least another hour. Anything is better than nothing."

"Maybe I will...," he said, folding his hands into his lap. He fell asleep immediately. Even with all the noise of all the people around him, he never stirred. Before he knew it, I was shaking him awake.

"Ephraim, Wheeler says it's time for you to go." He opened his eyes right away and had the look of someone who wasn't quite sure where he was for a moment.

"All right," he groaned, getting to his feet. Mercy Warner came over and handed him a small cloth bag.

"We put together some food for you. It's not much but it's the most we could do," she said apologetically. "You'll need it on your journey. May God keep you safe."

"Thank you," he replied quietly. I walked with him to the door and put my hand on his arm.

"Take care, my friend."

"You too, Jack. Take care of your wife and that baby you'll soon have." With that, he slipped off into the darkness and was gone. I said a little prayer for him that he would get safely to Marlboro as soon as he could.

On many a night, I've stood outside watching the stars twinkling and shining in the dark sky. I saw them that night through the window in the west-facing second floor room and the feeling it gave me was altogether different from past times. Instead of a pleasant sight that made me marvel, for I was always fascinated by nature's displays, I felt a pervading sense of loneliness and despair. There we were, 99 of us, crammed into a hot, stinking house surrounded by hundreds of Indians who wanted to kill us and see us dead. Instead of being just 25 miles from Springfield to the west and Marlboro to the east, we might as well have been hundreds of miles from any civilized place.

Chapter 22

There are some things that I will never forget, no matter how hard I try. One is the haunting sounds of animals being slaughtered; each horse screaming like a small child, pigs squealing in fright and terror, sheep bleating as they tried to run from the savages, and cows bellowing as their lives were cruelly taken away. The bitingly sweet, sickening stench of death was everywhere. Dead animals lay all around us, swelling and bloating in the hot August sun. The Indians left some of their dead; those that they couldn't reach under our sustained shooting. All of those smells wafted to us the entire time, every hour of the day and night on a light westerly breeze, added to the ever increasing, ever overpowering smells of so many people crammed into a single dwelling for three days during the hottest, most humid weather in years. They say the sense of smell is our strongest sense and that a certain smell can bring back memories of a time many years later. I certainly believe that because even now, just the slightest scent of a smell similar to that horrible, ghastly sweet smell makes those terrible days come rushing back to me as if I was there at that very moment.

Another smell that stayed with me is that of

gunpowder. Smoke from our guns filled every room in the house. It had a strong sulfur smell with a biting taste and gritty texture that mixed with the smells of sweat and blood and it stuck to our hair, skin, and clothes. It mingled with our sweat and ran down our faces, giving them black streaks that made us look evil. No matter how much we wiped it from our eyes and nose, the next few shots would bring it back again. It stayed there like something you'd never be able to get rid of, something that would never go away.

Then there is the noise - soft and faraway one minute, loud and angry the next. It rose and fell on the wind, seeming to move all around us. It was there all day long, louder in the daytime than at night. A continuous hum and buzz you couldn't ignore or shut out, no matter how hard you tried. It was the flies - millions of them - feasting on the bloated dead animals lying under the scorching sun. Sometimes you could see small black clouds moving above an animal.

Looking out at the destruction of our small village, we realized that, should we somehow survive, we would have nothing to eat. We saw the Indians pulling up plants and tossing them into the fires from our burning homes. They gathered armloads to eat, carrying them to the edge of the road where they had their fires, or walking around the meetinghouse across from us, eating the food we'd grown for our families as they waited to kill us. The animals running about before they were slaughtered trampled what the Indians didn't eat or destroy. All that would be left besides herbs was a few pounds of vegetables, not nearly enough to feed nine people, nevermind 99. It seemed we were in a never-ending nightmare from which we'd never awake.

The next day, Tuesday, August 3rd, the savages began to yell, scream, and shoot around 6:00 o'clock in the morning. None of us had much sleep except an hour here or there. Most of the men got less than that. Although we had set up watches, few of us could sleep for fear we would be attacked then. Our enemies continued yelling for the first couple of hours of the morning. They hurled taunts at us of every imaginable type, but mostly saying that our God couldn't and wouldn't protect us and that he deserted us. Every few minutes, two or three would shoot at us. Then a group of them went to the meetinghouse and began mocking us, telling us to come and pray with them and sing psalms. This was said with mocking laughter and insulting gestures. They began making a horrible noise that could only be singing, but exactly what, we were at a loss to describe.

Around mid-morning, Becky came upstairs to tell us that Sarah Coy was in labor. She was a young woman, only 14-years-old; plain but pretty. Her father and mother, Tom and Jane Kent, came to Brookfield four years earlier. They were good people although he pretty much kept to himself and was never much involved in the affairs of the settlement. Sarah was a twin who's sister Mary looked nothing like her. Sarah was taller, with dark hair and firm features. Jane was pregnant too, her belly sticking out farther than any of the other pregnant women.

Sarah's labor continued for many hours. The pain she suffered with her first child was apparent to all of us for she cried out often, attended by several women including her mother.

The fact that new life was being brought into the world at the same time the Indians were trying to take ours gave me hope and fear at the same time. I was hopeful because if we survived this seemingly endless attack, there would be new lives to be led. The babies would grow into children, then into young men and women and then into strong men and women. Not only was it the imminent birth of Sarah's baby that affected me but also Mary Trumble and her infant. She showed strength of character when we yelled to her of the attack as we dashed by her home. She carried her newborn baby a mile while herding her other young children in front of her. That she was able to escape the oncoming fury, saving herself and her children, is a testament to her courage and strength.

By late afternoon, Sarah was in great pain, her loud moaning and cries of pain were heard throughout the house. Two or three times when I was looking out the windows, I saw some of the Indians pause, listening to the sounds. It seemed to affect some of them for they lowered their weapons and went up behind the barn. After many hours of hard labor, she gave birth to twin boys. All of us were surprised at that although we shouldn't have been, given that her mother had nothing but twins. The birth made us men more determined to protect the women and children.

Throughout the day, the savages kept up the horrid singing, taunting us to come to join them at the meetinghouse to pray. It was a great joke to them as they laughed each time the taunt was made. That angered us; we prayed to God as we'd never done before to deliver us from this terrible situation. We shot at them as best we could, though they learned not to present too easy a target.

During the late morning, I looked out the window at the Indians across the road trying to see any that I recognized. As I watched, I saw one of them, and several others, down on the other side of the road about 200 yards from us. The size and build of the Indian looked like William, although I couldn't be sure. The more I thought about it the more sense it made to me that if he was forced to join with the others, he'd be as far away from the fighting as he could be. If that was him, and looking back, I think it was, I wondered what thoughts and feelings he had at that moment, as he watched his fellow Indians try to kill his friends and being powerless to do anything to stop it.

I brought my attention back to the warriors across the

road and saw Matchitehew standing at the side of the meetinghouse, watching us as the others sang their horrid songs. He had shot at us a couple of times but without much aim or care. This time he was joined by several others, all with guns in their hands, while two dozen more stood behind them with arrows in their bows, all getting ready to unleash their fire at us. Bullets came whizzing near my head slapping into the clapboards inches from my face. Splinters flew and some stuck into the back of my right hand. I ducked back and waited a moment. An arrow smacked into the clapboard just to the left of the window, so close I could have reached out and pulled it free.

Matchitehew was just beginning to reload when he looked at the tavern. I moved to the open window and watched him load his ball and powder. I realized there were no other shots being fired on either side, that all seemed to be waiting for this to happen. It was an expectant quiet with all of them watching us. The hatred he had for us, for me, came down to this moment. He brought his gun up and aimed at me. His shot missed, going into the clapboards just to the right of the window. I shouldered my gun quickly and fired, hitting the dirt to his side and not believing that I missed. We both loaded hurriedly. He took aim again as I was ramming home the bullet. I dropped the ramrod, threw my gun up, and fired just as he pulled the trigger. He staggered back, his throat gushing blood.

He dropped to his knees but looked directly at me as he was went down. I stared back and watched him die.

I slumped to the floor with my back against the wall as a flood of emotions went through me. Killing Matchitehew didn't bother me in the least because the world was better off without him. All the things that happened to me since my mother died went through my mind and I realized that I was afraid for the future. No one knows what it will hold for each of us but at that moment, it did not look promising to me. Coming from deep in my memory, I heard my father's voice; *Each of us has an inner strength that no one can take away unless you let them. The measure of a man is determined by how he responds to life's difficulties.* I didn't often think of him...but his words gave me courage and hope. I took a deep breath, hauled myself up, and decided I would prove him right.

Some of us, mainly the women, became hopeful that the Indians were leaving when they began removing their dead. While the shooting continued, it was not as fierce or frequent as before and lulled some into a belief that the worst might be over. Josiah, me and a few other men didn't think it was anywhere near over and shared our belief with the other men.

"There's no way they're just going to pick up and go away," Josiah told the men gathered on the stairs. "You think they'll just give up after all they've done trying to kill us? Don't be foolish," he said dismissively.

"They're up to something, I know they are," Tom Wheeler, Jr. chimed in. "They are the sneakiest bastards I've ever seen and won't stop until they run out of powder or shot or we kill them all...or they kill us." John Warner, known as Squire, moved to the center of the group on the first floor and looked up the stairs at us.

"Before yesterday, I wouldn't have believed that they would cause us any harm. Now I think they won't stop until they get us all. We shouldn't drop our guard for that's just the time when they'll attack us again. Mark my words...we aren't done with them by a long shot." His words couldn't have been truer since just then, one of the boys on the second floor yelled that they were shooting fire arrows at the roof. We scrambled to the attic and heard the flames licking the shingles above us as smoke began to come into the attic slowly at first and then more and more. Sam Warner grabbed an ax and began chopping at the planks a few feet to one side of the fire. He broke through in a minute, swinging the ax fast and hard, punching a hole in the roof. Tom Wilson scooted up into the opening, a bucket of water in his hand, and doused the flames. As he was just about to come back into the room, another arrow went by his head and landed at the edge of the roof on the other side. Sam still had the ax in his hand and guided by Tom, who'd stuck his head out the hole, began to chop wildly. Ed Ayres had a bucket in each hand ready to jump up once Sam was through the roof. We heard shots followed by Tom dropping onto the floor with a thud. He stood quickly with a surprised look on his face.

"They shot at my head. Just missed me, too."

Sam was through in another minute and Ed dumped the water onto the shingles. Only half the fire was out. He grabbed the other bucket from my hands and doused the rest of the flames.

"If they attack like this a couple more times we'll need more water," I told them. "We'll have to get to the well." Everyone agreed but no one volunteered. I went downstairs to let Wheeler know what was going on and that we needed to get more water. When I got to the bottom of the stairs, I saw Sarah sitting in a corner holding one baby to her breast while her sister Mary held the other. Becky saw me as soon as I got down the steps and came to me. She didn't say a word but just grabbed my right hand and squeezed it three times.

"How's Sarah?" I asked

"She's doing well. I hope I don't have to be in labor as long as she was when I have our baby. She took my hand and placed it on her belly. "The baby's been kicking today," she told me with a sad smile. "I hope we get out of this Jack. I want to have my baby." She whimpered softly.

"It will be all right....we'll get out of this. Ephraim should be in Marlboro about now," I said with more confidence than I felt. She gave me a weak smile. I didn't add that he would be there only if he'd been able to get away and we didn't know if he had.

"Jane started her labor too," she said, pointing to Sarah's mother, lying on the floor on the opposite side of the room from her daughter. "She's not due for another month…I hope everything is all right but…" she said, not finishing the thought.

"I have to see Wheeler. They shot two fire arrows into the roof. We put them out but need more water. Someone has to go to the well." She understood that this was very dangerous and that whoever went might be shot. I went and knelt in front of Wheeler; his face was pale and his breathing shallow. He was sleeping but didn't look good.

"Captain," I said shaking him gently. "Captain Wheeler, I need to talk to you." He opened his eyes and tried to sit up but the pain stopped him. It took him a minute to get his bearings.

"What is it?" he asked, his eyes closing.

"They shot fire arrows onto the roof; we chopped through it and put the fires out but we need more water. We need to get to the well." I knew he couldn't do anything for us but since he was the leader of the military force, I wanted to make sure he knew what was happening. I noticed that people had quietly gathered around me, listening closely.

"Ask for volunteers. If no one will go have Simon choose some men…we have to have water," he said weakly.

"His arm is getting worse," Elizabeth Prichard told me. "There's not much more we can do for him, at least not right now." I looked at his arm and saw it was swollen to three times its normal size all the way from the wrist to the shoulder. Someone touched me on the shoulder. I turned and saw Tom Wilson standing there.

"No need to ask for volunteers, Jack. I'll go." I stood there looking at him, feeling the people crowd behind me. We all knew it had to be done and realized Tom understood the danger involved. Simon came over and after I filled him in on the situation, he ordered all the men to come downstairs and those in the other first floor rooms to come close and listen.

"We need water. They shot fire arrows into the roof. Tom volunteered to go to the well," he said, cocking his thumb in Tom's direction. "Get all the buckets lined up at the back door." Turning to Tom, he said, "You understand you'll have to go out there a couple of times until all the buckets are filled?"

"Yeah, I know," Tom said.

"I want to make sure we keep the Indians busy while he's out there. Get your guns ready and be prepared to shoot. Get to the windows." With that, we all went back to our places.

Tom took four buckets, two in each hand, and slowly slipped out the door. He got to the well, filled the buckets, and was back without any trouble. He took another four buckets and was filling them when a few of the Indians behind the barn took shots at him. He hustled back and coming inside, put the buckets on the floor. Two of the young boys were given the job of moving the buckets to the various rooms. We fired at the Indians who quickly moved behind the barn. Tom waited a few minutes before going out again. He filled two buckets and turned back to the house. Three Indians ran out from behind the barn and shot at him while letting out a horrific scream. At that, others came running. Tom broke into a run but the buckets full of water banged against his leg, almost tripping him. The first two shots missed him, hitting the ground, throwing dirt in the air on both sides of him. The third Indian took careful aim and even though we were shooting at him, he never flinched. Right after he fired, Tom dropped to the ground screaming in pain at which the Indian made a great shout, rejoicing in his wound. Two shots rang out and the Indian who shot Tom dropped to one knee, holding his left leg. He scrambled back toward the barn as fast as his wounded leg would allow. Two of the soldiers, Ben Graves of Concord and John Fiske of Chelmsford, were watching Tom and seeing him fall, bolted out the door, grabbed him under the arms and dragged him back. When they got him inside, we saw that he'd been shot in the jaw on the left side of his face. The shot took all the skin off that portion of his face so it was a raw looking wound, the muscles and a small portion of the bone visible. On the side of his neck just behind his jaw, there was a thin red line where the ball had grazed him. Neither wound was bleeding at all. After a minute, he was able to stand, amazing and surprising us all by talking, although with some difficulty. He spit his usual venom, this time directed at the Indian who shot him in particular and all of the attackers in general. We thought, and I know some hoped, he'd not be able to speak for at least a few days. Some of the women took him into one of the other rooms and tended to him.

Two unfilled buckets were on the ground next to the well. We needed those filled along with two others the boys found. We all looked at each other, sizing up the situation, taking a minute to decide which one of us would go to the well to finish the job.

"I'll go," John Bates said as he made his way through the men. He was one of the soldiers; a small, square man with brown curly hair, and a diagonal scar on his forehead. "It won't take me but a minute. Make sure I don't get shot." We took up positions at our windows, ready to shoot any Indian that made a move towards him. To our complete surprise he was out and back in no time all four buckets filled to the brim.

"I told you it wouldn't take me long," he said with a shrug before moving into the right front room. We had no more buckets to fill so now we sat and waited, hoping and praying it would be enough.

A couple of hours later, a group of warriors charged the doors of the house in an attempt to prevent anyone from getting out. Smoke began pouring into the back rooms as flames climbed up the back of the house. With axes and sheer force, we broke down part of the wall on the side of the house where the fire was the biggest and using almost all of the water, we managed to put out the blaze. The Indians then shot a fire arrow into the attic that landed on a pile of flax, bursting into flames and scorching the underside of the roof. One of the soldiers in the attic put it out quickly with two buckets of water.

For the next few hours, nothing much happened, for which we were thankful. At least we had some time to eat and rest. I was exhausted and fell asleep as soon as I lay down on the floor in the upstairs room. I woke a couple hours later to Charity shaking me.

"Jack, Jack," she said quietly, not wanting to wake the others. "I came to make sure you're all right. I've hardly seen you. I was worried." I sat up and realized it was light out.

"How long have I been asleep?"

"At least a few hours. It's been light out for quite a while."

"It seems like I just laid down," I told her, feeling as if I could sleep for a week. The lack of sleep affected my sense of time because my mind told me it was the middle of the night, but my eyes showed me it was mid-morning. I stood and took her arm, leading her out to the landing at the top of the stairs.

"Thank you for worrying about me," I said with what must have been a weary grin. "I'll be fine. Is Becky doing all right?"

"She's fine; keeping busy helping everyone she can. It keeps her mind off things." We stood there for a moment in silence. She lifted her head and took both of my hands in hers.

"Josiah and I talked while you were sleeping. Actually, we've talked about things for a while now. If we live through this, and I pray to God every minute that we will, we've decided to go back to Ipswich." I didn't know what to say. The thought of where everyone would go when this was over never occurred to me.

"We're getting older and Josiah can't keep working like this. His leg hurts more and more. He won't admit it but it does. You've seen him hobble around. He just can't do it anymore. He won't say anything to anyone but I can see it in his eyes. Besides, you'll have your own family soon." I stood there trying to take it all in and not knowing how to respond.

"What about the Morgans?" I asked.

"I don't know," she said, looking down, wringing her hands. "I haven't talked to Elizabeth and Tom yet. People have nothing to stay for…everything's gone. For a lot of us it would be too difficult to start over. We all have to go somewhere anyway because we can't stay here. Even if Ephraim gets to

Marlboro and soldiers do come and we're saved from these savages, they'll just come back and attack again." I stood there slightly stunned as the realization came over me that Becky and I needed to make a decision about what we'd do when this was over, assuming we lived through it.

"I don't know what to say. I've been so concerned about helping us get out of this mess that I didn't think of what happens next. Assuming we get out of here alive. I guess I need to talk to Becky."

"I didn't mean to upset you. I just wanted to make sure you were all right. It's the mother in me," she said. For that moment I felt like a little boy again, my hand in hers as if she was taking me to meeting or to a neighbor's house.

"What is it?" she asked, tilting her head a bit to one side.

"Nothing. I was just thinking of when I was a little boy." A flood of childhood memories came to me now and I felt a lump in my throat. For the first time in a long time, I missed my mother. I could see her before me, her smile lighting up her face. I could feel her holding me, and I could still smell her special smell. I could hear her laugh and feel her hand patting my head as I sat eating my breakfast. I heard her calling me to come in from playing outside. I felt the tears coming to my eyes, wanting to be alone so I could cry because I missed her terribly. Charity seemed to know what I was feeling.

"It's okay, we still miss her too," she said, giving me a little hug before hurrying down the stairs.

I went back into the room and sat on the floor with my back to the wall. I pulled my knees up and wiped my eyes. I tried to stuff all the feelings down inside me but couldn't. I thought of how thrilled she would have been to see her first grandchild and began to cry softly, turning towards the corner so the others couldn't see me if they woke up. After a few minutes, I felt better and wiped my eyes several times, sniffled a bit and put my arms across my knees. I rested my head in my hands and thought about the predicament we were in; what Becky and I would do if we survived.

I guess my thoughts drifted because I found myself thinking of the river in Springfield and how good it made me feel to sit beside it watching the water go by. I always dreamed of buying land near the river; a lot of land, 100 acres or more. Yes, some land by the river…that would be a good place for a home for my family. A big home; something I built myself in a place I wanted to be. I'd build a good farm for my family and have my boys work it with me. I could see Becky and me when the children were grown and running the farm. I could feel the pleasure and pride at the sight of them continuing what we'd built. Mr. Pynchon mentioned several times that he always had good land for sale and that if I was interested to let him know. Becky and I talked of moving west some day; maybe now was the time. I was jolted from my reverie by the sound of feet pounding up the stairs. It was Sampson coming to tell us that the enemy was preparing for another attack.

"They've barricaded themselves in the meetinghouse and the barn. They're piling hay around the sides of both buildings that face us and putting boards behind the hay. They're definitely up to something."

"Oh, they sure are," exclaimed Ed Ayres looking out the window facing the barn. "Look, they're bringing things from the meetinghouse to the barn."

We crept to the window, looked out, and saw a small group carrying boards they must have gotten from some of the other barns and stored behind the meetinghouse. Two or three sprinted across the road with long poles in their arms. I recognized them as being the lug poles Tom Kent cut a couple of weeks ago for Jane to use over the fire. They were green and would not burn. I couldn't figure out what they'd be doing with them. Sampson was reading my thoughts.

"Why would they want those?" he asked.

"Tom Kent cut those no more than two weeks ago," I told him. "There's no way in hell they can use them to try to burn us out. What else are they doing at the barn?" I asked, squinting into the sun.

"I can't tell," Ed replied, putting a hand around the sides of his eyes to block some of the light so he could see better. "They're closing everything up tight…can't see into the barn at all now."

"We should keep them off balance and try to disrupt whatever they're doing," Sampson said, and we all agreed.

"Let's shoot at those around the edges of the barn…any that show themselves," I told them. "I'll take the first crack at them." I checked my gun to make sure it was loaded and took a bead on a short, heavy-set Indian whose shoulders and legs were just visible from the back left edge of the barn. He moved back and forth slightly as if talking to someone, gesturing to make a point about something. He was careless, stepping back just for a moment, revealing the right side of his body. I fired and saw him drop grabbing his side and scream for help, blood flowing from the wound. Two pairs of hands came out from behind the barn and quickly grabbed him by the legs, dragging him behind the barn. We were careful not to look out to see if there were any others creeping around. We learned after the attack started that they'd shoot at wherever they thought our shots came from, almost immediately after we fired. The best defense was for us to fire, and then quickly drop under the window so any shots they poured in on us would miss. We had to bide our time in order to make sure we got other chances.

We couldn't see anything but we heard banging and hammering. It would start, go for a minute, then stop, a quick rapping, tap, tap, tap, bang, bang, bang. It reminded me of a crazy woodpecker, one who couldn't make up his mind if he really wanted to drill at insects and kept changing his mind.

"What the hell are they up to?" I heard a voice behind us ask. I turned and saw Tom Morgan standing there. He looked shrunken and old; the time laying heavy on his shoulders, his face lined and wrinkled, and his hands hanging by his sides looked like cured leather.

"We're not sure," Sampson said, looking down at him. "They've been in the barn banging away for a while now. Jack just shot one," he said.

"You got one huh?" he asked. "You must be a better shot than I thought." He always made comments like that; not only to me but to everyone, his own family included. "Must be building something. I wonder what it could be?" he asked. "Probably find out after dark. You may not have a chance for much target practice then Jack," he cackled on the way out of the room. I heard him go down the stairs and looked at my companions.

"He's a real pisshead at times," I told them. "Best thing he ever did was father Becky." I let the matter drop as we began to wait for whatever came next. We didn't have to wait too long for the barn doors opened, framed by the light of torches inside, and saw a cart filled with hay, flax and pine wood. Behind the cart was a shield made of rough planks. It became clear to us that they would light the cart on fire and try to bring it against the house, the shield protecting them from our shots. It seemed to take a long time for them to get the fire started and when they did, the cart came on at an angle because they couldn't see where they were going. They stopped after 50 feet and tried to look from behind the shield but we were waiting for them and as soon as one stuck his head out we'd shoot. This happened a couple of more times until they got smart. One of them stood up past the barn out of range of our guns, calling to the others handling the cart, directing them which way to go. Between the shield and the good directions they got, there wasn't much we could do. When they were about halfway, 25 to 30 of them appeared from behind both the barn and the rock and began raining arrows down upon us. They aimed well, for several of them came through the window sticking into the wall opposite with the rest smacking into the side of the house. A few were fire arrows so we dumped water on them to prevent the fire from spreading. We hoped they wouldn't send too much more fire against us because we only had a few buckets left. When that was gone, we probably wouldn't be able to get anymore, because several of the enemy took shelter behind the big rock on the hill with a clear line of fire to the well.

The cart came rumbling down the incline, bouncing this way and that with the men running behind it almost losing control as it got closer to us. They let it go 50 feet from the house and gave it a push. As the two men ran from behind the shield, we were fired on by at least a dozen of them, which prevented us from shooting at them as they ran back to the barn. The cart came to a stop a few feet from the house and burned quickly causing little damage. Their next invention was more ingenious and more difficult to deal with, especially since they doubled their attack.

Twilight was coming on with sunset less than half an hour away. Starting in mid-afternoon, we heard them working in the barn again for three or four hours. In that time, we saw some of them running from behind the meetinghouse, across the road with poles of different lengths and diameters. There was some banging and pounding but not nearly as much as the last time. After a while, small groups took up positions on the sides of the barn, behind the big rock and at the meetinghouse across the road. Once they were in place, the barns doors opened and a heavy, cumbersome looking contraption sat at the rise above the tavern on our side. A barrel was in front through which an axle was placed through either end. The top had been cut off and the barrel stuffed with hay, flax, wood chips and kindling. Attached to the axle was a series of long poles lashed together at which they'd attached an axle; each was a set of small wheels they got from the various carts and barrows from our barns. The contraption was over 80 yards long and just beyond the reach of our guns. It was a clever device that would allow them to bring fire to the house while staying out of range of being shot. As we watched, the room crowded with people wanting to see what was happening. Several Indians wheeled a second contraption from the other side of the barn. This was slightly longer than the first with the barrel being much larger. They lit the fires as the Indians who'd taken cover began shooting at us with guns and arrows. We all ducked, many of the people running out and down the stairs. The sun had just set behind a wall of dark clouds gathering in the west. As I watched, I saw small flashes of lightning far in the distance. The distant sound of thunder came to us many seconds later indicating the storm was still a good distance away. The Indians saw it too, while doubling their efforts to burn us out. Their plan was obvious – wheel both carts at the same time to different corners of the house. They knew we couldn't have enough water to fight both fires at the same time and if either one of them caught, we'd be doomed and at their mercy. They would keep up a steady fire with arrows raining down on us like hail as they'd done several times before, which would prevent us from getting outside to put the fires out or push the carts away. All the while, they'd be just out of reach of our shot and able to continue their efforts to harm us.

They almost lost control of the second contraption as they began to move it into a position to begin the attack. There was yelling throughout the house, men scrambling to keep watch on all corners to make certain they weren't going to attempt some other trick on the other sides.

Some of the women were crying, believing that we could not defeat this attack while the young children whimpered, not sure of exactly what was happening but fearful because of their parents' response to the situation. I stayed where I was because I knew that, for the moment at least, I could do nothing to stop them. I went to the stairs and yelled for Becky who joined me a moment later. Even though many people left the room, it was still as crowded as it had been from the first day. She squeezed her way through and came to my side. A minute later Josiah and Charity came in followed by Becky's mother Elizabeth. They stood beside us as some of the others left the room. We looked out the window together, as best as we could, and watched as they moved the first contraption into place, the enemy aiming their weapons at us. I believed that it would be the most vicious attack yet. The Indians didn't know it, but we were slowly running out of ammunition. Our powder was nearly spent, and though we had enough lead left for another day, it would be useless without powder.

Becky grabbed my hand and squeezed three times; I squeezed back three times and gave her a tired smile. Out of the corner of my eye, I saw Charity looking at us. There was sadness in her eyes as she believed that none of us would ever get out of this alive and that we would never have the family we wanted so badly. Josiah stood behind her, gently putting his hands on her shoulders. Elizabeth came close to Becky and put her arm around her waist, drawing her close. It occurred to me that they were saying goodbye to each of us. I refused to accept that and continued watching the enemy prepare for their attack.

The black clouds in the west were growing bigger and the lightning was flashing more often, the crackling and booming could be heard much more clearly now. The top edge of the clouds was a line of gold lit by the last rays of sunlight. It was a stark contrast to the dark clouds that were growing blacker by the minute.

We were startled by the sound of a woman screaming in pain and agony. I had forgotten that Jane Kent was still in labor. We heard the women attending to her and trying to soothe her, talking in gentle tones. She continued this way for several minutes until the high-pitched cry of a newborn was heard. A minute later, it was followed by a second cry. Jane had given birth to two boys, a fourth set of twins. Both she and her daughter Sarah gave birth to twins within 24 hours of each other. It was truly amazing, but we didn't dwell on it as we would have if we weren't in this terrible situation. We had no time to celebrate anything.

Our attention turned back to the Indians' preparations for the attack. Three large and powerful-looking men now controlled the wheeled contraption. Two were on either side and one was in the middle. They were hurrying to try to get the house on fire before the storm came. However, the clouds seemed to be breaking up, giving the impression that the storm might fall apart and not provide any relief from the enemy's designs. A fourth Indian lit the contents of the barrel and, after a minute, it began to burn well. Many of the others began shooting at us but only for a moment. The barrel came closer and closer as they wheeled it down the slight hill. Within two minutes, it was a few feet from the side of the house. Just then, the other group began to light the barrel on their contraption and slowly wheeled it towards us. We began shooting but it had no effect because they were too far away, so we stopped after a few shots.

The storm was moving closer, the thunder growing louder and more ominous as the wind began to blow. The Indians seemed unsure of what to do, whether to retrieve their contraptions and try again after the storm or keep on with their efforts. They quickly talked it over it amongst themselves and decided to continue. The first fire barrel was right underneath us as the second got closer now only twenty yards away. Six buckets of water had been brought into the room and placed near the window. It was only about 10 gallons - enough, we hoped, to put out the fire. I wasn't so sure of that because the flames grew higher and burned hotter; we could feel the heat rising up to us. Josiah grabbed one of the buckets and prepared to dump it on the fire. Just as he put it out the window, a hail of arrows came down on us. He succeeded in dumping the water but it made no difference, the fire continuing to grow. Just as he brought the bucket in from the window an arrow smacked into it with a whistling noise, causing everyone to scatter and move away from the window so that any arrows that came through wouldn't hit us.

The second fire barrel was now near the other corner of the house. The men in the back room began yelling for more water buckets. You could hear the boys running up the stairs with the few buckets that were on the first floor. Lightning began to crash down, the wind picking up, blowing hard, showing the silver undersides of the leaves. The wind didn't do us any favors for it blew the fire against the house, fanning it into an ever-greater inferno. I took two buckets and dumped the water onto the blaze one right after the other. The water from both landed on the right side of the barrel and did little to put out the fire. As the other fire barrel began burning at the other corner, raindrops began to fall, a smattering falling through the few trees. It stopped almost as soon as it started.

The wind slackened and for a second, we felt the hair on our arms stand up followed immediately with a blinding, bright flash of lightning that seemed to hit just yards away, followed in a split second by a deafening clap of thunder that shook the entire house. Our ears rang from the noise as rain began to fall heavily; the skies opened at the moment we needed it the most. The rain dampened the fire in the barrels; soon both barrels were soaked, the fire completely out. The Indians took refuge in the barn, although a few were lying on the ground motionless between the rock and the barn. They must have been close to where the lightning struck, if it didn't hit them directly. I glanced out and saw a wide black hole in the center of where the Indians fell.

All through the house, people were laughing and crying, some doing both at the same time. The noise of our celebration erupted as the rain fell in sheets so heavy I couldn't see across the road. Everything was wet, water coming in through the holes in the attic, splashing on the floor above us and coming through the ceiling soaking everything. We couldn't have cared less. I grabbed Becky and squeezed her hard, holding her close to me. She pulled away, giggling like a young girl.

"Oh my dear sweet God," she exclaimed, stunned at our good fortune. "I can't believe it. They didn't get us."

"We're not out of the woods yet," Josiah told her. "Just because they didn't get us now doesn't mean they won't try something else. They may have left now but they could come back just as easily. The only way we're better off now than we were is that they didn't burn us out." That sobering statement brought us all back to our current situation. He was right; they still had us trapped and there was nothing we could do about it. My thoughts again turned to Ephraim. I'd been thinking of him off and on throughout most of the day, wondering if he had gotten through. I worried for my friend and hoped he was alive and safe. If he did make it to Marlboro, the militia might be on their way. Of course, if he didn't, no one would be coming to our aid.

Most of us were exhausted and decided we'd take the chance to get a little sleep. A few men were assigned watches of two hours. The rest of us lay down on the hard floor, trying to sleep. I really dozed more than slept. I've heard people say that sometimes you're too tired to sleep but I never believed it until that night. I was laying there half-awake when I heard a noise that, at first, I thought was thunder but it grew steadily louder. I stood up to listen, my muscles aching and bones creaking. I've always found that I hear better with my eyes closed so I did that and it sounded like horses pounding and galloping around the house. I was confused because the Indians killed or scattered most of ours and I couldn't figure out why some of horses would have come back to the tavern and been running around. Others heard the same thing and soon we were all awake, listening while staring out the windows.

John Ayres, Jr., slowly opened the front door, being careful not to present too big of a target. I'd made my way downstairs and stood behind and to the side of him, peeking out the door, trying to get a glimpse of something that would help explain the noise. If by the grace of God it was the militia, how could they have gotten through the Indians? Had they actually gone from us? Were they about to ambush the soldiers close to the tavern? A hundred thoughts went through my head as I listened.

Two shots rang out followed a few seconds later by several more coming from the direction of the road. The sound of horses got louder and louder, leaving no doubt that a large number were pounding up the road towards us. Within a minute, dozens of riders came up, stopping in front of the house. We heard someone give the order to be ready to fire. Captain Wheeler ordered John Buttrick, the trumpeter, to sound his horn, causing the militia to halt. John pulled the door open and stepped outside.

"We're the settlers! For God sakes, they'll be here in a minute! Get inside! Get inside now if you value your lives," he yelled at them. Captain Wheeler hobbled to the door his arm hanging limply by his side.

"I'm Captain Thomas Wheeler in charge of the militia," he yelled. "The townspeople are here. The Indians have besieged us for three days. Thank the Lord our most gracious God that you are here." Just at that moment, we heard guns that sounded like they were close by. "How many are you?" Wheeler asked.

"Fifty-three," a big, broad-shouldered man answered. He was tall and well proportioned with a sense of strength and confidence. "I'm Major Willard. Captain Parker is with me, 44 men and five Indian guides. We got word you'd been attacked and came as soon as we could." Several shots rang out, whistling as they passed by.

"The Indians are behind you! Get in now! Leave the horses. Now!" Wheeler yelled. The men began running coming in as fast as they could. Of course with 99 of us already there, it was next to impossible to accommodate more than half as many as we were but somehow we did it. We were elbow to elbow but didn't care. There were 53 more men to help us defend ourselves. They had powder and bullets enough to hold the Indians off for perhaps another day or two. The biggest problem now was food. Water was no longer a problem. Two of the boys, unbeknownst to us, had taken it upon themselves to go to the well and fill all the buckets. It was a foolhardy but necessary thing to do. They were scolded by their parents for doing such a dangerous thing but thanked by all of us.

After everyone was in, Wheeler gave Willard and Parker an account of what happened over the last three days. They stood dumbfounded, not believing what they were hearing, their men crowding as close as they could to listen in on the tale.

The Indians burned the Prichard's house and barn a

couple of hours after Willard arrived. Elizabeth was in tears at the final destruction of her family's home. First, her husband was killed at the ambush, and then her son was murdered and beheaded before her eyes, and now her home was burned to the ground. We didn't know what other tragedies could befall that poor woman. Even though we'd all lost everything, she bore the greatest hurt of all. They attacked by the light of the fire, shooting both arrows and bullets at us for a good while but then suddenly stopped. They screamed and yelled, taunting us once again, telling us that we could not escape and that we'd die at their hands. This may sound a little odd, but after hearing the same thing for three days, I got a little numb to it, so it had very little affect on me. The Indians were frustrated; we saw several arguing amongst themselves. When another one tried to step in to break up an argument, another began with even more of them joining in. After a while, they burned the meetinghouse and Ayres' barn, the light from the fire casting a dancing yellow shadow across the walls of the front rooms.

The noise slowly diminished until it was quiet.

There was no room to lie down so we stood shoulder to shoulder. Becky came to me just before the soldiers made it into the house. I held her all night long, letting her doze on my shoulder. I was so tired I felt faint more than once; my sight grew dim, and I began to sway on my feet. There was roaring and buzzing in my ears followed by the momentary blank silence of sleep. More than once, I felt a hand on my back or shoulder steadying me so I wouldn't fall down. Without that help, I'm certain I would have fallen, taking a few of my closest companions with me. The exhaustion and lack of food was beginning to take its toll on all of us.

The other thing I remember about that night was the quiet. After the Indians burned the buildings and drifted off, no one said anything. It was so quiet you could almost see the silence.

Slowly, we came to realize that the Indians may have left, whether temporarily or not we couldn't be sure, but as sunrise approached and the world began to turn gray, then lighter and lighter until we could make out the colors of things. From where Becky and I stood, I could see out of a corner of the window. There was blue sky and sunshine. After a lengthy discussion, the doors were opened; several of us went out, a few at a time, then the rest came tumbling out. We kept our guns loaded and ready just in case we were being duped. Everyone was ready to rush back inside if need be, but after a few minutes with no signs or sounds of our attackers, the women and children were let out.

It was a glorious morning and the air was fresh and clean. It was much cooler and far less humid than the last four days. A light, soft wind blew just enough to cause the leaves to flutter and ripple. From that time until now, I thought the air never smelled as fresh as it did that morning. We were hesitant to celebrate as we expected the enemy to come back, but they didn't. Surveying the scene around us, any joy we felt was dashed. Dead horses were lying all over the front and sides of the house. Clouds of flies, thousands and thousands of them, buzzed around them and the other dead animals in the fields. All our houses were burned, weeks of labor reduced to ash in a matter of minutes. The chimneys were the only thing left standing and seen from in front of the tavern, looked like gravestones, which in many ways they were. I heard one of Willard's men say the chimneys were like dead fingers pointing upward to the sky. I looked around at my neighbors and friends; every man's face was unshaven, grubby, pale, eyes red from lack of sleep, clothes reeking of sweat and gunpowder, and covered in grime. The women and children were no better.

I turned and saw Sam Prichard's dead, decomposing body lying across the road. His head sagged on the pole, the heat, and flies taking their toll on it. The women shielded his mother and sisters from the sight, taking them out back while we took the pole down. His head fell off and rolled a short ways. All of us stood there looking at it, unable to speak. One of Willard's men went over, gently picking it up by the hair and put it beside the body. They removed him to behind what was left of his father's barn until he could be buried. That act caused the rest of us to awaken from our stupor and realize all that needed to be done. I knew that I could do nothing until I got some sleep so I found Becky, took her hand, and walked around the side and found a soft area away from the dead animals and rotten smell. We lay down, like many others, and slept as we'd never slept before or since. Charity woke us up several hours later, lightly kicking me.

"Come on now, get up, there's work to be done. You've had enough of a rest," she said in a weary voice looking like she was about to fall down. "We don't have any food except what Willard's men brought with them."

"There has to be something left in the cellars," I told her. "Everyone one of us had barrels and baskets of all sorts of things. Even if the houses are gone the cellars are still there." She shook her head and wrung her hands.

"I don't know. I'm not sure about anything anymore," she said as she began to walk away to the front of tavern.

"Go help her," I told Becky. "Stay with her while I see what we can do about the food." With that, I headed in the direction of Wheeler and Willard, who were standing with a group near the edge of the road by the remains of Prichard's house. I was on edge and getting angrier with every step I took. When I got near to them, they turned to me.

"Major, I'm Jack Parker. My house was over there," I said, pointing in the direction of the charred ruins. "We need some food. We've eaten very little in four days. Can some of your men go with a few of us to try to find a cow or pig?" He looked at me for a moment before lowering his heard and kicking the dirt with his foot.

"We have nothing left," I told him. "The women are looking in the cellars since everyone had some type of food stored there. We can use it if the Indians didn't take it or it was ruined in the fire. If there is nothing left we have to get food somehow." Wheeler stood there scratching the stubble on his chin with his good arm, the swelling of the other had gone down quite a bit.

"If we can't find any animals then we either have to go to Springfield or Marlborough," Wheeler said to us. "But who knows where the Indians are? For all we know they could be a mile or two from here. A large number of us would have to go and that would leave the village almost unprotected. And, if the enemy came back…," he said leaving the thought unfinished for we all knew what he meant. "Let's see what's left here, it might be enough to last us a couple of days." Willard didn't say anything; he just nodded and slowly turned away, looking lost in thought. Perhaps he was beginning to understand the depth of the dilemma we were facing.

People began to wander around, some going directly to their houses and others looking at what remained of their neighbors' houses, slowly coming to grips with what little they had left. Everyone else was going through the same thing trying to find what they could, not knowing how much of their things, their life, was left. Everyone stared at the piles of ashes and burnt timbers crossing at odd angles, lying where they fell. All of the villagers had the same look of shock and disbelief, most of the women were crying, the men were angry at seeing so many years of labor gone, and the little children confused and worried. Becky and I, along with Josiah and Charity, wandered like the rest going to their house first. There was little left of their things, a broken clay dish, a piece or two of pewter, a small pot, hoops from a couple of small barrels in the hall and a few other odds and ends.

When we got to what was left of our house we stared in disbelief; everything was gone. There wasn't one thing left except the fireplace and chimney. Becky let out a small noise, a kind of half-cry as Josiah and Charity came up behind us. Becky began to cry so Charity comforted her as I jumped into the cellar hole and began poking around trying to remember what we had stored down here. I saw something round sticking out of a pile of stuff underneath the fireplace. It was a big, heavy kettle. I dragged it over to the edge and heaved it out. I stepped on two spoons and a toaster iron and handed them out to Becky.

"Did we have any food down here?" I asked her, scratching my head.

"There was a leather bag of peas and two small boxes

with dried parsnips in one and dried apples in the other. They were on the other side in the corner." I went where I was directed and found both boxes but not the bag. There were a few pieces of pewter lying in the grass and not much else. With a sigh, I handed everything to Becky. I crawled out and stood there, wiping the soot and ash from my hands on to my pants.

I saw the women and children going through what was left of their gardens seeing what they could find which hadn't been eaten by the hundreds of Indians or trampled by the scattered animals. Some of the men carried big kettles over to the tavern and built fires, and the women began preparing a stew of sorts, adding whatever they thought would taste best. At that point, I really didn't care for I was so hungry that I wasn't hungry at all. My stomach stopped rumbling two days ago and now didn't even do that. All this time, Willard and his men stood guard; ready to defend us if the Indians came back. Once the smell of the stew started drifting around, my stomach came to life again. We gathered in little groups eating out of a communal pot sharing spoons. We ate all there was and it wasn't enough. Everyone had a good meal but not nearly enough to make up for what we didn't have over the last few days.

Captain Wheeler came hobbling up next to me, his arm wrapped in an old piece of linen, patches of dried blood near the wrist and elbow.

"We have to get Henry and Sam buried," he said. "Henry's body has been in the house for three days now. Elizabeth Prichard, poor woman, is putting together a shroud for him. I don't know where she gets her strength, I really don't. Some of Willard's men will bring both of them over to the burial ground while another group acts as guards. Can you get a couple of others to bury them?"

"Of course I will," I replied. "Sam was a good man. Henry seemed like a good man too."

"He was...he certainly was..."

"I need to find some shovels or picks, anything we can dig with...I don't know if there are any left." I began to think of where I might find some tools. Tom Parsons quietly joined us.

"What about Jim Hovey?" he asked. "No one knows what happened to him." Wheeler turned, looking back at the groups of people gathered around the tavern, wincing in pain as he moved his arm a little too quickly.

"Your uncle," he said, nodding in my direction, "John and Ed Ayres and a few others have gone looking for him. Three of the guides and eight of Willard's men went too. I heard that Hovey was good friends with your uncle."

"Yes, he was," I told him. "They really took to each other even though Josiah was 25 years older than Jim. Josiah rode around their place when we came back from the ambush but couldn't find him anywhere. Of course, he didn't have a long time to look either." This made me think of how Ephraim and I became friends quickly and how I wished I knew if he was all right. Josiah worried about Jim all the time during the siege, alternating between hope that he somehow got away and the realization that he was most likely dead.

While Wheeler and I spoke, people began drifting back to their homes or where their homes were up until a few days ago. Everyone started digging through the rubble again and surprisingly to all of us we found quite a bit of our things. I saw a few men and boys carrying shovels so I went over, asking them if they'd help with the burials or at least let us use their shovels. All the men agreed to help. When we got to the tavern, they had wrapped Henry and Sam in their shrouds and put them in the back of a cart, one of two that the Indians hadn't destroyed. When everything was ready, thirty of us set out, all of us with guns in hand and four of us carrying shovels. A horse that belonged to Richard Coy wandered back and was immediately hitched to the cart. The poor animal looked worn and beaten but it, like the rest of us, had a job to do.

We went slowly so we wouldn't be surprised by any Indians that might be lurking around. It took us about three hours to get there, dig the graves, bury them, and get back. The digging was especially difficult because the land was full of rocks; some big, some small, some in between, but regardless of the size, there was plenty of them.

By the time we got back, it was early evening about an hour or so until sunset. There was a good deal of discussion about what to do that night, whether everyone should be in the house or if some of the soldiers would stay outside. The officers decided that everyone would stay inside just to be safe. Even though our attackers seemed to have deserted the area, we couldn't be certain that they wouldn't return at night to try to finish us off. I thought we'd never see them again anytime soon because they left frustrated and bored. They really didn't inflict much injury on us besides killing Sam and Henry, injuring Tom Wilson, and burning the buildings. It may seem like a lot, but for 400 Indians, it wasn't much at all. I realized that I hadn't seen Josiah or any of the others that went with him to try to find Jim and became worried that something might have happened to them. None of us was thinking clearly, for the effects of too little sleep were catching up with us. The energy we felt during the day was wearing off and the women got the children inside and ready for the night.

Becky and I found Charity and asked if Josiah had come back yet.

"No, they're not back yet. I'm getting worried, Jack. I know they can take care of themselves but after the last few days, I worry anytime anyone is out of sight. I hope they haven't gone too far looking for him. Priscilla said he went to the river about an hour before all of you came back. I don't think they'll ever find Jim."

The years had taken their toll on this wonderful woman, wearing her away bit by bit. I looked at her now, seeing the lines and wrinkles I never really noticed before. Her eyes were sad and no longer had the sparkle they once did. She looked weary all the time. Her dark hair was full of gray and she'd begun the habit of wringing her hands every few minutes as if to somehow make her worries go away.

"They'll be fine," I said, trying to comfort her as best as I could even though I felt uneasy about their prolonged absence. I looked at Becky and could tell that she saw what I did and it troubled her just as much as it did me. "If they're not back in a little while, I'll ask Major Willard for a few men and go looking for them. He'll be all right," I said, putting my arm around Charity. Her shoulders dropped and she leaned against me. We stood that way for a minute or two before Josiah and the others came up the road. Charity was overwhelmed with relief and left us, walking, and then running towards him. Everyone gathered around as the men came up to the tavern.

"Did you find him?" Jim's wife Priscilla asked, moving to the front of the crowd.

"No, Priscilla, we didn't. We searched down to the river and beyond the stream up past the swamp, up the hill and back again. Then we went behind your house and into the woods...looked all the way back there but didn't find anything.

We can look again tomorrow," he told her, casting a glance at Willard and Wheeler as if to say he didn't believe they would ever find his friend. The bond Josiah and Jim shared surprised us; sometimes it seemed like they'd known each other all their lives.

"Do you think they took him?" she asked hopefully. "I mean they took that Indian guide. They probably took Jim, too. It would make sense if they did." She was trying to convince herself that he was still alive. Those of us standing there were not sure what we could do or say to comfort her since there wasn't much of a chance he was taken captive.

"We'll look again first thing tomorrow morning," Josiah told her gently. "Don't worry…if he's out there, we'll find him." What he didn't say was whether they'd find him alive or not.

Night was coming on and everyone began going into the house in little groups. Even though I knew we wouldn't be able to get a good spot if we didn't get inside soon, I wanted to stay out as long as I could where the air was fresh and cool. The memory of the heat and horrid smells caused my stomach to turn. Becky and I were some of the last to go in. We stood just inside and to the right of the door, jammed into the corner with several of Willard's men, a couple of whom already seemed to be asleep on their feet. Like last night, Becky put her head on my shoulder and dozed off leaning against me. I didn't sleep at all. I kept fading in and out between the inadvertent pushing from every side, loud snoring, various smells wafting around, and my wife constantly adjusting herself first on my left shoulder, then on my right. I had my eyes closed but that's all. We kept all the windows open, letting in any fresh breeze that might come our way.

The best thing about being the last ones in at night was that we were the first ones out in the morning. I couldn't wait to get away from everyone. We'd been packed together for so long that it was starting to wear on everyone; you could see it in their faces and hear it in their voices. People wanted to be alone with their families but they had no place to go. The feeling was that of a rising angry bitterness, along with a growing sense of hopelessness. While that mood came and went during the day, the physical needs overcame any other feelings. Food was the greatest need. Several of the animals returned to the fields during the night. A couple of horses were on the hill behind the house; Mary, Jim Travis's little girl, spotted them right away. Some sheep and a cow were at the far end of the field across from the tavern down by the road. There wasn't much left from the scroungings; not even enough for a big pot of corn mush. Two of Wheeler's men found a pig wandering through the field by the brook near Coys' place and killed it, along with the cow, and dragged both all the way up the hill. They were butchered in a short time with some the meat placed in a big kettle with lots of water and the few vegetables the children were able to find. Tom Parsons, Jim Travis and a couple of others made two spits over a big fire so the women could roast the rest of the meat. The smell was wonderful and caused many of us to lick our lips more than a few times while it was cooking.

While we were waiting for the food, the decision was made that we should begin trying to find as many of the animals as we could. After the wonderful meal, we split into groups of ten and began combing the fields and woods. I was surprised at the number of animals that we did find - more than thirty horses, eight cows, fourteen sheep, and a few pigs. Since we had no way to contain them, several of the boys were made to guard them and make sure they were kept within the fields in sight of the house.

I kept an eye out for Bubs while we were looking for the animals but he was nowhere to be found. I began to think that maybe the Indians took him and the others animals we didn't find. They wouldn't have ridden him or the other horses but used them as food. The thought of Bubs being killed to feed the enemy made me sad then angry. I wandered around in a foul mood for the next couple of hours.

Ed Ayres came running toward me, yelling at the top of his voice.

"Jack, your horse is back! Bubs is here!"

I looked where he was pointing and saw Bubs plodding

up the path from the direction of the burial ground. The way he was walking made me think he might be injured. I began moving towards him and when we were 50 feet from each other, I could see the recognition in his eyes, a look of having escaped the carnage. It reminded me of the look I'd seen on people's faces when we realized that the Indians were truly gone. I rubbed him, feeling for any injuries but found only a few cuts along his right side from running through the heavy brush. I put my arms around his neck for a minute before guiding him to the tavern where he went into the small stockade with the soldier's horses. The return of many animals gave us a whisper of hope that our lives were slowly returning to as normal as they could be.

Towards mid-day, we heard two shots followed by three more coming from the other side of the hill behind the house and down towards the river. Not sure what we'd find, a group of us grabbed our guns and ran in that direction. When we got down to the bottom of the other side, three of Wheeler's men were helping one of Willard's who'd been wounded. They told us of how they were out looking for animals and saw two Indians skulking around. They shot at our men, who returned the fire and the Indians took off running down the hill across the brook, heading away from us. That caused us to get the women and children back into the house and to get our guns ready. We kept up a watch all afternoon but when nothing happened, we let everyone out, though no one wandered too far, ready to run to the house if the enemy should come back.

We were refugees plain and simple, true and complete. We had nothing left and nowhere else to go, although we knew we couldn't stay there. Talk began about where to go once we left the place. Quite a few decided to go back to Ipswich, Topsfield, or Gloucester for many had relatives they could stay with while rebuilding their lives. Others talked about going to friends in and around Boston. Some, like us, hadn't decided what we'd do. Josiah and Charity, Elizabeth and Tom Morgan, and Becky and I didn't talk about it, avoiding the subject. When people asked us what we were going to do, Becky and I told them that we didn't know yet. I was torn, knowing what I wanted to do but not wanting things to change. I wasn't sure I could leave Charity and Josiah, but I didn't want to go back to Ipswich. I loved them and this land, wondering how a man who loved both could leave either.

There comes a time in every man's life when he must face the reality of a difficult situation and make decisions that affect the remainder of his life and the lives of those around him. This was the first of those times for me. I had to decide whether to return to Ipswich or go west to the Springfield area to live my dream, our dream. Becky and I talked about it off and on all that day. The most difficult part was that if we decided to go west, there was a good chance we'd most likely never see Josiah and Charity or Tom and Elizabeth again. It is over 120 miles and six or seven days travel with a horse and cart from Springfield to Ipswich, too far to go to just to visit. While all of us farmers worked together and helped each other out whenever it was needed, none of us could afford to be away from our farms for that long. If Becky and I went to visit them in Ipswich, we'd be gone for at least three weeks counting the time we'd spend there. On a horse, I could make it in two days of hard riding but we wouldn't travel that way. It was a difficult reality to face, but it couldn't be avoided.

Becky and I had the biggest decision to make so we took a walk heading in the direction of where our house used to stand. When we got there, I stood shaking my head, feeling a sense of frustration and anger, that all of our work was for nothing. I looked at my wife and saw tears rolling down her cheeks. She looked up at me, the remaining spots of soot and dust on her face showing the tracks of her tears. I held her close and gave her a kiss on the forehead.

"Everything will be all right," I told her, taking her hands in mine. "It will be. Trust me." She shook her head from side to side.

"No, no it won't!," she said, suddenly angry, backing away from me. "All the years we've waited for this, trying day after day to make our dreams come true, working all day, every day until we're so tired we can't even keep our eyes open. It's all gone," she said. "Are we supposed to just start all over again? Go somewhere else and do this again? For what? To have something terrible happen to that too? I don't know Jack, I really don't." I knew that part of what she was feeling was all the bottled up emotions from everything we'd been through.

"I know how you're feeling. I wonder about it too…but we just have to keep going. We don't have any choice in that. One day follows another."

"No! No! No!" she spat at me, surprising me with the force of her words. "We have choices about everything. You're just saying that to get me to agree with you. What if I want to go back to Ipswich? What if I don't want to go to Springfield? What if I've had enough of this? Am I supposed to have my baby amongst all this ruin and slaughter? Am I? Well, am I?" she asked, sweeping her arm around at all the burned buildings. The thought that she might want to go back stunned me. I didn't know what to say.

"Maybe we should wait to talk about this. We don't have to decide today," I told her, looking at the fields and woods and knowing that I wanted to spend the rest of my life in this area. I realized that it would be better if her parents told us what they were planning to do but they hadn't. I already knew that Josiah and Charity would go back, for she told me just two nights ago, although it seemed like it was weeks, not days ago. I decided to let the matter rest.

I turned around and waited for her. "Come on," I told her, "let's go back now." She turned and walked with me, neither one of us saying a word, both of us lost in our own thoughts and feelings. I glanced at her to see if she was all right. She reached down, picked a stalk of grass and began peeling it apart as she walked. She was somewhere far away, seeing something in her mind's eye, not even aware of the grass in her hand. After a few more yards, she stopped and tossed the grass away and looked at me, her dirty, tear-stained face more beautiful than I could remember. There was something about her I'd never seen before; it was more than a look or how she was standing. Those things were part of it but then I realized it was her face. Her eyes shone and her cheeks glowed through the dirt and grime. She looked like the girl I knew years ago but different, somehow changed. It was a total transformation from the angry woman I'd seen a few minutes ago. She put her hands on her belly and smiled coyly.

"My place is with you, wherever that may be," she said. And that's how our decision was made.

Chapter 23

The next day was filled with talk about what people would do when they got to wherever they were going. The decisions were made, the plans discussed and a small glimmer of hope began to appear as the excitement took hold. Most decided to go back to the Ipswich area, while others decided to go to towns where they had relatives that would take them in until they could be settled. Then there was us. When we told people of our decision to go to Hatfield, they thought we were crazy and spent hours trying to talk us out of it. Many of their reasons were valid, from not knowing if the Indians would attack there next, to not having any family or friends to rely on in case of trouble, but it was our dream and we were going regardless of the risks.

It was very painful to think about the strong possibility of not seeing our families again. Josiah, Charity, Tom, and Elizabeth understood that we needed to make our own lives and didn't want to stop us but you could see the sadness in their eyes. All of us shared the same feelings of knowing we were going our separate ways and the reality of getting on with life. Never did I think of the day when I wouldn't be near Josiah and

Charity. They took me in all those years ago and raised me, giving me everything they had and could give. They taught me responsibility, compassion, and perseverance. But most of all, they gave me their love and affection. I couldn't imagine what it would be like not seeing them every day. I was sad and even though I wanted to go to Hatfield, it was very difficult. The days were sweeter though, for we knew our time together was ending. It reminded me of the clear, crisp autumn days when the sun still felt good but you knew that winter was on the way. Each day meant more to you and you remembered those days forever.

The only thing keeping people from leaving was not knowing if the road was safe from Indian attack. No family wanted to be the first to leave until the soldiers had gone through to Marlboro, the first town on the way back to Ipswich. It was 25 miles; you could walk it in a single, long day though it wouldn't be easy. If you couldn't, the thought of spending a night in the open with no shelter or escape was too much for any of them. Of course, Becky kept reminding me that it might not be any better for us because it was the same distance to Springfield. In normal times, stopping for the night on the way to somewhere would have held no fear for any of us, but times weren't what they had been and wouldn't be for a long time.

Starting early Saturday afternoon, the next several hours were a frenzy of relief, excitement, and energy. Captain

Thomas Watts rode in with a company of 70 men, 40 soldiers, and 30 Indians. About two hours later, Captains Thomas Lathrop and Richard Beers arrived with 190 men and three hours later, my friend Lt. Tom Cooper came in with 37 men including Judah Trumble. None of us knew what happened to him; for all we knew he might have been killed. To see him again caused a great sense of relief and joy in all of us. Mary came running from the back of the crowd when someone told her he was here. I'll never forget the sight of her rushing to him, the baby in her arms, the son Judah didn't even know he had. After a while, he told us what happened.

"I was on my way back from Springfield, and as I got closer, I noticed how quiet it was; no birds were chirping, the light breeze had stopped and everything was still. When I crested the small rise, I saw a light haze of smoke from beyond the Great Meadow. 'Now what the hell could that be?' I asked myself. I wondered what was burning, thinking that someone was burning something although I couldn't figure out what. When I turned past the far end of the meadow, I looked up the hill. I couldn't believe what I saw; Coy's house beginning to burn, then a bunch of Indians ran across the field in front of me not two hundred yards away. Scared the piss out of me I can tell you that." He cleared his throat and took a great drink of rum. "From where I was I couldn't see the top of the hill. Smoke wasn't coming from anywhere else. I saw more Indians just a few hundred feet away. I knew then that I couldn't do anything so I figured it would be best for me to get back to Springfield to let Major Pynchon know and to raise the alarm, so I took off as fast as I could and made my way back there as soon as I could. Went all night, didn't stop once," he said taking another swig from his bottle.

By early evening there were, with Wheeler and Willard's men, over 350 well-armed soldiers in Brookfield. For the first time in a week, we felt secure and safe for no harm could come to us now. The stories of our ordeal were told over and over again to the amazement of the soldiers. For the most part, the soldiers were kind and helpful, sharing their food and goods with us although some were ignorant and churlish, cranky, dirty, grubby men who didn't want to be there. They were the ones who seemed most afraid of any possible attacks.

Soon after the soldiers arrived, Major Willard held a council of the officers to discuss the situation. It lasted about half an hour after which we were all told to gather on the hill behind the tavern. All 450 of us gathered and waited for the Major to let us know what they discussed. Willard stood in the center of his officers, as the ranking officer, he'd taken command of the entire force. He had a powerful voice that reached us without any trouble.

"We now have 350 armed soldiers here," he began. "We don't intend to just sit here and wait for someone to tell us where the Indians went. From the information we have, it seems that they would have gone back to their villages at Menamesset. Early tomorrow morning, 300 of us will go there to punish the fiends for their wickedness and hate. The remaining soldiers will provide protection against any unforeseen encounters here. We see no reason we should not be victorious against the heathens. We will destroy them, as many as we can, and those we can't destroy we'll disperse so they are weakened and can't fight again," he yelled, his voice rising with every sentence. "They cannot be allowed to continue this war, for if they do, what happened here could happen elsewhere and that we can't allow! We will stop them tomorrow!" He took a breath, looking around at us as if measuring our fortitude. "After our successful assault tomorrow, we'll begin our task of securing other towns and villages. On Monday or perhaps Tuesday, Captains Lathrop and Beers will take their men to Hadley. Captain Wheeler and his men will return to Marlboro. Captain Watts and his company will go to Suffield, stopping in Springfield. Those of you wishing to go to any of those places will be able to travel with an armed escort. I suggest you make your plans accordingly." He turned and said something to Captain Wheeler who pointed in the direction of where I and 10 or 12 other village men were sitting. Major Willard shook his head, his back to us, evidently not agreeing with whatever suggestion Wheeler made. Lathrop and Beers joined in the discussion, which lasted a few minutes. I decided to ask the question I knew several of us were thinking.

"Major Willard," I yelled loud enough to be heard, causing everyone to turn to face me. I saw Becky staring up at me wondering what I was up to this time. The officers turned towards me. "Major, if you're going against the Indians tomorrow, I, and I'm sure there are other men here, who want to go with you." I stood waiting for his response. He took his hat off, rubbing his right hand over his face but didn't respond right away, which made me think he was going to say that he wouldn't allow it. However, he surprised us, not only agreeing to it, but also asking several of us to ride with him.

When we left early the next morning, it was already very warm and as we went on it got hotter and more humid. The breeze, what little there was of it, was fiery. Every man dripped with sweat; it ran down our faces and necks, making our faces shine in the burning sunlight.

Many of the soldiers acted as if they were going for a walk, a different type of walk to be sure. They acted as if it was more of an early morning hunt, which it was in a grim way. As we got closer, still a couple of miles away from the Indian villages, they seemed calm and not worried at all. Maybe our stories had no affect on them or they didn't understand all that happened, or they couldn't imagine the fear that wells up inside when you see a screaming Indian coming at you, war club in his hand, intent on beating you in the head until your brains fall out or the way you start to sweat when you see a gun aimed at your chest or an arrow aimed at your heart. My insides were like jelly; nervous and rumbling. All I could picture was the Indian I hit in the head at the ambush. He looked me in the eyes as he fell, never taking his gaze off my face. I could still see the red paint on the side of his head going up and over towards his neck, the little black turtle painted under his left eye. I have heard people describe war as glorious but it is not. It is anxiety, despair, excitement, boredom, impatience, weariness, hunger, pain, mind-numbing fear, death, and horror.

These soldiers were not as afraid as I was because they hadn't seen, heard, or felt what I had. I saw little sketches in my mind's eye of Coy being killed, Wheeler lying on the ground, his horse on top of his side, Indians pouring out of the swamp, men riding and running up the hill. All of it in flashes from one moment to another but a jumble of images that came together showing the whole terrible experience.

As we got closer to the sight of the ambush, there was no more talking as word that we were near where it happened passed from man to man until all were quiet. As the talk ceased the tension mounted, everyone keeping a sharp eye and keen ear for any sight or sound that might indicate an ambush. Our eyes wandered everywhere looking for any signs of the Indians, hunting for any sign of the enemy we stalked. On a hot, sultry day like that, even the birds didn't sing, adding to the feeling that something might happen to us. The only thing you could hear is the hum of insects. It is an odd feeling, as if someone is watching you or sneaking up behind you, but every time you turned to look, no one is there. The Major decided to halt, got off his horse, and spoke to the officers telling them that we'd prepare ourselves here. Willard ordered all men to inspect their guns to make sure they were ready.

When he asked us about what was up ahead, we gave him a good description of the route and the layout of the Indian villages. He got a more detailed picture from Joseph and Sampson who'd ridden ahead. Willard sent 20 of the Indians out as scouts, splitting them on either side of the swamp and ordering them to ride out in a line and proceed two miles ahead searching for any sign of the enemy. We needed to be very careful for even though we had 300 men, there were about 400 Indians that attacked the tavern. We had no way of knowing if their numbers had grown and if they did by how many. For all we knew there could have been 1,000 of them waiting for us.

Willard was taking no chances at all. He would rather go slow and make sure we knew what we were getting into before we got there. I, for one, agreed with him. A few of the scouts came back a short while later reporting that there was no sign of any of the enemy anywhere. This was a bit puzzling since we didn't think that they'd abandon such a large village as Menamesset. If anything, I thought there would be more of them than there normally were. The Major thought things over for a moment, then ordered his officers to move their men ahead. He sent the scouts back out telling them to get as close to the village as they could and report on what they found. After they left, we began our slow ride, every sense on edge waiting for a scream, a yell, or a gunshot that would signal an attack.

Our horses plodded along, seeming to understand the need for quiet movement. The flies kept bothering Bubs, getting in his ears and eyes causing him to flip his head back and forth trying to get rid of them but without any luck. I tried to calm him so the movement wouldn't be seen by any of the enemy if they were near but I realized that if there were any Indians around, they'd see 300 men before they noticed my poor horse tossing his mane. I felt sorry for him; I could tell he was out of sorts not having gotten enough to eat for over a week; the sudden appearance of hundreds of other horses; the hot weather and the long, slow ride were taking their toll on him. It was taking a toll on us too. I could taste salt in my mouth from the sweat rolling down my face and I kept wiping my face with my sleeve but it did no good. My throat was hot and dry. Joseph and Sampson rode in at full gallop and slid to a stop in front of us.

"The lower and middle villages are empty," Sampson

told us. "They're gone…there's not one person there."

"What about the upper village?" Major Willard asked.

"Two of the guides that came with Captain Watts are there now and should be back soon. We thought you would want to know about the villages being empty rather than wait for them. The upper village is three miles up the river," Joseph said, pulling on the reins.

"We'll continue on," the Major told the officers. I could hear the word being passed down the line about the villages being empty. It was like a great sigh of relief as if the soldiers were one man. We were only a couple of hundred yards from the swamp. I was so upset at the thought of what happened here a week ago that my stomach hurt. Grimacing, I turned to the Major.

"Sir, are you planning to stop at the swamp?" I asked with a bit of a tremor in my voice.

"You mean to find your men?"

"Yes, sir."

"Do you really want to do that? You don't even know if they're still there." I could hear it in his voice that he was trying to soothe my anxiety. "From what you told me," he continued, "the swamp is large and impassable in some places. How do you propose to proceed?"

"I don't know…I thought I'd just go in and start looking for them. I know where they fell." I sat there, holding the reins in my hand, thinking about what I might find. "We have to at least try," I told him.

"All right, since the villages seem to be empty you can take some time. We'll stop here for another rest. Take a few men with you," he said, sliding off his horse with a weary groan. He ordered the company to dismount and rest. John Ayres, Jr. was with us along with his two of his brothers as was Rich Coy, Jr. They gathered near me.

"I want to go look for them," I said. "There's no need for you to. It might be better if you don't."

"Jack," John said, looking at me, "it's kind of you to do this but they were our fathers and we should be the ones to find them and bury them." With that, he walked by, followed by the other three, so I turned and followed. Rich was the first to spot something. It was a bone, an arm bone, sticking out of a bush. As he picked it up something fell into the water with a plop. He bent down to look, stood up, turned, and vomited. It was a hand. He dropped the bone and made his way back to the horses, gagging and coughing all the way. What we found wasn't pretty. The weather and animals had done a great deal of damage. The stench was so overpowering that we smelled the remains before we ever saw them. We gathered those parts we could find and buried them on the other side of the road at the base of the hill. It was a horrible chore that will haunt me to my dying day. Even though so much time has passed, I sometimes wake, even now, soaked with perspiration from bad dreams.

The scouts from the upper village came back right after we finished with the burial. They said that it was as empty as the other two so we continued on our way, moving at a fast pace since we knew there would not be any opposition. Willard ordered us to burn everything. A third of the company went to each village and set fire to anything and everything. We got off our horses, watching as the flames began to catch, the smoke billowing up, adding to the already hot, sultry sky. As it burned, I could feel the heat growing and watched with great satisfaction as it destroyed everything that might be of use to our enemies. After an hour, it was all gone; we left nothing but heaps of smoldering ashes. We turned and rode back to the village. The thought came to me that it was time to head for home, until I realized I no longer had a home.

Chapter 24

When we got back to the village, everything happened too fast. We were all tired, hot, and hungry. With a start, we realized that we'd be leaving tomorrow, Monday.

Becky and I were too anxious to sleep much that night. As I lay there, thoughts running through my mind of the past and future, I began to consider my beliefs, those things most important to me. I came to realize that it was love.

Through all the troubling times of our lives, it is a true constant, helping us to weather the winds of uncertainty. Knowing you are loved - truly, deeply, eternally loved, can cause the greatest fears to recede, to take their place amongst the scale of good and bad. Love, sweet love, the kind filled with warm summer sunshine and cloudless blue skies, soothes your upsets and fears. To have people love you, not for wealth or power or things you can give them, but for being yourself and offering the gifts you have, however humble and small, those that make you truly you. I believe that love is the greatest gift you can give or receive.

The dawn came too soon; everyone was up, moving about, excited but sad at the same time. We'd said our goodbyes to many of our neighbors last night. We realized that we were all setting off on long voyages and adventures, lifetimes really, and there was heartfelt crying and weeping for loved ones and friends we would never see again.

I told Josiah and Charity to take Bubs because Becky and I wanted them to have him. We knew they wouldn't have an easy time if they had to walk all the way to Marlborough then on to Ipswich. Josiah refused the several times I offered, saying we'd need him more than they would.

Elizabeth, Tom, Young Tom, Nate, Josiah, and Charity gathered around us. The tears began, first Elizabeth, then Becky, then Charity. Josiah got a little teary eyed and I will admit that at that moment I came close to deciding that we'd go back to Ipswich with them. I gave both Charity and Josiah a hug, trying to thank them for all they had done for me. Josiah made a bit of a speech saying he couldn't have asked for a better son than if I were his own. I shook hands with the men and hugged the women one more time. Captain Watts' men were forming up and he called out that we were leaving so to finish our goodbyes. Becky got on Bubs as I took the bridle in my left hand and with my gun in my right, began walking away.

We never saw any of them again. My last view of them was waving goodbye to us as we made our way down the road. Charity's hand went to her mouth; I could tell she was crying.

She and Elizabeth comforted each other. We waved one more time and turned around, heading west to our future. I looked back once more but they were gone. We made it to Springfield by mid-afternoon without any trouble. A great sadness was upon us but it was mixed with a small spark of hope and excitement for our future life together.

But that's a story for another time.

Acknowledgments

No author writes a book alone and I am no different. I have many people to thank for helping me along my journey.

My wife Barbara, for always being there when I needed her.

To all those who spent hours reading and re-reading the many drafts and giving invaluable advice, comments and encouragement: Tom and Lois Londergan, Marcy Supovitz, Maureen Milliken, Bill Jankins, Kerri Lundberg, Greg Jackman, Jeff Lubs, Natalie Hildt, Cynthia Kennison, John Salem, Muriel O'Rourke, Pam Earle, and Denise Desplaines.

CPSIA information can be obtained
at www.ICGtesting.com
Printed in the USA
FFOW01n0923091014
7890FF